BOOK YOUR PLACE ON OUR WEBSITE AND MAKE THE READING CONNECTION!

We've created a customized website just for our very special readers, where you can get the inside scoop on everything that's going on with Zebra, Pinnacle and Kensington books.

When you come online, you'll have the exciting opportunity to:

- View covers of upcoming books
- Read sample chapters
- Learn about our future publishing schedule (listed by publication month *and author*)
- Find out when your favorite authors will be visiting a city near you
- Search for and order backlist books from our online catalog
- Check out author bios and background information
- Send e-mail to your favorite authors
- Meet the Kensington staff online
- Join us in weekly chats with authors, readers and other guests
- Get writing guidelines
- AND MUCH MORE!

**Visit our website at
http://www.zebrabooks.com**

Surrender

Patricia Rice

Zebra Books
Kensington Publishing Corp.
http://www.zebrabooks.com

ZEBRA BOOKS are published by

Kensington Publishing Corp.
850 Third Avenue
New York, NY 10022

First Printing: October, 1998
10 9 8 7 6 5 4 3 2 1

Printed in the United States of America

Dear Reader:

I first tried my hand at writing historical romance when I had no car, no job, and a house full of kids running around underfoot. I had a degree in accounting but attitudes at the time frowned on female accountants. To keep my brain from deteriorating to my children's conversational level of "One Fish, Two Fish," I wrote. And wrote. And wrote some more.

The result of some of that determined scribbling is in the pages that follow. In 1983, Kensington Publishing converted my laboriously typewritten story into print, and I became a published author. Since then, I've gone on to write twenty-six currently published books, a dozen novellas, and have won numerous industry awards in the process. But this baby was my very first, and I'm thrilled and a little scared to introduce it to the readers I've gained since it first appeared on the market.

According to my bookseller friends, this is a classic romance of the period, but I've modernized it slightly to fit current publishing practices. I think it's better than the original, but what makes it classic is still there—the love and tears and laughter.

I hope new readers will enjoy discovering an old book and old readers will enjoy rereading it. Thank you for all the hours of delight you've given me over the years.

Patricia Rice

One

The good Lord preserve us from Saturday night. This thought ran inanely through Jennifer's head as she rushed through the kitchen, staying just beyond her mother's reach and preferably out of eye range. Just the sight of her daughter was enough to remind the harried woman of a dozen other chores left to be done, and Jennifer already had her hands full, literally as well as figuratively. The tray of dirty dishes teetered as she lowered them to the wooden table beside the sink.

The thin woman at the stove turned at the sound, catching Jennifer before she could slip outside to catch a breath of fresh air. The kitchen was filled with the smell of frying food, the unbearable heat and humidity of mid-July capturing and holding the smells in a steamy cloud. Not a breeze stirred through the open back door where the flies swarmed; the very air itself was oppressive. Jennifer sighed at the black look on her mother's face and turned to pour more hot water from the stove into the basin of suds.

Taller than her mother, Jennifer was more slender than thin, her faded calico dress clinging limply to well-rounded breasts and hips. Shamelessly, she wore little in the way of undergarments, knowing the kitchen heat would be her only companion; her mother's sharp eyes kept her from straying much farther than the back stairs. Since she had started developing the attributes of a woman, her mother had kept her from the front rooms of the inn, never ex-

plaining the reasons why she could no longer sit behind
her father's polished mahogany bar, wiping glasses and
joking with the more jovial boatmen who wandered in.

A tired, small-boned man, James Pell's gentle nature was
much to be preferred to the constant sharp tongue of Jennifer's overworked mother. But he bowed to his wife's demands on the matter of his daughter as well as most
everything else that touched their lives. Mildred Pell had
once been one of the most beautiful women in Paducah,
or so it seemed to James when his handsome eyes and
gentle ways had swept her into marriage. He worshipped
the ground she walked on, but by the birth of their first
and only child, worship was all he could do. For Mildred
was horrified by the physical nature of marriage and men,
and the torture of the birth of their daughter was the final
blow to their marital bed. James weakly succumbed to her
wishes, fading into the background as the once profitable
inn became a victim of the times and the location, and his
once beautiful wife turned into a shrew with red hands
and stooped shoulders while attempting to do the work of
a staff they could no longer afford.

Jennifer knew little of her parents' relationship; to her
it had always been thus, and she had few opportunities to
compare it with others. They lived in the inn by the river
in an area inhabited by few other respectable families. Jennifer's life had been spent with the rise and fall of the river
and the coming and goings of the riverboats instead of in
the everyday world of sunshine and warm grass and laughing children. Once or twice her mother's childless sister
had attempted to persuade Mildred to let Jennifer go back
to the farm with her, but her mother insisted every pair
of hands was needed at the inn.

And it was the truth. From the time Jennifer was able
to walk she remembered helping in one way or another,
learning the duties of maid, housekeeper, cook, and clerk.
Until she was twelve, she was allowed the bliss of learning
from the inn's one resident boarder, an elderly English
lady with an active mind and a limited pension. From her,

Jennifer learned the beautiful penmanship that embroidered the inn's business letters, the quick mental calculations that kept the inn's books balanced, and a thorough respect for good grammar and pronunciation that caused the inn's usual inhabitants to look at her strangely when she spoke. But with true Victorian practicality, all these refinements had their uses and were learned only at times when she was not needed elsewhere.

They came to an abrupt end one day when she was twelve, after her mother discovered Jennifer was learning not only to read, write, and do sums, but how to think and question. More specifically, the lessons stopped when Jennifer, after reading *Silas Marner*, had the audacity to ask her mother where babies really came from. After that, she was never allowed to return to the boarder's room, and soon after, the old lady died. With her went Jennifer's last friend and ally.

Now, at the age of seventeen, Jennifer Pell had become a more beautiful woman than her mother had ever been, combining her father's almond-shaped, long-lashed brown eyes with her mother's thick, auburn tresses, and her own characteristically firm mouth, full lips, and delicately bridged nose. But it wasn't the delicate features or elegant carriage that made her beauty so noticeable, it was the inquiring light in her eyes when she listened to someone speak, and the humorous upturn of her lips that spread so rapidly into heart-stopping smiles that made men turn when she passed by. Her churchgoing mother called it the devil in her and saw to it that Jennifer was seldom seen on the streets or anywhere besides the back room of the inn.

So Jennifer's days and nights were mapped out for her by the demands of the inn and her mother, each one blending in with the next, only the twenty-four hours from sundown Saturday to sundown Sunday standing out as any different to the rest. On Saturday the riverboats emptied and the men poured into the crude, growing riverport town. The bar filled to overflowing with drunken laughter and raucous cries, and the guests spilled over into Sunday with their riotous demands for food and service. Jennifer toiled in the kitchen while her mother kept up with the tavern until they collapsed in exhaustion in the wee hours of the morning.

It was approaching that time now. Even in the middle of the night the heat hadn't dissolved, and as the last dish was washed, Jennifer could feel the sweat pour down her back, tendrils of hair sticking about her face where she had tried to wipe it away. Longing for a cool bath and knowing she would have to haul the water for it up three flights of stairs to her attic room, she watched for the opportunity to slip out from under her mother's ever-watchful eyes. A quick dip in the river, down past the docks where no one ever strayed, would serve the purpose much better than the pump.

With the ease of experience, she found her opportunity. Her mother thinking her safely on the way to bed, Jennifer ran swiftly and silently to the riverbank, avoiding darkened streets by taking alleyways and backyards familiar only to her. Arriving safely at the water's edge, she waded cautiously to a tree-darkened bank. Water lapped sensuously at her toes as she found familiar ledges. The night air was heavy around her, but the gentle breeze off the river cooled her sweating brow as she slipped into the shrubbery on the water's edge. Divesting herself of the sweat-dampened dress, she stood only in a light shift as she listened to the sounds floating over the water. Certain there was no boat or person near, she dove into the water, bobbing up to take the pins from her hair and fling them to the bank where her clothing lay. Waist length hair spreading across the water, she lay back and floated, allowing the coolness to penetrate every pore and muscle as she stared at the night sky above her.

Listening to the tree frogs, the lapping of water against the bank, and distant sounds of laughter and revelry from the gaily lighted steamboat at the dock, Jennifer felt her usual midnight restlessness begin to stir. The urge to do

something, to strike out and move, go, be somebody, cou-
pled with a desperate longing for she knew not what drove
her muscles into action. Flipping over and stroking into
mid-stream, she battled the current until she was breathless, driving out the demons that overtook her.

Thoroughly exhausted now, she paddled toward shore,
rising from the river like a freshwater mermaid, dripping
hair spreading about her shoulders and down her back,
the short shift clinging to her slender body, serving only
to smooth the outline of her curves into a single form.
Behind the bushes, she stripped it off and wrung her hair
out, letting the night air dry it slightly before donning the
now cooled cotton dress. Without benefit of even the shift,
the modest dress became a tool of the devil her mother
so often invoked. The soft cloth rubbed her breasts; the
tips, already taut from the cool breeze, now ached at the
touch of the flimsy material which rolled across them and
down around her thighs, winding itself about her legs as
she stretched tired muscles. There would be no avoiding
the restless urges tonight; she knew it would be one of
those nights where even her dreams betrayed her and she
woke exhausted with the need still in her.

Hair streaming behind her as the river breeze picked
up, Jennifer ran back the way she came, enjoying the feel
of movement as she had the swim against the current. The
freedom from prying, suspicious eyes urged her on as she
jumped small walls and fences, heedless of the damage
done to bare feet, shoes and stocking dangling uselessly
in her hands. Some nights she felt the urge would drive
her to keep on running, out into the streets and down the
road, past the city into the open country, away from everything she had ever seen or known. But tonight was Saturday and aching muscles would not allow her to go
farther than the back door of the inn.

The kitchen was dark as she slipped up the back stairs
to the first landing. Now came the tricky part. There was
still an occasional shout of laughter from below, a shuffle
of footsteps or a brief cough from behind closed doors.

Other than that, the inn appeared quiet, most of its guests asleep. Her mother would have long since gone to bed; to take the back steps the rest of the way meant passing by her room. The only other choice would be to traverse the deserted hallway and up the main staircase to the attic where she slept, risking being seen by one of the guests.

Fearing her mother more than the guests, Jennifer slipped quietly into the hallway, nearly gaining the stairs before she heard the drunken stagger of heavy footsteps on the lower landing. Her heart jumped as she hesitated, uncertain whether to continue or turn back. Too late, she realized the unseen man had reached the top stair and could see her standing there, shoeless and shiftless, her hair streaming down her back instead of in the severe knot her mother insisted on. Terrified, Jennifer ran toward the nearest staircase, praying his room was on the first floor and that he would ignore her.

But her luck had finally run out. She could hear the drunken chuckle behind her as the man negotiated the final steps and turned to follow her up the next flight. He reeked of cheap whiskey and some sweet scent she couldn't identify as she scurried faster up the stairs out of reach. More nimble than his staggering speed, she didn't stop to look back, figuring to outdistance him before reaching the next floor, not counting on the threadbare carpet at the top of the steps.

Her bare toe caught in the worn threads, and she sprawled across the floor, her shoes clattering against the wooden planks, terrifying her more than the muttered obscenities from behind. If her mother heard the commotion, it was all over; she had to get back to her room before she was seen. Grabbing her shoes and scrambling to her feet, Jennifer started for the next flight of stairs when a rough hand seized her from behind, twisting her around with startling strength to meet his stinking breath, coarse lips crushing down on hers.

In horror and revulsion, Jennifer shoved at his chest, struggling against his groping hands, but he only grasped her tighter. With all the instincts of a wild animal, Jennifer brought her knee up, catching the drunk with a painful blow to the crotch, causing him to gasp with pain and slacken his grip. Jennifer reeled backward at his release, smacking against the door of what her mother sarcastically referred to as the bridal suite.

Larger and once more elaborately decorated than the remainder of the rooms, it rated a higher price than the cheap waterfront rooms the inn normally dealt in. Since the inn was never full, the room was never used. Remembering the wooden bolt that rendered it inaccessible (thus, her mother's reference to the bridal suite for undisturbed newlyweds), Jennifer grasped gratefully for the door handle and nearly fell through the door as she leaned her weight against it. Slamming the bolt home, she drew a deep breath and leaned against the door, listening to the stranger's outraged curses as he attempted and failed to open the door. Obviously not too drunk to understand the need for quiet, he contented himself with a foul string of epithets before stomping off down the stairs.

Jennifer listened to his retreating footsteps with relief, conscious now of the trembling that swept through her body. The only man she had ever been that close to before was her father, and not even he had held her since she was twelve or thirteen. Filled with revulsion at the taste of that foul mouth against hers, she swiped it with the back of her hand, trying to drive away the memory. Her arm ached where he had held it, her body protesting at the abrupt invasion of unwelcome hands.

In an attempt to calm herself, she glanced around the room. It was totally dark, the heavy drapes drawn against what little light might enter from the street. Making her way in the direction of what she knew to be the window, Jennifer had the sensation of being watched and shivered at the thought of rat eyes staring balefully from beneath the furniture. Glancing nervously at where she trod, she could see nothing, but she had no desire to return yet to the deserted hallway until she was certain her attacker was in a drunken stupor somewhere in his own room.

Reaching the window, she pulled the drapes back slightly, allowing a small glimmer of light to creep through. She searched for its source, deciding it had to be the moon for the street below was dead and dark. Her hair hung heavily down her back as she moved about. Unaccustomed to its weight, she pulled her fingers through it in an attempt to free the tangles the night swim and running breeze had caused.

A whispered exclamation split the silence, and nearly screaming, Jennifer swirled about with fingers pressed to her lips, searching for the source of the sound, only to be caught once more in the strong grip of masculine arms. But these were different. Hard and firm, they wrapped around her, molding her against a well-muscled chest, the thin cotton of her dress making a mockery of protection as her breasts crushed against him and her thighs encountered the warmth of naked skin. Her scream caught in her throat as lips once more pressed upon hers, but these were soft and warm, almost gentle as they plied her mouth with sweet kisses, becoming more persistent when she did not respond. Whiskey flavored them, but this man was not drunk. He held her with firm assurance, oblivious to her struggles as he bent her backwards, catching her loose hair in one hand and stroking it over her shoulder, his mouth tracing feathery caresses down her throat.

She couldn't scream. He had crushed the breath from her and sucked the air from her lungs. She couldn't breathe with the awareness of his body touching every inch of hers, only the thin piece of cloth preventing total exposure. Then his mouth covered hers again and she realized with a shock that she was responding, trembling, tentative, but answering to his pressure with unaccustomed weakness. Strong hands moved across her back as their lips locked and held, rendering her breathless as they twisted and parted, the burning brand of his tongue searing the insides of her mouth. She felt her knees go weak,

and her hands no longer beat against the hard chest, but
clung to it for support, while the longing need inside grew
and churned and demanded more.

With a gasp, she realized his hands no longer stroked
the soft material of her dress, but bare skin, the dress unfastened and gaping as rough fingers caressed her shoulders, slipping lower to the small of her back, holding her
gently while fanning fires she hadn't known existed. As
the hand slipped even lower, she pushed away wildly, the
sensation of strong fingers where no man's hand had ever
been driving her into a panic. Her movement only served
to loosen his hold, giving him more freedom to slip the
dress from her shoulders and over bare breasts where it
fluttered softly to the floor. Crying, paralyzed with fear,
she allowed him to draw her back into his arms, the folds
of material no longer offering any protection as skin
brushed against skin and the tips of her breasts rose taut
and aching under his touch.

Jennifer clutched at broad shoulders as his arm slipped
under her knees, lifting her from the floor. He carried her
to the bed, depositing her gently before lowering his
weight beside her, capturing her with one strong limb
across her legs. She was grateful for the curtain of darkness
draping them as his hands explored bared breasts and re-
cessed curves while his lips followed their path, adding an
exquisite pain to the aching need welling up inside her.
She wanted more, wanted something she could not put a
name to, and when his fingers found the moist entrance
between her thighs, she ceased all pretense of fighting
him, her hips rising against him of their own accord.

With sudden terror at the degree of need he aroused
in her, Jennifer's eyes flew open to search the darkness for
what manner of man tried to possess her. Perhaps her
mother's threats of the devil taking her soul were true.
This painful longing had called him to her side, drawing
him from the midst of darkness to consume her soul and
condemn her forever to hell.

A sliver of light from the window reflected in the eyes

above her. A blue-gray gleam of smoking desire bent over her before lowering to send shivering chills down her spine. His lips made trails across her cheek and down her throat, settling on the tender flesh of her breasts. If this be the devil, he had eyes more beautiful than any god or man, and his touch felt too right to be wrong. Perhaps she was the devil's own, then, and he had come to claim what was rightfully his; she only knew she had no wish to deny him. If this be hell, she would burn forever. Her hands slid softly over smooth shoulders, feeling the strength rippling beneath them as she surrendered.

Soft words whispered reassuringly in her ear as he lowered his body over hers, parting her legs with his knees. Strong hands lifted her hips to meet his, but the first touch of his hardness frightened desire into retreat, and Jennifer jerked away. But it was too late to resist now. He held her firmly, pinning her with hands and body. Then he was forcing an entrance, pushing deeper inside until Jennifer felt she would be torn asunder, and she uttered the first sound to pass her lips since entering the room. The piercing cry straggled into a whimper as he eased his movement, propping himself on one elbow to lift some of his weight from her. He stroked her hair, his surprise too great to offer comforting words.

With cautious patience, his lips fluttered across her forehead. His warm breath blew against her eyelids as his mouth came down on hers, and his hands returned to their caressing, forcing her body into response once more. With frightening ease he rekindled the fire, and she moved with him, slowly, awkwardly, until the longing to envelop this stranger, to become part of him, became so strong she could no longer think, was no longer conscious of the pain, but only of the need to have him. With another soft groan, she clung to him, her hips rising and falling with his ever-increasing demands until her need boiled up from deep inside and burst in a rising tide of waves with a final sharp thrust and shudder from this Satan who had, indeed, consumed and possessed her.

There were still no words between them as he kissed her, rolling to one side and pulling her with him so she lay curled against his chest while his hand stroked the long, silken hair that wrapped about them. What words could there be? They knew no names, no faces, nothing of each other but that their needs were satisfied. Jennifer lay content against his chest, the longing stilled for the first night in months as she felt his arms around her and his kisses pressed against her hair. She closed her eyes and slept.

With the first gray light of dawn, Jennifer awoke, images of her mother pounding at her door flitting uneasily through her mind. The stranger's arm lay wrapped across her breasts, one leg intertwined with hers, the intimacy bringing a flush to her cheeks as she attempted to ease herself from under his restraints. The drapes made it still too dark to see, but there was little imagining between them, his lean strength and firm muscles were imprinted on every inch of her body. Cautiously, she removed his arm and slipped from beneath his leg, planting a soft kiss on his shoulder before sliding from the bed. He stirred slightly, shifting his position, and she held her breath, afraid he would wake before she could make good her escape, but he fell further into sleep.

With a sigh, she returned to hunting for her clothes in the dark. If her mother found her missing from her room, she would turn the inn upside down in her search, embarrassing all and sundry. There was no choice but to scurry back up the stairs and be prepared when her mother came to find her for the morning breakfast ritual. Jennifer located the sadly wrinkled calico dress and pulled it on, only half fastening it before hunting for the remainder of her clothing.

She found the shoes where she had dropped them, but the shift and stockings eluded her, and no amount of crawling in the darkness could locate them. She had no choice but to leave them and hope she could get back before her mother cleaned the rooms and found them. With one last backward look, she slipped from the room.

Scurrying up the back stairs, Jennifer met no one, gaining access to her own room before anyone could miss her. She washed in the tepid water on her night stand, reluctantly washing the lingering man scent from her body, stirring new feelings deep within her. She did not know what she had done last night, if she had been possessed by man or demon, but his scent was evidence that it was no dream. She pulled out a clean shift and stockings, drawing them over her body, remembering the freedom of being without and the sensuous softness of his skin caressing hers. She shook her head to drive away such thoughts, there was much to be done. She searched her wardrobe for a suitable dress. If she must return to his room she wanted to be as presentable as possible; it would be devastating if he looked on her with distaste in the morning light. But there was little selection to be had. She could not wear her one Sunday dress to work in the kitchen, and the only others were matching duplicates of the one she had on yesterday, only the material changing. Drawing out the yellow and praying it would suffice, she slipped it over her head, fastening it securely behind her.

Jennifer studied her reflection in the tarnished mirror of the dresser; the thin material molded to ripe breasts, clinging about her waist before draping in folds across her hips to her ankles. The material was old and worn, but the yellow went well with the golden highlights of her hair as she brushed it thoroughly, wrapping it into a respectable knot at the nape of her neck. She wished she dared wear it loose, or with wisps of curls about her face as she had seen other ladies do, but her mother wouldn't hear of such finery.

She was just pulling on her shoes when the knocking sounded at the door, her mother's voice calling for Jennifer to rise. Answering with her usual cry of awakening, she heard her mother's footsteps continuing on down the hallway. Now she had the few minutes usually spent in washing and dressing to run back down the stairs and find the incriminating evidence she had left behind. She wondered if he would still be sleeping, what he looked like, or if she really wished to know.

The carpet of the second floor deadened her footsteps as she approached the door. Should she knock? Hesitating only a moment to see if anyone was about, she turned the glass knob and slipped in. The drapes were pulled, the room flooded with light, and she knew instantly that he was gone. Disappointment pulled at her heart strings as she realized how much she had hoped to see him again. It was a bitter pill to take as full realization swept over her that she would never see him again, wouldn't know him if she did. He had disappeared as he had come, seemingly with a puff of smoke. Her eyes swept the room for some visible trace of his presence, only the rumpled sheets of the bed showing that anyone had slept there at all.

With resignation, she searched the floor for some sign of her clothing, finally going down on hands and knees and hunting under the furniture before deciding it had disappeared in the same manner as the creature who had inhabited the room. Her gaze fell across the bed again, catching on the spots of blood that represented the only evidence of last night's passion. Her cheeks flushed with heat at the thought of her mother finding the stained sheets, but there was no way of hiding it. Hastily, she threw the covers over them and prayed her mother would strip the bed with her usual dispassionate efficiency, all in one stroke.

One quick glance around the room before she left, and her attention was drawn to the dressing table. Crossing the room, she stood before the mirror and read the message on the bundle she found there. In a carefully scripted hand, the words "For the beautiful, auburn-haloed angel" were inscribed on the back of what appeared to be the page of a book or a diary. Jennifer touched the note with gentle fingers, afraid to do more or have it disappear with another puff of smoke. But it was time she was down in the kitchen and she couldn't leave it here for all the world to see.

Grasping it gently, Jennifer lifted the package and uncovered three gold pieces, more money than she had ever held in her hands at one time. With a low cry, her eyes clouded, the image in the mirror reflecting a lost and bewildered waif instead of the beautiful female who had just achieved womanhood. She slipped the money into her palm where it burned as the fires of hell. Gripping the package in her other fist, she peeked out the door and escaped into the hallway, racing up the stairs as if the devil were truly in hot pursuit.

Once in her room she had to resist the urge to fling herself across the bed and burst into tears. There wasn't time for emotion. Hastily, she tore at the wrappings of the bundle, dropping the paper into the fireplace and setting it afire with the kitchen match kept by the mantel. The note she tucked safely into her bodice.

The wrappings unfolded, a sea of pale green cashmere floated before her eyes. Not ordinary, coarse wool of the kind her mother used in her knitting, but the finest yarn she had ever touched, the fibers like silk between her fingers, crocheted into delicate patterns, forming a shawl finer than the ones of the ladies she had seen at church. Half afraid to unfold it, she brushed it gingerly, knowing she could never wear it. Once more, tears threatened to overflow her eyes, but from years of practice, she held them back. She could not present herself to her mother with red eyes this morning, not if she wanted any of her questions answered.

Lovingly, she lifted the shawl and tucked it into some tissue paper in her drawer, hiding it behind the cheap cotton shifts and stockings where her mother never trespassed. On the off chance that she might encounter her demon and know him in the rooms below, she tied the gold pieces into her pocket where they wouldn't clink or rattle, determined to return them. Then she hastened to return to the kitchen and the morning chores.

Her mother eyed her suspiciously as she dashed into the kitchen, but said nothing as Jennifer threw herself into her work with extra energy. She wished for just one chance to escape into the main room, certain if she could have just one look around she would be able to find him, but the chance never came. Orders piled up faster than she could cook them, the smell of frying ham thoroughly permeating her hair and clothing before the morning was over.

Not until breakfast was out of the way did she have a chance to speak to her mother, and then she wasn't sure how to start. Surely there was some reason for a man to be staying in a room that was so seldom used. Certainly her mother would remember a guest wealthy enough to pay the enormous rate she expected for it. Jennifer chose her moment carefully, bringing her mother her mid-morning coffee before commenting on last night's crowd.

"Did we do more business than usual last night, Mama?" She leaned against the back door frame, welcoming a cooling breeze from the river.

"Not so's I noticed. Why?" Mrs. Pell's ordinary voice was sharp, no sharper than usual was her question.

"Just wondering. Thought I saw the door to the bridal suite open when I came down. I figured if someone was using it, the place must have been full." She sipped her own coffee, not tasting the hot liquid as it poured down her throat.

"No such luck. Just some crazy riverboat captain with grand ides. Wanted our best room and didn't even ask the rate." Her mother snorted her disapproval of such wanton waste. "Didn't even give his name, just plunked the money down and took hisself off with a bottle of drink in his hand. Drunken bunch of louts they are." She'd reached one of her favorite topics and Jennifer knew she would get no further information, and let her mind drift as her mother's tongue rattled on about the evils of drink and river men, the two seemingly combined.

A riverboat captain. That could mean anything from a smelly barge to the *Robert E. Lee* around here, not that the *Robert E. Lee* would bother with a tiny port like Paducah.

But there was a steamboat at the dock last night; she whirled the fantasy around in her mind. The captain of a fancy steamboat would be used to lovely ladies around him, dancing them around the huge ballroom, the sounds of orchestral music floating out over the cool night air. He would be handsome, debonair . . . And he would not spend the night at a riverfront tavern.

But what did the fantasies hurt? She carried them with her to her room that night, wrapping the elegant shawl about her shoulders as if it were the affection she craved and trying to imagine how she would look in a lovely gown to match. If he was the captain of a riverboat, he had a job to do, places he had to be at appointed times. But he would be back. All she had to do was figure out how she would know he was back, not an easy task. But she was clever, she would think of something.

The restless longing had left her, dissipated with the night's adventure. Now she knew the solution to the driving need within her. She had only to wait for him to come back to put an end to it once again. Somehow, it relieved her to know that there was a solution to it, that she was not insane or unnatural, not a daughter of Satan. It had been natural and right, leaving her satisfied and content.

She allowed the fantasies to build as the days wore on, the sweltering heat of July melting into August no longer oppressive as long as she had dreams to occupy her. The restlessness was replaced by calm patience as she devised a method of determining if there were a guest in the bridal suite. If he were to return, it would be to that room, she was certain of it. A carefully placed stalk of broom grass would let her know if the door had been opened and was easily replaced after her mother's weekly cleaning incursions.

With a light heart and easy conscience, Jennifer drifted through the weeks, catching herself singing as she washed and dried the dishes, spurts of song on her lips as the steam rose around her at the stove. Undaunted by her mother's black looks, she would switch her love ballads to a traditional hymn and restore peace. In the back of her mind, she knew it was all nonsense—she was nothing if not sensible—but there was so little to lighten her life, so little to hope for, it couldn't hurt to dream just for a while. Smoky blue eyes haunted her dreams.

The cool morning of September broke the heat wave, much to everyone's relief but especially Jennifer's. With no letup in the weather, the staggering build-up of heat and kitchen odors had become almost dizzying. At least now the mornings were comfortable, and the evening's heat more bearable with the thought it would soon pass. By the time the last dish was dried and put away, Jennifer could barely stand to climb the stairway to her room, her head swimming with the stench of fish and fried potatoes.

As the weeks passed, the fantasies she wove faded ever so slightly. She still checked the position of her broom grass, calculated the distance and time it would take to go to New Orleans and back—the farthest port she could think of—but it was more a mechanical response, something to do with her time as she lay in her bed staring at the ceiling. When the familiar ache began to grow again in her, she would slip to the bridal suite, her bare feet making no sound on the wooden planks as she let herself in and closed the door on her darkness. Running idle fingers over the bedcovers, she would try to remember how she had felt that night, how it had felt to have a male body against hers, to be held by strong arms and caressed lovingly, but the memory was fading like the fantasy. She sighed and crossed to the window. It wasn't easy to satisfy a physical need with a memory.

It never occurred to Jennifer that any man could cure this need to be held and loved. The river man was the only one she could imagine in her arms, the only one whose body could make her feel as she had that night. For the first time in her life, she looked at other men with curiosity whenever the opportunity offered, but the men on the streets outside or in the church were not the image of her dreams. They were all too soft or flabby, too short, too hairy, too bony, too rough. None of them matched the lean toughness, the muscular strength, the gentle tenderness she remembered. Or had she dreamed that, too?

And somewhere on the vast waters of the Mississippi, a lonely riverboat captain stared out the narrow aperture of a porthole, daydreaming like some lovesick schoolboy of an auburn-haloed angel once held and loved and lost forever.

Catching himself at it again, the man ran his hand through dark curls and smiled ruefully. It had been a long, long time since any woman had captured his fancy as this one had. His hands could still feel the silken texture of those young firm curves as they molded to his touch. In his drunken ecstasy at her discovery, he had made some serious misjudgments, but the joy of her eager willingness lingered with him still, like a small flame in eternal darkness. He nurtured the faint gleam carefully, with no small amount of awe. He seldom held respect for the types of women to whom he usually made love, and those he respected, he did not bed. He had not thought it possible to combine the two. Maybe—just maybe—he was wrong.

It was a foolish assumption and the cynical part of his mind scoffed at such romantic notions in a man of his experience, but still, he could not snuff that light. Rummaging in his trunk, he produced the evidence that night had not been a drunken fantasy. A worn and threadbare cotton shift caressed his palms, and he stared at it thoughtfully. What quirk of fate had placed such innocent beauty in his hands for one night, and torn her away so abruptly?

He didn't know, but he meant to find out. Closing the trunk, he stood, broad shoulders squaring determinedly as he jammed his fists into his pockets. Silver blue eyes glimmered and sparkled like the sun on the waters. Fate had dealt him worse hands. With luck and skillful maneuvering, he would someday find that gleam again, and find out for certain if it were a once in a lifetime flame.

* * *

September passed, and with it went the heat. But instead of the crisp chill of early morning causing her to jump up and face the day as it once had, it forced Jennifer further into her blankets, an uneasy weight pressing her down against the bed. She had no energy to face the coming day, no fantasies to make it easier to while away the hours, no idea how she had once tolerated her life before the river man had shown her there was another side to it.

Lack of rain slowed the boat traffic and with it, what business they had. Jennifer listened to the frustration in her mother's voice, heard the tense arguing in other rooms when her parents thought she could not hear, and wondered if once her mother had known a river man as she had. She had a lot of questions she would like to ask, but did not dare. Her mother answered every question with another, making it impossible to pry completed answers from her. But she could turn to no one else and her mind was desperately filling with a thousand wondering thoughts.

By October she was almost convinced her mother had been right on a lot of matters. River men were not to be trusted, that much had become perfectly clear. To Jennifer, the shawl had been a promise, a gift of love. How could anything so beautiful be anything else? But if it had been a promise, it was an empty one, and she tucked it away, no longer caring to conjure up fantasies that would never be. She saw now it must have been an idle thought, a passing fancy to leave so valuable a gift for one night's love; he probably already regretted it.

And perhaps her mother was right about the devil and hell, too. Maybe they weren't meant to take their pleasures in this world, maybe she was the devil's daughter to wish for what she couldn't have. With more care than in the past, Jennifer listened to the preacher's sermons on Sunday mornings, looking for some wisdom in his words to guide her through this morass of doubts she found herself in. But her teacher had schooled her too well in the art of questioning, and the threats of hellfire and damnation that poured like brimstone from the pulpit left her unconvinced. She spent chilly October evenings with her Bible in efforts to confirm the preacher's message, but nowhere could she find passages condemning all pleasures. Perhaps the message was lost in the words and phrases she couldn't understand.

So she watched the brilliant colors of the October leaves along the river drifting down the current out of sight to places she would never see, could never go, could no longer even dream about. If only days could drift aimlessly as the leaves there would be no need for this restlessness inside her, and she could be at peace.

November presented no new challenges. The leaves were gone now, but not her restlessness. Each day Jennifer dragged herself from the bed with more difficulty, performing the day's routines with less energy, a fog of mindlessness replacing her questioning curiosity as she cooked the meals, cleaned the kitchen, and forgot to place the broom stalk in the bedroom door. There was no point in it any longer. The river traffic was slowing down earlier than usual for the winter, the showboats had long since gone, and the steamboats came less often than ever. He would not return.

The need for someone to confide in was overwhelming, but her mother rebuffed every attempt with the cold scornfulness of her answers, and her father was even more withdrawn than usual. With dismal desperation she watched the days go by, each one dragging into the next with no break in the monotony, no relief for her misery.

Until a clear, mild day in mid-November, a harvest day that turned thoughts to wheatfields and cornshucks, pumpkin pies and turkeys, brilliant autumn berries and the smell of smoking leaves. In the kitchen, the only concession to the season was the aroma of mincemeat cooking, overriding the ever-present stench of frying fish. Into this autumn day broke the patter of unfamiliar feet on the hallway outside the kitchen where no one walked but Mrs. Pell, and she was already in the kitchen, scrubbing the stove as Jennifer rolled pastry. They both looked up in time to see the door fly open, a cry of greeting bringing smiles of delight to their faces when they recognized the intruder.

"Trudy! What are you doing up here? Why didn't you warn me you were comin'?" Mrs. Pell screeched, caught up in a bear hug by the well-padded woman who kissed both her cheeks, greeting her joyously.

Clad in her best rust-colored silk, the woman was a monument to the season, plump and well-dressed, exuding good health and well-being. Jennifer waited in ill-concealed delight for her aunt to turn to her, eager to welcome her and let her cheerful conversation sweep away the dinginess surrounding them. Like a shaft of sunlight on a dreary winter's day, she brightened everything around her.

Releasing Mildred from her embrace, Gertrude Boyd swept around to face Jennifer, throwing her arms out to be hugged. "My goodness, girl, you've grown! Just look at you!" She squeezed Jennifer to her ample bosom, then pushed her to arm's length for a better look. Her look of delight quickly dimmed, and the light left her eyes as she searched Jennifer questioningly, all trace of gaiety gone. Uncertain what had caused the change, Jennifer lowered her eyes in dismay, afraid her aunt had read right into her mind. The hands on her arms tightened. "Jenny, you're a beautiful girl, your mother must have her hands full chasing the beaus away." The facade of jollity hid the question in her voice.

"I don't have time for beaus, Aunt, there's too much work to be done around the inn," she answered quietly, hoping that would satisfy her and she would go on to another topic.

The eyes only sharpened with more concern. "Why don't you go on out and help your uncle carry in some of them things from the wagon? Don't you go carryin' those heavy baskets; bring in some of those yard goods I brought up for your mother." She dismissed her, sending

Jennifer out of the room before striking up the conversation again.

Jennifer heard the low murmur of their voices as she ran down the hallway and into the main lobby, empty except for her father and uncle. Worried about the change in her aunt's manner, she still couldn't prevent herself from smiling in pleasure as she greeted the only men in her life. She seldom saw her uncle, but she remembered him as a gentle man, soft-spoken, sometimes stern, but always having a kind word for her. His tall build towered over her father as they turned to meet her, their smiles indicating she was welcome.

Communicating her aunt's message, she followed them out to the wagon, nearly skipping with the joy of their arrival. Her uncle knocked the ashes from his pipe before stowing it away and swinging down the first bushel of corn from the wagon bed, allowing Jennifer to scamper up into the back and search out the material asked for. Locating it, she hopped down without assistance, leaving the men shaking their heads at her unladylike behavior as she danced back through the doorway.

In the hall, she could hear loud voices coming from the kitchen and her brow puckered with worry. Her mother never argued with her older sister, and her aunt seldom had a hard word to say to anyone, but as she drew closer, it was apparent there had been a break in tradition. Her mother's voice was furious, nearly shrieking, and her aunt sounded ominously cold. Jennifer hesitated by the door, afraid to interrupt but not willing to eavesdrop. An outraged lull fell over the room, and she took advantage of it to enter.

Both women swung around to stare at her as she entered, and she nearly dropped her burden with the intensity of their gazes, fright filling her as she realized she had been the topic of their argument. Not giving Jennifer a chance to turn and run, her mother's voice shrieked in accusation.

"How *dare* you shame your family like this!" Her face

was ghastly pale as she faced Jennifer, her eyes burning with something akin to hatred.

Before Mildred could continue further, Trudy grabbed her sister's arm and shoved her firmly toward the door. "Get out of here and let me handle this. It's too late for you to talk to the girl now, you should have done it a long time ago." She maneuvered her sister from the room and turned back to Jennifer, a look of sorrow on her face as she motioned Jennifer into a chair. "Sit down, child."

With a sinking feeling in the pit of her stomach, Jennifer sat. Her eyes reflected her bewilderment, but in the back of her mind she knew what this was all about. Images of blue-gray eyes pierced her thoughts.

Concentrating on her aunt's kindly face, she focused her attention on the questions being asked.

"When did you have your last monthly, child? Don't be embarrassed, women may talk of these things." Trudy sat down across the table from Jenny, covering the delicately boned hand with a large, plump one.

Biting her lip, Jennifer lowered her eyes to the table. That had been one of the questions she had so desperately wished to ask about, but now that there was someone to talk to, she was afraid. When her regular time had stopped coming, she had tried to count back to the last one and realized it was before the night with the river man. She'd wondered if what they had done had some way harmed her, remembering the pain, but it was nothing she could explain to her mother. How could she talk about it to her aunt?

"In . . . in July, I think . . ." she stumbled out, conscious of the weight of her aunt's hand on hers, keeping her head bowed, unable to face this woman she knew was only trying to help.

Trudy sucked in her breath and held it, closing her eyes and praying for guidance. "Listen to me carefully and don't be afraid to tell me anything. I know you know little of these things." She shook her head at the foolishness of her sister to let a girl as beautiful as this one work in a

tavern without ever explaining the facts of life; it bordered
on the brink of insanity. She waited for the girl to look up
at her, brown eyes soft and hurting like those of a wounded
doe. The answer to her question was already there before
she even asked it. "Jenny, have you lain with a man? Has
one touched you in any way?" Her voice and eyes were
filled with concern as she squeezed the hand beneath hers.

With shock at the directness of the question, Jenny
stared at her aunt in wonder, color flooding her face. She
nodded her head, unable to trust her voice.

Her aunt's head bobbed in acceptance as she phrased
the next question. "Will you tell me who?"

Again, Jennifer lowered her eyes as the words stam-
mered out. "A . . . river man, I think. Why? What is the
matter with me?"

Anger boiled up within the normally cheerful Trudy,
anger at the man who would take advantage of such innocence, anger at the girl's parents for not taking better care
of her, anger at Mildred for shirking her responsibility to
the child's knowledge.

"Jenny, you're going to have a baby. We need to know
who the man is so the child may have a father. Can't you
tell me his name?"

Before she could reply, James Pell burst into the room,
slamming the kitchen door against the wall. "Which one
of the bastards did it, Jenny? I'll have his hide nailed to
the wall before the sun's down!" He pounded an angry
fist on the table, scattering polished silverware across the
room.

Her mother and uncle followed behind and the room
erupted into violent argument, with her mother's shrill
voice shrieking accusations. Tears filled Jennifer's eyes, but
she refused to let them fall, holding her head with her
hands, blocking out all sounds as the information sank in.
A baby! She was going to have a baby. That was something
that only happened to married people; a baby had to have
a mother and father. A man and a wife. How could one
hot, summer night make a baby? Her aunt's voice domi-

nated the argument now, soothing angry male voices, biting angrily at her mother, bringing the attention back to her.

"Jenny, are you listening?"

Jennifer nodded wordlessly, still holding her hands to the sides of her head, trying to contain her thoughts before they all slipped away. She knew they stared at her, could feel her uncle's sympathetic eyes on her back, her mother's furious bitterness, but she couldn't look up and see the hurt in her father's eyes again.

"Do you know who the father is?" Her aunt's voice was gentle, but persistent.

Jenny just shook her head in response, what could she say?

A shriek of rage escaped Mildred Pell. "There's so many you don't know which one? Who you protectin', girl? I'll see the two of you in hell before I let you bring this shame down on us!" The bitter torrent halted abruptly as her husband's hand clamped across her mouth.

Jennifer looked up in surprise. She could not remember ever seeing her father lay a hand on his wife, in anger or otherwise. It was to him she finally spoke, wishing there was some way she could erase the pain from his eyes. "I don't know his name. It was too dark to even see him." She watched with anguish as her father turned away, unable to conceal the hurt she had caused.

"Rape!" The word whispered from her aunt, and her uncle's hand came down on her shoulder. "Why didn't you tell someone, child? Maybe he could have been caught."

Jennifer didn't know the word, but she could guess its meaning. They had jumped to the wrong conclusions, but she didn't know how to tell them that. "I was afraid. I . . . I didn't know what to say . . ." Her voice died out, not knowing how to explain, afraid they would condemn her more.

"And that, dear sister, is what comes of spreading ignorance." Her aunt's voice was flat and cold as she stood in all her majestic glory, sweeping her eyes scornfully around the room.

"Our mother never told us anything, she said it was a husband's duty to teach these things. There ain't no sense in puttin' ideas in a girl's head beforehand." Mildred's voice had become defensive. "Now what are we going to do? I won't even be able to hold up my head in church no more, everybody knowing my slut of a daughter is swole up with child and no husband to blame for it." The bitterness was back, the accusations barbed and painful.

"She'll be going back with us. Go on, child, pack your things." Her uncle's voice filtered down from somewhere above her, his big hand patting her shoulder awkwardly.

Jennifer was too numb to respond; looking at her father for support and getting none, she stood and did as her uncle instructed, leaving the room in silence. Upstairs, she mechanically drew a trunk from beneath her bed and began emptying drawers, laying each item of clothing carefully in the bottom of the trunk before reaching for the next, the motion soothing, mindless. It wasn't until she reached the bottom drawer and the tissue-wrapped shawl that the pain hit her, racking her body with great, wrenching sobs, all the pent-up fury and sorrow boiling up inside and pouring out. She buried her face in the soft cloth, stroking it for comfort, unable to control the tears that flowed endlessly, tearing her to tiny pieces and dashing her into a chasm so deep she despaired of ever coming out. It wasn't until she hit bottom that her mind began to clear, thoughts wiggling their way out of crevasses, surfacing aimlessly.

She was being cast out in shame. Her parents no longer wanted her. Her father couldn't even look her in the face. And why? She had a baby in her. She had never even held a baby before, never seen one at close range. How would she care for it? What does one do with a baby? What would her aunt and uncle do with her? Had she really been possessed by the devil? It was the only explanation she could find for the hell she was being cast into. How could such a short pleasure be so evil as to cause all this?

She stood before the cracked mirror, looking for some sign of the devil on her. Her hair was glossier than ever, her cheeks flushed, but her eyes were red and swollen; something had died from them. The full lips were tight and pale, no longer turned up at the corners, giving her appearance the severity of her hairdo. But despite the austerity of her expression and dress, the ripeness of her body was evident. Her breasts had developed a firm fullness that threatened to expand the seams of her gown. There was a new roundness to her hips and belly; she smoothed the fullness of her skirt to look for the swelling her aunt had seen so quickly. With an awed wonder, she stroked the small bulge, trying to imagine a new life in there. The thought dried her tears.

With firm determination, she finished her packing, tucking the shawl away beneath the meager supply of clothing. It was all the baby would have of its father; she would have to keep it. She looked around the room to see if she had forgotten anything. She had so little: a few books, a few ribbons, her clothes, the gold pieces tied safely in a handkerchief. She could ill afford to leave any of it behind; she knew she wouldn't be returning. Her quick inspection revealed nothing. Gathering her old coat into her arms, bonnet tied beneath her chin, she slowly advanced down the stairs, head held high.

Her uncle met her on the landing and gave her a silent pat before continuing up to collect her trunk. It wouldn't do to let his sympathy reach her; she could not break down again. Keeping her calm reserve, Jennifer walked the length of the hallway and went down the main stairs, refusing to enter the kitchen again. They were all there waiting for her; her aunt came bustling up to help her put on a coat, scolding her anxiously for not wearing gloves. Her parents held back, standing in the shadows of the tavern doorway, watching her go without a protest. She would not go to them. Hearing her uncle's feet on the staircase, she loosened herself from her aunt's hovering administrations and walked out the front door, not once turning back to look at the faded inn she had called home for seventeen years.

Two

A cold March wind blew against the sun, sending a sudden shiver through Jennifer as she stood on the dock watching the magnificent sidewheeler idle up to the pilings, its decks filled with waving passengers, whistles screaming their arrival. No gingerbread wedding cake design to this one, it was streamlined and elegant, all strength and little excess, white paint blinding to the eye as the sun flashed off sparkling railings. It was a breathtaking sight, but to the girl standing small and silent amidst the bustling crowd, it loomed threateningly like a great, white beast.

Jennifer tried to calm her fears with thoughts of the last few peaceful months, a time of rest as she gathered her strength for the event due in little more than a month. She'd had no idea it would lead to this while she was sitting by the flaming fireplace in the old farmhouse, watching the snow drift outside the windows as she knitted tiny sweaters and caps, listening to her aunt's chatter. If she had known, she would never have enjoyed the plans they had drawn up in anticipation of the baby's arrival. Her aunt had lost her only child when it was still an infant; unable to bear more, she was as thrilled with the idea of the baby as Jennifer had been, once she had time to get used to the idea.

Isolated on her uncle's large farm, there was no one to condemn her for what had happened, no one to call the baby by its rightful name of bastard. Jennifer could enjoy the pleasure of feeling the baby's first movements, ask excited questions of her aunt, dream of the day when she would hold the miracle to her breast. The restlessness had fled, leaving only peace and anticipation—until the day her father had descended on their idyll, totally shattering all dreams and hopes with one blow.

That was two days ago. Now she was here, in a strange city, on a strange river, waiting for strangers to take her farther away to places stranger still. It was too incredible to think about. Jennifer didn't want to think about it, because then she would have to think about what would happen when she got there, and she couldn't do that without screaming yet. The scream was there, hovering just behind her eyes, dropping to her throat every time she opened her mouth or closed her eyelids, ready and waiting to leap out any time she lowered her guard.

Why couldn't they leave well enough alone? Aunt Trudy wanted the baby; Jennifer knew she did. She would have worked hard, made herself useful, hired herself out to other farms if necessary to provide for the infant's needs. Why, why did her parents have to interfere again? They didn't want her, Jennifer was certain of that. And that was the key to it all. Her mother wanted her gone, not just out of sight, but out of mind. No longer existent. As long as Jennifer and the infant were with Trudy, there would be no forgetting their constant reminder. No forgetting the constant shame she endured at having a child who bore a bastard.

So her parents had grabbed at the first opportunity to get rid of their burdensome daughter, a heaven sent opportunity, as her father had patiently explained. Jennifer had listened with disbelief, refusing to comprehend his words until she realized both aunt and uncle were nodding in agreement, forced to honor the wishes of her parents. That was when the scream had started forming. She had clamped it down inside her, not opening her mouth to let it out, clenching her hands and biting her lips to give her strength to hold it back while she listened to the three of them throw her life away. Not just her life, but the life of her child. Through eyes black with grief, she watched her aunt give in to the arguments of the two men, agreeing it would be best for everyone, and Jennifer had known her fate was sealed.

Her parents weren't here today to see her off. They had agreed it would be best to take the ferry across the river to Cairo and board the boat there, where no one would recognize Jennifer. Her aunt and uncle stood by her side now, waiting to help her to the cabin and see the trunk loaded before walking out of her life. They had made the last few months comfortable, she should be grateful. But she had to concentrate all her attention on the scream— she couldn't let it out now, not here in the midst of all these people who had never done anything to harm her. She must hold it in until she was alone or until it dissolved of its own accord. Jennifer's eyes rested on the turbulent waters of the Mississippi, high and icy from the spring thaw. If she could hold her head under that current long enough, she could scream and scream and no one would ever hear. It was an interesting thought, one worth contemplating.

But there wasn't time to continue with it. Uncle John was grasping her arm now, leading her down the dock, toward the plank leading up to that huge white whale that would swallow her up and spew her out again hundreds of miles from here. Jennifer followed obediently, hearing her aunt's sobs but not acknowledging them. Her new caped coat billowed out behind her, revealing the smooth gray silk covering her enormous belly. Jennifer tugged the coat back around her, not ashamed, but protective, keeping the infant warm. Her bonnet caught in the high breeze, whipping back from her face, letting the warm

March sun strike against her hair. She let it flap, not caring if the wind whistled about her ears, fastening her attention on the gleaming magnificence before her. She had once dreamed of sailing away to far places on a boat such as this. Was this the only way dreams ever came true, when she no longer cared about them?

At the foot of the plank she halted abruptly, startling her guardians and causing muttered oaths from the surprised passengers in line behind her. Holding her chin up, pulling her wrap tight, Jennifer uttered her first words in two days.

"I'm on my own now, I'll find my own way." Freeing herself from John's grasp, gathering her skirts in hand, Jennifer marched proudly up the plank, not looking back.

Taking the hard, brown hand offered her, she climbed aboard, the scream falling silent while she looked blindly about.

"Well done, madam."

A mocking gaze focused on her, and startled, Jennifer realized she still held the stranger's hand. Hurriedly, she released it, not wishing to encourage further attention from its tall, dark-haired owner.

"Thank you, sir," she replied absently, dismissing him from her thoughts, wondering where to go from here.

"Would you care for some help finding your stateroom?" The mellow voice again intruded on her thoughts, and Jennifer looked up, surprised to find the stranger still there.

Tanned and handsome, the man was no longer looking at her with laughter, but with professional concern.

"Yes, please, I would appreciate that."

Signaling a cabin boy to act as guide, the man turned back to greet the other arriving passengers, unconscious of her departure.

Jennifer's room was small and dark with none of the elegant fixtures of the staterooms at mid-deck, but it was a private room, more than her parents could normally afford. Her uncle had insisted on it, she knew, and she was grateful for the privacy, but she couldn't find it in her heart to thank anyone for her position.

She loosened the ties on her bonnet and took off her coat, stroking the soft material of her first silk dress. Its voluminous folds couldn't hide her advanced condition, but the gown was a thing of beauty, one of few she had ever owned. Only once had she looked at the green shawl since it was packed away in her trunk so many months ago; it was a broken promise she had no wish to remember. Now the only other beautiful things left in her possession were this dress and the life inside her, and soon even this last would be denied her. The scream spurted to life again, and she hastened to muffle it, covering her mouth with her hand and biting hard on a finger until the pain drove away all thoughts.

She paced the room, wishing for the nerve to stroll about the upper decks and admire this machine she had once so longed to see. But she was out of place there, belonging with the lower deck passengers, and respectable ladies did not parade their pregnancy for all the world to see, especially when there was no ring on their fingers. So she was confined to this cabin for the duration of the trip. Or at least until nightfall, she thought rebelliously, throwing her gloves down beside her coat. She could not stay cooped up forever, and she would walk the deck at least once, even in the dark if necessary to maintain everyone's sense of decorum.

As nervous exhaustion blanketed her, she carefully lay down on the small bunk, hands caressing her swollen abdomen. It wouldn't be long now and she would be free, they had assured her. In a few months she would be eighteen and no longer her parents' chattel, she would have a job and be able to support herself, lead her own life. Wasn't that what she had wanted? All it would cost her was the baby. She couldn't raise a child and work. The baby needed a father and a full-time mother; she couldn't provide that. Give up the baby, that was all they asked. All. The word echoed in the canyons of her mind as darkness descended upon her, the silent scream filling the crevasses of her sleep.

Jennifer woke to find the room muffled in darkness, even her small porthole showing no trace of evening light. Hunger gnawed inside, but she had made no arrangements to have meals sent to the cabin as her uncle had directed her to do. She would have to locate the dining area or a steward, preferably the latter as she had no wish to sit alone in a hall full of strangers.

Throwing a coat over her shoulders to keep out the chill night air, Jennifer stepped into the passageway. The cabin boy had shown her the way to the main cabin if she could only remember what he had said. She had been in too much of a daze to pay much attention. Now, with pangs of hunger driving her on, she was wide awake and repentant of her inattentiveness. With a bravery she didn't feel, she marched down the passage determined to tackle the first person she ran across.

It didn't work in quite that way. The first person she ran across tackled her, his limp form flying with unavoidable speed from the darkened doorway of the saloon, crashing into her shoulder, sending her caroming into the far wall with a frightened scream and sickening thud. As she lost her balance and grabbed blindly at the walls to steady herself, angry curses exploded behind her, and strong arms caught her, their grip tightening as she struggled to right herself. With firm assurance someone helped her find her footing, then left her standing bewildered and alone, watching with amazement as a tall, furious figure stalked past. He grabbed her drunken assailant by the shirt collar, dragged him to his feet, and shoved him into the hands of a waiting companion.

"Get this damned drunk out of here and don't let me catch him back in here again." The tone was low and deadly, with the command of someone used to giving orders and having them obeyed.

Towering over the two hapless drunks, hands behind his back, the furious figure waited until they staggered out of sight before waving an imperious dismissal at the crowd gathering in the doorway. Not until the crowd dispersed did the dark-haired stranger return to Jennifer's side, his gray eyes cold and icy with anger. With a slight bow, he presented himself, a dark curl falling across his brow as he unbent his lengthy frame.

"Madam, I beg your pardon for the incident. Are you safe? Would you care for some assistance in returning to your room?" His voice conveyed cool courtesy, but the twitch of a muscle over sculptured cheekbones bore evidence of a still simmering temper.

Jennifer recognized the handsome stranger who had so effectively come to her aid twice now, and naively wondered what his position could be on this boat. It would have to be one of importance to make other men run and jump as she had seen them do at his command.

"I'm a bit shaken, but well, thank you, sir. If you could just tell me whom to talk to about having meals sent to my room, I would be grateful." Shyly, she lowered her eyes away from his penetrating gaze; he seemed always to be staring, and with an unnerving intensity.

"Forgive me for not introducing myself earlier," he apologized coldly. "I am Captain Marcus Armstrong, officer in charge of the *Lucky Chance*. If you will give me your arm and direct me to your stateroom, I will see you safely back and a meal sent up at once." Mentally, he cursed whatever idiot had allowed this child to roam his boat alone and in her condition. All he needed was to have her giving birth on deck after being knocked down by one of those drunken oafs in the saloon. Husbands and parents could come crawling out of the woodwork then, suing him for everything he had and then some. His gaze flickered idly over slender fingers clutching at an inexpensive coat, abruptly noticing the absence of a ring. Puzzled, he quickly took in the rest of the obviously pregnant girl, her high-necked gown, the severely wrapped hair, and those disconcerting almond eyes. She was an enigma. He could place her in no particular category with his usual passengers.

"Thank you, Captain, but I only have a small room just down the passageway. I can find my own way back. I hate to bother you about dinner, but I . . ." her voice wavered.

Peremptorily taking her hand and placing it in the crook of his arm, the captain guided Jennifer in the direction indicated. "It is no trouble and I have no desire to see a repeat of this incident. You will be much safer in your room and I would advise you to leave it only in the company of someone else for your own protection." His curiosity aroused, he didn't have time to pursue it; there were more important things to be done on this trip.

A trifle irritated at the man's superior manner, Jennifer said nothing. His strong arm encased her hand, and she did not dare risk his ire by pulling away. Tired of people telling her what to do, she was thankful the walk was a short one; this stranger had the irritating habit of making every word a command. It did not make for peaceful conversation. Stopping at her door and turning to dismiss him, she was slightly startled to discover his eyes were no longer the icy shade of gray she had noticed earlier, but a softer color approaching blue.

Ignoring this hesitation, the captain held her hand a moment longer before releasing it. "A lady eating for two should not be kept waiting for her dinner; I'll see that it is sent up at once." With a gentle squeeze, he returned her hand and strode rapidly away, once more the perfect facsimile of a busy man with many things on his mind.

Jennifer watched thoughtfully as he disappeared around a corner. Had there been a trace of a smile on his face as he left her? Her cheeks reddened as she looked down at her ringless hand, and she whirled and let herself back into the darkened room. She should have worn gloves, a proper lady would have, then there would have been no need for that smug look on his face. Flinging her coat across a chair, she returned to pacing the room in angry frustration.

After refusing the bottle of wine brought up with the meal, Jennifer was left to eat alone in the privacy of her room, only to discover she was no longer hungry. She picked at the meal until the decision to walk the decks reasserted itself, and with a tight smile of decision, she cleaned her plate. Darkness would hide her from prying eyes, she could get her exercise without disturbing anyone's idea of propriety, and the captain would never know the difference.

As she had suspected earlier, the chilly deck was deserted, and Jennifer strolled easily without further "incidents" as the captain had termed it. Everyone had taken refuge from the cold in the gaudy entertainment rooms, the sounds of loud laughter, tinkling glasses, and music floating out on the night air in the same magical way she remembered from summer nights past. Only this time, she was only a few feet away, had only to step through a doorway to be swept up in the glitter and merriment. But it was a step she could never make.

Wrapped in her warm coat, the silk of her dress rustling about her feet, Jennifer walked on, circling the deck twice before giving in to the cold and returning to her lonely room and the blissful escape of slumber.

Sleep did not come easily, and once there, it was a restless slumber at best. Dashed awake by an ear-splitting crash of thunder, Jennifer threw herself from the bed, clutching the blanket in terror.

The floor rocked furiously beneath her feet, and the ever-present scream pounded at the walls of her mind, seeking release. Tossed about like a leaf on a raging tide, she had nothing to cling to, nothing sturdy to grab for support, nothing to prevent the scream's escaping. It was as if her worst nightmares had come awake with her. Darkness and uncertainty crashed around her like the thunder, and all her soul cried out to give vent to that violent scream. It tore at her throat, choking her like an unseen hand, and she would go mad if she didn't allow it to rip from her.

Terrified by her own insanity, Jennifer tore open the door, letting the stormy wind fly into the cabin and pelt her with ice cold drops that didn't cool the burning sensation of fear. She let the wind tear her from the safety of the room, heeding its mad call as she searched for a gale to drive away her madness. The river pounded against the lower decks as she leaned over the railing, the urge to scream growing stronger, pushing her forward, surging upward and outward as her hands gripped the railing tighter and tighter, denying the deep, dark waters swirling far below . . .

Rough hands grabbed her rudely from behind, jerking her from the railing. Jennifer plunged into a swirl of total darkness, awakening again only with the awareness of angry voices and the sensation of being carried. She struggled to free herself from a pair of strong arms. The blinding scream retreated, slipping back into its hiding place, allowing her head to fall limply against the security of someone's broad chest.

"What in the damn hell were you doing out there, woman?" The furious voice was accompanied by a swift upward movement, the rain still beating down about their heads, the wind whipping her hair from its long plait. "Of all the goddamn insane things . . ." her captor cursed on, not expecting an answer as he found solid footing once more and strode purposely along an upper deck.

A foot kicked open a door and a blast of light hit Jennifer's face before she could bury it against the warmth enclosing her. She could struggle no longer, the depth of her panic and the strength of the storm had left her weak and limp, without the will to fight back. She closed her eyes and tried to hide in the darkness enveloping her.

But the arms were rudely loosening their grip, lowering her to a sitting position on the feathery softness of a bed, pulling the wet blanket from her hands. The voice was silent now as strong hands pried her fingers from the soggy wool. Flinging the blanket from the bed, the hands began impersonally unbuttoning her soaked gown.

Startled at the swift assurance of her invisible captor, Jennifer raised a hand in protest, her eyes flying open at the unwelcome intrusion. Automatically jerking away, Jennifer hurried to secure the loosened buttons, her gaze settling reluctantly on the face of her captor. Icy gray eyes stared back at her.

"I don't suppose you'd care to explain the reason for this latest escapade of yours." The captain's voice was hard with sarcasm as he caught Jennifer's hands behind her and proceeded to undo the buttons again, more swiftly this time. At her continued struggles, he added gently, "You can't keep those wet clothes on, we've got to get you into something warm before you develop pneumonia."

"Take me back to my cabin," Jennifer finally gasped, finding her voice while continuing her fight against confident hands. "I can find dry clothes without your help. Let me go!" She wrenched from his hands just as he slipped the wet gown from her shoulders, and it fell over her breasts revealing shimmering water droplets across ivory skin.

Icy eyes held no hint of admiration at the sight. "And have you go out there and throw yourself overboard the next time my back is turned? Not on your life. Sit still, damn it." His limited patience had apparently worn thin. "I'll get you a blanket and you can finish your own undressing since you seem to have regained your energy."

He stood up and rummaged in a chest, pulling out a heavy woolen cover and throwing it in the direction of the bed. "You're in no condition to plead maidenly modesty or to worry about your virtue, but I'll yield to your whims if it will get you dry any faster." The tall dark-haired captain stood away from the bed, hands behind his back as he watched her arrange the blanket around her shoulders and attempt to peel the damp nightgown from her soaked skin while hanging on to the protection of the cover.

"If you'd turn your back, I could do this a lot quicker," Jennifer snapped, sanity returning with anger.

"I'm not taking my eyes off you for a minute," he stated firmly. "This is my last trip up this river and I'm not going to end it with your suicide on my conscience. Now get

those things off before I do it for you." The eyes narrowed
again, the muscle twitching as he paced the floor, never
taking his gaze from the bed.

"I have no intention of killing myself now or in the future, but I'm developing an overwhelming urge to do away
with you!" Jennifer snapped. "Why can't you mind your
own business and leave me alone? I can't turn around on
this blamed boat without you behind me." Jennifer disentangled the clinging garment, dropping it into a puddle
on the floor and wrapping the blanket around herself, covering her confusion with an outburst of anger. Kill herself?
Was that what she had been doing? She couldn't remember anything but the burst of thunder and the silent
scream. The thunder was still rumbling outside the room,
but the scream had slipped into oblivion.

"I can think of no other good reason for an unaccompanied, unmarried, pregnant child to be hanging over the
railing of my boat in the middle of a raging thunderstorm.
And don't tell me you were seasick." With an angry jerk,
the captain stripped off his wet coat. Dropping to the sofa,
he began tugging at his boots, apparently satisfied his prisoner would be making no further attempt to escape.

Jennifer turned away, dismayed at his heedless undressing, embarrassed by the obvious state of her plight being
tossed so casually into the conversation. "I had a bad
dream," she whispered hoarsely. How else could she explain her actions?

"You won't mind my not believing that, will you?" His
other boot dropped to the floor, and she could hear him
padding lightly about the room. For a man of his size, he
carried himself with easy grace, well accustomed to the
rocking of the floor beneath him.

A long nightshirt fluttered down on the bed, and Jennifer looked up to find the captain standing over her.
Soaked, his starched shirt clung transparently to his chest,
revealing the broad strength of muscle beneath. The pants
were little better, fitting snugly to his masculine lines, and
Jennifer averted her eyes once more. For all the gallant

tales she had heard, this riverboat captain was no gentleman. But then, he assumed she was no lady, and he was
probably more right than she.

"I knew that thing would come in for some use someday.
Put it on, it will be more comfortable than that scratchy
blanket. I'll send for your trunk in the morning. There's
no point waking anyone for it this time of night." He
turned away again, his footsteps indicating he crossed the
room.

"My trunk?" Jennifer turned to stare after him in bewilderment.

He was rummaging in the chest again, pulling out more
blankets. "Your trunk, madam," he repeated, matter-of-
factly. "You obviously cannot be trusted on your own, and
I cannot keep an eye on you while you're on the deck
below; the only other solution is to keep you here where
either I or my man can see that you remain safe until we
reach St. Louis. I take it that is where you are going?"
Stacking the blankets on the floor, he returned her gaze
as he began undoing the fastening of his shirt.

Jennifer gulped at the sight of the dark mat of hair appearing beneath the soaked cloth. How far would he go
before calling a halt to this charade? Afraid to find out,
she buried her face in the blankets in an attempt to pull
the nightshirt over her head while keeping the blanket in
place. Without warning, the room fell into darkness, and
she gasped in fright before realizing he'd blown out the
lamp.

"Will that suffice to save your modesty?" The tone was
lightly mocking.

Jennifer hurriedly donned the shirt and wrapped herself
in the blanket before replying, "Nothing will suffice until
I return to my room. What gives you the right to hold me
prisoner here?"

The leather couch across the room creaked as he lay
down and arranged the blankets about himself. "As captain and sole owner of this vessel, I am in complete com-

mand of everything and anything that goes on aboard it, including you. You do have a name, don't you?"

Warily, Jennifer lay back against the pillows, still clutching at the blanket. The storm outside was receding, flashes of lightning few and far between, the roar of thunder muffled and distant, but static electricity still charged the air. What chance had she of escape under these circumstances? It was better to acquiesce for now, at least partially.

"Jennifer Lee Boyd, Captain," she replied unwillingly, giving the name under which she had registered. "But I cannot believe your passengers will approve of your keeping me locked up in here, no matter what my circumstances might be," she added with a trace of defiance.

Marcus gave a short laugh. "There are several who definitely will not, but not for the reasons you're thinking. Now go to sleep, Jennifer. I've got to get up and go to work in the morning."

She wondered at his words, but could find no satisfactory explanation for them. Surely he would relent in the light of day. He could not have the time to run a boat and watch after her, it was too ridiculous to contemplate. The baby kicked sharply in agreement, and Jennifer almost smiled as she rubbed the spot where it lay.

Then memories erased by the last few hours galloped back, and tears slowly, and at long last, rolled down her cheeks. The silent scream crumbled into choked, muffled sobs, and Jennifer buried her face in the pillow in a fit of weeping for the first time since she had left home. She poured out her misery and loneliness for a time and place that would never be again.

Three

He was gone when she awoke. Last night's storm had chased away the chill gray wind of the day before, and now sunshine poured across the cabin floor as the shrill whistle of the steamboat leaving port announced the break of day. Jennifer swung her legs over the side of the bunk, clutching the blanket around her for warmth as well as protection, and cautiously surveyed the room. Almost immediately, she spotted her trunk sitting in the corner, and she stared at it with dismay. He really meant to carry out his threat.

On swift feet, Jennifer crossed the room and tried the door; the knob turned easily, causing a smile to flit about her lips. Finding a basin of warm water waiting on the table, she washed, then searched for a brush amongst her clothes. Brushing out the tangles from last night's storm, she pinned her hair into a knot, leaving a curl or two dangling about her ears, a ploy her mother abhorred.

She had only one other good dress besides the gray silk, a high-necked soft brown cotton that matched the color of her eyes. She drew it on, thankful the buttons marched down the front and not the back where it was now difficult to reach. The empire waistline hid the bulky width of her waist, but nothing could conceal the now prominent bulge of her stomach. Jennifer patted it affectionately and checked the mirror. Brown eyes sparkled with mischief for the first time in months, and pregnancy brought a creaminess to her complexion that had never been there before.

She needed no artifice to create color in cheeks or lips. Jennifer understood that her mother considered her looks wicked and that the curls about her ears would condemn her as vain and sinful. But her mother was not here to see, and she was about to make a handsome captain angry, so she was inordinately pleased with herself.

Hand resting on the brass knob, she turned it slowly; there was no mistake, it wasn't locked. Silently, she pulled the door open a crack and peered out. Seeing nothing or no one along the rail outside, she opened the door enough to step out and feel the sunshine soak into the dark color of her dress, luxuriating in the warmth before making the next step.

"Beautiful day, ain't it, ma'am?"

Startled, Jennifer swung around to confront a gray-bearded man of small stature, his old navy jacket and cap a relic of earlier days. He immediately doffed the cap and gave a slight bow.

"Cap'n said you might be wantin' some breakfast, and I was to wait for you to come out before gettin' it. If you'll step back in the cabin and wait, ma'am, I'll have a tray up here for you in a jiffy."

Tiny black eyes peered at her with curiosity, but his expression remained friendly. This was no giant of a guard to keep her imprisoned.

"Thank you, but I'd prefer to return to my own cabin, Mr. . . . ?" Jennifer's voice trailed off inquiringly.

"Henry, ma'am, just call me Henry. I'm powerful sorry, but Cap'n's orders are to keep to the cabin until he gets back." His tone was apologetic, but there was a merry light in his eyes; the captain had already warned him what to expect next from the fiery redhead, pregnant and young as she might be.

Jennifer tilted her head slightly to the side and contemplated the man with some sympathy; working for a man like Captain Armstrong must be a tedious chore, and she wasn't about to make it any simpler. "Henry, I have no wish to cause you trouble, so you can tell the captain anything you like, but I'm not staying in this cabin a moment longer." Catching her skirts up with both hands, she took two steps toward the forecastle where she knew the stairs between the hurricane and main decks were located before Henry's words caught up with her.

"Ma'am, Cap'n says to tell you he's got a man posted at the stairwell, and he knows how you hate to be bothered by strangers, and you can look for yourself if you like, but then you better get back in the cabin, or he'll come down and put you back in." Henry spurted all this out with a frown of concentration, grinning with relief and embarrassment when he stopped to catch his breath.

Jennifer swung around in amazement and stared at the old man, then slowly turned to investigate the truth of his statement. A few more steps allowed her to see into the angle of the stairwell and verify the presence of a rather bulky boatman slumped casually against the wall in front of the stairs. The captain was right, she wasn't about to put herself into the hands of that character.

With determination, she retraced her steps and looked out over the rail onto the main deck below, searching for a kind face she could call to. Keeping her back to the man who waited patiently for her to return to the cabin, Jennifer remarked off-handedly, "You can tell the captain I'll go back in there when hell freezes over."

The man gave an embarrassed cough, and she shot him a sharp look.

Henry gestured upwards. "You can tell him yourself, ma'am. He's right up there."

With surprise, Jennifer tilted her head back to gaze up to the pilot house, only to confront the laughing eyes of the lean figure draped over the top railing. He tipped his hat to her, his broad smile dominating the rough cut features of his face. Without the angry, stern look of last night, he looked years younger and much more charming, but Jennifer was in no mood to bandy compliments. Glaring at his cheery expression, she stomped her foot in a fit of temper and flounced back into the room, slamming the door behind her.

The man was despicable, little better than a pirate or a kidnapper. Jennifer looked around for something to throw, but the place was immaculate, and if she heaved the water jug against the wall, she knew he would make her regret it later. Fury mounting with no way of venting it, Jennifer paced angrily, an action not easily suited to her condition. Giving up, she turned around just as a light knock barked against the door.

"Come in," she snapped irritably.

Henry eased the door open, his hands full with an overloaded tray. "Breakfast, ma'am. Where would you like it?"

"I've got a good answer for that one, but I guess there's no point in taking it out on you. Just set it down, Henry. There's more there than I could eat in a week." Jennifer turned her back on the old man and studied the book shelf above the captain's desk; it was an odd assortment for a river man.

"Yes, ma'am. Cap'n said to tell you he'd be down in a bit to join you." Henry had the tray set out and was backing out the door as he completed his sentence.

Jennifer bit her lip with frustration. Now the arrogant beast was coming down to laugh at how neatly she had fallen into his trap. He couldn't even let her eat in peace. What in the world was the matter with a grown man who had nothing better to do than torment a defenseless woman, one who couldn't even be of any use to him, at that? Surely, with his looks, he could have half the women on this boat, probably already had, she thought cynically. He certainly couldn't be lonesome. His concern for her safety was admirable, but she didn't believe it for a minute. She had learned the hard way not to trust another person, not even her own family, let alone a river man. No, she had just irritated him, and now he was getting even. That was the only other explanation.

A short rap on the door interrupted her thoughts before the door flew open and the captain walked in, a small bouquet of wild daffodils dangling in one hand. His suit this morning was crisply clean and tailored to fit neatly over his well-proportioned figure. The cabin shrank in size with his entrance.

"Good morning, Jennifer. I trust you slept well?" he asked casually, throwing his cap against the bunk and searching for a water glass for the flowers, making no move to present the delicate bouquet to her.

Disarmed by the golden beauty of the early blooms, Jennifer forgot her urge to fling something at her patronizing captor and timidly reached to touch a soft petal. There were no flowers near the inn; her mother had no time for them and the river trash that lived nearby had no use for them. When she turned inquiring eyes to him, he smiled and handed the bouquet to her.

"A peace offering. I was afraid you would throw them at me if I offered them first." The small flowers looked incongruous in the captain's large hand as she reached for them.

Conscious of those startling eyes on her, Jennifer could only blush and admire the flowers, avoiding the touch of his hard brown hand. Someday she would have a whole field full of flowers for herself, she resolved, setting the glass carefully on the desk. She arranged the flowers so all could be seen, and kept her back on that tanned face with its assured smile. She was already losing the battle and had yet to speak a word.

"I had to get up early and inspect the boat for storm damage, I haven't had time to eat. Would you mind if I joined you?" Marcus remained formally polite, but laughter lingered behind his words.

Keeping her eyes lowered, Jennifer accepted the chair he held out, allowing him to seat her at the small table that had materialized under Henry's guidance.

"Simple conversation is not too difficult." He pulled up another chair and seated himself across from her, uncovering and inspecting the various dishes between them. " 'Good morning, Captain,' would be good for a start. A little show of interest perhaps, would be nice: 'Did the storm do much damage?' for example. Would you care to try it for a while? Or I can keep it up all by myself for the rest of the morning, if you would prefer." He ladled a heaping spoonful of eggs onto his plate and did the same for Jennifer's.

"Since even the most inexperienced passenger can see the boat is making good time against a rough current, there would be no point in asking such an inane question as to the damage of the storm. And the phrase 'Good morning' is not necessarily applicable in this situation. I do thank you for the flowers, and you were right, I would probably have thrown them at you. And if all you have is simple conversation, I'm not interested." After this haughty outburst, Jennifer refused to look at him, preferring to keep her concentration on the eggs which were considerably less disturbing than the man sitting across from her.

"You're a puzzle, Jennifer Lee." He stared at her bent head. "One moment, you're in the midst of a childish temper tantrum, and the next, you express an aptitude for conversation exceeding that of most adults I know. Would you care to explain?"

"It probably has a lot to do with the company you keep." She took a sip of coffee and dared a careful glance at him.

Amusement was written on his face as he looked back, black hair curling rakishly onto his forehead. "Yours, or mine?"

"Both. I was raised in the company of adults, I was never allowed to be a child, therefore I never learned to talk like a child. But if you can find no one to carry on a decent conversation with you, I must assume you keep company with some pretty childish people." Jennifer returned his stare more boldly now. Actually, she had seldom been allowed a conversation with anyone but her elderly teacher and her aunt and uncle, but since she knew none of the pitfalls, she knew no fear, either.

"Well, then, that gives me a good excuse to keep you

around for the next two days, you can improve the level
of my conversation. Now what can I do to convince you it
wouldn't be disastrous for you to stay with me?" His smile
was gentle, framed by the dark sideburns that accented
his tanned face.

"Captain Armstrong, I value my privacy. If you truly have
my well-being in mind, you will allow me to return to my
room where I promise I will remain for the remainder of
the trip. Please do not embarrass me any further by forcing
me to share this room with you," she pleaded.

"Do you have any idea how many women would consider it an honor to share the captain's cabin?" Marcus
asked mockingly. "And you, who have nothing further to
lose by it, consider it an embarrassment. I admire your
modesty, madam, but I cannot grant your request."

He watched with curiosity as the girl's complexion paled,
then grew pink with rage. Originally, Marcus had felt sorry
for the obviously abandoned child, but now he was fascinated by her open display of emotions. She held nothing
back: a marked contrast to the sophisticated women he
dallied with who concealed their claws in velvet gloves and
raked his back when he turned.

Jennifer flung her fork down and pushed away from the
table, rising to cross the room as far from him as possible.
Straining to see out the porthole and to control her rage,
she managed to choke out, "It is not gentlemanly to continue to mock my plight, sir. It seems I have no more power
over my life than I do that river out there. You do me an
injustice to continually point that out."

"You are little more than a child, what you say is possibly
true," Marcus stated coldly. "But you have a choice now.
You may make yourself at home here for the next two days,
read whatever book there catches your eye, order up whatever meal touches your fancy, and I will place myself at
your disposal as much as possible. Since it is apparently
going to be a warm day, perhaps I can even arrange a
better place for you to watch the river than that hole you
cannot see out of without breaking your neck. Or you can

continue to try to escape me and make life miserable for both of us. You wish some control over your life, start by making that small decision." He was no longer sitting at the table, but standing behind her, some small part of him saying she needed comfort, not cold logic, but his experience with women left him wary of betraying any emotion, even to one this young.

"If I am a puzzle to you, Captain, imagine what you must be to me. You come in here bearing a gift that must have caused you some trouble to obtain, ask me what I would like to make me happy, and refuse the one thing I request. How can the same man be at once so kind and so cold?"

"Because, little one, you ask the one thing of me that would be most harmful to you. So now be a good girl, sit yourself back down and finish your breakfast, and afterwards, I will go talk to Mr. McQueen and see if he won't tolerate you a little while in the pilot house." With the same self-assurance he had used the previous day, Marcus put a hand on her shoulder and steered the girl back toward the table. But this time, before she went any farther, she looked up at him with those soulful brown eyes, the hurt so far ingrained in them Marcus nearly flinched at the sight. This was no lying temptress, but a badly wounded child, and he immediately regretted his harsh words.

Obediently, Jennifer returned to her place at the table, having decided it would be easier to give in than to fight. She would only have to put up with him for two more days, then surely she would be free to do as she pleased. And the prospect of seeing the river instead of being cooped up all day was a pleasant one, almost worth the loss of her privacy although she would never admit it to him.

"Will you only speak to me when you are angry? When I try to be pleasant, you seem to lose your powers of speech. Do I have to constantly raise your ire just to have the pleasure of your voice?" He spoke teasingly again, sitting down to his interrupted breakfast.

"I am still angry now, but trying my best to curb it so

as not to be accused of childish temper tantrums again. Have you not ever wished to be in control of your own destiny? Or is it forever the fate of women to be dominated first by parents, then by whatever man happens to be within her vicinity thereafter?" Jennifer kept her voice low, talking as much to herself as to him.

He had to give the girl credit for admirable restraint; except for last night's terrified outburst and the silent sobs he heard for some time after, she had not once given him full benefit of all the emotion he could see reflected in her eyes. Any other woman might be expected to break down and sob bucketfuls of tears, real or otherwise, and at the very least, slap his face for his rude comments. But although the anger and the hurt were evident, she had given vent to only words and then, only at his instigation. She showed remarkable maturity for one so young.

"Pardon my mentioning the matter once again, but you do not look like you have done very well in the realm of managing your own destiny. And from what I saw last night, you are still in need of someone to look after you." He held up his hand for silence as the signs of vigorous protest appeared on her face. "I could very well be wrong, I realize that, I do not know you well enough to make in-depth judgments. But in my hasty opinion, it would not hurt for you to stay here with me for a few days. So let's not argue any more about it, but discuss what you would like to do with this day."

Jennifer rested her chin on her hand and studied the handsome face before her. He could not be much more than thirty, but he spoke with the authority of one well used to giving commands. It might prove some distraction to find out more about him; if she had met him eight months ago, he could easily have swept her off her feet, now she could only look at him with curiosity.

"All right, Captain Armstrong, I will surrender to your whims after making this one last statement: the only mistake I have made in the management of my destiny has been one of ignorance. I intend to do everything in my power to avoid that mistake again, providing I am ever allowed the freedom to do as I wish, of course." She looked at him calmly now, the anger fading under his cool scrutiny; she could sense a small change in his attitude toward her and allowed herself a tiny feeling of triumph.

"My name is Marcus, Jennifer, if we are to be sharing a room together, we should at least be on a first name basis. And for some reason, I am willing to believe what you say and that you are a victim of grave injustice. That is a very large admittance for me and one I do not make readily. Just the same, I am glad you will honor my whims, as you call them, because you will be doing me a service as well as yourself. Now, would you care to make a date for lunch at the pilot house? The sun should be sufficiently warm by then to keep you from getting a chill." He laid his napkin on the table and smiled agreeably at the solemn girl across from him, well aware that she did not return his look.

Instead, she continued to stare thoughtfully at him. "Thank you, Captain . . . Marcus. I think I would like that if I won't be too much of a nuisance." She would not give him the pleasure of sharing the delight she felt at the idea of spending a sunny day on the river at the top of a great steamboat, truly another fantasy come true.

"You already are a nuisance, Miss Boyd." He stood up, a flash of white teeth in a tanned face showing there was no objection on his part. "But we'll see what we can do to rectify that error before the trip is over. I'll be back at noon, Henry will be right outside the door if you need anything." He retrieved his hat, bowed slightly, and left the room.

She spent the morning awkwardly perusing a volume of Dickens while propped in the narrow bunk. Sunk in the vivid tale, time passed rapidly, and the quick knock at the door surprised her until she noticed the desk clock. Without further preliminaries, the door swung open, and Marcus stood there filling the opening, laughing down at her undignified position.

Marking her place and setting the book aside, Jennifer struggled for a more dignified position. He crossed the room to give a hand, then picked up the book she had set aside.

"Have you read Dickens before?" He towered over her as he returned the volume to her hands.

"Not for a long time and not this particular tale. You do not mind my borrowing the book?" she asked anxiously, afraid he was already going back on his words.

"Certainly not, books were made for reading. Now do you have a shawl or something to wrap around you? Our lunch will be cold if we do not get there shortly." He helped her to stand, his callused hand enclosing her smooth one as she steadied herself against his strength.

When he did not release her hand of his own accord, Jennifer slipped free of his grasp to kneel beside her trunk, searching for an appropriate wrap to protect her from March breezes. The green shawl lay dead and buried in the bottom of the trunk, and she allowed it to remain there, pulling out an old woolen one her mother had created some years ago. She was having enough trouble fighting off this new fantasy without dredging up old ones.

She sat back on her heels and remembered the night last December when she had been overcome by an overwhelming urge to look at the shawl once again, to caress its softness and allow her mind to reach out in search of that presence that had once possessed her. She had been struck by a loneliness so acute she could almost feel her lover's arms reaching out for her, and she wanted with all her might to run in search of what she could never have. She had never taken the shawl out of its wrapping again.

Silently, Jennifer accepted the captain's offer of help once more in returning to her feet, his large hands taking the shawl and wrapping it carefully about her shoulders. He did not immediately remove them. "Jenny, do you feel all right?" His voice reflected concern.

Jennifer smiled sadly at him and stepped out of his grasp. "About as well as can be expected, Captain. You do not have to worry about the baby being born aboard your boat on your last trip. Or is that better luck than a suicide?"

His expression was quizzical as he opened the door to allow her to exit. "I was not thinking of that. You looked somehow pained and I wondered if I had done anything to hurt you. Purely selfish thoughts, as usual."

The smile brightened imperceptibly. "If nothing else, I must give you credit for your honesty." She swept past him, out into the bright light of sun and water, attempting to absorb all the stimuli that ravished her long deprived senses. Early smells of spring and damp earth drifted over the river, a stink of fish and water came up from below, the warmth of sun against her skin, and the myriad colors of green along the riverbank fed her delight.

"I was beginning to think you couldn't do that." His hand was at her back, guiding her toward the stairwell.

Jennifer looked up, a trifle startled. "Do what?"

"Smile." Marcus grinned down at her.

She ducked her head and allowed him to guide her, wishing he wouldn't look at her like that. How could she ever think his eyes were cold and gray? They were as open and blue as the sky above, sometimes she even imagined frank admiration in them, and that was more than she could bear.

From the pilot deck, a panorama of the Mississippi Valley spread around them. Trees still bare from winter, with only here and there a touch of new green leaves to add softness to the view, concealed little of the fields behind them. Those that had been plowed were still barren and brown from the spring floods, others were tangled jungles of last summer's weeds and awakening honeysuckle. Occasionally the roof or chimney of a house or cabin peered out from dense thickets of trees or hidden valleys, often children waved from the hillsides beside their homes, excited with the mystical magic of the exotic steamboat. Jennifer twirled in delight, taking it all in at once.

"Hold still now, you're making me dizzy. Come here and meet Mr. McQueen, one of the best pilots on the Mississippi." He led her into the pilot house, introducing her to the burly man at the helm. Broad as he was tall, the man had a twinkle in his eye as he turned to nod a greeting, a full red beard dominating nearly every inch of his face.

"Sam, this is Jenny Lee. You won't mind if we lunch up here with you today, will you? She claims to have never steamed up the river before, and I thought she would never get a better view than from here."

"Glad to meet you, Miss Jenny." McQueen kept both hands on the wheel but gave her a delighted grin. "Captain don't often bring his pretty girls up here for me to meet, 'fraid I'll steal them away, I guess. Make yourself to home s'long as you like."

"Thank you, Mr. McQueen, for the compliment as well as the invitation. It shouldn't be hard for you to steal a girl's heart away with a line like that and a view like this to offer."

His grin grew broader. "That's what my wife said. Now we got seven kids, and she don't care if she never sees another view in her life. Or so she tells me."

Steering Jennifer to a lounge brought for her comfort, Marcus perched on a low seat running along the back wall before distributing the contents of their lunch basket. Haltingly, not wishing to be accused of sullen silence again, Jennifer began questioning this handsome, but rather frightening man.

Submitting to her inexpert interrogation with amusement, the captain revealed his intentions of selling his boat upon arrival in St. Louis, thus making this his last trip up the Mississippi before returning to his parents' home in California. Responding to her interest, he explained the dangers and failings of the steamboat business now that the railroads had spread their steel tentacles across the country and into land bound areas where river travel could never go.

Jennifer frowned at his explanations. "I have never been on a train, but surely they can be nowhere as impressive as all this . . ." Her hand waved to encompass her glamorous surroundings.

"They're impressive all right, but most of all, they can go where boats can't," Marcus replied. "Steamboats are a pretty risky business at best, and I'm afraid in a few years they won't be at their best. Besides, I'm eager to take on something new, the challenge has left this business. My father died a few months back, and I'm going to California to straighten out his financial affairs. It should give me a chance to look around and find a better place to invest my money."

Jennifer observed him with interest. The picture of riverboat men her mother had drawn did not include well-to-do businessmen; his looks fit her mother's picture more than his words. "I'm sorry to hear about your father, but if he lived in California, how did you get into the riverboat business?"

Marcus raised a quizzical eyebrow while chewing a piece of tough chicken. "Curious little brat, aren't you? But I suppose it's better than arguing. My family is originally from St. Louis, some of my relatives are still there. I left home when I was twenty to work on my uncle's steamboat line. I saved my wages, made a few lucky gambles, got a good deal on a small boat, and worked my way up from there. Does that answer your question?"

Jennifer smiled serenely in return, aware that his sharp tone was a cover-up and not for her. "Quite nicely. It must be nice to be a man and be able to go out in the world and make your own way. Of course, I don't have an uncle in the steamboat business to start me out, but it would be nice to think I could."

Her ironic tone caused the captain's eyes to harden suspiciously, but after only a few further mild skirmishes, lunch continued peacefully, ending with the sudden arrival of Henry. At the captain's questioning look, the old man spoke hesitantly.

"Lady down on the deck askin' fer you, Cap'n, and there's a row brewin' in the saloon that's gonna need lookin' to 'fore long." Henry stood, hat in hand, speaking almost apologetically. He had never seen the captain so intensely involved in a conversation with a woman before, and he was afraid he had interrupted something important. If the rumors already floating around below deck were true, maybe the captain was father to the girl's babe, but Henry had never seen the girl before, and he thought he'd seen them all at one time or another. And this one certainly wasn't the captain's usual type, much too prim and proper for all she was with babe and unwedded.

Marcus made a wry face. "I can just imagine the lady you're referring to, Henry. I'll come down and get her off your back in a minute." He dismissed the man and returned his attention to Jennifer.

"Much as I hate to interrupt this pleasant interlude, duty calls me. Perhaps you would care to join me for dinner and we can continue this discussion?" The eyes were blue and laughing again as he stood and took her hand.

Too aware of the warm pressure of his fingers, Jennifer could barely meet his eyes. "Do I have a choice?"

He returned her smile. "No, madam, you don't. I'll send Henry up with your book if you would like to stay here a while longer. Would you?"

"If I could, please?" she asked eagerly.

"You won't try to run away again?"

With surprise, Jennifer realized the thought hadn't even occurred to her, she was enjoying the privileges he offered too much. "I promise," she answered fervently.

"I will be back about two to help you back to the cabin. I wouldn't want you getting chilled after that soaking last night." He squeezed her hand gently, releasing it to follow Henry back to the lower decks.

The warmth of the sun and the dancing characters on the page of the book Henry brought served to make Jennifer sleepy as the afternoon drew on. Her eyes became increasingly heavy until she finally rested them. The next thing she knew, powerful arms carried her and she recognized a familiar masculine voice.

"C'mon, sleepyhead. You had a rough night, you'd better take a nap downstairs out of this chill." Comforting arms carried her across the deck, and a faint smell of cigar smoke filled her nostrils.

"If you need any help undressing, let me know, I'm very good at it," he whispered teasingly as he lay her down on his bunk.

Jennifer blinked sleepily and curled around a pillow. "Get thee away from me, Satan," she murmured, closing her eyes.

She heard him chuckle and leave the room before she awoke enough to remove her dress and smooth the wrinkles out. Then she returned to the bunk, curled up, and went back to sleep.

An irate pounding startled her to wakefulness some time later. "Who is it?" she cried out, pulling the covers over her.

A golden head with a magnificent hat seemingly woven of feathers peered around the corner of the door. "You all alone, honey?"

"If you would close the door, I would be." Jennifer glared at the apparition with resentment. It was bad enough being forced to share a room with a strange man, but having his women callers appear unexpectedly was more than a person should have to take.

The woman did not take the hint. Dressed in a dinner dress of raw silk, the cut of a daringly narrow design with generous decolletage to expose the fullness of her breasts and the long curve of her creamy neck, she filled the room with sweet perfume as she closed the door behind her. Moving gracefully across the small expanse of floor between door and bunk, she blinked to adjust her eyes while staring with astonishment at the girl in the bed.

"My God, he's taken up with children now! How old are you, child?" she asked, aghast.

"Old enough to know better than to ask your age," Jennifer replied. "If you would please step back outside, I could dress and greet you in a more respectable manner."

She knew better than to make the suggestion but felt she had to try if only to divert the conversation onto more innocuous lines.

The woman stood over her, eyes round with disbelief, bowed lips turned up in a smirk of triumph. "My God, the rumor is true, then. Not only a child, but a pregnant child, this is unbelievable! Well, you're certainly in no shape to keep the captain entertained, honey, why don't you be a nice girl and let me borrow him for the evening?"

Jennifer's mouth fell open in total amazement at the woman's indecent suggestion. She wasn't certain what assumption the woman was making, but her sheer audacity was breathtaking. Out of spite, she played the line she had been given. "Of course, do what you will with him." She shrugged. "He's of no earthly use to me anymore."

A wicked smile of delight crossed the woman's face; she hadn't expected such quick surrender. "Well, then, come child. Get up and get yourself dressed. I'll take you to the main cabin for a while. I'm sure you'll find some amusing fellows there to keep you company. Where are your clothes?" She was moving about the room, finding the dress over a chair and carrying it back. "Here, let me help you. Don't be shy, we're all women here," she chattered as Jennifer stood, allowing the bedcovers to fall back from her. "Dear me, how could you let him get you into this condition?" she clucked sympathetically, observing Jennifer's pear-shaped figure while holding out the gown.

"If you could tell me how to prevent it, I would be eternally grateful," Jennifer muttered sarcastically, lowering the dress over her head.

"I'm sure I wouldn't know, honey; I've been lucky, I guess. I surely can't understand what Marc sees in you in that condition." She shook her head as she watched Jennifer pull the material of her dress taut over milk-laden breasts, buttoning it with some difficulty.

Jennifer looked at her disdainfully. If this was the type of woman the captain preferred, she couldn't understand his odd predilection either, but she wasn't about to let this creature know.

"Maybe motherhood appeals to him," she suggested caustically.

The woman ignored this, hustling Jennifer toward the door. "Come on, let's get you out of here before the captain comes back, I want to surprise him."

Jennifer caught the handle of the door, opening it and politely allowing the woman to step through first. Still holding on to the knob, she glanced around for Henry, spying him at the end of the deck and coming closer. She waited for him to reach hearing range, then called sweetly, "Henry, this charming lady wants to show me the main cabin. Surely it will be all right for me to go with such an old friend of Marc's." She emphasized the pet name with a touch of irony, giving the woman a malevolent look behind her back.

Henry shook his head. "No way, mum, captain's orders were for you to stay in the cabin until he comes back. He's already sent down word to cook he'll be dining here tonight."

As the woman exclaimed in fury, Jennifer beamed with malicious mischief. "So sorry, I guess he prefers motherhood, after all." Stepping back into the room, she slammed the door and waited as angry footsteps clattered down the deck and out of hearing. Then she eased the door open and looked for Henry.

He was leaning over the railing, obviously watching with enjoyment the furious figure below him. At the sound of the door, he swung around, still snickering. "Anything I can do for you, ma'am?"

Jennifer grinned in collusion. "Will you stop that ma'am nonsense and call me Jenny like that abominable captain of yours does?"

He returned the grin. "Yes, ma'am, Jenny. Anything else?"

"Did I do the right thing? Or is the captain going to be awful mad?"

"Oh, no, you did just fine. I couldn't of done it better."

"Thank you, Henry, but I couldn't have done it without you. Do I have time to wash before the captain comes back?"

"Yes, ma'am. Let me get some warm water." Then he hurried off, leaving Jennifer to her own amusement.

After washing, Jennifer donned the gray silk once more. It could not compare with the fashionable ladies below, but neither could her figure at the moment. Brushing out long, auburn hair, she stroked it until golden highlights sparkled against deep, gleaming red. Twisting it on top of her head, allowing small wisps of curls to escape about her face, Jennifer decided her mother would be properly horrified at the result. She wrinkled her nose at the reflection and went to find her book.

She was ensconced in a more dignified position this time when the captain's knock rattled at the door. Instead of entering without pause, as before, he called out, "Are you decent?"

Jennifer rose and opened the door for him. "More decent than some people, I suspect," she replied cryptically as he strode in, flinging his hat into the corner.

Hooking thumbs in his vest pockets, Marcus looked down at her through laughing eyes, a grin spreading across his chiseled face. "Does that commence round three or are you referring to the lovely Lady Lassiter?"

Jennifer returned to her seat and picked up her book, returning his look with innocence. "Is that what that menace is called?"

"Among other things. I understand you two didn't hit it off too well. As a matter of fact, my ears are still burning from the product of that episode. You wouldn't be interested in explaining, would you?" Marcus remained in the center of the room, watching the mischievous flicker in her eyes with delight. If he could return laughter to this beautiful creature, he would have accomplished something this trip. The child desperately needed something to cling to and a little laughter couldn't hurt.

"Obviously, somebody already has," Jennifer observed sardonically. "I wouldn't want to bore you with the details. Are you going to have a seat or stand there staring at me the rest of the evening?"

"I think you better give me your version of the tale or chances are good they'll haul me off the boat at St. Louis and have me arrested for child molesting. Gwendolyn just happens to be the wife of a very important judge there, and she's used to getting her own way." He pulled up a straight back chair and straddled it, resting his arms on the back as he continued contemplating her. He'd already heard the various versions of all the rumors floating about on the lower decks, and he wasn't particularly worried about their outcome, but it would be interesting to see how the girl had reacted to them.

The mischief swiftly fled Jennifer's face and her brow puckered. "I'm sorry, I didn't know that. I hope I haven't caused you more trouble. How could the wife of a judge be such a . . ." she struggled for a polite word.

"Bitch?" Marcus supplied helpfully. "Being married to a man thirty years her senior may have something to do with it. Marrying him for his money maybe a little more. See, I told you you would come in handy around here. I won't have to put up with her for the rest of the trip now, so don't be too sorry."

"She won't really have you arrested, will she? I mean . . . you didn't have anything to do . . ." Jennifer floundered in her embarrassment.

"It would be a pity to pay the penalty and not have had the pleasure," he assured her, turning embarrassment to outrage. "No, I wouldn't worry too much about that nonsense," he continued, quickly soothing ruffled feelings. "I brought it on myself when I hauled you up here. It didn't bother me then and it doesn't bother me now. I'm just curious to know what you said to her to get her so riled up."

"I didn't really say anything. She came up here laboring under that outlandish misconception and I just let her have her way." Jennifer shrugged laconically. "Maybe I did make a nasty remark or two, but as long as she was getting her way, she didn't seem to care. It was when she found out that I wasn't in a position to give her what she wanted that she got mad." Jennifer met his eyes easily, a grin tugging at the corner of her mouth as she remembered the woman's irate glare.

"Tricking her out of the room and slamming the door in her face didn't come in to it anywhere, then?" His eyebrows inched up quizzically.

"I told you I value my privacy. If you wish to entertain any more of your paramours, I suggest you return me to my room so I won't be tempted to repeat the performance."

His laughter rolled across the room as he stood and pushed the chair back. "Not a chance, lady, you're too valuable a commodity. I would like to see you repeat the performance several times a day if you would. It's not often that female gets what's coming to her." Marcus crossed the room to the door and opened it, retrieving a bucket of ice from outside, a bottle of champagne carefully buried within. Carrying it into the room, he twisted the cork. "Now, the cook tells me you refused the bottle of wine I sent you yesterday. I'm not going to let you get away with it again today." The cork fizzed open, and he removed two goblets from the bucket, pouring the wine into the glasses.

"I've never tasted anything alcoholic before, are you trying to make a confirmed sinner out of me?" Jennifer watched the fizzing liquid in awe. It looked like nothing she had seen in her father's bar.

"Nonsense. There is nothing wicked about champagne. It may tickle your nose a little, but it will drive away all thoughts of our charming Gwendolyn." He put one goblet in her hand and drew his chair up close.

She accepted the glass gingerly, watching the bubbles float to the top. "My religion teaches that all alcohol is the work of the devil and he who imbibes is lost."

"They probably also told you fornication is evil, but that

didn't stop you. Now drink up." Marcus tilted the bottom of her glass slightly, bringing it to her lips.

Jennifer took a small sip, wrinkling her nose at the bubbles, her dark eyes studying his tanned face and winning smile with caution. "At the time, I didn't know what fornication was," she admitted.

Marcus laughed, "What, the word or the act?"

Her gaze didn't falter. "Either."

Momentarily stunned, her remark this morning of being guilty only of ignorance smacking him with new meaning, Marcus fell silent. He had believed her then, but the full extent of her ignorance had escaped him. Was it possible to make love and not know what one was doing? Gazing at the clear innocence of those breathtaking eyes, Marcus knew the possibility existed. He grew furious at the idiocy of the people in her life all over again.

"What manner of man would take advantage of such total innocence!" he cried with stunned outrage. "If your mother neglected your education, why did your father not see to it that the man responsible was made to shoulder his share of the burden? Do not make such statements without expecting to make full explanation," Marcus demanded.

"What difference can all this make to you?" Jennifer asked. "It is done, and I am the one who must pay. For all I know, it was the devil himself who possessed me. I was thoroughly convinced of it at one time; for all I know, the babe will be born with horns and tail. It doesn't matter anymore."

"Doesn't matter!" His surprise at her complacent acceptance was interrupted by Henry's entrance with their supper tray. The conversation broke up and deteriorated into idle mealtime chatter as the table was set and laid. There seemed nothing left of importance to say.

But the lady Gwendolyn nagged at the back of Jennifer's mind. It mattered little what this stranger thought of her, but she would know what attracted him to such a creature, and why he no longer desired her. As the delicious little bubbles of champagne effervesced in her veins, it grew seemingly more important that she know until the need to understand grew stronger than her natural reserve.

"Do you mind if I ask something appallingly ignorant?" she asked abruptly. At the captain's questioning gaze, she continued, "Mrs. Lassiter—she is a married woman, a lady with a respectable husband, yet she comes to you like . . ." Jennifer shook her head and held her hand up to halt any reply, there was more to it than that. "And you, you must once have given her some reason to expect this . . . familiarity, but now you want nothing more of her. Why is that? There must have been some feeling to make you do these things. If she left her husband for you, why did she not stay with you? Or once you possessed her, why did you not want to keep her?" Jennifer questioned desperately. If she could understand this relationship, perhaps she could better understand what had happened to her.

Marcus looked thoughtfully into troubled dark eyes, covering her hand with his and tracing small patterns on the delicate wrist. "Jennifer, you have a lot to learn about love, more than I can possibly teach you in two days. But there is a vast difference between the physical act of love and the kind of love that holds two people together for the rest of their lives. It is possible to have one without the other. Do you understand?" He answered as honestly as he was able. The child deserved that much.

"I'll have to think about it. It is so difficult to imagine the one without the other . . ." Jennifer's thoughts wandered off to that dark midnight when she had willingly placed all she had into a stranger's arms. She had thought he had given love in return. How had she been so easily deceived?

"You loved the man very much, then?" Marcus asked gently, hoping to find some clue to the girl's desperate melancholy.

Jennifer stared into her own thoughts unseeingly. "At the time, I thought he was showing me what love is, and yes, I thought I felt love. I could have sworn it. But I guess I was very naive," she said sadly.

She still hadn't told him what manner of man she had fallen for. The champagne had loosened her tongue, but not enough for her to unbottle all the unhappiness she held inside. Marcus filled her glass again. "You are very young, Jenny, there is plenty of time for you to learn about love."

She gave him a forlorn smile as she rubbed the protrusion where the baby rested. "Now you are being very naive, Captain. No man would ever marry me now, and I will have no man again without marriage. I would not go through this again for any amount of love."

"That's ridiculous. You're too young and beautiful to go unmarried long. Any man would be glad to have you and the child for his own."

Perhaps he had drunk too much himself. Marcus almost believed that. She was hauntingly beautiful tonight despite her condition, the lamplight throwing shadows across delicate cheekbones and deepening those mysterious almond eyes. But in this strait-laced society, her reputation would ensure many proposals, none of them for marriage.

Jennifer's face closed at his unsuspecting words. She carefully set the glass down. "Thank you, Captain. The meal was delicious but I cannot sit in one position for long. If you would excuse me . . ." Before she could lay the napkin aside, the tall captain had jumped to help her from the chair.

"Let me get Henry to clear the table, then we will go for a walk about the deck."

Her protests were imperiously silenced, and before Jennifer could seek escape, she was being guided along darkened upper decks on the arm of this domineering man who had so abruptly taken charge of her life.

From the deck below drifted the haunting melody of an old ballad sung by some unseen troubadour, backed by the strumming of a guitar. The night was warm, and a few people strolled the lower deck, their voices murmuring on the still air. But the hurricane deck with the officers' cabins and larger staterooms was empty, leaving the early spring moonlight to the couple promenading along the deck's edge.

Marcus walked straight and tall, his thumbs hooked in coat pockets as he listened to the familiar sounds of the boat. He'd left his hat in the cabin, but he took no notice of his appearance. His gaze was on the awkward figure beside him, her eyes shining in the moonlight as she listened to the love ballad, a smile playing about her lips as she recognized the words. In a low, sweet voice she sang the accompaniment, the sound carrying on the night air like the call of a bird. It was a melody meant to stir the heart strings.

When the song ended, Marcus glanced down into her dark eyes and whispered thoughtfully, "I wish there was someone, somewhere who could sing that song for me. Can you still feel that much passion for the man you left behind?"

"I sing only for a figment of my imagination and no mortal man, Captain," Jennifer murmured.

"Then Jennifer Boyd, you are more innocent than I believed."

They leaned against the railing, looking out over the dappled moonlit water, the sound of the steam engine drowning out the music from below. Marcus drew a cigar from his pocket and gestured inquiringly. At her nod, he prepared and lit it.

"Where are you going after this, Jenny? To relatives?" If she would venture no information on her own, he would drag it from her. There would never be a better time: with champagne to relax her guard and moonlight and music to distract her thoughts, he could surely entice her to reveal everything. Marcus propped a boot against the rail and waited.

Jennifer's eyes became two deep, dark pools, unfathomable and reflectionless. "Does it matter, Captain?"

"Could you not call me Marcus and pretend I'm your

friend? I only wish to help." His fingers caught a stray wisp of her hair, wrapping and unwrapping it as he watched her.

"I am going to a man in St. Louis my parents have spoken to, a man of the church who takes in women . . . like me," she offered hesitatingly. "He . . . he finds good homes with . . . with couples who cannot have children for . . ." Her voice grew ragged from the effort of trying to speak.

"For the baby? And you don't want to give it up?" He quieted his voice, soothing her over the hard places.

Jennifer shook her head blindly. "I had hoped . . . my aunt had said I could . . . but my parents didn't wish the shame, and she could not go against their wishes." A deep sigh escaped her as she went on. "It is for the best, I suppose. The child should have two parents. I could never support it without working and could not care for it while working, there is no other choice. I had just hoped . . . I was being naive again, I guess." She bowed her head, then pulled away from the rail, pacing restlessly down the deck.

Marcus swiftly caught up with her, putting his arm around her once more, pulling her close to his side. She was trembling, and he knew he had reached the source of her distress, but there was little that could be done to relieve it. "Surely this man knows what he is doing. You say he is of the church and has done this for others, he must know what is best for all concerned. And what of you, then? Will you return to your parents?"

"Never. My parents would prefer to forget my existence. No, this man has promised to find me a suitable position so I may support myself. Then I will no longer be dependent on anyone for anything, and I can live my own life for a change." Her voice was clear and defiant now.

"Is that what you want then? Will you be happy on your own?" Her words rang with startling familiarity in his ears, echoes of his own many years ago.

"Eminently so. Of course, I have no rich uncle to rely on . . ." Jennifer paused and grinned as she ribbed him gently, "But I think I shall manage. It is not as if I have never worked before, only this way it will be for myself with no one to interfere."

"A woman like you needs a home and children, a husband to offer you his protection," Marcus muttered, half to himself.

The suddenness of her attack left him stunned.

"Then who is there to protect me from the whims of my husband?" Jennifer demanded angrily. "I am no fool, Captain, and I am rapidly learning the rules of your game, the hard way, possibly, but learning. I will never marry, Captain. If you are so fond of the state of matrimony, why have you never married?" she asked tartly. Her skirts rustled as she matched his quick pace.

"I prefer loneliness to the charms of scheming women," Marcus replied grimly. "Eventually, when I have established myself in a more stationary occupation, I might consider it, but only for the advantage gained. I am simply not ready for a nagging wife and screaming children yet." He unbent enough to give her a small grin. "Would you have me succumb to the tender mercies of a woman like our Gwendolyn?"

Jennifer arched her eyebrows. "Would you see me dominated by a pompous rogue such as yourself?" Then remembering her idle conversation with the pilot, McQueen, and the rumor of an ill-fated love affair in the captain's past, she asked, "Are scheming women the only type you have known?"

His glance was quizzical, half laughing. "Until I met you, anyway. You defy categorization. I doubt seriously that you know the meaning of the word scheme, yet you exhibit more intelligence than any of the single women I have had the misfortune to meet. You tell me you are a working girl and your manner of dress tells me this is so, yet you speak with the accent of a well-educated Englishwoman and obviously have the education most working people would seldom know existed. Then you top it off by telling me you are from an extremely religious family, but you show all the signs of a rather irreligious nature. You are definitely a dangerous new breed of woman, and the sooner you marry, the safer the world will be."

They approached the door at a slower pace than they had been practicing this second trip around. Jennifer allowed him to continue his grip on her hand, finding it easier to fight him with words than useless struggles. His underlying laughter kept any discussion from being serious.

"I pity any woman you decide to take as wife. You had best choose some meek-mannered, dutiful creature willing to obey your every whim for you would surely make any woman with a mind of her own miserable." She stopped by the door and turned to face him, her smile not reaching her eyes. She meant every word and felt an inexplicable sadness at the thought.

Marcus released her hand only to grasp her shoulders, sliding warm fingers beneath the heavy material of her coat so they rested on the silk of her dress where she could feel them pressing into her flesh. A long buried hunger stirred deep within her, but she denied its pressure.

"Jenny Lee, you have a sharp tongue for one so young," he chastised her softly. "Now I have other matters to attend to before I retire, so I will leave you to your privacy. But before I go, I demand some payment for this evening."

Jennifer's eyes widened as he lowered his head to hers, but the gentle brush of his lips caused her to steady herself momentarily against his hard chest. At this unprotesting response, his lips plied hers with more insistence, and Jennifer shuddered with the electricity of her own response. The aching chasm inside cracked open, and the burning heat of her reply surged through them. She felt his hard lips twist more urgently against hers, his fingers digging deeper into her shoulders with a need to match her own, and then he twisted away with a suddenness that left them both gasping.

"Whoever the man was, Jenny, he was a fool to let you go," Marcus whispered softly, releasing his grip on her shoulders. "Now get some rest, we'll be in St. Louis by tomorrow evening."

Jennifer made no response, slipping silently into the room without further acknowledgment of his words, closing the door on the hurt he had stirred inside her. She had thought the pain buried in the winter snows, the longing lost with her advancing pregnancy, but just the touch of this stranger's lips brought it all back with painful clarity. She could easily hate him for this reminder, and as easily love him for his touch. It was lucky they would be in St. Louis tomorrow, or she would be hopelessly ensnared once again in this tangled skein of emotions.

It was hours later before she heard Marcus return, bringing with him the smell of whiskey and expensive cigars. He was muttering incoherently to himself, and she knew he was drunk, although his footsteps remained light as he approached her bed. Terrified, Jennifer didn't move, keeping her eyes closed and her breathing even in the hopes he would think her asleep. He only lingered there a moment before returning to the couch, its creak telling her he'd found its safety. Boots dropped on the polished floor and the mutters ceased as he sought a comfortable position.

With a small sigh of relief, Jenny dropped off to sleep.

Four

The cabin's gradual lightening woke Jennifer and a soft snore told her Marcus still slept. She opened one eye, peering in the direction of the couch. He had thrown aside shirt and coat, but had the decency to keep his trousers on, for the blanket had slipped to the floor as he lay half on and half off the small couch. She watched the rise and fall of those hardened muscles with curiosity. His chest was tanned as darkly as his face. He must have wintered in the south, she thought, drawing her eyes away from the thick mat of hair covering him.

Her one encounter with a man had been in total darkness, and she had not had the opportunity to see him unclothed; she wondered if the father of her child resembled in any way the handsome figure across the room from her now. She could almost feel the sensation of soft hair against her palm, lean hard muscles pressing against her breasts. If she would have her lover look like anyone, it would be this captain. Without the arrogant smile playing on his lips or the cynical laughter in his eyes, he appeared almost likable. With a father like that one, the child would have to be beautiful.

A sharp pang of misery brought Jennifer to her feet. It would be better to be moving about than lying here thinking, and if she moved quickly enough, she could dress before he awoke. Struck by a sudden thought, she slipped from her nightgown, dressing herself as rapidly as possible. Untangling the long braid of hair, she brushed it out, wrapping it into a long curve of hair at the back of her head. That would do for now, until he left and she could wash properly.

Quietly, she let herself out the door, looking around for Henry. She didn't have far to look—he scurried up the deck at first sight of her.

"Anything I can do for you, miss?" he asked as he puffed up to the door.

"Henry, would the cook mind terribly if I visited his kitchen?" Mischief danced in her voice.

"If cook didn't, Cap'n would. Kitchen's down below, that be too far for you to climb." The captain had assured Henry the child was not his, but Henry wasn't totally convinced. It would be better to protect the young lady as if it were the captain's child, then he would have no reason to regret it later.

Jennifer didn't lose her smile; she had made up her mind, and there was no one there to stop her. Henry presented no problem. "Unless the kitchen can only be reached by ladder, it will not be too difficult for me. I am used to climbing four flights of stairs every day of my life, these few will have no effect. I cannot let the captain be the only bearer of gifts around here, I wish to surprise him. Please show me the way, Henry."

The slight plea in her voice and the winning smile nearly convinced the old man, but the captain's rage was a definite deterrent. "The Cap'n will be powerful angry if I let you go anywhere without him, I daren't do it, miss."

"I don't believe the captain will be up and about for quite some time, Henry, and when he does, he will be needing something to relieve a powerful headache. My father taught me an excellent antidote for what ails him, and if the captain likes hotcakes, I can make them better than anyone east of the Mississippi and then some. That should settle his anger somewhat, shouldn't it?" The idea had only come to her, but the French cook's attempt at fried chicken yesterday had triggered it. He might provide excellent French cuisine, but American cooking apparently eluded him.

Henry grinned in return. The captain had had a hard night of it, that was for certain. Between the judge and the judge's pretty lady, he hadn't had much choice but to get well-oiled, not that the captain needed an excuse lately. When the bug bit him, he could drink any man under the table and walk off standing. It wasn't something he did frequently, but Henry had been with Marcus a long time, and he'd begun to notice it was happening more often than usual lately. He wasn't leaving this river life any too soon, was the old man's opinion.

At Henry's reluctant agreement, Jennifer smiled and allowed him to lead the way. This was her last day on the boat, and she was determined to show the captain he wasn't the only one who could do anything around here. He would have to admit she had a few more accomplishments besides getting pregnant. It was a shame she couldn't show off her knowledge of math and bookkeeping, but that would be a little difficult to exhibit.

The cook was surprised at her appearance and not particularly pleased, but after being softened by a few brazen compliments and a proposal to trade recipes, accompanied by the flicker of long lashes and a grin, the Frenchman gave in. With amazement, he watched the concoction of juices and gin she created, gingerly accepting a taste before nodding in approval. If that didn't wake the captain, nothing would.

But he observed her American method of making pancakes with horror as the great fat cakes sizzled in a bed of grease. But with a deft hand, Jennifer flipped the cakes onto a platter and they nearly floated to a stop. Dipped in honey, they were a match for the finest crepes he had ever made.

His enthusiasm grew as he helped her decorate the tray, using the finest china and crystal, adding a pot of freshly brewed coffee and a bowl of fresh fruit, the last of his supply. But it wasn't until Jennifer explained the method of frying chicken southern style and the secret ingredient that made her apple pie a gourmet delicacy that he would let her go, eager to top her efforts.

Half an hour nearly gone, Henry carried the tray anxiously, knowing the captain's habits too well to believe he could oversleep much longer. But Jennifer clattered blithely along in front of him, unconcerned by the curious stares about her and to the possibility of the captain's anger. It was too beautiful a day to spend worrying about people she would never see again, and her sense of accomplishment carried her through.

Marcus had just drawn on a white frilled shirt and was searching hurriedly for his boots when she opened the door.

"Goddammit, woman, I was just coming to look for you! Where's that damn fool man of mine?" Marcus irritably threw down the boot he'd located.

Jennifer stepped aside to allow Henry in, not taking her amused gaze from Marcus' unshaven face. His look was thunderous as the old man set the tray down and began to back out of the room.

"Where the hell do you think you're going? I want some explanations before anyone goes anywhere." Marcus dumped water into a bowl, splashing it to his face in a vain attempt to clear the fog in his brain.

"Before drowning yourself, I would suggest you sit down and try a sip of this. Then perhaps you will be in some condition to understand what is being said." Jennifer presented him with the glass of drink she had mixed, a smile still curving her lips. How could anyone be frightened of a man with a curl in the middle of his forehead?

Gray eyes observed the glass suspiciously as he toweled his face. "Before I submit to your poison, I suggest you tell me where you got it. I have already warned you of the folly of wandering these decks without me." Marcus took the drink from her hand and eyed it closely, sniffing it and wrinkling his nose while waiting for her reply.

Relieved of the glass, Jennifer sat down at the small table and began uncovering dishes, setting out plates, and pouring coffee. "I believe you warned me of going alone, and I was not alone, I was with Henry. Now let the poor man go back to his work and sit down. Your breakfast will get cold if you stand there much longer." She winked at Henry, and he again edged toward the door, a frown still on his face but the faintest glimmer of a smile appearing in his eyes.

Marcus glared as the old man attempted to escape. "I want warm water to wash with, I haven't got all day to play around in," he barked.

"Yes, sir!" And Henry disappeared, leaving the beast to the beauty.

Marcus sipped his drink and grimaced. "What is this stuff? It could scald the hide off a buffalo."

Jennifer sat back and watched as he drained the glass. "An old family recipe. Feeling better?"

"No thanks to you. I nearly killed myself getting up off that couch when I saw you were gone." He rubbed the back of his skull wryly.

"I meant to be back before you woke but your cook is too much the Frenchman to allow me to leave easily. Now will you please sit and quit glaring at me so hatefully? I only wished to pay you back on more satisfactory terms than I could offer last night." She smiled at his raised eyebrow.

"Would you not prefer that I wash and dress before I offend your maidenly modesty?"

She cast a wicked eye over his shirt-sleeved garb before replying, "My maidenly modesty has been more mortally offended than that, but my culinary artistry has not, and it will suffer greatly if you do not eat while the food is still hot."

"By that, I take it to mean you tripped down to the kitchens to cook this meal." Marcus slid into the chair and began to examine the contents of the various dishes. "You could have broken your neck on all those steps. You had no business going down there."

"I could negotiate those steps better than you could in the state you were in last night," she replied calmly, filling his plate with the cakes and handing it to him.

"Yes, but if I fall, the only party injured is myself." He took a bite of the hotcakes, completing his mouthful before continuing.

"How did you persuade Henrì to allow you in his kitchen? I'm lucky to get within whistling distance of it." He sat back in his chair after helping himself to another cup of coffee.

"Henrì knows the value of a good bargain when he sees one," Jennifer replied circumspectly.

"Just what exactly did you bargain with, if I may be so bold as to ask?"

"If you plan to eat dinner aboard tonight, you might find out. I couldn't stay to show him, so I hope he understood and doesn't attempt to upstage what is basically a simple process. Unless, of course, you will let me go back and show him how?" She asked the question with full knowledge that it would be refused.

"Not a chance. But you remind me of something I wished to ask. Is your arrival on this boat expected? Will someone be there to meet you?"

Jennifer's brow wrinkled at this unexpected turn of the conversation. "No, the decision was too recent for anyone to be properly notified. What has this to do with my recipe?"

"It was dinner I was interested in." The laughter was back in his face now, and he was young and carefree once more, light dancing in his eyes as he watched her puzzlement. "I would ask you to accompany me for my final meal and evening as owner of the *Lucky Chance*. Tomorrow morning, I will see to it that you are delivered safely to your new home. Will you oblige me?"

Jennifer rested her chin on one hand and observed him thoughtfully. What trick had he designed now to impose on her? "You have given me the choice of the lesser of two evils, Captain. Why would you choose me to spend your last night on the river with?" His unfastened shirt no longer bothered her, and she wondered if she was as wanton as her mother claimed; the intimacies he had imposed on her in the last few days failed to shock her as she supposed they should. If anything, they fed her curiosity and eagerness to learn more. She was going to hell at a fast run, especially since she was considering his proposal instead of running away as fast as she could.

"Because, my dear, you are the most intelligent and beautiful woman on this boat at the moment, and I prefer to submit to your hatred than to the wiles of the scheming women out there." Marcus gestured toward the door while keeping his eyes on her, laughter hovering just beneath his words.

"There are more than one, now?" His laughter was irresistible; despite the problems that would face her on the coming day, she knew she would enjoy whatever scheme he anticipated for this one.

"May the saints preserve us from mothers with spinster daughters and wives with senile husbands. Every time I walk into the main cabin I get the feeling of a thorough-bred on the auction block, eager mommies waving their fortunes in my face to blind me to their darlings' defects. I'm afraid someday I will become so desperate as to take one up on their offer and end up murdering their little darling before the courtship ends. So if you would save me from myself, you will do me the honor of sharing my meal this evening."

For the first time in what Jennifer felt to be eternity, she laughed. For a moment, she felt alive again. His arrogance was almost endurable when he put it like that, the images he evoked ringing true, and Jennifer could not resist falling for his charm.

"Your conceit is so magnificent as to be admirable. It is not my intelligence or beauty you seek, but my disinterest that tantalizes you. We should make a well-matched pair this evening. I am in no condition to be seduced and you are safe from the possibility of entrapment. I guess I will have to choose the known evil to the unknown one and stay this one more night." Jennifer smiled with delight as he raised his glass of juice to toast her decision, but stayed his hand before he could drink it. "But you must promise to try and treat me with some respect. I'm tired of your discourteous insinuations."

He grinned. "Fair enough, if you promise to not insult me any more than necessary." She nodded in agreement, and he drank the juice in one swallow, his wicked gleam returning as he set the glass down. "This should add some challenge to the day, to see who gives in to their anger first. Perhaps we should place a wager on it?"

"And add gambling to my list of sins? I really am beginning to believe the world is beset with demons to tempt me, and you're amongst the foremost."

"Yes, I believe you expressed that opinion before, 'Get

thee away, Satan,' or something to that effect I believe it was." He chuckled at her blush and caught her hand against the table. "When will you learn that everything pleasurable is not sinful?"

"When you can prove to me that one night of pleasure will not reap the wages of sin." Jennifer rested her hand provocatively on the bulge of her stomach before rising from the table. "Now we are bordering on the disrespectful already and you will have to excuse me, I cannot sit in that chair any longer."

Marcus rose with her, a small frown puckering the ridge over his nose. "I will leave momentarily. Are you telling me that you have only had one night of pleasure to pay such a high price?"

His laughter disappeared as he looked at the proud figure across the room, standing straight and tall under such a heavy burden. His admiration for her multiplied as she dipped her head in acknowledgment and turned from him to hide the color in her face. He was treading dangerous waters once more. "Well, I cannot offer you the same pleasures tonight, but I will throw in a free night of entertainment for you to enjoy without fear of paying the 'wages of sin' as you call it."

He came up behind her and put one hand on her shoulder, tilting her chin up with the other. "I cannot repair what is done, but for the sake of someone I once knew, I would like to see you smiling today. Now I must get back to work. Make yourself comfortable with Mr. Dickens and if the weather holds, I will be back at noon to take you to Mr. McQueen. Will you greet me cheerfully?"

Jennifer smiled. "I will make no comments about the condemned prisoner and his executioner, if that is what you mean."

"You are no longer my prisoner, the guards are gone. Now I will gather my shaving gear and do likewise." He released his hold on her and departed, satisfied that she was no longer dangerous to herself or the babe.

At lunchtime, they had another pleasurable picnic in

the pilot house, listening to the previous evening's troubadour sing the songs of the showboats, but soon after,
she was forced to retire to the captain's cabin for her now
necessary afternoon nap.

Awakening gradually from dreams of dancing blue eyes
suddenly turning stone cold gray, Jennifer drifted from
the mists of slumber. Adjusting her position, she caught a
glimpse of green where nothing else had been earlier, and
forced herself to wake.

Spread across the couch in a billow of light green satin
lay a gown of extravagant loveliness. Marcus must have
been here while she napped.

Blushing as she looked down at herself, imagining what
she must look like in her threadbare shift, she rose hurriedly to distract her thoughts. She touched the rich material gingerly, not certain if she should disturb it. Enjoying
the slippery smoothness between her fingers, she lifted the
bodice, only to jump, startled, as a piece of paper fluttered
from its folds.

Jennifer sat to examine the nearly illegible scrawl.

"This was a gift for a faithless lady; you would do me a
favor by wearing it." There was no signature, but there was
no need of one. The captain's bold style was self-evident.
Jennifer stared at the writing and wondered mindlessly if
all men wrote so carelessly of things of such value, remembering another similar note she had once received. She had
learned now that men meant nothing by these little epistles,
they were simply an excuse for their arrogant behavior, but
she continued holding the dress lovingly.

She had never worn a dress with such a low cut neckline
in all her life. She couldn't possibly wear such a thing in
her condition. The captain must be quite insane. Dresses
like this were made for ladies with corsets and eighteen
inch waistlines. It would never do, but it was nice to dream.
She stood, longingly holding the folds of material in front
of her.

Despite the low neckline, the style was almost girlish,
simple, without all the immense bustles and bows she had

observed on the ladies below. It was almost Grecian in cut, with only a ruffle of satin about the neck for adornment. The long sleeves puffed at the shoulder and narrowed to a small ruffled cuff, and it lacked the fitted waist required by current fashion. Where could Marcus possibly have found such a thing? With some stretch of the imagination, it might almost fit her.

It couldn't hurt to just once try on such a costly thing. Then she would return to the gray silk. Slipping out of the cotton dress, Jennifer washed slowly, still seeing the filmy green from the corner of her eye. Another fantasy coming true, but only when she was in no shape to appreciate it. Was that the meaning of hell? Steamboat travel, glamorous gowns, and handsome captains made a wonderful storybook romance, but not when you're seventeen years old, eight months pregnant, and cut off from your family forever. Sadly, she let her hair down from its knot and brushed it out, thinking what radical changes had come into her life as a result of one night with a man she didn't know and would never see again.

Giving into temptation, she let the material slide across her breasts and arms and drop to the floor. The satin rubbed against her skin, and Jennifer revelled in the sensation, smoothing it against her hands and arms. It was like being clothed in a cloud. She looked in the shaving mirror to try and determine the effect, but she could not fasten the buttons in back. With the gap in back held closed, the gown gathered tightly beneath her bosom and fell in soft folds about her thickened waist. It would have clung wickedly to a narrow waistline, but it partially hid her protruding stomach. As usual, the captain knew what he was doing. This gown was not only made for a younger girl her age and size, but it fit even in her condition. He was obviously well aware of women's sizes.

But it was much too daring for her. Still not willing to take it off, she stood in front of the mirror and attempted to fix her hair as she had seen the other ladies wear theirs.

Absorbed in this occupation, she didn't notice the rapid knock at the door as it swung open.

Marcus stopped, entranced by the scene before him. Dark red curls tumbled about the graceful column of her neck, supported by the smooth expanse of shoulders above the unfastened gown. Arms lifted to smooth a curl in place, she exposed the creamy ripeness of young breasts against the silken bodice. It was a sight to feast sore eyes on, but looking was not sufficient. Marcus crossed the room and efficiently began fastening the bodice.

Jennifer dropped her hands and tried to swing around, but he held her fast until he completed his task, then turned her around to admire his handiwork. It was obvious she wore nothing beneath the gown, but she needed nothing to cover such loveliness.

"If you were any kind of a gentleman, you would knock before entering, and you wouldn't stare at me like that." Jennifer reddened under his gaze.

Marcus smiled at her upturned chin. "I did knock, but you were so busy imitating those old ladies downstairs you didn't hear me. And there isn't a gentleman alive who wouldn't stare at you."

"There isn't a gentleman alive who would enter a bedroom knowing a lady was asleep within, either. You told me I would have some privacy, but you're obviously not a man of your word."

Sliding his hands into his coat pockets and cocking one eyebrow, Marcus sprouted a crooked grin. "You are both angry and insulting, my dear. You lose the wager. I simply wanted to surprise you when you woke, but perhaps you weren't pleased?"

Jennifer reddened but refused to back down under his mocking gaze. "The gown is beautiful, though your manner of presenting it is as rude as your words. But you must know I cannot wear it." Jennifer ignored his reference to their wager. "If you would unfasten it for me, I will be more comfortable in my own gown." She presented her back to him.

Marcus brushed her hands away. "If you wish to please me, you will wear what you have on. Now find your petticoats and shoes, dinner will be waiting while you play your silly games."

Already she was being punished for her sins, Jennifer thought. She should have known better than to allow this devil to tempt her again with his luxuries. Now she would suffer the torment of the damned while he gazed on her nakedness the rest of the evening.

"At least have the decency to turn your back while I finish dressing, then," she replied haughtily, ignoring his laughing look. But he turned obediently while she donned the remainder of her clothing.

Checking the mirror of a final time, she thought of the green shawl; it would be a perfect match. That shade of green must be popular, but she wouldn't give in to the urge to wear it. The shawl belonged to the baby now, she wanted no part of it or the memories that clung to it. When she gave up the baby, the shawl would go with it, and she would be totally free of her past; only the gold coins knotted in her handkerchief would remain, and they would serve as a reminder of her folly.

She saw him watching her in the mirror and swung around to face him. "Your faithless lady must have been much my size. I thought you were not in the habit of associating with children?" Her voice was slightly mocking, uncertain of his thoughts.

"Let me assure you, she was all woman, and, I dare say, twenty pounds lighter, but the dress was apt, or so I thought at the time. Now put a wrap on, it's cooling off rapidly outside." The laughter was gone from his eyes, but there was no irritation in his tone at her questioning.

"Outside? I cannot go outside dressed like this . . ." Her voice was filled with dismay. It was bad enough to be exposed to his gaze, but she could not bear to have others see her.

"Don't worry, I have no intention of sharing you with those maggots below." He picked up the woolen shawl and placed it about her shoulders. "But I told you I meant to enjoy this last day, and you've agreed to my whims. So, come, dinner awaits us."

Lit by flickering candles on an overhead chandelier, the room they entered contained only a velvet love seat and two matching chairs separated by a linen covered table. The tinkling prisms of the chandelier chattered in the draft of the open door. Enchanted, Jennifer almost didn't hear his words.

Amused, Marcus watched her lift a finger to the moving crystal, its dancing color creating a pattern on the darkened walls. Wherever she came from, it didn't have chandeliers; he should have brought her down earlier. But then she turned back to him and the sadness was there in her eyes again, a dark curtain of blackness covering the illumination of her brief joy.

"I do not deserve all this," she whispered miserably.

"You deserve all this and a husband to go with it," he admonished. "Do not talk like a fool."

"You would see me tied to a husband who would come home once every few months and leave me with another mouth to feed once a year while he spends his time in port drinking," she replied with distaste.

"In my experience, it is women who drive a man to drink. You could possibly drive a man to drink without much more practice. For someone who has had no experience of men, you are rapidly learning how to turn them inside out." Marcus tasted his wine.

"Is that your excuse for your behavior last night? Would you blame me for your swollen head this morning?"

His face became an impenetrable mask. "You, someone very like you, Gwendolyn, what does it matter? In truth, it was the old judge that drove me to it last night. It was either that or risk hurting the old man when he struck at me. Does that satisfy your curiosity?"

A knock at the door signaled the arrival of dinner and Jennifer made no reply as their places were set and the

tray of food rolled in. At a glance from the captain, the
waiter bowed himself out, leaving them alone again.

"I did not mean to inquire into your business as you do
mine, but I wonder that you think drinking with the man
better than fighting with him. At least the latter would allow
him some self-respect, which I assume you demolished by
dallying with his wife again." Jennifer's voice was cool and
distant; there were miles between them tonight, and she
intended for it to remain that way. She was too vulnerable
to his polished charm, a fact he obviously never considered,
apparently playing with her just to keep in practice.

A twinkle appeared in his eyes as he looked at her. "I
don't detect a tiny bit of jealousy speaking there, do I?"
He didn't encourage her frown further, but continued,
"After I left you last night, fair Gwendolyn found me and
shortly thereafter, so did her husband. Since I had not
quite disentangled myself from her charms, he assumed
the worst and struck first. I am not very pleasant when
angry, and I tend to become angry when attacked, but out
of respect for the judge, I restrained myself. Matters led
from there to the bar, and I will admit to keeping the judge
company when he sought to drown his sorrows. That is
the whole sordid story. Do not condemn the entire sex for
my behavior."

"Do not hold yourself so important that I would judge
an entire sex by your behavior. What little experience I
have of men leads me to assume there is very little difference between them. I would prefer to not rely on any one
of them for any reason," Jennifer replied stiffly.

"Does this mean you will join the WCTU and the suf-
fragettes and vilify all us cowardly weaklings that do not
bend to your whims? I cannot see that. You are too beautiful to be a part of those disappointed old maids; you
simply need a man's arms around you to rid you of your
strange ideas." The laughter was back in his eyes again as
he watched her reaction to his words; she could not remain
cold for very long.

Jennifer lay her fork on her plate and folded her napkin

beside it. "I did not agree to help you enjoy this last evening by listening to your insults. If you will excuse me, I prefer to return to my room." She rose, but her attempt to leave the table was halted by a strong grip on her wrist.

Marcus stood up and pressed her firmly back into her seat. "By your room, I assume you mean that uninhabitable little hole down the hall. No, you won't escape me that easily, little one." His hand stroked her stiff neck before returning to his seat, still maintaining his grip on her wrist. "I will apologize for trying to arouse your anger; there is something about that stiff upper lip of yours that urges me to mischief. But you still owe me for losing that little bet, and I mean to collect before I let you go."

"I agreed to no bet, it was all of your making." Jennifer jerked her wrist away and surprisingly, he let it go. She returned to her food, refusing to meet his laughing eyes.

"The idea was your suggestion, and you did not deny my wager. I am a gambling man, madam, and I always collect my debts. Now I would make one final wager with you, and I will mention the subject no more. I would wager, Jenny Lee, that if I should return within a year, I will find you married. And just to show the strength of my conviction, if I am wrong, you will have me at your beck and call for twenty-four hours. I will make a special trip back here just for the satisfaction of seeing this bet out." His lopsided grin was infectious.

"You are an arrogant man, Captain, I'm not sure I would be gaining anything by winning that bet. But since I cannot possibly lose, I will take you up on it." Anger simmered in her at his assumptions, but his grin and his arrogance—instead of being irritating—were too engaging to be resisted.

"That's the Jennifer I know." Marcus patted her hand before adding, "You do realize what the alternative is if you should—God forbid—lose?"

"I'll simply see to it that my husband is bigger and stronger than you and with me every minute of those

twenty-four hours." Falling in with his humor and the idea
of such a ridiculous future, Jennifer relaxed.

"That's an unfair advantage, but I'll take you up on it,
for where I may not be worth the wager, you, madam, are
worth every minute of it, if I have to marry you myself to
win it." He held the wineglass up in toast to their agreement.

Jennifer finally gave in to her laughter, holding her
water glass up to meet his. "You would have to hold me
at gunpoint to accomplish that, and then the twenty-four
hours you collected the debt would be the last peaceful
twenty-four hours of your life, Captain. So I suggest you
practice losing gracefully."

"I can well believe that, you little vixen. So perhaps it
would be best if we just remain friends." Marcus sipped
the wine, watching Jennifer smiling and laughing the way
she should be. He didn't know what demon drove him to
antagonize her to fury, other than preferring any response
from her than a cold one, but this laughing sprite was
much more pleasant than the angry fury.

"Friends, then, until the next time you insult me, anyway." She sipped her water and set it down. "While I'm
keeping an eye out for that big, strong husband, what will
you be doing with yourself? You said your father died . . ."
she ended the sentence questioningly.

"He left a business out in California; that's where my
family is. I'll have to go back and untangle the lawyers, see
that my mother is being looked after, then I'm going to
look around for a stake of my own. I'll have my money
from the *Lucky Chance,* and if I play my cards right, maybe
a little extra," he grinned at this thought. "And with no
one depending on me, I figure I can throw it into one
thing or another until I find something I enjoy doing."

Jennifer looked at him with curiosity. "I don't know how
you can give up the *Lucky Chance.* It seems like the ideal
life for you, railroads or not."

"That's because you have me all wrong, little one. I'm
no river man; I'm all business, and romantic dreams don't

fill my pockets. Railroads are the future; what I need now is another uncle in the railroad business . . ." he chuckled at her shy smile. "Then someday, like I said, I'm going to settle down and find that dutiful wife you told me about. But not until I've got things going the way I want them, until then my time will be too limited to play house."

"It sounds very much like you're not planning to marry for love, then." She bit a thumbnail and rested her chin on her palm while studying his face. He could be so dynamic and charming, but underneath he must be made of cold steel. She remembered the gray look of his eyes when angry and shook off a mental shudder. She would not wish to see that look again soon.

"Love only muddles the mind and complicates the thinking processes and usually comes to naught, as you can attest for yourself. No, the wise businessman finds a wife who will further his ambitions as well as tend to his household and raise his children. Now you're frowning at me." He swirled the wine in his glass.

"I'm sure you will have no problem finding a wife to fit that description, and you will probably get what you deserve, just don't expect to be happy with it." Her response was rather tart.

"If it's what I have chosen, I will be happy enough with it. I'm getting too old for the romantic ecstasies you thrive on, I outgrew them long ago." He ignored the ironic lift of her eyebrow and went on, "Now I have some business to tend to in there," he nodded toward the cabin door. "I want you to finish eating; I'll be back in a few minutes to collect that debt you owe me." He rose from the table and smiled down at her.

"We specified no payment, how do you have the right to claim whatever payment you prefer?" She looked up into his smiling face and prayed he didn't hear the loud pounding of her heart; if he exacted the same toll as the previous night, she was in danger of losing what was left of it.

"Because I am the captain and an arrogant man and I

like things done my way." He left, laughing at her expression of distaste.

The sounds of an orchestra tuning up drifted through the thin door of the room and Jennifer realized it must be near the stateroom where the dance music was performed. From there came the music and laughter she had so often longed to join. She could imagine the enormous chandeliered, gilded room filled with elegantly gowned dancing couples, as the strains of music drifted in through the door with little loss of power.

When Marcus reentered the room, he found her face shining with a radiant aura. He approached cautiously, not wishing to disturb whatever enchantment she wove about herself. As he touched her hand, she smiled up at him, and the aura reached out to encompass him, the magic of the music and the loveliness of her smile working its charm.

She was much too young, and she carried another man's child, but for just that magic moment he was hers. She curled her fingers about his, and her smile of pleasure repaid him for all he had done.

"Come, my love, I've come to claim the debt you owe." He tightened his hold on her hand and lifted her to her feet.

Jennifer stood, uncomfortably aware of her lack of covering. The shawl lay tossed over her chair, a casualty of the room's warmth. "What payment would you exact, sir?"

"I claim one full dance with you, my lady." His arm went about her as if to sweep her into the music immediately, but she pulled away.

"You are insane. Have you not taught me enough sins that you need to add to them? Besides, I not only do not know how to dance, I am in no condition to attempt it." She tried to retreat to her chair, but he still held her hand.

"There can be nothing sinful about it when I cannot even get close enough to press my amorous advances on you, so now is the ideal time to learn. Besides, if I am to see you married within the year, I need to provide you with all the skills necessary to trap a husband." He was laughing at her again as he drew her back into position.

"I cannot, please . . ." she pleaded, her eyes finally looking up to his.

He disregarded her plea. "You can," he insisted. "Just listen to the music and let my hand guide you."

"The last time I trusted a man's hands, I ended up in a most unfortunate position," she murmured.

He laughed out loud and began to move slowly. "You do not have that worry this time, so relax, I will not harm you. Just follow where I lead and we will be spinning about the room in no time."

It took a little longer than that until Jennifer learned to relax and move with the music, giving herself to his guidance as they moved sedately about the room. As the music became more lively, he increased their speed. Jennifer gave in and floated in his arms, supported by the music and oblivious to everything else. Visions of blue-gray haunted Jennifer's imagination as his dark head bent over her, and she closed her eyes against this devil-sent illusion. The music carried them on until she was left gasping, collapsing in his arms at the end of the set.

Marcus lowered her to the cushioned covers of the sofa. Her breasts heaved with the need for air, and she held one hand to her stomach to steady the movement within. He covered her hand with his, feeling the thrashing movement of the baby. Her eyes sprang open at his touch, and they smiled at the shared pleasure.

"I believe I understand now why dancing is sinful, Captain." Jennifer's words were dreamy and far away, but quite clear.

Marcus gave her a questioning glance, and she looked up, relieved to find his eyes as blue as she remembered.

Jennifer smiled mischievously. "And now I will know better than to let any fast-talking man lure me into such sin again, or I will find myself losing another wager or worse. Now I suggest we go outside where we may cool off."

His eyes danced with triumph. "I finally release the

woman in you, and you wish me to cool off? Nonsense, madam, not while I have the advantage.'' And he bent his head to hers.

Jennifer succumbed to the pleasure, totally incapable of resisting anything he did any longer. Her lips clung and parted beneath his pressure, sending a shudder down Jennifer's spine. Strong arms held her in that embrace, tightening perceptibly when her lips parted to allow his urgent invasion. Jennifer returned his excitement, thrown back to an earlier midnight when lips like these had pressed their point so triumphantly. She could almost imagine the kiss was the same, and her heart leapt erratically in her breast.

The touch of his tongue singed her soul and Jennifer clutched his coat, feeling herself plunging into the same aching chasm as before. She wanted the moment to last forever, ached for a more intimate touch, and knew the impossibility of her wish. Her hand wrapped itself tightly in his vest.

The touch of that small hand against his chest brought Marcus abruptly back to reality, and with regret, he moved his lips to brush a soft cheek. Pressing her head against his shoulder, he did not loosen his embrace.

"You are too trusting and much too tempting, my darling," he murmured in explanation. "I'm afraid your parents have made a grievous error in allowing you out on your own. Now I think I'd better follow your advice for a change and go outside before I give in to the urge to ravish you further." He stroked a stray hair from her cheek and kissed her forehead, then stood and helped her to her feet.

Jennifer followed obediently, letting him wrap her in the old shawl, his hands lingering at her shoulders before he offered his arm and led her from the room.

Cold night air hit them after the excessive heat of the small room, and Marcus wrapped an arm about her shoulder, drawing Jennifer closer to his warmth. The night was bright with stars as they made their way down the deck, the lapping of the river the only sound as tension grew with the silence.

"Jennifer . . ."

"Marcus . . ."

They laughed and looked to each other, the tension dissipating as their friendship returned to a more familiar footing.

"Ladies first," Marcus offered magnanimously, strolling easily beside her.

"I . . . I only wanted to thank you for being so kind these last few days, you've gone out of your way, I know," Jennifer ended timidly, not certain what she had wanted to say but knowing she had to release him from whatever burden she had placed on him back in that cabin.

"That's a different tale than what I've been hearing. Am I no longer the arrogant conceited, rude . . . what else was there? . . . person I've been all along?" Marcus looked at her with amusement, apparently relieved that she expected no explanations for his behavior.

"Oh, you are all that still and more. I am not even sure if you are a good man or a bad, although, like my erstwhile lover, at times I'm sure you're the very devil himself. But I think, perhaps, the good outweighs the bad."

"That's a relief, to know there is still some hope for me." They mounted the darkened stairs to the upper deck.

Outside the door of their shared room he stopped. "I will leave you here to your privacy, but I warn you I will be back early; there will be no rude awakenings from me tonight. You'll need to be fresh and pretty to meet your new family in the morning, so I want you to get lots of sleep."

"If you wish me to sleep, do not remind me of tomorrow or the days to come." Jennifer rested her hand on his arm, and Marcus brushed her forehead affectionately with his lips before opening the door for her.

"You'll be taken care of, little one, don't worry."

The door closed, and he was gone.

* * *

Henry drove her away from the dock while Marcus stood on the upper deck and watched her go. She didn't turn back once; head held high, sunlight glinting off the reddish cast of her hair, coat wrapped tightly about the gray silk, she left as she came, and he was sorry to see her go.

The green satin packed in her trunk upon the captain's insistence, Jennifer felt the weight of leaving once more creep upon her, the old worries and fears returning as the horses marched relentlessly toward their destination. Time stood still for no man, her teacher had taught, and her time of pleasure had passed; now came the time of trial.

Henry stole a glance at the proud figure beside him and saw a tear trickle down one soft cheek.

Five

Jennifer dug her fingers into the soft plush of the maroon velvet drapes as she stared unseeingly out the upper story window. On first arrival, she had been overwhelmed by the luxury of her new surroundings, but now that she had some vague glimmer of the truth, the opulence repulsed her. She strove to hide her terror from the dapper man filling the room with the scent of his sweet cologne. Fear was a weakness she could not afford.

"I want to meet the people who will be parents to my child," she whispered raggedly, not daring to face the emptiness of her host's eyes. He had treated her genially from the first, but Jennifer had sensed an unwholesome current of excitement beneath his kindnesses. Now, with Bess's words chilling her heart, she was forced to recognize the truth. Her newly acquired friend's warning rang with enough sincerity not to be taken lightly.

"That's quite impossible, I'm afraid," Delaney answered smoothly, advancing further into the room. "They wish to remain anonymous, to raise the child as their own. They have no desire to meet you." There was an inflection of scorn to his chilly tone.

"Then I will not give up the child," Jennifer answered decisively, her chin going up defiantly, though she still refused to face her tormentor. Fear coursed through her veins, and her fingers wrapped nervously in the heavy velvet. Delaney had come closer, she could sense his nearness without looking, and she had to check a shiver of revulsion.

"You have no choice, my dear. You are still a minor, and under my jurisdiction. The child will be gone before you are in a condition to follow it." The smooth tones held a hint of satisfaction, the first real sign that all was not as he feigned.

"Then I will leave now, before it is born. I cannot give my child up to people I do not know." Jennifer swung around furiously, only to be checked in mid-tirade by the cruel slant of Delaney's lips. Never before had he appeared in this light to her, but now she could see the evil in his eyes and her lungs constricted, her words choking in her throat without being uttered.

"You have no choice. You cannot leave this house. You are mine now, to do with as I wish. Behave nicely, and you shall have all that money can buy. Disturb me, and you will be sorry." The icy steel of his voice replaced earlier velvet tones as his hand reached out to stroke her cheek and cup her chin.

Jennifer's eyes widened in horror at his words, and she flinched perceptibly. "Then it is true?" she asked in horrified whispers. "You're not as you told my parents?" Unable to speak the words phrasing the question more precisely, she clung to these unsatisfactory and illusory ones.

Dark eyes gleamed as Delaney's fingers crept down to caress her neck. "Did you really think a man of your church could live in such splendor? Look around you." He gestured. "You will grow quickly accustomed to living in such style. Giving up the child is a small price to pay for such comfort."

"Why?" The tortured word was drawn from Jennifer's clogged throat.

Instead of answering immediately, Delaney pushed the cloth of her robe down over her shoulders, revealing rounded breasts laden with advanced pregnancy. His fingers pinched at honey-brown tips, and Jennifer shrank in horror against the window, away from his touch, trying frantically to rearrange her clothing. Delaney slapped her hand away and proceeded with his molestation.

"Because it's my business to do so," he replied enigmatically. "The child will bring a tidy sum from people whose uses I do not intend to question. That will serve to cover the expense of properly training you until you start paying your own way, though I imagine you're young enough and if we're careful enough, we can pass you off as a virgin and collect another tidy sum to advance your education." His chilling gaze moved assessingly over fair skin, smooth hands following the path of his gaze. "There are ways of doing that, you know. You'll profit handsomely in the long run, so don't cringe away as if I'm some demented monster."

Humiliated and terrified beyond all power of reason, Jennifer shook her head violently and edged away, trying to escape his clammy hands, trying to escape the horror of his implications, but Delaney held her cornered, and she was in no condition to fight or run.

The life he planned for her loomed in all its horrifying reality when he lowered his head to taste her nipples. Jennifer screamed, pushing at his shoulders.

Delaney stood up abruptly and cracked his palm across her jaw. "Shut up!"

Immobilized by the force of his blow, Jennifer crumpled

against the wall, fighting just to maintain her balance. Taking her silence for defeat, Delaney ripped open the remainder of her robe, flinging it to the floor as he glared in derision and disgust at her misshapen figure.

"A slut like you has no right to quibble over who takes her, especially if she's paid generously. Once you get rid of that repulsive burden, I'll see to your training personally. That's why you're here and not with the other whores. You're going to be mine to do with as I wish until I'm ready to let you join the others, so you might as well get used to the idea."

His fingers twisted cruelly in her hair as he bent her head backward to meet the onslaught of his hard mouth. He jerked harder when she did not yield to his pressure, forcing her to part her lips with a cry of pain.

With her last fading strength, Jennifer reached for the bedside lamp. The bulbous base was difficult to grasp, but desperation provided the impossible, and with a single swing, she brought it down with as much force as she could muster against narrow shoulders.

Delaney bellowed with astonished pain, but did not release his tight grip on Jennifer's long hair. With a vicious curse, he cracked his fist against her jaw, sending her reeling backwards to the bed. In her last moments of consciousness, Jennifer heard him cursing for his bodyguards. Then she sank into welcome oblivion.

In the days and weeks that followed, she tried vainly at every opportunity to escape, finally forcing Delaney to post twenty-four-hour guards in her room. Only one other avenue of escape remained. Jennifer quit eating. A nurse was hired to force feed her, but the task was tedious and not overly successful. Jennifer longed for the oblivion that came now more frequently than ever.

But even the bodyguard did not attempt to prevent her staring out the bedroom window. During periods of consciousness, Jennifer focused her gaze fixedly on the street below, praying for a deliverance she could not voice even to herself. When it came, she was weak, but ready.

* * *

The month of March can be interminable, hovering between winter and spring in gray gloom and cold while the earth aches to burst open with new life. Time hangs heavily, waiting for something to happen, for some sign of hope that this too will pass, but the impatient observer sees only the blustering, windswept trees and the futility of eternity.

But for others, it is a time of renewal. Each day produces new signs of life, green shoots appear and grow larger, and time passes swiftly with the scurrying of clouds across sunlit skies. Before he is aware, the month is gone and April bursts upon him with the suddenness of a spring shower, drenching him in its joy.

For Marcus, March had gone largely unnoticed while he closed his dealings with the firm buying the *Lucky Chance* and prepared for the journey to California. He woke up to find it mid-April, his bags packed and ready to go, only the matter of the train tickets left to be settled before he was on his way. It was at this point he remembered one more piece of unfinished business needed tending before he left.

It was on this business that he found himself in the old residential district of St. Louis, stone and brick mansions set amidst towering trees and masses of shrubbery, the first forsythia and azaleas just coming into bloom. Following Henry's directions, he urged his horses down one tree-lined street after another, the first new leaves just showing their color against winter-bare branches. The neighborhood gave a feeling of well-secured gentility, and he was relieved that the girl had found a home in such an area. With a snort of amusement, he realized his jest about some young businessman snatching her up could very well come true. It wouldn't take long for every young man in the district to notice that one after she was up and about, and if she would only put half a mind to it, she could probably have any one of them. For a moment, he was almost jealous of their opportunity to see her as she ought to be, with slim waist and happy smiles, dressed stylishly and teasing the boys who came to call. But then, if she were living with a family that belonged to that church of hers, she might still be wearing those dreary dark dresses and tying her hair back in a knot. What a waste that would be. But obviously, their religion had nothing against living well, these houses weren't built by the will of the Lord.

He wondered if she'd had the baby yet, if they had allowed her to hold it long enough to prove to herself it wasn't the product of a devil. Such nonsense they put in the heads of children. He would like to see her again, but he supposed they would frown on gentlemen callers seeing someone in her condition. But he was determined to see for himself that she was well taken care of and had everything she needed. Maybe he could assist them in finding her the kind of employment she would like; it was a shame they would probably disapprove of a job with the steamboats—she would be in heaven. Remembering the fried chicken and apple pie Henrí had finally confessed to making from her recipes, he knew of several places right off hand who could use her.

Pulling the carriage up in front of the massive house fitting Henry's description, Marcus looked around. Ostentation seemed to be the architect's only consideration in the building's decor, a fact that was hard to associate with the somber sect to which Jennifer belonged. But if this wasn't it, they could always give him directions. Swinging down from the fashionable two-seater, he brushed off his hat and proceeded up the walk, observing the well-manicured lawns. Marcus did not question his acceptance into whatever manner of household he might find within, but he had taken pains with his appearance. It mattered little what these people would think of him when he came to call, but a good impression might create an easier atmosphere for the little girl if they thought she had someone to protect her, and he had dressed accordingly, setting aside his usual rakish air and dress for a more somber business suit. Holding hat in hand, he rapped the knocker. The door opened immediately, indicating his approach had been observed. A nervous Negro maid stood in the opening, waiting for him to state his business.

Marcus handed her his card and asked, "Is Mr. Delaney in?"

The maid took the card and ushered him in, leaving him to stand in an open central hall while she disappeared through another doorway. A grand staircase led to a second floor balcony opening over the hall. Noticing the huge central chandelier, he chuckled, remembering Jennifer's awe at the small one on the *Lucky Chance* and wondering what her reaction had been to this magnificence.

The man approaching him was not what Marcus had expected. Thin and sallow, he sported an expensive fitted suit with ruffles protruding inelegantly, his long mustaches just a trifle ostentatious to be in good taste, as was the rest of him. As he came closer, Marcus could smell his heavy cologne and an undercurrent of whiskey. Delaney did not fit the established pattern of a charitable pillar of any church, and certainly not the rigidly strait-laced southern sect to which Jennifer belonged.

"Captain Armstrong, happy to meet you." Delaney held out a heavily ringed hand. "What can I do for you today?"

The words seemed to slide out of the corner of the man's mouth, and his eyes flickered over Marcus' costume as if to judge his total worth from the cut of his clothes. Obviously impressed, his handshake became firmer.

"I've come to ask after a friend of mine, Jennifer Boyd. I believe you have been so kind as to take her in?" Marcus felt the urge to wipe his hand against his trousers after dropping the man's hand. His gambler's intuition rang clarion warnings.

Delaney's black eyes narrowed. "Miss Boyd?" Then suddenly comprehending, he replied unctuously, "Jennifer is in no condition to see visitors. If you are truly a friend of hers, you will appreciate that."

Marcus had come prepared for that, but not for this sudden determination to see the girl no matter what was said. He didn't trust this viper, and he would see for himself that she was well and happy. He replied firmly, "I understand that, but if you would send someone up to her while I wait, I'd like to know that she is well and if I can be of any assistance." He would also like her to know he was here, just in case.

A violent crash in the hallway above caused both men to glance up to the balcony, Delaney a trifle uneasily and Marcus with instant suspicion. Seeing nothing untoward, Delaney answered coldly, "This is just a trifle presumptuous, is it not? As you can see, we are in a position to provide Miss—Boyd—with everything she needs, and I can assure you she is quite well under the circumstances."

A torrent of vituperous curses cut off his words, followed by a wailing cry of despair and anguish so piercing it penetrated every nerve of Marc's body.

"M-a-r-c!" The wail pounded in his ears as he shoved aside his startled host and dashed toward the staircase, taking the steps three at a time in his haste to reach the source of the sound.

Ascending into the upper hall with a final bound, Marcus discovered a red-haired woman tugging at the bulk of a white aproned amazon. A second glance showed the amazon bent over Jennifer's half-conscious body as she clung to the rails of the balcony. Stubby fingers tore painfully at her slender white ones, threatening to break them with their ferocity. At Marc's growl, the amazon swiftly surrendered her charge, departing rapidly without testing the fists he clenched in fury.

Jennifer remained crumpled and senseless on the floor, her hands still clutching the rails. The green satin he had given her spread in a rumpled puddle across the carpeting, and a pale green shawl trailed dishevelledly from her shoulders. With a mighty curse, Marcus pried her fingers loose and gathered her into his arms, barely aware of the red-haired woman's presence until she spoke.

"Get her out of here now, for God's sake, she don't belong here," the woman whispered, shoving him toward the staircase. "Watch out for Delaney, he's got a pistol on him, but he's a coward. Run for it!" Then she disappeared into the dim recesses of the hallway.

Marcus didn't linger. Hugging Jennifer's limp figure to his chest, he stormed down the staircase with murderous tread, his heart pounding erratically. The soft cashmere of Jennifer's shawl burned an irrational pattern into his consciousness, but his rage was too great for a closer inspection of his thoughts. His first thought was to get her out of here. Then there would be time to ask the frantic questions springing to mind.

Delaney blocked his path. As the woman warned, he held a small derringer at waist level, aimed at Jennifer. "You are mad, Armstrong. She is my property, put her down."

Marcus glared at the sallow gun holder. Without warning, he crashed his polished boot into the derringer, sending the gun flying out the open doorway, bringing a yelp of pain from Delaney. Shoving the cringing man aside, Marcus sped out the door and down the walk he had so calmly strolled just moments before.

Setting Jennifer in the passenger seat of his carriage, and praying she had the strength to hold on, Marcus climbed in over her and whipped the horses into a frenzy. Delaney wouldn't stand around for long, and he wanted to be well away before reinforcements appeared.

The carriage raced through quiet residential streets, raising startled glances and chasing pedestrians to the curbs as it hurtled around corners. Jennifer gripped the side of the carriage as she had the railing, as if her entire life depended on it. Marcus threw her a quick glance, then urged the horses faster, driven by blind despair and irrational fury.

Memories of Jennifer's straight, proud back as she drove away from him, hair shining like burnished copper in the sunlight, haunted his agonized thoughts. Other memories, too, long ago memories that he shoved aside as he saw again her crumpled figure in the house behind him. Whatever Delaney had done to her back there, he had destroyed the Jennifer he knew. There was no proud lift to this bent head, those terrified eyes held no laughter or even a sign of intelligence, the bloom on her cheeks had become a ghostly pallor. He had delivered a healthy, beautiful woman to their door, and returned to find a pathetic shadow. What had he done to her? The thought painfully struck him in all its ambiguity.

He slowed the carriage as it came in sight of the hotel. Pulling to a halt in front of the doorway and throwing the reins to a boy lounging in the dust, Marcus jumped down and lifted the half-conscious girl into his arms. She scarcely felt larger than she had a month ago. If anything, she was lighter.

The desk clerk came running but backed off after seeing the captain's face, his questioning look becoming one of fright until Marcus informed him, "My wife's had an accident and needs to rest before returning home, send my servant up when he arrives." Thinking bitterly that that should cause some vivid consternation around the hotel for the evening, he stormed through the lobby. It made no difference to him, he was leaving this cursed town anyway.

Entering his room, Marcus studied it a moment, finally deciding Jennifer would prefer the overstuffed chair to the bed and acting accordingly. She collapsed like a limp doll where he put her, only her fingers showing any sign of life as he loosened their panicky grip on his coat.

"Jenny, honey, it's me, Marcus. I'm going to get you a drink and I want you to drink it slowly and get it all down. Do you understand me? You won't like it, but it will help, I promise." He settled her into the chair more comfortably, arranging her clothing into some semblance of order, brushing wisps of hair back from her face, anything to reassure her.

The bottle was on the far side of the bed and as Marcus moved to retrieve it, Jennifer pulled him back, her hand catching weakly at his coat sleeve. Reassuring her again, he freed himself and poured a large tumbler of whiskey, taking one swig for himself before returning to her with the remainder. It wasn't going to be easy to get the answers to his questions, but it had to be done and soon. He had to get her to a doctor immediately, but first he had to tackle that filthy bastard back there, and he needed ammunition with which to do it.

Placing the tumbler in Jennifer's hand, he helped lift it to her lips, watching as a small amount slid down. She made a face and pulled away, but he urged her to take another small sip. The burning liquid left her gasping and coughing. Seeing her eyes water from the strong taste, Marcus watered the drink slightly, realizing it was a long jump from a small glass of wine to straight Kentucky bourbon for one not used to spirits of any kind. He forced her to take several more small sips until she was able to hold the glass on her own, then he sat down on the bed beside her, occasionally urging her to take another drink until he was satisfied she was coming around.

Her head rested weakly against the back of the chair, but her eyes began to show signs of life as they wandered around the room, finally coming to rest on him. A puzzled frown wrinkled her brow. "Marcus . . . ?"

He smiled in relief, taking her hand and squeezing it. "How are you feeling, little one?"

The frown didn't leave her face. "Groggy. What is this stuff?" She looked at the glass with distaste.

Marcus took it from her and set it on the bedside table. "When recovering from a faint, a lady is supposed to ask 'Where am I?' You have a lot to learn, Jennifer Lee. But right now I want you to tell me a few things, starting with what happened to your man of the church? If Delaney is a religious man, I'll eat my hat."

The frown disappeared as Jennifer screwed her eyes shut with a shudder, rolling her head back and forth against the chair as if to banish the thoughts within. Marcus dropped her hand and cupped her pale face between his palms.

"It's all right now, Jenny. I'm here. I won't let anything happen to you, but I've got to know what's happening if I'm going to help you." He stroked her frightened face until her eyes opened again with a look of terror so profound that he wished he could bear the pain for her.

"The baby." She wrapped her arms about herself. "He was going to *sell* the baby . . ." her voice cried with anguish and then fell to a whisper, "to the highest bidder." She started shaking again, her head thrashing back and forth in violent rejection.

Anger boiling up within him, Marcus found it hard to concentrate on anything but the need to crush Delaney from the face of the earth, but for the girl's sake, he had to keep control. He smoothed her hair and waited for her to calm down, offering another drink.

She refused it and continued, brown eyes wide with horror at her thoughts. "He . . . he was going to sell *me* . . . that was the work he had for me." Her eyes pleaded with him for understanding.

Suspicion dawned instantly. "Sell you to whom?" His voice was hard and unyielding.

Long lashes hid a private pain as she answered, "He owns a place called the Magnolia House . . ." The sentence dropped off as explanation enough.

The Magnolia House. Marcus knew the place from word of mouth, but had never felt the need to drown his loneliness there in the arms of some stranger shared by hundreds of men before him. It had developed a reputation as a house of distinction, discreet and well run, attended by the wealthy and respected of the city. But a whorehouse just the same. At the thought of Jenny's fair innocence being mauled by the lusts of the city's degenerates, revulsion ripped through him.

Jennifer saw the look on his face and turned away, branded now for what she really was, a whore. She knew now what that meant, but it was hard to accept that one night with a stranger could turn into such a monstrous nightmare. At Marcus' touch, she refused to face him.

"Jenny," his tone was warm and coaxing, his fingers gentle as they brushed against her cheek. "Just one more question and I'll let you rest. It's very important, and I want you to answer truthfully. I've got to know if I'm to help you."

She stared stonily at the far wall and wished hell would open up and claim her now. Impatiently, he caught her chin and turned her face to meet his.

There was no nonsense in his voice as he demanded, "Tell me where you got that shawl, Jennifer. You didn't wear it on the boat. Did someone here give it to you?"

She stared into his stony gaze with amazement, her fingers convulsively clutching at the soft folds of cashmere. "It . . . it belongs to the baby. I would not wear it, but Bess made me to keep warm. She . . . has a fondness for pretty things." Surely he would not take it from her? What could it mean to him?

His eyes softened. "Who gave it to you for the baby?"

Lowering her head, she replied so softly he had to strain to catch her words. "It was a gift . . . from the baby's father."

His reaction startled her into submission. With gentle fingers, he slowly unpinned her hair, pulling the long tresses down about her shoulders, only a slight intake of breath betraying his emotion. Smiling quietly with a strange sadness, he brushed her forehead with a light kiss.

"All right, Jenny Lee, I won't ask you anything else right now. I'm going to find a place for you to stay . . ." He patted her hand when she grabbed his arm fearfully. "Delaney will not dare touch you there, and I think you will like these people." She fixed her eyes on his imploringly. The odd smile crossed his face again. "You will be able to keep the babe, Jennifer, I will see to it, I promise."

Tears finally fell as she gave him a look full of relief and gratitude.

The torment she had been through, and she was grateful to *him* . . . It was hard to restrain himself from telling her everything, but she'd had enough excitement for one day; it was in her best interest to see she got peace and a doctor's care, and he had to do it now, before Delaney found them.

Marcus cursed Henry's absence, but he could not delay while waiting for the old man's appearance.

"Now, I want you to lie down and rest while I am gone, Jenny. Are you listening?" Through a veil of tears, she nodded, and he continued, "I'll be right back so there is no need to undress, there are plenty more gowns where that one came from. Henry will be up later. I'll leave word for him to knock when he arrives, but he'll wait in the hall until I return. All right?"

Not totally comprehending all that was happening, Jennifer nodded her head again.

Satisfied that she had recovered sufficiently to be left alone for a short while, Marcus crossed the room and opened the dresser. Drawing out a pair of pearl handled revolvers, he examined them, saw that they were clean and loaded, and buckled on the holster they rode in. As he turned to retrieve his coat, he saw the look of terror return to the girl's face. He had no taste for guns himself, but he was brought up in a region where they were necessary for survival, and he not only knew how to use them, but use them well. If Delaney was going to draw guns on him, he would be prepared the next time. There was little that could be done to ease the girl's mind.

It wasn't just the guns that returned Jennifer to reality, it was the twitching muscle in his cheek and the raw look of hate in steely eyes that made her tremble. She had seen his anger lash out before, but it had been controlled and brief. Now she realized that gray look had been there the entire time he had questioned her, and it wasn't going away with the buckling on of those guns. This anger was too tightly confined and needed only a small spark to set it ablaze; there was murder in those eyes. She shivered at this thought and sank back into the chair.

"Don't let anyone in while I am gone," his voice was cold and distant now, his thoughts already far ahead of his actions. His gaze fell on the child in the chair, and his anger flared anew. He would have his revenge on that whoremonger, but first he would see her to safety. He lifted a rifle from a corner behind the door and with one backward glance, left the room.

Clattering down the hotel steps, his hard look stopping any questions, Marcus left instructions with the desk clerk and returned to his carriage. His aunt would hear his tale with calm aloofness, her air of sophistication and refinement unruffled by his sordid story, then she would proceed to chastise him severely and set the wheels of action in motion. He knew his aunt too well to be fooled by her cold manner; she would accept the girl as one of her own, and there would be hell to pay if Delaney made any interference. A grim smile crossed his face at the thought of the reception of his news, but it was the only way he could assure himself of the safety of the girl and her child. He urged the horses on.

Returning from the interview with his independent-minded aunt, Marcus had to grin at the accuracy of his estimate. Ears still burning from her tirade, he acknowledged the veracity of her opinion of him, matched only by the candor with which she stated it. Even now, the maids were stripping a room and making it ready while a doctor was on call and waiting for the arrival of this newest example of the correctness of her opinion.

As he approached the hotel, a shadow flitted from an alley, flinging itself to the floor of his carriage with an awkward thump. "Keep goin', Cap'n, keep it goin'." Henry's hoarse whisper hurtled up from the confines of the limited floor space. At a sign of protest from his employer, he sat up and grabbed the reins himself, whipping the horses past the hotel at a dangerous speed.

"Henry, what the hell . . . ?" Marcus grabbed the reins back before the old man ran a fine pair of horses through the courthouse wall, directing them to a quieter street.

"They got the girl and they're waiting for you," the old man gasped from the effects of his acrobatic efforts.

Marcus swore long and vigorously and whipped the horses in a different direction. He had been wrong; he should have taken on Delaney first instead of being so damned cautious. The horses beat a furious dust behind them as his curses flailed their ears, and the whip sung about their heads.

"Delaney's got police back there waiting to pick you up for kidnapping." He gave his employer a second glance, observing the murderous mask of rage. "Where're you goin'?"

"I've got two choices, Magnolia House or Delaney's, and with the law in tow, he wouldn't dare involve the first. He's still playing it respectable, he'll have to take her back home." Marcus was thinking out loud more than answering the question, ignoring his friend's puzzled expression. With Delaney, his bodyguards, and the police surrounding the place, there wouldn't be any chance of sneaking in. He would have to confront them all, brazen it out, and pray he didn't get killed in the process. The girl had no other hope.

Once more his steaming horses raced through quiet residential streets; he was no longer aware of the stares they aroused or the passage of time or of anything else beyond the one consuming desire to get the girl back where she belonged. And he would do it or die trying.

Marcus jerked the winded animals to an abrupt halt at his destination and reached behind the seat to retrieve his rifle. Throwing it to Henry, he jumped down from the carriage and signaled for him to follow.

"Stay outside the door and back me up whatever I say or do; no matter what happens, your first concern is to get the girl out of here and to my aunt—you got that?" The words were terse, thrown behind him as he strode rapidly up the walk, Henry trailing after at a slower pace.

There was no time for reply. Throwing open the massive front door, Marcus entered the hallway with both guns drawn, centering them on Delaney and one of his henchmen as they looked up in surprise from their conversation with two blue-clad officers of the law.

"I've come for the girl, Delaney, try to stop me and you'll have a bullet right between your eyes to drain out all the putrefaction you call a brain."

His broad-shouldered, towering figure seemed to grow to immensity with the help of his swaggering belligerence and two loaded revolvers. The men backed off.

The older of the two police officers held his ground, one hand resting on the pistol at his side. "Captain Armstrong, you can't be behavin' like 'tis a Wild West Show," he protested mildly.

"I have no quarrel with you, Sergeant, only Delaney here. And I'm not lowering these guns until I have the girl." He stepped forward a few feet, forcing them to retreat toward the staircase.

" 'Tis a serious quarrel we have with you, Captain. You're in the way of bein' charged with kidnappin' and assault." The sergeant's voice remained reasonable although his expression revealed uncertainty about the rationality of the gentleman behind the guns.

"I'll settle any charges you may have against me once I have the girl, Sergeant. Move it, Delaney!" He gestured menacingly with the gun and stepped forward again.

The sallow-faced brothel owner stopped at the bottom step. "The girl has been sedated, *Captain,*" he sneered the word. "She was seriously disturbed by this morning's episode, and I had to call a doctor to calm her. Sergeant, I demand that you have this man removed before he causes the child more serious harm."

If Marcus had ever wanted to drill a hole through a man's head, it was now, but once the shooting started it wouldn't end until they brought him down. He would have to find the room she was in himself . . . or maybe there was someone up there to show him the way, like that red-headed creature he had seen this morning. He raised his voice to a bellow that rattled the chandelier. "Jenny!" The sound echoed through upper passages, but he had been right: it brought a shadow flickering from a darkened doorway, flattening against the upper hall wall.

The four men facing him stared as if he'd gone mad, then threw themselves from his path as he dashed head-long through their formation and up the stairs, his long stride carrying him to the upper level before they could do more than stumble to their feet.

Still wearing the pink fantasy of the morning, the shadow waved him down the left side of the hall and un-locked the last door before disappearing into the next room. Holding his guns up, Marcus kicked open the door, the sight within filling him with such rage he swung around at the first footstep behind, blowing the gun out of the bodyguard's hand before realizing what he was doing. The man grabbed his injured hand with a wail of pain and fell back into the hall. Marcus filled the doorway, one gun smoking, the other aimed at Delaney, ignoring the two policemen hovering behind. Jennifer's unconscious body lay on the bed behind him, her gown ripped where she had fought off her captors, auburn hair in tangled knots across the sheets.

"Delaney," his tone was ominous, his words threatening. "If I ever, *ever* find you've touched one hair of this girl's head again, I'll blow *your* head clear into the next county." With that warning out of the way, he turned to the police officers. "Sergeant, I intend to leave with this girl in one manner or another. If you will ensure our safe conduct, I will accompany you to your headquarters where this matter can be straightened out."

The sergeant had worked the city's police force ever since it had official status; he knew the Armstrong family, and he knew what Delaney was despite his pretense. What-ever the rights of this matter might be, he would stake his bet on this headstrong son of a respectable family over the whey-faced "businessman" beside him. Let the chief sort out the wrong-doers.

"All right, lad. Lay down your guns and bring the colleen and we'll be seeing what the chief has to say." The sergeant's hand still rested on the butt of his pistol, but his attention was now on the irate Delaney.

"Sergeant, I'll have your job for this. That girl is under a doctor's care; she cannot be moved. You can see for yourself what condition she is in. I'm her legal guardian, and I have the papers to prove it. You can't let this madman carry her out of here like this." His sallow complexion turned a deep purple bordering on apoplexy.

"Aye, and I'm seein' what condition she is in. They tell me it took two of your men to be gettin' her here and her a screamin' all the way. You might not find it so easy to be gettin' her back." He turned back to Marcus who was still waiting with guns poised. "If you'll be so good as to carry the lass, Captain . . ."

Marcus eyed the man thoughtfully, then holstered his guns, his long coat swinging in place to cover them. Swinging around the room without taking his glare from Delaney, he came up behind Jennifer and lifted her from the bed as if she were a baby, her head lolling against his shoulder as he pulled the shawl around to cover the torn bodice of her dress. Lifeless, she was an awkward burden, but he could feel a feeble kick through the layers of material separating her swollen belly from his side, and he clasped her tighter. If she could bear the heavy burden within her, he could surely manage this much lighter one. With a tight smile at the sergeant, he led the procession from the room.

Descending the staircase, Marcus spotted Henry slipping from a back hallway into the main foyer. He had found the servants' stairs and had been prepared to attack from the rear at the first sign of battle. Marcus gave the old man a genuine smile and gestured with his head to indicate he should follow. Henry joined the procession leaving the house, rifle slung warily over his shoulder.

Outside, the sergeant took command, ordering Marcus into the police wagon with the girl, sending the younger officer with Delaney and his crew, leaving Henry possession of the carriage. Marcus settled back against the hard wooden seat of the wagon and adjusted Jennifer to a more comfortable position in his lap. She stirred uneasily, and he hugged her closer, tucking her head beneath his chin. The day wasn't warm enough for the revealing evening dress, and he wrapped her more tightly in the shawl, its soft threads stirring unbidden memories as he felt her body close to his.

They arrived at the courthouse police station in a flurry of dust and horses, their little procession swelling as the drugged girl drew the attention of bystanders, and newspapermen saw visions of headlines captioned "Sleeping Beauty." Marcus stared stonily ahead as he heard his name bandied about in whispers while they walked the halls to headquarters. The gossips would have a field day with this one, but there was little he could do to stop it, and he prayed for the patience and understanding of his long suffering aunt.

The desk clerk looked up in astonishment as the room filled with the sergeant and his party. A young man, he could scarcely tear his eyes from the limp figure in the gentleman's arms. Even in her disheveled state her beauty was apparent. But the cold, hard gaze of the face above her left him shaken; this was no grieving lover but a vengeful fury.

"Don't be dawdlin' there like some dimwitted son of a seafish, be gettin' the chief for me now, will ye?" The sergeant's brogue blustered the clerk into motion.

The small room filled with the heat of a dozen bodies, and Jennifer moaned as her hand pressed against Marcus' chest in a fitful attempt to get away.

Marcus broke his silence to address the sergeant. "Is there a private room where we can make the lady comfortable? There is no reason she should suffer this treatment." His tone was arrogant and hard, carrying easily over the hubbub in the room.

The sergeant glared at his irritating prisoner, then his glance fell on the struggling form in Marcus' arms, and he relented. "There's a place in the chief's office," he answered reluctantly, moving toward the railing that separated offices from lobby.

Marcus shoved his way through the crowd, and not to be outdone, Delaney and his two bodyguards followed. Henry brought up the rear, slamming the gate effectively after him to cut off curious bystanders and reporters.

The chief's office was smaller than the lobby and poorly furnished. A dusty parlor reject behind the office door apparently served as the chief's napping place, its curved arm piled high with ancient pillows. It was there that Marcus lay his sleeping burden, sitting by her side on the wide cushions, effectively blocking her from the view of the remainder of the room's occupants. The others milled about, resting against the file-covered wooden desk at the far wall or leaning on the grimy walls, none of them occupying the big chair behind the desk. Henry rested his rifle inconspicuously behind him, standing by the doorway in a position where he could watch both hall and office.

Marcus rubbed at Jennifer's wrists, hoping to bring some sign of life to the closed eyes and deathlike pallor of her face. The drug had removed her consciousness, but she moved restlessly. Looking up, he caught Henry's eyes. Henry nodded and slipped from the room.

He returned bearing a cup of coffee at the same time the police chief walked into his overcrowded office, staring at the motley collection invading his privacy.

"What the hell is going on here? Sergeant, you'd better have a good explanation for this circus," the chief demanded before wading through the room to his desk. Raising a surprised eyebrow at Delaney's presence, he sat down in his chair before noticing the couple behind the door. Silence fell as he stared at the pool of pale green satin covering his faded sofa, his gaze broken from reaching its source by the elegantly dressed man with a cold gray stare.

"Damn it all, O'Hara, what's the meaning of this?" The chief returned his glare to the sergeant for explanations, leaving the insolent gentleman to return to his occupation of reviving the girl.

As the story stumbled out, interrupted by the chief's rude interjections, Henry produced the coffee and returned to his post, leaving Marcus to figure out how to get it down the unconscious girl. Oblivious of the tale being told, Marcus concentrated his attentions on returning Jennifer to life. Putting one arm behind her, he gently lifted her from the pile of pillows, brushing away the tendrils of hair that clung to her face. At the change of position, her eyes fluttered and for a moment, looked directly into his, then the fogs of sleep closed in again. Patiently, he held her up, bringing the coffee to her lips, urging her to drink as he had earlier with a much different potion. Perhaps some remembrance of that distasteful drink still lingered. She turned her head away, nearly knocking the cup from his hand.

Dust motes floated in the sunlight from the window behind the desk. The monotonous tone of the sergeant's report continued uninterrupted, providing a distant background to his efforts.

With careful patience, Marcus administered the bitter stimulant a sip at a time, succeeding only in gentling Jennifer's restless motions. He could hear the chief questioning the arresting officer, but he ignored the words, knowing the time wasn't right to state his case. He let the argument flow on around him, his silence stirring the violent winds of anger further.

As the hot fluid worked its way through her system and the effects of the drug wore off, Jennifer gained consciousness of the room around her, its dusty smell and overheated air telling her first of its unfamiliarity. But the strong arm around her was solid and real, the low voice caressing her ears decidedly familiar, and she ventured to open her eyes, focusing on Marc's tanned and unsmiling face.

With the lift of long lashes, some of the tension drained out of him, and he breathed a sigh of relief; she was returning to him. Pressing her hands around the still warm cup, he whispered gently, "How are you feeling, little one?"

Staring blankly into gray eyes above her, Jennifer took a minute before his words reached her. She was conscious only of a need to see behind his eyes, mindlessly ignoring everything in a futile struggle to see what wasn't there. But the moment passed, and she became more aware of her present state and dared not look him in the face again.

"My back aches a bit, could you help me up?" she murmured, too softly for any ears but his to hear.

She clutched at her shawl as he lifted her to a more vertical position, resting most of her weight now against the back of the sofa. Delaney's irate explanation halted in mid-sentence at this unexpected movement, but then continued as he produced the papers he had spoken of earlier, handing them to the chief. The air remained silent except for the rustle of papers.

Marcus still sat with his back toward them, half holding the cup in Jennifer's hand while she tried to fight off sleep. As the conversation around them picked up, he took the opportunity to whisper to her. "Jenny, I'm going to need your help to get us out of here, can you understand me?" He straightened the tangled hair about her shoulders, pushing it neatly behind her ears, knowing she preferred it that way.

She nodded groggily, and he didn't think she fully grasped the situation.

"You've got to wake up. Here, finish the coffee—drink it all up." He nodded approvingly as she drank from the cup. "Now don't let me down, Jenny, just listen to what I say and tell them the truth if they ask you anything, do you understand?" Concern dominated his expression— she was barely conscious and apparently in some pain. It was no time to do this to her, but he was left no choice if they were to get out of this situation safely.

"Chief, I object to that madman's conversing with my ward. I've stood here and waited patiently long enough, now I want him away from her and preferably locked up." Delaney's voice penetrated loud and clear into their little haven of peace, disrupting the tranquility and blowing them into the hurricane's rage.

"Captain Armstrong," the chief's stentorian voice rang out over Delaney's protests, "I presume you are related to the steamer line Armstrongs?"

"My aunt operates that business now, Chief." Marcus shifted his position to face his interrogator, finally exposing Jennifer to the watchful eyes of the room's occupants.

"Then I knew your uncle and father, both fine, upstanding men of the community." His words were meant as a reprimand, although said in a calm voice to prevent insulting a member of the city's aristocracy.

"My father died a few months back, I represent the head of my family now." Marcus understood the man's hesitancy and played it against him.

"I'm sorry to hear that, sir." The chief spoke cautiously, glancing uneasily at Delaney. Armstrong was a fine, old name in the community, but Delaney had used his wealth wisely in the protection of his business. The policemen's benevolent society coffers brimmed to overflowing with his support, and full service was expected for the money. Now it was the chief's job to separate that grim young man from his plaything and return her to her rightful owner. It wasn't a task the chief looked forward to accomplishing.

"Now, Captain, I have the papers here appointing Mr. Delaney as Miss Pell's legal guardian, and I've heard the sergeant's full report on your behavior this morning. Have you some good reason for your actions?"

Marcus showed no reaction to the unfamiliar name of "Pell," instead, focusing a steely glare on his antagonist as his words thundered through the room with the force of a lightning bolt.

"I need no reasons. She carries my child."

The angry murmurs of hurricane winds halted abruptly, and into the silence a cup crashed to the floor, shattering into a dozen pieces. Marcus wheeled about just in time to catch Jennifer as she pitched forward, a low groan escaping her lips as he lay her against the pillows. It was a cruel blow, but there was no other way. Once again, he cursed his cautiousness in not telling the truth earlier.

As irate words once more blew about the room, Marcus bent over Jennifer's inert figure, the flicker of lashes telling him she was awake but not yet ready to face him.

"Jenny, I'm sorry . . . I didn't know until today." His hand cupped the fine mold of her head, cradling her as he whispered hasty words. "This devil and your first are the same, my auburn haloed angel," he admitted regretfully, deliberately using the words of that first fateful note.

Jennifer opened her eyes with a mixture of fear and horror, comprehending the truth of his words before he explained them. There was room for only one devil in this world, and she had found him; it was her fate to suffer the torments of hell forever. Why had she never guessed? The truth had been there for her to see all the time. Gray eyes of icy coldness hovered above her, and she knew she no longer had a single friend in this room. She shuddered, forcing the next word from her lips. "How . . . ?"

"The shawl, Jenny. If only you had worn it on the boat . . ." Marcus spoke gently, but Jennifer's eyes were frozen with fear, and he could feel the pain of it cut through him like a knife. It was his child she carried, and she would never forgive him for that one fateful night, but for the moment, it was more important that they escape. And for that, he needed her cooperation. "You must believe me, Jenny, the child is mine, and I will let nothing happen to it." He attempted a smile as he touched her cheek, but she turned away, the anguish of that first betrayal destroying all her hopes.

He understood and contented himself with holding her hand. The one man in this room she trusted and relied on was the same man whose actions had put her there in the first place. All the months of hurt and misery she had suffered were caused by him, how could she expect him to save her? He would have to try and make it right later, but now he had to concentrate on what was happening here.

The chief was shaking his head at Delaney's indignant demands, and Henry was looking at his employer with a queer expression. Marcus gave him a small shrug of his shoulders and nodded his head to the old man's inquiring glance, but the servant's reply was unreadable as he looked quickly at the young girl and then shouldered his weapon. Whatever happened, Henry was ready to defend the girl and her child as willingly as he would his captain, without further need of explanation.

"Captain Armstrong," the police chief redirected his attention now that Marcus had his charge in hand, "is Miss Pell able to answer a few questions?"

Marcus placed an arm behind Jennifer's shoulders for support, casting her a quick look as he did so. She nodded, and he gave her a smile of reassurance, hoping she would understand.

Turning back to the policeman, he replied, "If we're quick about it; she's in pain and really should be under a doctor's care."

The chief looked vaguely alarmed and gestured to the sergeant, holding a whispered consultation before speaking again. "In that case, Captain, I think we better call in someone more experienced in the law than I am. The judge is in the building, and I think we'll have him take a look at this situation. I'll go get him myself and explain the case on the way over here to save time. If you'll excuse me, gentlemen, I'll be right back."

Jennifer collapsed into the pillows, turning her face to the back of the sofa and pulling up her shawl to hide herself from this river man who had so suddenly changed from friend to executioner. Her life was in his hands now, and even if he should rescue her from the Magnolia House, she could expect no better fate than to be left on her own in this strange and frightening city. Only his promise to allow her to keep his child kept her from retreating entirely from his side, that and the certainty that the child would be born before this day was through, and she would need whatever help he could give. She bit her lip and let the rolling ache move across her, trying her best not to cry out in this room full of men.

Leaning one arm against the back of the sofa, Marcus looked down uncertainly at the huddled figure beside him—her hand pressing tightly to her abdomen—and a worried frown creased his brow. Covering her hand with his, he felt her fingers grip it convulsively, and at the same time, her panic-stricken eyes flew open, telling him all he needed to know. If they didn't get this over quickly, his first child would be born in police headquarters.

Loud, arguing voices preceded the footsteps of the returning chief and as the sounds separated into two distinct speakers, Marcus felt his confidence in the outcome dwindle. He should have known Judge Lassiter would be the man the chief sought out, and the whole picture finally became clear to him. St. Louis politics had smelled of corruption for some time now. He had already assumed the relationship between Delaney and the police chief: no self-respecting whorehouse could operate without the police in its pocket. But it had not occurred to him that the corruption would extend as far as the courts of law. Now his last chance was dissolving before him as the chief brought in the man he had chosen to decide the case, one of his worst enemies, Gwendolyn's husband.

Rapidly, Marcus considered his chances of shooting their way out of here, holding off the police and Delaney while Henry got the girl out and away to safety. It might have been possible at any other time, but Henry could not carry Jennifer, and she would be in no condition to walk out on her own. Rather than allow the whoremongering bastard have her and his child, he would shoot them himself if it came to that. His hand rested momentarily on one pistol as his eyes met Henry's.

Their only hope was that Lassiter was too old to be blackmailed by Delaney and too rich to be bought. That, and too honest to allow his hatred of Marcus influence his decisions, and that was asking a little too much for even the good Lord to do. Gritting his teeth, Marcus looked up just in time to catch the judge's entrance.

Obviously well prepared by the chief, the judge found the couple in the corner immediately, nodding to Marcus as he stood in front of the sofa and looked down at the girl. Feeling the presence of a stranger near her, Jennifer opened her eyes, the image of a wounded doe in their liquid softness even greater under physical pain. The lashes lowered under the judge's brief stare.

"This the girl you had on the boat that last trip?" His voice was gruff, revealing nothing.

At Marc's brief nod, he turned and walked to the desk, settling himself in the chief's chair and picking up the papers in front of him. Delaney was already seated in the chair his man had brought back, and he gave Marcus a look of triumph. It hadn't taken long for rumor to circulate about Marcus and the judge's wife.

Marcus stared stonily ahead, holding Jennifer's hand and revealing nothing, although his mind raced through all the possibilities open to him. Whatever happened, he would not let this child be lost to him, or it would destroy him as surely as it would the girl.

Jennifer felt the poised tension in the man beside her, saw his hand resting on the gun at his hip, hidden by the long tail of his coat, and knew something had gone wrong. The devil had turned into a determined man prepared to defend what was rightfully his.

The change frightened and awed her, but it gave her something to think about besides this waiting for the next contraction to take over her aching body. If she should survive this and be allowed to keep the child, at least she would be able to tell him something of his father. It was good to know he was courageous as well as handsome; the other flaws in his character would be easily forgotten with the passage of time. She clenched his hand tighter and gave him a fleeting smile when he turned his concerned gaze to her.

The judge cleared his throat, bringing the attention of

all the room's occupants to the desk where the square of sunlight had lengthened, marking time spent. He raised his glasses to his nose and looked from Delaney to Marcus, finally fastening a forbidding stare on his young rival.

"Captain, it appears to me that this gentleman here has all his papers in order and properly signed giving him complete guardianship over this young woman and her child until she comes of age or marries. That is evidently the express intent of her parents and they have full power of law over her until such time."

The glare of light behind his balding head prevented Marcus from getting a good look at the judge's face, but the eyes behind the glasses seemed to soften as they turned to Jennifer. Marcus helped her up so she could meet his look.

"Miss Pell, how old are you?"

"Eighteen in June, sir," she murmured. She clung tightly to Marcus for reassurance.

"As you can see, Captain, she is still a child in the eyes of the law and therefore ward to Mr. Delaney here."

Delaney started to rise, and Marcus pulled the girl behind him, his gun instantly half out of his holster. The judge waved the triumphant guardian back into his seat.

"Miss Pell, is there any question that this man is the father of your child?"

Frightened eyes stared up at Marcus, and he nodded for her to go ahead and speak. "He is the father, sir." The words were so soft as to be almost inaudible, but they fell into deafening silence.

A sigh broke the quiet as the judge turned his attention to Marcus. "Then, young man, there are only two choices here, and it does not matter to me which one you make since you have brought them both down on your head by your careless and irresponsible actions." He waited a moment to be certain his words were being fully heeded, but Marcus didn't flinch. "One, you may leave the girl and her child to Mr. Delaney's care and face the charge of kidnapping and possible imprisonment, or two, you may marry the girl and thus transfer her guardianship to your-self, making the charge of kidnapping a moot point."

A groan escaped Jennifer's lips, and Marcus lay her back against the pillows, not knowing whether she moaned from pain or the choice of fates that lay before her. It made no difference, there was no choice involved. He squeezed her hand and stood up, exuding calm authority.

"I will marry her, but let us get this done quickly so I may get her out of here at once."

Delaney jumped to his feet, his face purple with rage, but the burly sergeant stepped in front of him, deflecting his tirade. The judge ignored the outburst, standing to meet the captain's challenging gaze.

"I will gladly perform the ceremony myself." There was almost a twinkle in the old man's eye, but the light on his glasses kept Marcus from being certain. "Sergeant, see these other men out and fetch my clerk with the proper forms for a civil ceremony."

Marcus stepped aside and allowed the policeman to usher out the furious Delaney and his men before return-ing to Jennifer's side.

The police chief and Judge Lassiter remained at the front of the room, idly talking and throwing an occasional glance to the sofa in the corner as they waited for the court clerk to make his appearance. There was little to be seen of interest since Marcus had again planted himself in the way of their view of the girl, turning his back on them as well.

Jennifer had given him one piercing, horrified look of anguish, and cried out an amazed "No!" before crushing her eyes shut. Marcus could do nothing but look down in sorrow and brush the fine hairs from her forehead. He knew well her thoughts on marriage; to be forced into that state with a man she now despised could never bring hap-piness to either of them. She would have been content with his aunt, and he had given brief thought to her as mistress, but as his wife she would be miserable, all hope of freedom crushed from her, and with it, the joyous spirit he knew had once existed, the same joyous spirit that had created this living being inside her. Not to mention the effect it would have on his own plans.

The clerk returned swiftly. The chief of police and Henry served as witnesses as the judge performed the ceremony. The young, country bride—in a torn and tattered green dress of fine satin—could barely utter the words that sealed her to the forbidding gentleman at her side. The groom remained expressionless as he removed a heavy ruby ring from his finger to place on his bride's, finalizing the act of making her his own. It was a solemn ceremony from first to last and ended, after the last signatures had been affixed to the papers, by the silent groom sweeping his young bride up in his arms and carrying her from the room without waiting for a single congratulatory handshake.

The sun was dipping low in the sky by the time they returned to the waiting carriage. Jennifer was in no condition to remain seated on her own. Marcus carried her on his lap while Henry drove the horses and the newly married couple home. Urging his man to drive as carefully but as quickly as possible, Marcus wrapped his arms around his new wife, resting her head against his shoulder with every outward sign of tenderness. Only Jennifer could sense the rigid tension in the muscles beneath his immaculate jacket and see the cold, hard set to his jaw. Her baby had a name now, but it was not willingly given. She buried her face in the rough cloth covering his shoulder and willed herself back to unconsciousness.

But the cool wind as the carriage moved into a lane shadowed by towering evergreens brought her back to awareness, however unwillingly. She moved in her new husband's arms to see where she was being taken, and she felt some of the tension go out of him as they came within sight of their destination. Would this be her home, then? She was almost afraid to look.

In the growing darkness, there was only the impression of a massive stone front, its wings extending far out into the overgrowth of shrubs. Perhaps this wasn't a house at all, but a hospital or some place where you took unwanted relatives, or heaven help her, another form of Magnolia House. If she had learned anything of men at all, she knew her husband to be more ruthless and less afraid of anything than Delaney had ever been, and quite capable of anything at all. As a friend, he was a fine man to have on her side, but as a furious and unwilling husband, he was no longer her friend. And she was in no condition to put up any more fights.

With a small moan, Jennifer held on to him as he lifted her from the carriage. Henry scurried ahead to throw open the door, diffusing a warm light into the gathering dusk outside. Jennifer could hear hurrying footsteps down the marbled passageway and as they stepped into the warmth of a heated foyer, a majestic voice carried in before them.

"Marcus Stuart, you had me worried ill. Where have you been?" A rustling of heavy skirts against stone floors followed, and then Jennifer was looking up into the warmest pair of gray eyes she had ever encountered. If only her husband's could look like that, she thought incoherently, before the pain raked through her, leaving her unaware of any thoughts other than surviving this tormenting upheaval ripping at her insides.

"My Lord in heaven, what are you thinking of—riding this child around in carriages while she's in this state! Get her up to her room immediately." The voice was scolding, but not harsh, and Jennifer was aware of a deep current of affection between her husband and the source of this voice despite the sarcastic tone he used to mention that there had been some slight delay that he would explain later. Jennifer wondered what he would tell them, but the pain was coming back again, and she could not think farther. A scream formed in her throat as the pain grew instead of abating, and she was no longer aware of anything but the blackness inside her head and the ripping at her belly and all the voices and sounds swirled into a whirling vortex of agony and disappeared.

After depositing his limp burden in the bed Marcus was forced from the room, even the doctor ignoring him as he raced up the stairs, black bag in hand. Jennifer's pale young face and bloodless lips biting back screams of agony swam before his eyes, and he descended the stairs hurriedly, heading for the liquor cabinet. That was where Henry found him when he returned after putting up the horses.

Empty glass in hand, Marcus sat slumped in an easy chair dazedly listening to the distant moans echoing from the bedroom. A wife and a child in one day was more than should be asked of any man, no matter how strong that man might be, and Henry refilled Marc's empty glass without being asked. The two men sat in the flickering gaslight until well into the night, watching the scurrying of maids up and down the stairs, too far gone to do more than exchange relieved glances when the first weak sounds of crying replaced the screams of agony.

Six

An April breeze blew through the open window, caressing a face still flushed with sleep, and Jennifer stirred restlessly amongst soft sheets, drawing the covers closer about her sore and aching body. But the moment's consciousness had done its damage, and her hand flew to her flattened stomach, eyes opening in distress to search the room. The baby, what had happened to her baby?

A soothing voice spoke from the side of the bed, reassuring her as she turned to meet the source of the sound. Warm eyes smiled down at her from the face of a woman in her fifties, smooth skin unwrinkled by age except for tiny lines of laughter about her eyes, gray hair piled majestically upon her head.

"Your son is sleeping in the next room. We thought it best that you not be disturbed for the night while you recovered from yesterday's ordeal. Shall I send for him?" She smiled at Jennifer's eager nod of assent, and stepped to the doorway to call a servant.

The woman was taller than Jennifer, and more sturdily built despite the disguise of her tightly corseted attire. Calm gray eyes studied her thoughtfully for a moment. Then drawing a chair to the bedside, the woman sat down, her gaze level with Jennifer's.

"I am Marc's Aunt Josephine, although he usually calls me Jo in that disrespectful manner of his." The lines crinkled deeper in amusement. "What would you prefer to be called? I have not made much sense of my nephew since he brought you in last night."

"I was christened Jennifer Lee, but Marcus only calls me that when he is angry," she replied shyly, wondering if she was expected to call this elegant woman Aunt now, also.

The woman decided the question for her. "Then I shall call you Jenny and you may call me Jo, and whenever Marc shows his temper, we shall both take him on at once. You must learn not to be frightened of that dreadful temper of his, it only encourages him to worse rages."

A maid appeared in the doorway carrying a small bundle of whimpering blankets, and Josephine jumped to her feet as lightly as a young woman. Taking the bundle from the maid and dismissing her, she returned the infant to the hands of his waiting mother.

Jennifer struggled to a sitting position against the pillows as she took the tiny bundle, unwrapping the blankets from her son's face and admiring the lovely shock of dark curls that adorned his red and wrinkled form. There was no doubt as to whose son he was, and to emphasize the fact, he let out a loud squall of temper that caused Jennifer to look up in amusement.

Josephine was watching, and the two women looked at each other in understanding before dissolving into laughter. Jennifer sighed with the relief of finding someone she could talk to, although it would be a while before she could grow accustomed to Jo's air of elegance.

"Here, let me help you with this bed jacket; then you may feed young Marcus, Junior there with some privacy. I still have a few things to ask if you don't mind my curiosity, and I don't think I care to wait until your man wakes with aching head to ask him."

She lifted a heavy lace jacket from the bedside and placed it around Jennifer's shoulders. Someone had removed her tattered green satin gown and replaced it with a white lawn nightdress with slender straps that easily unfastened.

Shyly, Jennifer took the infant into her arms, and wrapping the enveloping jacket about them both, held him against her. His seeking mouth soon found its place, sending chills through her at the intimate touch she had felt before in not so innocent a manner.

When her unseen devil had just been a dark memory, he had been easy to accept as some fevered fantasy that had overcome her one night. But now he was a living, breathing human being, father of this child at her breast, and all the things they had said and done together came rushing back in one swift flood she could not sort out. She could not picture the man she knew as the lover who had so tenderly taught her the art of love.

"Jenny, Marc has told me very little of you. Would you mind if I knew more?" Josephine asked.

"I would tell you all, but I do not know if he would approve. Is he ill?" His aunt's reference to his waking with aching head led Jennifer to believe otherwise, but it would be best to know for certain.

Jo grimaced. "Only with an illness he brings on himself.

It seems he could not bear your agony last night so he eased it with some of his good whiskey. He was in no condition to answer anything sensibly by the time I returned downstairs. I understand there was some tremendous altercation that delayed your departure yesterday." The last was stated questioningly.

Jennifer considered this before replying. "I am afraid it will all be public knowledge shortly, and it might be better if you heard it from him. I fear I have not made him very happy; that was the reason for his drinking last night, not any agony I may have felt." She did not state this bitterly, but thoughtfully, trying to understand what he must have felt at being forced into a position of which he wanted no part.

Jo did not give up so easily. "I cannot believe you would do anything that would make him unhappy enough to drink himself into such a state. Marc may be a hard man, but he has a weakness for women, as you may have noticed . . ." Her eyes twinkled in understanding.

But Jennifer did not return her merriment. "I have noticed, but this time it was nearly fatal for him and most certainly would have been for me if he had not come along in time. As it is, the results are not pleasing to either of us, and he is likely to come down very out of temper with or without his headache."

This bit of information caused Josephine to lose all semblance of patience. "Jenny, you cannot leave me hanging after a statement like that; now either you tell me what went on yesterday, or I will go shake it out of Marcus and Henry. Those two rogues have been in more scrapes than I care to remember and eventually, I find out about every one of them. I am that like my brother that I do not give up once I set my mind to something, and his son seems to have inherited the same irritating trait. So you may as well give in and tell me now. It will save a lot of trouble. You might wish to start by telling me why you are wearing the ring that I know Marcus was wearing the last time I saw him."

Jennifer looked at her left hand in surprise as if she had never seen the ring before, and in truth, she had scarcely noticed it at the time it was given. Its heavy weight fell loosely against her finger; there was no reason for it to stay on at all. And this was what it took to make an honest woman of her, to give her baby the grand name of Armstrong. Remarkable. But she did not feel married. It was simply another one of her fantasies, and he would come in soon to tell her so.

Seeing the puzzlement on the face of the woman who had been so kind to her, Jennifer groped for an answer. "I do not intentionally keep anything from you, but I'm afraid much of what happened yesterday is not very clear to me, either. Did he tell you where he found me?" she asked hesitantly, afraid if this grand lady found out about Magnolia House, she would run shrieking from the room.

"He told me everything, including the fact that you are as innocent as you appear and your whole predicament is due entirely to him. Marcus can be brutally candid when the situation requires it. He said only that you were about to bear his child and he would see you taken care of before he returned to California. I cannot say that I approve of his cavalier attitude, but it was better than leaving you at the mercy of those slave merchants. Surely you must remember something of what happened after he left here?"

Marcus had still planned on going to California when he left here yesterday! Jennifer was not given to unreasonable angers, but if he had known then that she was bearing his child, he could have at least offered to do the decent thing instead of being forced into it. But he had not wanted a wife to get in the way of his ambitious plans, particularly not one whose parents were innkeepers. What would he do with her now? Damn the man, anyway. Suddenly, she felt immensely tired.

Lying back against the pillows, Jennifer looked to the anxious woman beside her. "I was a legal ward of Delaney's; they said Marcus had no right to me or the child and threatened to charge him with kidnapping." Josephine's sharp intake of breath told her she understood the situation to some extent. "He had no choice but to marry me to save the child." Jennifer looked at the sleeping infant in her arms, the cause of so much trouble to so many people, was it possible? "At least, that is the way I understand it. I remember little of what actually happened," she murmured, talking more to the infant than Josephine.

"Oh, my God." Josephine got up, her dress rustling over voluminous petticoats as she paced back and forth, her smooth face drawn up in a wrinkled brow.

"I guess he really is Marcus, Junior, then," she finally admitted, taking the sleeping infant carefully in her arms. "Now, I'll put him in the cradle over there," she nodded toward the wall by the far side of the bed, "and I want you to get some rest until it's feeding time again." Then she leaned over and kissed Jennifer's forehead, "Welcome to the family, Jenny."

When Jennifer next awoke, there was a maid waiting to take her breakfast order. She waited until the maid was gone before gingerly swinging her legs over the bed to explore her new surroundings.

After taking care of her first urgent needs and washing hastily in the luxury of a room with running water, Jennifer helped herself to the brush and comb lying on the dresser and returned to her bed. Drawing the brush through the tangled skeins of her hair, she watched the sleeping infant at her side, his tiny fists curled into little red balls and his face puckered in a deep frown. His father could have no doubt of his ownership of this one, she thought, there is not a trace of his mother in that pugnacious little mug. Grinning at the thought, she flung her hair back over her shoulder and looked up to find Marcus standing in the doorway with a breakfast tray in his hands.

Looking no worse for wear, he was immaculate in his suit of light dove gray instead of the usual dark colors he affected. With his tie evenly knotted and his hair carefully combed into place, only the cloudy gray of his eyes indicated that all was not right with the world.

Setting the tray down on a low table, Marcus sat down on the bed and touched a large finger to the tiny fists of his son. Jennifer watched him closely. Could she imagine this tanned, handsome man as her husband? It was too impossible to be true, and she knew the moment he spoke he would destroy the fantasy, but it was so beautiful while it lasted. She would like to spend the day dreaming she might have an ambitious and handsome husband who would love her son and allow her to make a home for him. She must have sighed for he suddenly switched his attention from the baby to her; she could almost imagine for a moment his eyes were gentle as he gazed upon her, but then they hardened into their familiar focus, and the fantasy broke without his saying a word.

"Is it possible to pick him up without waking him?"

Jennifer lifted the child, leaning forward to present his son to him. A little more color in that pale face and Marcus could almost imagine she had entirely regained her health. Last night he was almost certain he would lose her, and now he was presented with a picture more tempting than the ones he carried in his head. She would have made a most desirable mistress.

Marcus took the infant, cradling him awkwardly in his arms as he inspected tiny fingers and toes, aware that Jennifer waited nervously for his reaction. Unable to take his angry frustration out on her, he lifted his head and smiled at her eager expression.

"He seems to have the makings of a fine Armstrong, little one. What will we name him?"

The relief in her eyes was painfully obvious; she must think him some kind of ogre who would deny his own child. But then, she had little to build hopes on, as he knew better than anyone.

"Your Aunt Josephine is already calling him Marcus, Jr. Would that please you?" she asked carefully.

"Jo has a way of taking things in her own hands sometimes. You will have to beware of her or she will walk all over a tender bud like you. I have no objections to giving him my name, but to avoid confusion, I would prefer calling him by the middle part." Marcus handed the sleeping bundle back to her and watched her gaze adoringly at the product of their one night together.

"Stuart?" Jennifer touched a tiny nose.

"Imagine that, you remember my name. I thought perhaps you would think it Satan." Moving about restlessly, Marcus stood and walked to the window, looking out before turning and walking back.

Returning to the tray he had carried in, Marcus placed it on her lap. "I have been given strict orders to see that you eat every bit of this, so if you're in some hurry to rid yourself of me, you'd best start eating."

"And if I dawdle?"

"You'll be spoon fed and none too gently. Now behave." He pulled up a chair and made himself comfortable, sipping at his tomato juice. "I suppose if I were at my best this morning I should have asked how you are feeling?" he asked abruptly.

"I am in no hurry to repeat the performance, but I will survive," Jennifer replied in the same curt tones he had used.

"There we find ourselves in agreement. I take it you have met my aunt already. How did you like her?" He examined the food on his tray, spearing a bite here and there as it appealed to him.

Jennifer's enthusiasm for his aunt bubbled over. "She's a fine lady; I think I shall like her very much. You are lucky to have someone so understanding to confide in. Only . . . Have you spoken to her this morning?"

"Don't worry yourself, she has confessed to having beaten the news out of you and says to tell you she is very sorry, but she isn't, you know." Having finished his juice, Marcus started on his coffee, leaning back and studying the girl before him, her enormous eyes filling her drawn, pale face. With waist length hair draped about her, she did not appear old enough to have borne a child, no less to submit to the tremendous pressures she had been under these last months. "Jo has an insatiable curiosity and hates it when I try to keep anything from her, but I would not have kept this secret, little one. So you are excused."

Jennifer stared at him with an expression of dread. "Then, I did not dream it? We really are . . ." she hesitated at saying the word, letting it come out as only a whisper, "married?"

"I'm afraid so, Jenny Lee." The panic on her face surprised him. Despite her earlier protestations he had not thought she would find the idea so displeasing, and the knowledge that she did annoyed Marcus further. "Was it too high a price to pay?"

"No higher than I have been paying, I suppose, only now you are paying, too." She shoved the tray away.

Marcus leaned over and pushed the tray back into position. "Eat. You must practice being that dutiful wife you once spoke of. I have no intentions of paying any more than necessary, so don't worry about me."

Jennifer had no idea what he meant; it could mean one of a thousand things. Perhaps he intended to pretend he had no wife, she would not put that past him in the least. But what would he do when he eventually found the rich and dutiful wife that he so obviously expected to marry instead of her? Was there some way he could end this marriage?

He could do as he liked, she decided, but only if he left the child to her. She had nothing else in this world but that living, breathing bundle she had fought so long and hard to keep, and if she had to put up with this monstrous man to keep him, she would. Only, she wished she knew what he expected of her.

Marcus cleaned his plate and got up to stride around the room again, stopping over the cradle to watch his sleeping son. Jennifer kept her gaze to her plate as she forced the remainder of her breakfast down, aware of his every movement. He was like a caged beast, restless and eager to be set free. Finishing her food, she pushed the tray away and looked up to find him staring at her. His gaze fell to the ring she twisted nervously and he crossed the room to pick up her hand and examine it.

"I will have to find you a more fitting ring. That one somehow does not quite suit you." He spun it around on her finger. "You realize if you are to be accepted as my wife, you will have to dress and act like a lady, not a Bible-toting farmer's daughter?"

Jennifer jerked her hand away. "If you expect me to act like your friend Gwendolyn, you would be better off locking me in some corner of the house and declaring me insane." Why did he persist in his insulting stare?

"Actually, I had my Aunt Jo in mind for teacher, but locking you up might not be a half bad idea. I will remember that," he replied irritatingly, lifting the tray from the bed and setting it on the table out of the way. "I have business to attend to today and may not return in time for dinner. You probably should spend the day resting, anyway, and I am obviously not a suitable nursemaid. If you get bored, send someone to find you a book in the library."

Marcus stared down at her, one hand in his pocket with an expression of perplexity on his face as if he did not know what to make of her or do with her. Then he turned to leave.

"Marcus!" Jennifer reached out a hand to halt his departure. He was not an easy man to understand, but she owed him more than her life, and she could not bear to let him leave angry. He looked at her quizzically, and she struggled to say what was on her mind, but under his cold stare, she could only offer a small, "Thank you."

The frown softened and he kissed her forehead. "You have little enough to thank me for, angel, I only claimed what was mine." Abruptly, he left.

As he had foretold, Marcus did not return for dinner. Jennifer was kept company by his aunt's chatter and the coming and going of various servants for various reasons, most of them involving the infant. He was scrubbed, cleaned, and changed enough times to satisfy the mothering instincts of an entire army of maids. Jennifer could only sit by helplessly and observe, wondering if she would ever be allowed to take care of the child herself.

But finally he was cleaned, fed, and asleep, the room cleared of all its visitors, the lights darkened, and Jennifer lay alone, listening to the distant ticking of the clock. She had been informed she now had a husband, a home, and a child, but only one of them seemed half real to her, and she wondered how long it would be before the other fantasies were destroyed. She had once indulged the fantasy of having a lover who would return to her and take her away, but it had led to months of misery and despair before it became even partly true. Did she dare pretend that this house could be her home and these people be her family? Or that the frightening man with guns on his narrow hips and a tongue that lashed like a whip could turn into the laughing, blue-eyed devil she had known on the river or the tender lover who had fathered her child? None of this seemed possible even to her overactive imagination, and she closed her eyes to block the thoughts from her mind. Sleep was her only friend.

The room was empty of visitors when Stuart's whimpering cry warned of an impending hunger tantrum, and Jennifer smiled at finally having something to do. She had already been up and washed, brushed her hair, and pulled it back in blue ribbons she had found in the dresser, and had been lying there wondering idly if anyone else was up yet. Now she pulled her bed jacket about her and gingerly slid to the edge of the bed. Just as she was about to put her feet to the floor, a powerful hand on her shoulder pushed her back against the pillows.

"I'll get him, you're supposed to be resting," he said gruffly, going around the bed to pick up the wailing infant.

"I need exercise, I'm not used to sitting still." Jennifer watched nervously as Marcus bent over the cradle. She was not used to seeing him less than fully dressed, either, but this morning he was still in shirt sleeves, his collar unfastened and exposing a portion of his broad, tanned chest. Unbrushed, his hair stood in rough curls, falling onto his high forehead in the rakish manner she remembered too well, and her heart skipped a beat.

"I noticed that. You've been in here puttering around for an hour this morning; if my aunt found out, she'd have one of the maids sleeping in here to prevent any further episodes." Marcus held the baby in his arms and made a face. "He's wet!"

"Generally, babies don't dry themselves. Bring me one of those cloths from the dresser." Calmly, Jennifer pointed them out and accepted the sodden infant from her husband's hands. "I did not mean to wake you; I thought I was quiet. You will not tell your aunt?" This last was asked anxiously; she enjoyed her few moments of freedom and a full-time nurse would be death to her privacy.

Marcus handed her the diaper and sat down on the bed as she inexpertly made the change. "You were quiet, I wasn't sleeping, and I won't tell my aunt unless you start overdoing it. I know how you value your privacy."

She looked up at him, almost startled into believing her blue-eyed captain was back, but the same bleak, gray eyes were watching her. She ducked her head and returned to her task, trying to control the flailing limbs of the wailing child. "Thank you, I will be careful," she said quietly.

"Apparently changing babies isn't on your list of accomplishments." He caught the infant's tiny fists, letting the small fingers twist around his large ones.

"I have never even seen one until this one came along, and your aunt and her maids have successfully kept him from my reach except when he's clean and dry and hungry. But I learn quickly." With a smile of satisfaction, Jennifer fastened the last corner and bundled the wailing infant in his blankets again. Looking to Marcus to see if he intended to stay put, she decided he showed no sign of moving. Embarrassed, she lowered her gaze from his lean face to the crying child and requested shyly, "If you would turn away, I could give your son his breakfast."

A smile flickered across his tanned faced. "I believe I told you once before that you have nothing that I have not already seen, and now that I know better, nothing that I haven't more than seen. Do not be so ashamed of your body; you weren't that first night if I remember correctly."

Deciding his perversity was no reason to let the child starve, Jennifer loosened the ribbons of her gown and brought the baby to her breast, carefully covering herself with the jacket. As the babe pulled hungrily at the tender nipple, she could feel her husband's gaze on her. She could not meet it as she replied, "It was dark that night or I would have died of embarrassment." Remembering how her dress had suddenly fallen to the floor at his hands, giving her no time to protest, Jennifer's cheeks burned with the memory.

Marcus hid a smile at the color on her face. Married and having borne a child, she was still as innocent as she had been that first time. He practically had a virgin bride on his hands. "You have never explained what you were doing in my room that night. Did you make it a practice to visit all the rooms in that way?"

This brought Jennifer out of her embarrassment as she threw him an angry glare. "I never entered any of the rooms unless they were empty and then only to clean them in the broad light of day, what do you think I am?"

"At the time, I thought you were an angel sent down from heaven just for me, but you still haven't explained why you were there that night." Marcus rested a hand on the far side of her legs, leaning casually across her as he admired the process by which his son fed himself, enjoying the partially revealed loveliness of ivory skin and a fleeting moment's pride in possession.

Jennifer squirmed uncomfortably under this unexpected intimacy. "I had been swimming . . ."

He interrupted, looking at her with new interest. "You can swim?" Then the laughing look returned to his eyes. "What did you wear when you were swimming?"

She gave him a swift, angry look which softened into a

half smile at her own expense. "That's not part of the tale, do you wish to hear it or not?" Ignoring his knowing grin, she continued, "I was trying to sneak up the stairs without crossing my mother's room when some drunkard came up behind me."Raised eyebrows wiped away the grin as he waited for her to continue. "He was barely able to stand, so I could outrun him easily, but I was barefoot and my toe caught in the carpet just before reaching your floor." She shrugged as the raised eyebrow turned into an ominous frown; he had asked for the tale, now he would hear it all, but her stomach churned at the memory of those grasping hands touching her, and her brow knit at a new thought. "It's strange, but when I think of that night now, I think of Mr. Delaney, but I could swear I never saw the man before I came here."

"Perhaps you are somehow associating what almost happened that night with the fate Delaney planned for you; do not worry any more about him." Marcus dismissed the thought peremptorily. "How did you get away from this man?"

"Crazed fear, I suppose. I shoved him off and ran to a room that was always empty and I knew had a bar to it; only, this time it wasn't empty." His gaze was so intense, Jennifer had a hard time meeting it.

"Then it was the bar closing that woke me. Thank God I was in no state to fasten it when I came in."

Jennifer shrugged. "Then it would have been someone else's bastard I would have borne instead of your own, and you would be a free man today."

Shocked into speech, Marcus snapped, "My God, Jennifer, do you hate me so much that you can speak of such an alternative?"

Calmly, she replied, "I cannot hate anyone who would save us the way you did the other day, but I can hate having been taken advantage of and deserted and then being dependent on that person for the rest of my life. It is an awkward situation for me, at best."

"Damn it!" Marcus sat up, cold eyes hardening as he

stared at her. Then he stood and crossed to the window, saying "I believe our son is asleep."

He kept his back to her as she lifted the sleeping infant to her shoulder and refastened her gown with shaking fingers. She hadn't intended to offend him, but he had to understand her position in this also.

"All right," he swung around as suddenly as he had moved away. "I suppose I had that coming. It gives me a better idea of what kind of arrangement we have here." He yanked the bell pull, returning the baby to his cradle before resuming his impatient pacing.

"You made it quite clear before that you had no wish whatsoever to get married or have anything further to do with men, particularly someone as rude, arrogant, and tyrannical as you seem to find me. I take it your opinion has not changed to any great extent?"

Jennifer laced her fingers together and tried to remain calm; if he were going to throw her out, it might as well be as soon as possible; it would be easier now than after she had grown dependent on this life here. "I have not changed any more than you have."

Marcus stopped at the bed and grinned. "Touché. That makes things a bit easier, then. It seems we are in agreement on more points than I thought possible. We should make a most interesting partnership. If you promise to not throw anything at me when I turn my back, I forgot to bring something from my room that I intended to give you this morning." He waited for her reply.

She looked up in surprise. He went from one extreme to another faster than she could keep up with him; would she ever learn what to expect next? "You do not ask my permission to enter the room, I see no reason why you need it to leave," she stated frostily, still irritated by the annoying grin that grew wider the angrier she became.

"I should have known better than to expect my Jennifer to be the weeping, sobbing fair maiden in distress, although you had me worried there for a little while. I'll be right back." He went off whistling, and Jennifer hugged herself in exhilarated relief. She was not cast out yet.

Marcus arrived one step ahead of the breakfast tray, throwing her a small, carefully bound package before drawing up a table for the maid to set the dishes on. Dismissing the maid, he settled himself in a high-backed chair to watch her wrestle with the wrappings. When the string proved too strong for her efforts, he reached over with a pocketknife, and slit the package open with one sure stroke.

Jennifer removed a blue velveted box from the wrappings and turned to him inquiringly, receiving no explanation other than his impatient gesture to open it. Snapping open the lid, she caught her breath at the sight of the contents. Through tear-filled eyes she looked up at him, unable to find the words for which the gift called.

"You're not proving me wrong, already?" With concern, Marcus moved to sit beside her, removing the rings from the box. "I told you we would have to find more appropriate rings than that thing you have on. Here, give me your hand."

Jennifer found her hand encased in his large, brown one as he slipped the oversized ruby ring from her finger and replaced it with the diamond and gold wedding bands. They fit securely, oddly heavy and comforting. "Marcus, I . . . They're so beautiful." The words were inadequate to describe what she was feeling; the magnitude of the gift overwhelmed her, but just the fact that he thought of her in such a way was enough to render her speechless. The reality of the fact that she was actually the wife of this overbearing river man was just now being impressed on her.

Marcus brushed a tear from her cheek and kissed her forehead. "They simply tell the world you are mine, so don't go getting sentimental on me. And to be fair, here, I will put this one on my left hand and now we are properly bound." The ruby slid difficultly over his left knuckle.

"Well, I'm happy to see you two are getting along a little better this morning, but that's no excuse for you to be

wandering around half dressed, Marcus. You'd better go
back and put on something more suitable before you give
the maids ideas." Josephine stood in the doorway, taking
in the tender scene between the newlyweds with an appraising glance.

"Please, let him eat his breakfast before it gets cold, Jo."
Marc's teasing glance fell on her as Jennifer pleaded with
the older woman.

"He'll do what he wants anyway, there's no talking to
him, so have it your way. I just wondered if you might know
anything about this, Marcus." Throwing a folded newspaper at him with a meaningful look, Josephine backed from
the room, closing the door on the sight of a half-dressed
male in a lady's boudoir, even if she was his wife.

Marcus caught the paper and chuckled. "Now I know
you have at least one use, not only keeping the ladies off
my back, but Josephine, too. This might work after all."
Tucking the newspaper out of sight, he brought the tray
to Jennifer's lap.

"I haven't made her mad, have I?" Jennifer asked anxiously, glancing at the closed door.

"No, I dare say she's tickled pink, actually, but that's
another matter. Now eat your breakfast." He drank his
coffee as he scanned the front page, his eyes fastening on
one corner while he read the fine print.

Jennifer watched, wondering what had captured his and
his aunt's attention. Unable to restrain her curiosity, she
asked, "Is there something of importance in the news today?"

Refolding the paper, he grinned at her. "Nothing of
particular importance. Pulitzer is an old friend of mine,
he's just up to his usual scandal-mongering best." He lay
the paper beside her and started in on his breakfast. "You
can glance through it when you get bored, perhaps you'll
find something to amuse you."

After Marcus left for the day, Jennifer eagerly spread the
newspaper out around her and began searching for the
article that had brought Jo up here in search of her

nephew. The only item that looked to remotely have anything to do with them at all was a local one on the front page concerning a new series to be conducted on the scandalous corruption prevalent behind the facade of city government. The only reason that one caught her attention was that it contained the name of the police chief who had threatened to charge Marcus with kidnapping. She read it over more carefully, but she had little experience with newspapers and could not see how Marcus could have anything to do with such a series. She shrugged and read the rest of the paper for more interesting news.

The afternoon proved more entertaining. First, her trunk arrived, bearing not only what few clothes she possessed, but the entire wardrobe she had spent the winter making for her child. Jennifer wondered if Delaney had sent it or if Marcus had to go after it, but there was no message included in the delivery.

These were no sooner stored away in drawers when another delivery arrived, scattering stacks of boxes about the room. It took several maids and trips to bring them all up and sort them out, and Jennifer didn't have the heart to send the maids away when it came time to open the boxes; they were as excited as herself at the prospect of more gifts than they had seen on Christmas Day. Josephine laughed at their elation and removed herself from the chaos, sitting in a far corner to observe them with cool amusement.

Box after box of the finest children's clothes flew open, soft cambrics and delicate laces as well as sturdy broadcloths for an older, more active infant. Jennifer had never seen so much clothing in her life and never of the quality of these. She smoothed a soft, cotton blanket between her hands as she watched in amazement while they brought still another box. Out tumbled an assortment of infant's toys, cloth animals and rattles and a music box of lullabies. This last brought even Josephine out of her detachment as she wound the delicate mechanism and listened to the tinkling music with childlike rapture. Jennifer simply

hugged one of the stuffed animals and broke into peals
of laughter.

While the maids played dress-up with the outraged infant, Josephine brought the last and largest box to the
bed—having recognized the label on it, she had some idea
what it contained. Bemused by this side of her nephew she
hadn't been aware existed, Josephine watched with expectation as Jennifer unwrapped the last gift.

From folds of tissue paper, Jennifer drew out a filmy
cloud of palest apricot, accompanied by a matching silk
nightgown cut with severe simplicity designed to emphasize the attributes of the wearer and not the gown. Beneath
these lay another similar gown, but of the same light apple
green as her shawl, with silken dressing robe to match.
Jennifer drew them from the box with wonder, holding
them against her and spreading the delicate fabric across
the bedcovers. Her eyes lifted to the benign face of the
older woman and their eyes met with understanding. With
a quavering smile, Jennifer smoothed the green silk, whispering half to herself, "He must have a fondness for this
color."

Josephine perched at the edge of the bed, folding the
gowns back into the box. "Marcus has an eye for beautiful
women; unfortunately, until now, they have all been married. But he knows what looks good on them; with your
hair and skin, that is the perfect color. I shall send my
maid up this afternoon and have her do your hair before
dinner and you can wear one of these new gowns. You'll
show him he has chosen well."

Suddenly tired, Jennifer said nothing. She allowed the
other women to take over and clear the room, settle Stuart
back to sleep, and one by one depart as they thought her
sleeping. Instead, Jennifer's mind raced, trying to understand what was happening to her and why. Had Marcus
truly accepted her as his wife, buying her the gifts a husband would buy for his wife and newborn child? But he
had admitted not being pleased at marriage, that his feel-

ings on the matter had not changed, and there was certainly no question of love between them.

Once before he had attempted to buy her with beautiful gifts and then deserted her to her fate. Was he about to repeat that performance? It seemed the more likely solution considering her small knowledge of his character, and she found her heart sinking at the thought. She could not let him trick her into complacency as he had before. She would have to steel herself against his charm and gifts and be ready for whatever would come next, even if she had to fight her own feelings every inch of the way. She bit a knuckle to prevent the tears from falling and eventually fell into a restless sleep.

True to her word, Josephine sent her maid up later that afternoon with perfumed soaps and colognes and a knowledge of hairdressing learned through many years of experience. Jennifer found herself scrubbed and scented, dressed in the apricot nightdress as if it were an elegant ballgown, and her hair arranged so skillfully in wisps and curls in a pile on top of her head that Jennifer was afraid to touch it lest she disturb one hair of the creation. Then she was left alone to amuse herself with Stuart's new toys and a book sent up from the unseen library.

It was thus Marcus found her, auburn hair layered in shimmering copper curls, pale, oval face drawn into a thoughtful expression as almond brown eyes stared unseeingly at a book in her hands. The filmy cloud of apricot about her shoulders did little to conceal the creamy skin beneath; full, young breasts pressed temptingly against the silken chemise of her gown. Marcus knew that she was unaware of the seductive picture she posed and appreciated the sweetness of such uncommon innocence, but this unwitting teasing of his baser desires could prove a problem in the future. She was only a child. He had taken advantage of that fact once; he was not coarse or cruel enough to do so again, not if he were to continue with his plans. It was something he would have to deal with when he came to it; for now, he would take his pleasures as he found them.

"That color looks well on you, angel." He kissed the peak of hair on her forehead as she looked up at his entrance.

"Thank you, sir." Setting her book aside, Jennifer lay a small hand on his arm and looked at him appealingly. "Will you sit and talk with me a while? There are so many things I don't understand and would like to know, if you will not be too upset at my impertinence."

He sat beside her, taking in the fresh fragrance of her cologne and wondering at the serious set of her face. This was not the reaction he had expected from her, but he hid his concern. "I will help in whatever way I can, but I do not promise anything."

She knit her fingers together and stared at them. "I've thought about this all afternoon, and I cannot decide what to do or say to make you understand without making you angry. You have been very kind to me, and I don't wish to make you angry again, but . . ." She parted her hands and looked to him for guidance. "I know you as a riverboat captain, nothing more. You have told me of your plans to sell your boat and take your savings to California to make your fortune . . . yet, today, you have showered me with gifts of such cost I cannot even imagine . . ." She gestured helplessly and looked away.

"Well, no one can say you married me for my money if that's all you know of me." Marcus turned her chin back toward him. "Perhaps I have not played quite fair with you, but surely even an innocent such as you should have understood that as a simple riverboat captain, I would now be sitting behind bars in St. Louis' finest while you graced the place of honor at Delaney's."

He watched the fine eyes widen and marveled at such naivete. "Jennifer, my love, this house we are in is not my aunt's, but mine, left to me by my father. After my uncle died, Aunt Jo returned here, the place where she had been raised, to run the household for first my father and now for me. It is her home, and she loves it here, but it is mine to do with as I will, along with my father's share of the riverboat line and the businesses in California. The money I spent today was not even a portion of my pocket money. If anything should happen to me, you and Stuart would be well taken care of for the rest of your lives without having to do anything further, but that is not the life I prefer.

"As owner of my own enterprise, I am an independent man, and I intend to continue that independence even now that my father is dead. It does not suit my nature to rely on the wealth of my father for my needs, I rather provide for myself. Do you understand any portion of that?" Her face had paled even further if that were possible, and Marcus released her chin to rub warmth into cold hands.

"I understand that it is even worse than I imagined." Jennifer's voice was cold and hollow, coming from a distance. "It would have been better for us if you had been an extravagant riverboat captain with a wealthy aunt." She lowered her head and stopped the motion of his hands, holding them tightly as she struggled with all the thoughts spinning about in her mind. The daughter of a bankrupt innkeeper might possibly expect to be the wife of a river man, but never that of a wealthy scion of society. She remembered now his aunt's horrified reaction to the news of their marriage and understood it; it was no wonder he had to be forced into the marriage. He could have had an heiress; instead, he was shackled to an ignorant nobody.

Marcus said nothing, waiting for further explanation of her statement.

Jennifer took a deep breath and quickly composed her declaration of independence. "I told you I have changed none since you saw me last. I have no wish to be owned by any man, but now I owe you a debt I can never repay, and you compound it by surrounding me with a wealth of luxuries I cannot earn."

Determination flashed in her eyes as understanding began to dawn in his. "No matter what you may think, you did not buy me with a few mumbled words and these rings, no more than you bought me with your coins the first time."

Jennifer leaped from the bed, throwing open the trunk and rummaging about in it until she withdrew a knotted handkerchief. Marcus had stood when she threw herself so precipitously from his side. Now, with surprise, he caught the bundle of coins she flung at him.

"I *gave* myself to you then! If I could have found you later, I would have thrown those things at you. I was not for sale then, and you cannot buy me now. I do not choose to give my body or sell my soul in exchange for rings or riches. I will work to pay the debt I owe, but do not think of me as yours. A wife belongs to a husband out of love and respect, and you hold neither of these for me. I want you to understand *clearly,*" Jennifer set her lips in a firm straight line as she stared up into the hard face of her husband, "that I will obey your wishes for the sake of the debt I owe and nothing more."

Marcus crushed the coins in his hand, staring at her for a full minute before responding to her challenge, and then his words were as scornful as hers had been brave.

"My dear child, your lack of knowledge in the laws of man and nature is astounding, but since you choose to wave your ignorance in my face, I will recognize it." He sat down in his high-backed chair and made a tent of his fingers as he studied her face.

"I don't seem to have convinced you that I am not the devil, and I have no need of your Puritan soul. Perhaps you would feel better if you knew I left these coins," he had removed them from their wrapping and now dropped them one by one on the table, "simply because I had nothing else to give, and I wished you to remember me. But whatever you want to believe, let me assure you I have no other need for your body or soul but their *presence*. These last few days have been an enlightening experience for me, and I'm beginning to think that a wife might be useful, after all. As a matter of fact, for the first time since I came back to town, the dowagers and their unpleasant daughters have left me blessedly to myself, and I am enjoying the peace."

He chuckled, and Jennifer glanced up quickly to see that the muscle in his jaw was no longer twitching, and he was watching her with amusement. He had been cut off by society for his scandalous marriage, and he was laughing about it; the man is obviously mad, she decided.

Marcus caught her look and laughed as he reached for the bell pull. "Don't worry, pet, they'll be back before long, dying of curiosity to meet the new bride. St. Louis doesn't stay scandalized for long. Unfortunately, you will be the one to bear the brunt of society's charms, that's one of the ways you'll earn your keep. I have better things to do. When you're stronger, we'll have a long discussion of your duties, but for now you'll have to put up with my amusing myself by dressing you and our son to suit my tastes. Do you object strongly to my choices?"

"I have never seen anything more beautiful," she murmured, surprised by his reaction into admitting it. What duties were there left for her to perform if he did not want her body? He already had someone to run the house, and she would act as nursemaid to their son willingly for nothing. But he had promised she would have to do nothing to compromise body or soul. She would have to be content with that.

"Neither have I." Pearly teeth contrasted with tanned skin as he grinned at her, and she blushed. "Have I satisfied most of your worries so we may eat dinner in peace? Or do you have more questions burning holes in that active little mind of yours?" Marcus moved his chair out of the way so the maids could finish setting up their dinner trays, not acknowledging their presence otherwise.

Jennifer waited until they were left alone to reply. There were thousands of questions she could think of, any one of them likely to send him back into a rage. She gave him a cautious glance, but he seemed more amused than outraged at her earlier attempts, and there was only one way to find out. "If I ask, do you promise not to be angry?"

"Only if I'm under no obligation to answer." He sat back, sipping his wine.

"Fair enough. You have asked me why I was in that room that night, it is my turn to ask you the same. Why would the captain leave his boat for a seamy water-front inn?"

His grin broadened. "It did not seem so seamy to me; it had some advantages I found particularly pleasing." Marcus raised his glass in toast at her irritated frown. "But you have our charming friend Gwendolyn to thank for my presence; she would be most amused to know she was responsible for bringing us together. Should I have told that to the judge?" At her impatient look, he went on, "It's quite simple, really. Our not so brilliant judge allowed his bride to ride unaccompanied from her parents' home in Louisville, and I had no strength left to resist her temptations, so I removed myself from them. Your inn happened to be the closest place in sight in which to drown my sorrows and get some much needed rest. Does that answer your question? I did not promise you would like the answers."

Jennifer stirred the food around on her plate; it was extremely vexing to think she owed her son to Gwen and her marriage to the judge, a star-crossed fate if ever there were one. "It's not my place to judge your actions. I was just curious. Why were you carrying a shawl with you?"

"A gift for my mother I had just purchased the day before and had not bothered to pack away yet. When I saw the color of your hair as you stood in the window, I knew the color was made for you."

Jennifer frowned. That was sensible enough by itself, but . . . "The gown you gave me was the same color, but you did not buy that for your mother?" It was an inquiry, not a statement, as she tried to remember the words he had used when giving it to her.

"No, that was for someone else, and here I use my pre-

rogative to refuse answering further. Why don't you eat
your dinner like a good girl and not worry yourself over
such trivia? Surely you cannot be jealous."

That successfully ended that line of questioning. With
a startled sweep of long lashes, Jennifer turned back to
her food, reluctant to give up such a profitable opportunity
but unwilling to risk his anger again. Jealous! He would
have all the Gwens he wanted just as long as he left her
his son.

Observing the outraged flare of her otherwise lovely
aquiline nose, Marcus could guess the path of her thoughts
and hastened to distract them.

"This is part of a suite of rooms, yours and my room
are connected by the washroom, there is a sitting room
on the other side of this one, use them as you will. I'm
afraid the front staircase is much too long for you to attempt right now, you will have to be content with our meals
here for a while longer. That way, you will not have to
worry about dressing properly until you are in better shape
for wearing the confounded clothing women get themselves up in."

Marcus halted her protests with a finger across her lips.
"I know, your dresses have the lovely advantage of not
needing all that cursed whalebone, but you must remember you are my wife now and not the preacher's daughter
or whatever. You will be expected to dress fashionably, and
I have no wish to see you harmed by the whims of fashion.
So stay here a while longer and take good care of Stuart
until the day comes you are well enough to brave the more
social world. One of your tasks as my wife will be to learn
to conduct yourself as a proper lady, not a little hooligan
who takes midnight swims in the river."

He was so close, it made her nervous, and Jennifer was
too aware of the transparency of her clothing, the warmth
of his hand on hers stirring feelings not long buried. He
could be so arrogant and cold, even now his words were
insulting and dictatorial, but she could not summon up
the image of the gray-eyed stranger when he was close to

her like this—the memory of warm blue-gray eyes and tender kisses were too fresh, causing the blood to heat in her veins.

She had to remind herself that despite the charm with which he phrased it, he was keeping her prisoner in these rooms, going so far as to deny her access to clothing to satisfy his own prurient whims. She was his wife now and must obey his orders, whether she agreed with them or not. All hope of independence and freedom were gone forever, and *he* had to be the one to hold the key. A tear trickled from one corner of her closed eyes, and Jennifer withdrew her hand from his grasp.

"Despite my age, I am not a child, there is no need to treat me as one. You have already made it clear that I should use Josephine as a model; if you will have sent up whatever etiquette books you may possess, I will learn them rapidly. I have no wish to disgrace you." Her chin held high, she opened her eyes and stared boldly into gray ones that hardened at her cold words.

"You won't disgrace me or I'll take a switch to you. Two brats on my hands are more than I have patience to deal with. I'll see the books are sent up in the morning and speak to Josephine about allowing you up for short periods." Marcus stood towering over her, his dark coat molded to powerful shoulders, his face dark with displeasure, and Jennifer marveled at her own temerity: he could easily crush her into oblivion with one hand and probably get away with it. Instead, he left without so much as a parting gesture.

If she had been the weeping type, she would have cried, but months ago she had resolved to shed no more tears over this monster. He saw her only as a childish nuisance, and she must not allow her imagination to see otherwise. But it was so lonely when he left, the room seemed so large once emptied of his enormous vitality, it was difficult to think of his sardonic smile and cutting wit, she only remembered his closeness. It was a long time before she slept.

Seven

Comforting her wounded spirit by curling the dark locks of a sleepy infant the next morning, Jennifer glanced up to find Marcus standing in the doorway. The informality of yesterday gone, he was dressed once again in his immaculate gray suit, a small diamond stickpin flashing against a dark waistcoat as he stood, hat in hand, obviously prepared to go out. Lines were once more etched about his eyes, and they were hard and flinty as he stepped into the room.

"I am on my way into the city, is there anything I can get for you while I am there?" His tone was icy as his gaze rested on the infant in her arms.

This is the man I will have to learn to deal with, Jennifer decided, the true man behind the blue-eyed charm. In any case, he was the one who looked on her as his property to be used as he saw fit, and it was best to learn to deal with him on an employer-employee basis. If she could concentrate on this relationship and no other, she might survive the constant battle of emotions.

"In my ignorance, not that I am aware of, thank you. Is there anything I can do for you while you are out?" She kept her voice polite, but could not resist the urge to be sarcastic; it would take practice to gain control over her need to strike back when struck.

"Not that I know of," he replied acidly, turning on his

heel and preparing to leave when suddenly confronted
with the determined figure of his aunt.

"You're not getting away that easily again, Marcus. I demand an explanation of what you and this friend of yours
are up to. It may be easy for you to go muck-raking in your
own backyard when you do not intend to stay here, but I
have to live with these people . . ." Josephine waved a
folded newspaper in his face, finally striking him in the
chest with it before Marcus tore it from her hands.

"You know very well what my intentions are and if you
need them in clearer terms, we'll discuss it downstairs."
Marcus shoved the newspaper under his arm and guided
his aunt firmly by the elbow, closing the door behind him
without another glance back.

Jennifer stared after them with astonishment instantly
diverted by the baby's choosing to burp part of his breakfast over his new gown. She forgot the incident for the
moment, but revived it later over a lonely breakfast when
she asked a maid to bring her a newspaper.

Again, the only local news of interest was the series on
corruption in city government, and Jennifer wondered if
the names mentioned happened to be friends of
Josephine's, but what would that have to do with Marcus?
Just because the man who owned the paper was a friend
of his didn't mean he had any influence on the articles
written. In one of the last paragraphs Delaney's name
caught her eye, but it was mentioned in the same breath
with several others, and she could find no significance.
That he was corrupt, she already knew, and could find
nothing newsworthy in repeating common knowledge.

At lunch, she donned her new silk dressing gown and
dined with Josephine in the sitting room. The room was
decorated in dark woods and blues and greens and was
obviously intended for a man's use, but she felt comfortable there. The stuffed chairs were large enough to curl
up in with a good book and the library table made a sturdy
substitute for the trays from which she had been eating.
Her main concern was her appearance, and there was little

to be done about that, if she had a choice of her old gray
silk or the dressing gown, she would have to choose the
gown as being more appropriate to meet Jo's elegance.
The etiquette books she had spent the morning studying
said nothing about making such an incongruous choice.

Having spent the morning at the steamer line offices,
Josephine was dressed in full regalia, and she chattered
on about the business while Jennifer listened politely, until
mention of a distrust for bookkeepers came up, and she
tuned in more attentively. Perhaps this was the opportunity
for which she had been looking: she had little experience
in bookkeeping outside of the inn, but with a little practice
it couldn't be too difficult. If Marc's aunt could work in
business, there was no reason it wouldn't be ladylike
enough for his wife. After all, he had said to use his aunt
as example.

"Jo," Jennifer interrupted the monologue tentatively,
setting her tea down. "I have some experience in bookkeeping. Could I . . . Would it be of any help if I . . . ?"
The question was halted by Josephine's cry of delight.

"You don't mean that! You can do something besides
adding up the dollars and cents it takes to buy a new bonnet? Wherever do you come from, child?" Her face
beamed with surprise.

"I come from a hard-working family who couldn't afford
to hire help to do their work. I've been keeping books
since I was twelve, and I'm sure yours must be much more
complicated, but if there's anything I can help you with,
it will ease my idle brain." Jennifer tried to hide her eagerness. If Marcus said no, she didn't want her disappointment to be too obvious.

Josephine's mind was following the same track. "Marcus
finds my preoccupation with business unladylike, but he's
too much of a gentleman to say so to my face. And it's
one area I'm not backing down to him in. I enjoy the
business, it was part of my life before I got married, and
my husband greatly appreciated my help after I got married, and it's too late for me to give it up now. If I bring

home a little work now and then and you offer to help with it, I can't see that he can object too strenuously, especially if you're confined to the house for a while. And despite all his modern notions, you will be. I'm not exposing an inexperienced child like you to the teeth of society so soon after this latest scandalous episode of his, they'll eat you alive. And not satisfied with that, he seems bent on creating another." She shook her head in dismay as she stirred her coffee.

Jennifer pricked up her ears; this lunch might be more informative than she had anticipated. "I heard you scolding him, but I do not understand what it is about."

Josephine shook her head again. "It is nothing for you to be concerned about, and Marcus would have my head if I told you. Anyway, I assume he will be taking you to California with him, and you will not have to worry about it any more than he does."

Jennifer bowed her head. She wished she could be as sure as his aunt about her husband's intentions. He had not once mentioned California in her presence since that time on the steamboat, but she knew that was where he was headed sooner or later. It was inevitable. It would be better if she prepared herself for a life here; if she could carve out a niche in this household, perhaps Jo would allow her to stay on in one capacity or another. To plan a future with Marcus in it was unthinkable.

Josephine went on, "I think maybe it's time for us to have a little discussion about Marcus. Are you tired? Would you like to lie back down?"

Jennifer smiled at her kindly expression and rested her head against the chair back. "No, I'm fine. What did you want to tell me?"

Josephine looked at her skeptically, then settled back on the sofa with her coffee as she gathered her thoughts together. "I can only tell you what I have observed: Marcus is an extremely reserved young man, except for his temper, of course. He has not ever told me any of his reasons for doing anything, and I can only make assumptions, although I'm getting better at that now than I was when he first came here.

"I still haven't pieced together the reason he came back here. There was some sort of break with his father, and I understand there was a broken engagement involved, but whatever it was, he came back a man at age twenty, told his uncle he wanted a job working on the docks, took a room in town instead of here, and he has supported himself every since.

"We've grown closer since my husband died. I've always been fond of Marcus, but he supported me through a very rough time then, and I learned there is a lot more compassion in him than readily meets the eye. Since that time he's actually condescended to stop by here on occasion to visit, although this is the first time he has taken up residence here since he came back East. And as far as I know, the only communication he keeps with his family is a business letter every few months to his mother. It's only since his father died that he's had any urge to return to California."

Jennifer listened intently, watching the woman's face for all the nuances behind the words, trying to fit this image to the one she had of her husband, but all she could see was the tough, ruthless stranger in this description, and a fondness for an exceptional aunt. Perhaps, somewhere, somehow, he had been badly hurt by someone, but that vulnerable boy was long since gone, and in his place was this hard businessman who would marry for advantage and visit his bereaved family only to conclude a business arrangement. She could find no hope in these words. Her expression revealed her disappointment.

"I have not helped much, have I?" Jennifer's silence spoke for her. "Jenny, I do not know what you fear, but Marcus is a good man and given a chance, he will be a good husband. He has his moods, I admit, but if you think he is bad now, you should have been here last winter when he came home in a dreadful temper! That lasted up until he ran that last trip. I am sure this temper will blow over sooner. Marcus just hates being forced into anything—the judge did you a disservice when he forced this marriage. But there's nothing that can be done about it now, short of death or divorce, and he'll soon learn to accept it.

"Actually, I think he had grown rather fond of you before all this happened. He spoke of you in very glowing terms, and I am sure with a little time, you can return his affection. Just have patience, child, things will work out."

Jennifer barely heard the words following "divorce." She had not heard the term before but if it were a means of escaping marriage, then there was every chance Marcus had already thought of it, and was probably planning on it. He could use her for whatever purposes he might wish until the time came when he decided he needed that advantageous wife, and that would be the end of this empty marriage.

She was thankful he at least had the decency not to use her as wife if he had no intention of keeping her as wife. Perhaps he would have the decency then to see that she had a proper position somewhere before letting her go. But just in case, she had better look after opportunities for herself.

Aware that his aunt had stopped speaking and was waiting for some reply, Jennifer pulled out of her gloomy study. "Thank you, Jo, for trying to explain things to me. I know so little of men, and Marcus thinks of me only as a child, that I have no opportunity to learn what pleases him. And I'm afraid my temper is not much better than his sometimes. I wish I knew what magic formula makes him happy so I could return him to that state for you."

Josephine looked at her oddly as she set her cup back on the table. "Judging from the timing, it was that last trip up here that returned his humor. Didn't he exhibit it while he was with you?"

Surprised, Jennifer stared at her for a moment before replying. "He was very charming whenever we weren't fighting; unfortunately, I do not like being forced either, and he spent much of the trip forcing me into positions

I found unacceptable. As a result, we spent a good deal of time fighting. I don't know how that could restore his humor. Why was he in such a black humor in the first place?"

"Heaven only knows," she shrugged. "He came back from a trip last December in the foulest mood I'd ever seen. There had been some trouble with the boat and he had been laid up in New Orleans for quite a long time, but that never bothered him before, so I just figured it was woman trouble again. Whatever it was, it disappeared like magic on that last trip; so find out what you did then, and try it on him again. Right now you'd better get yourself back to bed, you look exhausted." She stood and pulled the bell to have the dishes cleared away.

Reluctantly, Jennifer returned to her room, her thoughts spinning from the implications presented by this indomitable woman.

After Stuart's late afternoon feeding, a maid carried in a large package addressed to Jennifer. She opened it more cautiously than she had the ones the day before, afraid her words may have provoked Marcus into something outrageous. The tissue wrapping fell away, revealing a dark emerald glow of velvet. Jennifer stroked the material lovingly; it was impossible to imagine material so lustrous and rich as this. Drawing it gently from the box, she laughed ecstatically at the contents. Instead of the filmy, revealing dressing gowns of the day before, he had sent her one to cover her from head to foot, with even a hood to be tied about her neck with soft ribbons. Whatever hardness there was in his heart, it was well covered by his sense of humor, and she welcomed its return.

When Marcus entered her room that evening to find it empty except for the sleeping infant, he strode rapidly to the sitting room door, throwing it wide in his haste. Wrapped snugly in her new dressing gown against the evening breeze from the open window, Jennifer sat curled in an easy chair, engrossed in one of the volumes of etiquette littering the table beside her. The last rays of sun sent shafts of light across the dim room, illuminating the red and gold fall of hair and catching on the bouquet of yellow flowers she'd arranged before her. The table was already set with crystal and china for two.

She looked up at his entrance, brown eyes dark and impenetrable, the fairness of her skin contrasting with the deep emerald velvet where it fell open at her throat. Her voice was studiedly low and mellifluous as she greeted him.

"Good evening, Mr. Armstrong, would you care to have a seat?" She gestured gracefully at the high-backed chair she had brought in from the bedroom. "Shall I ring for some wine?"

His moment's irrational panic dissipated into equally irrational irritation.

"That's quite cordial of you, Mrs. Armstrong, but if you practice that crap on me I'm quite likely to wring your pretty little neck." Marcus snatched the book from her hand and snapped it shut, throwing it down to join its companions. "You'll ruin your eyes reading in this light," he offered as explanation before taking the seat indicated and drawing it nearer.

"You said you must have a lady for wife, so lady I will be. Unfortunately, I have not yet reached the part in dealing with insulting, threatening gentlemen, so I'm not certain of the ladylike response required." Jennifer folded her hands in her lap and met his eyes calmly.

The piercing loveliness of the vision before him warred with his turbulent emotions and lost, and the conflicting desires to strangle or to kiss that lovely throat dissolved into sharp words.

"It won't take you long to learn the art of the subtle cut, but I prefer you to tell me what you think outright. I have quite had my fill of muddle-headed coquettes and vipers disguised as the fairer sex; turn your charms to other uses besides me."

"Such as?" Jennifer looked at him inquiringly, trying to pretend calm but her hands clenched nervously.

Marcus gave a snort of disgust and shoved the chair back, getting up to pace the room restlessly. "All right, Jennifer, it's obvious we will not be able to conduct a civil conversation until we come to some mutual understanding of our roles in this farce. I would like to propose a business contract between us, since you do not accept our marital one."

"I didn't think I was alone in that feeling since you have admitted no need for a wife, let alone one who is a childish nuisance, a brat, and a hooligan." Her eyes flashed as she watched him, but she kept her voice cool.

Marcus stopped before her, hands behind his back as he looked down at her slight figure curled childishly in the overlarge chair. He had once expressed a desire to see her without the heavy burden of pregnancy; now he had the opportunity but could do nothing more than look. The velvet robe hadn't been a joke, it was self protection.

"You cannot deny any of those charges, but at the same time I am also prepared to admit you are intelligent, talented, and more mature than most children your age. It is to this side of you that I am appealing. You wished to be independent, to work and support yourself, and to be obligated to no one. Am I correct?"

Jennifer felt the heat of his gaze and nervously clutched the lapels of her robe; it was difficult to think when he looked at her like that, his enormous masculine vitality permeating the senses, with stirring longings that could never be quenched. What would it be like if he suddenly swept her up in his arms as he had that first night? She shivered and whispered uneasily, "That was what I had hoped to do."

Marcus strode off again, returning to his pacing as he spoke. "Then I suggest a business arrangement between us, a partnership. I have already given you my name, I will also see that you and our son are well provided for. In return for my support, you are to first and foremost, look after the welfare of our son." He silenced her wordless protest with a gesture. "I could hire a governess and a covey of nursemaids for him but I think you better suited for the job. I have already told you I will have little time for wife and children; you will have to provide all the love and support a child needs with little help from me. But I expect him to be raised with a healthy, inquiring mind and not crippled by the hellish beliefs of your religion." He stopped in front of her again, his gaze boring through to her soul.

Jennifer wondered if this was the aspect the devil took when he came to earth, if smoke would spew forth when she contradicted him. "I will not raise my son as a pagan! I am no great believer in my mother's church, but he shall learn of God and the Bible if I have to starve to see to it."

Marcus dismissed her words with another quick movement of his hands before shoving them into his pockets and resuming his pacing. "I have no objection to that; I am not totally without morals. But besides nursemaid and governess, you must learn the task of being my wife in public. I did not give my name to have it bandied about loosely. As my wife and mother of my son, you have a position you must uphold, I will not tolerate any behavior that will lessen it. Do you understand?"

Jennifer spoke coldly. "I may only be an innkeeper's daughter, but I daresay I have more morals than I have noticed in you and will create less scandal than you have already associated with your name. I will try my humble best not to shame your precious honor." The last was spoken with increasing sarcasm as all the implications of his words began to sink in. What did he think she was that he would speak to her that way?

"I did not think that would be too difficult a part of the bargain since you had already swore off all men as being detrimental to your independence. Unfortunately, you will find you have very little independence in my employ either, although the job pays better than any you might find on the street. I cannot guarantee any days off since the child represents a full-time job. I cannot even promise evenings off if a social engagement involves your presence with me. But you are free to set your own schedule without my interference within that limited framework.

"You will also train yourself for the position of running

a household once I establish a residence of my own. At the moment, your main concern will be learning to meet our social obligations and dealing with the servants appropriately instead of making pets out of them as you are inclined to do. Managing a household such as this requires a lot of other responsibilities, and you must be ready to assume them when the time comes. Am I asking too much of you?" Marcus dropped into the chair in front of her and waited patiently for her reaction.

Jennifer drummed her fingers against the arm rest. "You seem to be under the impression that the magnitude of the job should impress me. Well, it does not. Caring for Stuart is something I am prepared to do on my own, the rest is no less than I have done every day of my life for years, only under less formal circumstances. I am also quite capable of being cook and maid if you require them. You must have extremely pressing social obligations to pay such high wages, Mr. Armstrong."

He smiled faintly. "At the moment, I am a pariah in several circles, including my aunt's. But if I am to maintain my connections with the business community, that situation will be rectified, with your help, of course. Perhaps your most unpleasant chore, then, will be putting up with my humors and attempting to disagree with me as little as possible. Will you agree to this contract?"

The obvious question here, Jennifer thought, is whether or not this contract has an expiration date, but that would only infuriate him, and she had no wish to lose such a lucrative position so easily. Only he hadn't named the hardest part of her job; somehow she had to balance in the precarious position between wife and employee without getting hurt. This might require more skill than she possessed. "No marital obligations?" she asked cautiously.

"Separate bedrooms, if that's what you mean," he agreed grimly.

She nodded thoughtfully. "I cannot afford to turn it down, as you are well aware, but for Stuart's sake, I will play the part of your wife in public better than any dutiful lady you can possibly find. I will earn my keep."

The sun had set, leaving only the flickering of candles to shadow their faces as they concluded their agreement with a handshake, Jennifer's long, slender fingers crushed firmly in her husband's strong grip.

On the day Jennifer was first declared well enough to descend the stairs, a box arrived early in the morning containing all her clothing needs for the first day out. Her husband's ability to judge size was rivaled only by his superb taste in clothing, and Jennifer spent her morning's exploration dressed in a fashionable morning gown of yellow silk, long train and petticoats rustling behind her as she followed Josephine about her morning duties.

She could not tell if Marcus approved of her new attire. His manner remained neutral and businesslike in the presence of others, and now that she was allowed the freedom of house and grounds, there was no further need for their private confrontations. At first, Jennifer was relieved at this arrangement: their arguments were few and small in the presence of others, and she no longer felt pinned by his icy gaze or nervous at his nearness. She was free to treat him as other members of the household, and she rejoiced in this protection. But it did not take long to discover that she missed the intimacy of their old relationship, however rocky it might have been. He was more than ever the cold stranger, with no sign of her friend the riverboat captain.

There was no other mention of California either, in public or private, by Josephine or Marcus. Jennifer dared not open the discussion with Marcus, and judging by the coolness that had grown up between aunt and nephew, felt there was little chance in obtaining information from Josephine. So she chose the role of silence and waited patiently, never quite certain if this would be the last she saw of her husband or not.

Telling herself it was just a matter of time before she regained her own innate confidence, Jennifer was convinced she would soon be ready to step out into the world with or without Marcus' support, but every night she awaited his arrival more eagerly than the night before. He had taken to stopping by her room before retiring, playing with his son for a few minutes or just exchanging a few words before taking the connecting door to his room. He said little, laughed less, but it was the only time during the day they were together and alone, and daily her need for these few moments increased.

The rest of her day was spent in learning Josephine's housekeeping routines, studying her manuals of etiquette, taking care of Stuart, and helping Josephine with the company bookkeeping. She was soon relieving Josephine's duties in several areas, but it still seemed more like play than work. It was a long way from sixteen hours of nonstop work under her mother's watchful eye.

As May grew longer and the days became warmer, Jennifer took advantage of the weather to stroll with Stuart in an old carriage about the gardens surrounding the house. The trees were fully leafed now, and the gardeners were busily moving tender plants from the greenhouses to the grounds.

Thick hedgerows formed garden paths, giving the impression of privacy and seclusion that Jennifer cherished when bouts of springtime restlessness drew her out of doors. Enclosed by towering evergreens and thick masses of azaleas and rhododendrons, she could lose herself in the wilderness of greens and scents to dream impossible dreams, drink the lush sensation of nature's opulence, and ease her troubled soul with silence. While Stuart slept in the sunshine, Jennifer paced out the longing that pierced her more poignantly than ever before, stirring emotions better laid to rest, resurrecting memories that could only make her more miserable when she should be grateful with happiness.

Her bustled yellow silk splashed against the backdrop

of green boxwood like a late-blooming forsythia, alabaster hands stroked a marble nymph implanted in the shrubbery, the deep rich glow of auburn hair caught in a sunbeam in a cascade of curls and ribbons to form an etching that burned itself indelibly into the darkest corner of his mind as Marcus came around the shrubbery in search of her. It was a classic study, "Girl in Garden," only the wicker carriage on the crushed gravel path appearing incongruous.

The gravel crunched beneath his boots as he approached, and Jennifer turned swiftly, interrupting the low song pealing unconsciously from her lips. It was so natural a part of the setting as the bird's songs that Marcus had been unaware of it until she stopped, and he regretted his interruption.

Jennifer watched his tall figure approach in polished boots, with wide brim Stetson hat pulled down over his curls at a rakish angle, and the white frill of his shirt providing a bright contrast to the somber hues of waistcoat and jacket. He was a striking figure that could easily set any woman's heart aflame, but she was his wife and could not even allow her thoughts to turn in that direction. It was a case of living one more dream only to find it a nightmare.

Gray eyes softened as he stopped before her. "You look lovelier than any flower here. Do you enjoy the gardens?"

"I don't know how you can stay away from them." Jennifer moved toward the carriage, out from under that steady gaze, her slippers barely disturbing the gravel.

Marcus followed behind, his hand resting on her shoulders as she bent to inspect the infant sleeping with tiny arms outstretched. Jennifer found the gesture of familiarity unsettling, and straightened to move from under it.

"If I'd known the place was inhabited by angels, I wouldn't have." Marcus caught her waist before she could elude him, guiding her around the pathway. "Come, show me what I've been missing, and tell me how you've been getting along. Does your new job suit you?"

Jennifer's arm brushed against her husband's solidity, and his hand felt warm and strong about her waist as she smiled hesitantly up at him. "So far, it is child's play to what I am used to. My only objection is the price I must pay to wear all the finery you flatter me with; I'm sure these bones fit the whale better than they do me."

Amusement glittered in his eyes as he ran his hand over the stiff length of the offending garment. "I must admit, I prefer your natural curves to these artificial ones; if you were cinched much tighter I swear you would break in two. But console yourself, you look lovelier than any of the St. Louis maidens who came out this spring; you will be the envy of all female society with a figure like that and I will be the envy of all males."

"Does that mean you are back on speaking terms with society again or are you just talking through that extraordinary hat you're wearing?" Jennifer knew too well that his compliments were meaningless, but she thrilled at the thought of his actually noticing her at all. He had said equally silly things when she had been eight months pregnant and at her worst, but though he might not mean the words, he would have said nothing at all if he had not been thinking of her.

"You like my hat?" Marcus took it off and dusted the low crown before returning it to his head. "No holes, so I couldn't be speaking through it." He grinned, and the gray faded ever so slightly from his eyes as his smile was returned. "How would you like to take a brief carriage ride to the city? Your dressmaker informs me she is about ready to empty my bank account."

Jennifer stared at him, brown eyes wide with momentary panic. "You want me to ride with you to town?" After all these weeks of practicing the role of fine lady behind closed doors, was he finally about to expose her to the critical eyes of the world?

"It's just a short ride to the dressmaker's and back for a fitting. If it worries you, I will have her come out here. I just thought you might like a change of scenery." He took her hand absently, freeing her waist from close confinement.

"No, no, I would love to go!" Anxious to please, Jennifer hurried along beside him. "Do you mean today? Will it take long? I cannot leave Stuart . . ."

A corner of his mouth turned again. "It will not take long if you do not spend so much time talking. Stuart will be fine in the hands of the maids until we get back." He tucked her hand in the crook of his arm and grasped the baby carriage handle, pushing it at a merry rate back toward the house.

Before Jennifer was well aware of what was happening, Marcus had sent the infant off with a maid and packed Jennifer into his two-seated carriage, bearing her off down the dappled lane toward town behind two aristocratic bays, their mettlesome gait throwing her more than once against her husband's rocklike arm. Grinning down at her, he urged the horses faster until trees and lawns were left far behind and warm sun burned against rocky pavement.

Marcus slowed their pace as they entered the city, and Jennifer clutched at the reticule in her lap as she tried to absorb all the images bombarding her at once. The few times she had been through here before were only hazy impressions, and she had been in no state then to observe anything outside herself. Now she was eager to learn all she could about what promised to be her new home.

Marcus glanced down and smiled, slowing the pace further before coming to a stop before his hotel. Jennifer looked at him questioningly, then spotted the small figure unfolding himself from the shade of the porch steps. Marcus threw the reins to Henry, then swung down from the seat, giving Henry further instructions in a low voice before coming around to help his wife from her seat.

"Come, my love, it's just a short walk from here, and you can admire the beauty of our fair city without worrying about my driving." Pulled down over his eyes to keep the sun out, the hat threw shadows across his face, and Jennifer could not tell if the smile on his lips had reached the grayness of his eyes as she took his hand.

"Do you still keep your room in this hotel, then?" Her glance flickered over the imposing brick structure, trying to remember the few details of its interior she had caught that day in another age and time.

"It is paid for until the end of the month; old habits are hard to break." His words were abrupt as he led her away, but then he seemed to have second thoughts and looked down at her quizzically. "Is there some reason for that question?" The crooked grin showed he could think of several, but he refrained from stating them.

"It's not my place to question your activities. I simply wondered why we stopped there." Jennifer ignored his grin and turned to gazing in shop windows. A room in town would be convenient for entertaining his paramour, but then, she had no right to expect anything else.

"Rest assured, madam, my purpose was entirely innocent," Marcus promised. "The dressmaker is right here, as I said, only a short distance from the hotel. I hope you're prepared to be quick because I have no wish to stand around all day." He pushed open the shop door and held it for her.

Recognizing Jennifer, the seamstress bustled up, ushering them in with a torrent of greetings. Marcus eyed her impatiently, then bowed over Jennifer's hand.

"I will wait for you outside. I believe I will find the atmosphere more congenial there," he muttered under his breath before squeezing her hand and departing, leaving Jennifer to smile after him.

The fitting dragged on interminably; Jennifer found it hard to admire the beautiful materials while being stuck with innumerable pins and turned this way and that, so it was with relief she greeted her husband's impatient figure when he reentered the door. She was wearing the final dress, a delicate ivory batiste summer gown, as he came in and circled her, nodding his head approvingly.

"That will do nicely, a far cry from those abominations

you came with," he commented. "Now hurry and get it off so we can get out of here, I'm tired of admiring the street life."

The dressmaker fluttered about, anxious to please her most demanding and most profitable customer. The last few pins in, she rushed Jennifer into the dressing room and out again with a minimum amount of fuss.

Jennifer strolled down the street on her husband's arm in a bubble of happiness, the brilliant sunshine and the strong arm under her hand serving to drive away all dismal fears while she floated in the pleasure of being out and about and in Marcus' company. She counted this moment one of the highlights of her life, a small dream come true without the pain accompanied by the others.

"Shall we find a bonnet to match that dress you had on? There's a millinery a few blocks away." The excited dance of Jennifer's eyes was all the response Marcus needed to lead his wife with a light step toward the shop, giving an occasional wave or nod to passing acquaintances and smiling inwardly at his young wife's excitement. But gray eyes hardened when his glance fell behind him as they turned to enter the shop.

Jennifer failed to notice the change as she surrendered herself to the pleasant task of choosing one bonnet from among many, trying on several before turning to Marcus for approval of her choice. He stood with arms crossed, leaning against the door while he watched her make a selection, finally nodding approval at her decision and paying for it with a sudden air of impatience.

Jennifer had learned to expect these abrupt changes of mood and followed him out unquestioningly, content that he had been pleasant for this long. With brisk step, he guided her farther down the street and away from the hotel, stopping before a sidewalk cafe.

"I see a friend across the street I would like you to meet. Why don't you have a seat here and order something cold while I go get him?" Marcus helped seat her in a position facing the street, his words more an order than a question.

Jennifer sat obediently, watching the swing of his broad shoulders as he crossed the street and disappeared behind a parked carriage, praying his friend was someone extremely amiable and not likely to scorn her. Concentrating on finding Marc's familiar figure amongst the crowd, she failed to notice the approach of a man behind her until a hard hand squeezed her shoulder, and the terrifying chill of cold metal pressed against the nape of her neck.

With a shudder, Jennifer recognized the rasping voice— one of Delaney's men. Echoes of that month-long horror reverberated in her mind, jarring loose nightmarish memories only recently buried, and she barely suppressed the desire to scream.

Through the noise in her mind, she understood his illiterate demands. Reality bruised her shoulder and sent shivers of fear through her numbed brain with the touch of the cold gun barrel against her skin. Frozen in panic at the mere thought of Delaney's name, Jennifer was beyond thinking; only pure, cold reaction flowed through her veins.

"I'm not going." Her voice was flat and firm as she clamped the table top with nerveless fingers.

"Goddamn it woman, you'll get your ass out of there now before I put a bullet through you. Now move." The rasping voice was vicious in its nervousness.

"Shoot me, then, I'm not moving." That wasn't true, she was shaking with terror, every nerve ending quivering with near-hysteria.

The hand crushed her shoulder, attempting to drag her to her feet as Jennifer hung on to the table with deadly intensity. "Delaney wants to talk to you, that ain't no cause to get your head blown off. Now be reasonable and come along with me before you make a scene."

"He can talk to me when I'm dead and not a minute before!" Jennifer's knuckles turned white as her fingers grasped the table tighter, her eyes closing in silent prayer and desperate horror, waiting for the searing flame that

would end her torment, praying it would happen soon
before her strength gave out.

"I'd suggest, Griffith, that you move away from the lady
before you get two barrels of shotgun shell in the middle
of that yellow streak." The voice was calm and clear, almost
a drawl and distinctly familiar.

Jennifer gasped and her eyes flew open. Marcus was
standing directly in front of her, accompanied by a shorter
man with a full beard and an astonished expression on his
face. Neither carried a gun, but Marcus appeared amaz-
ingly calm as he stared icily at a spot over his wife's head.

Without so much as looking at her, Marcus held out his
hand and gestured for Jennifer to come to him. "Get up
slowly, Jennifer, and come here."

The bruising grip on her shoulder had already slack-
ened, now the gun backed away as she edged slowly to her
feet, obeying Marcus' orders in a daze of incomprehension. His hand was warm and sure as it caught hers, and
she collapsed against his broad chest. His strong arms instantly circled her, squeezing her tightly against him before
gently pushing her behind him. Jennifer clung to his coat-
tails, too terrified to think rationally, aware only of her
husband's protective masculine presence. The gentleman
beside him clucked sympathetically and shook his head,
waiting for the remainder of the performance before expressing any opinion.

"The next time I find you or any of your cronies molesting my wife, Griffith, I'll shoot first and ask questions
later. Got that? Now get the hell out of here and tell your
boss if he wants to talk to anybody, it better be me. Henry,
escort this man out of here before I change my mind and
call the police." Marc's frigid tones hid a molten current
of hot rage, and the man moved swiftly to remove himself
from danger, Henry and shotgun following close behind.

Not until they were well out of range did Marcus take
Jennifer in his arms again, crushing her close and muttering against her hair as he stroked her back. "Damn, why
can't you just faint or scream like other women? Telling

him to shoot you—I swear, I thought I talked you out of that death wish of yours. What am I going to do with you, Jenny Lee?"

She buried her face against his coat, letting the flow of warm words wash over her, soothing her hysteria as his strong arms secured her against fear. If only she could hold this moment forever . . . A detached cough sounded in their ears, and Marcus drew away, not releasing Jennifer entirely while she composed herself.

"Marcus, if I'd known I was putting your family in jeopardy by running that series . . ."

"If I'd known Delaney would hang around after we closed him down, I would have found a better way of hanging him. It's not your concern, Joseph."

Marcus bent his head to examine his wife's face. "Jenny, this is the friend I wanted you to meet, Joseph Pulitzer. I believe you've developed a recent interest in his newspaper, haven't you?"

He still hadn't released her, holding her tightly to his side as he spoke. Jennifer was glad of the support, her knees still weak with trembling as she realized the extent of the danger she had just been in. She had difficulty comprehending what had just been said, but it stirred an uneasy feeling within her as she extended her hand to the stranger.

"How do you do, Mr. Pulitzer? I apologize for my performance just now . . ."

"Don't be absurd, my dear, your performance was superb, I admire your courage. We really must get to know each other better, Marcus has kept you to himself long enough." The man took her hand and bowed politely over it, his eyes sparkling with ill-concealed interest.

"I think it best wait until another time, Joseph, my wife has had a rather bad shock, and I would like to see her home."

"Please, Mr. Pulitzer, come to dinner with us sometime, would you? Then we would have a better opportunity to become acquainted." The phrases rolled off her tongue without thinking, and it wasn't until they were out that Jennifer wondered if she had gone out of the bounds of her duties. She glanced surreptitiously at her husband to find him looking at her with a strange glow, and she basked delightedly in its warmth.

"I would be delighted, Mrs. Armstrong. Just send me a card naming the time, and I will await it eagerly."

"You shall receive one in the morning, sir. It's been a pleasure meeting you."

Within minutes Marcus had her in the carriage and jouncing down the street, his hand holding hers while guiding the horses with the other.

"I'm sorry, darling, if I'd known that was going to happen I would never have brought you to town. I'm afraid I'm going to have to make a few changes in my plans."

The term of endearment was lost to Jennifer in the confusion of emotions the last half hour had generated, but the reference to his plans caught her attention. "What plans? Marcus, what were you and Mr. Pulitzer talking about? Why would Delaney want me now? What's happening?" Her voice rose slightly as she saw the warning signals in his face, the clenched jaw and darkening eyes, but she wasn't letting him off that easily. She had some right to know what was going on, it had been her life in danger, not his.

"Can you not guess the answers to those questions? Is your hatred of me so great you would think I would leave Delaney's treatment of you unchallenged?"

"Unchallenged!" Jennifer's eyes grew round as she stared up into his face; what possible madness lay behind that icy mask? Wheels of thought turned around, piecing together his words with others. "Surely you did not write those articles for the paper?"

Her tone of amazement brought a grim smile. "Pulitzer writes fine on his own; all he needed was the information to work with. I have not been entirely idle these last few weeks."

Jennifer let these words sink in before replying, a puzzled frown of thought upon her brow as she spoke. "I am trying to remember what was said in those articles, the names were mostly unfamiliar to me, but Josephine said you implicated some of her friends. How does that tie in with Delaney?"

Marcus snorted at her innocence and explained the tangled web of blackmail and threats Delaney had used to entrap so many of the town's officials, payoffs and scandals that kept the dishonest wealthy and the honest silent while providing Delaney with enough ammunition to keep his immoral businesses profitable well into the next century. There was scarcely a prominent businessman or official untouched by Delaney's chain of extortion. It was small wonder that some of Josephine's circle of friends were included. And Marcus had made it his task to expose them all and bring the rambling house of intrigue and ill-repute to a crashing halt.

"So you closed Magnolia House," Jennifer said wonderingly, amazed at the amount of evil lingering beneath Delaney's sordid exterior, unable to comprehend the herculean task her husband had set himself. Instead, her mind jumped to more pragmatic questions. "Then what did he want me for?" It had been the threatened horror of Magnolia House that had kept her glued to the table, preferring a clean, quick death to the life of whore. "And if he did all that, why isn't he in jail?"

The grim set of her husband's jaw told her his answers weren't pleasant, but Marcus replied calmly enough, answering only the last question. "That had been my intention, locked safely behind bars or driven so far away we would never hear of him again. Now I fear your safety is in jeopardy, after all." He grew silent, making no further explanation.

"Marcus?" Jennifer touched his arm timidly, trying to bring his attention back to her again, not satisfied with his curt answers and worried about where his thoughts were traveling. The knowledge that he had tumbled a veritable institution for her sake sent a thrill of pleasure through her, but practicality prevailed.

He grunted absently, and she took that for encouragement.

"How did Henry get there?"

Dark eyebrows pulled together in a frown. "Get where?"

"He was at the hotel. Why was he at the cafe with a gun?" She hated being so persistent, worried that the next question would send him flaring into a temper, but dark suspicions were forming in the back of her mind.

"When I saw Griffith in town, I had Henry follow us as guard. You were never in any danger if that's what you were worried about; Henry had a rifle trained on him every minute." His tone was still abstracted as he pulled the horses to a halt at the front steps.

"He could have killed me! What do you mean there was nothing to worry about? You set me up!" Jennifer was irate at this callous use of her person, instantly forgetting the comforting warmth of his arms and the earlier worried concern in his eyes.

Now Marcus just looked at her with stern gravity. "I suggest we continue this discussion in the house. Your unhappiness may increase with what else I have to tell you."

She stared at him, open-mouthed; surely he wasn't already getting rid of her? If that's what he wanted, why hadn't he let Delaney have her?

Taking her into the library, Marcus slid the doors closed behind them. It was a room Jennifer had browsed through frequently these last few weeks, loving the atmosphere of well-read books and the masculine smell of comfortable leather chairs, but now there was a chill in the air as she seated herself and watched Marcus open the liquor cabinet.

"Would you care for some sherry?" His back was to her as he took out the decanter and poured the drink without waiting for a reply. He took nothing for himself, carrying the fragile goblet to her side and placing it in her hand.

"I'm afraid your first outing wasn't as pleasant as I had hoped. You might need this to steady your nerves."

The wine was warm and mellow, the taste giving Jennifer something to think about besides the disquieting proximity of her husband. His hand rested on the chair back, sending nervous vibrations up and down her spine; she could sense his tension, and her stomach knotted with apprehension.

"Jennifer, you knew from the beginning that I intended to return to California. I have postponed the trip in an effort to be certain you are happy and comfortable here, but I have already made arrangements to leave at the end of the week." Her head jerked nervously but he continued determinedly. "I did not wish to force this decision on you before I was prepared to offer you some semblance of this same comfort out there, but today's events have made me more concerned for your safety than your comfort."

He paced restlessly for a moment, then drew up a chair in front of hers and sat down. Taking her hand, he spoke in measured tones. "I know you and Josephine get along well, and you seem to be happy with the work she's found for you to do, although I'm not sure bookkeeping is what I had in mind." A touch of irony crept into his voice. "But it may be difficult to see that you are properly protected under the circumstances. If you choose to stay here, I will leave Henry here and provide other precautions, but it will mean curtailing your activities to a great extent. I fear Delaney and his men will not give up easily if they have chosen to seek revenge."

Jennifer searched Marc's face for some clue to his thoughts, but his eyes were enigmatic. There was nothing she could say, so she remained silent, more conscious of the hard grip of his fingers on her hand than of the terror his words should inspire.

"The only other choice I can offer you right now is for you to make the arduous trip to California with me. I am aware that you have not fully recovered your strength, but

I cannot postpone making the trip any longer. I cannot even promise you agreeable living arrangements once we arrive. The house in San Francisco where we would reside is run by my mother and unless she has changed drastically since we last met, I do not think the two of you will get on anywhere near as well as you and Jo do."

Marcus rose, hands in pockets, and walked across the room to the front window. "I am not painting a pretty picture, but I wish you to know all the facts before making a decision. I will be busy and won't be around much to help. Until I have the time to locate a proper establishment for us, and it may be months before that occurs, you will have to put up with my mother's society. I will do my best to ease you into her good graces, but I seldom enjoy that state myself. Arrangements must be made immediately, so you must give me your decision at once."

Jennifer tried to listen calmly, rationally, to weigh one word against the other before reacting, but the knowledge that he had intended returning to California leaving her on Jo's hands as if he were a free man had destroyed all possibility of rational reactions. Logically, she had known that was what he wanted to do, even understood why he wanted to do it. She had no illusions about this marriage; he had done it as the most convenient alternative in a bad situation and thought no more about it. Now he intended to follow through his plans as previously arranged, set himself up in business in California, and find an advantageous marriage.

But logically wasn't the way she wanted to look at it; he was her husband, the father of her son, the one and only person in this world she had to turn to, and she wanted desperately to be able to trust him. Sometimes, she could almost feel as if she could, as if he really might be the friend he claimed to be, but then he would hit her with something like this and all the fragile tentacles of trust she had sent out would be crushed.

The silence grew in the thickening gloom as Marcus turned to face her, trying to read her thoughts before she could speak them. The sadness in her liquid brown eyes stunned him with its intensity and filled him, surprisingly, with despair: she had decided against him. He settled in his desk chair and leaned back, propping his feet up on the desk in a display of casual indifference, waiting for her to frame her reply. The room's remaining light seemed to focus about her hair, and it glowed like banked coals, the young face pale and strained below it.

"You are giving me little choice, as usual. I may stay here and be a nuisance to Josephine and take my chances with Delaney, or go with you and be a millstone about your neck and take my chances with your family. Does your mother even know of our marriage?"

Marcus swung his feet down. "We correspond little. Unless Josephine has written, she knows nothing of you. There is not much that can be done when she is faced with accomplished fact, and with a child in question . . ." He shrugged his shoulders and spun the chair away, unable to bear the pain in her eyes, knowing full well he'd placed it there, again. "If it is of any use to you in your decision, you will not be a millstone about my neck; you will perform the same functions there as you would here. I would rather you decided on your own preferences and not mine. You have been uprooted and tossed about too much these last few months. I do not want to do it to you again. California is a long way from your home. Many women would object to being taken so far from their family." He pressed his fingertips together and stared at them as if he could press hard enough, he could get the answer he sought.

"I have no family other than Stuart, that is scarcely a factor in the decision."

Jennifer's words were cold and far away and Marcus swung around to stare at her again. Just what was going on in that inscrutable mind of hers?

"You are being childish now. You may have a right to despise what they have done to you, but they are still your family. I return your question, do they even know of our marriage?"

"I have written my aunt to tell her that I am well and the baby is fine, I have said nothing more. You do not need to fear being invaded by a horde of greedy relations."

Marcus slammed his fist against the desk, jarring a vase halfway across its surface. Then he jerked open a drawer, rummaging angrily through it until he found pen and paper. "What is your aunt's name? And your uncle's?"

Jennifer looked at him, puzzled. "Do you intend to send me back to them?"

Marcus groaned in dismay and covered his eyes, forcing words out from behind clenched teeth. "Will you tell me what I have done to deserve this opinion of me? I simply intend to write your family and inform them of our marriage. It is something I should have done weeks ago, but I seem to have been otherwise occupied. Will you trust me to do this one thing properly?"

Shocked by the intensity of this declaration, Jennifer silently rose and crossed to him, kneeling at his feet and resting her head abjectly against his knee. Startled, Marcus placed his hand at the nape of her neck, stroking the silken hairs that escaped their pins.

"Forgive my distrust. You have done everything you possibly can for me, yet I still bite and growl at you whenever you hold out your hand. If you really have no preference in the matter, and I will not interfere with your business, I would like to go with you. Your son needs a father, and we have a contract. I can carry it out best if I am with you." Not until all the words were out did she look up. He was her world, and it cost her considerable pain to admit it, but that look in his eyes was worth every minute of it. She ached to be swept up into his arms, knowing the futility of her desire.

Marcus set the pen aside and cupped her chin in his large palm. "There is nothing to forgive, angel, you have every right to distrust me and growl and bite to protect your interests, just so long as you understand when I fight to protect mine. Now get yourself up from there." Gently, he helped Jennifer to her feet, keeping her at a circumspect distance as he led her back to the chair. "You will not interfere with my business, and I shall be glad of your company, although I fear you will be trapped into my mother's dismal entertainments in my place. Are you certain you are well enough for the trip?"

He still clasped her hand as he sat near her, but Jennifer was more awed by his change of mood—where did he hide this self when he was coldly castigating or laughing at her and calling her fool? This was the man she had so foolishly loved, and the current of electricity coursing between their fingers told her nothing had really changed. She did not dare look him in the eye again, for then he would surely see what was so shamelessly written in hers.

Shakily, she disengaged her hand from his, lacing her fingers together to control their trembling. "I am well enough. It will not be unhealthy for Stuart?" Now that the connection was broken, her mind was clear to receive the myriad other questions tumbling to the forefront.

"I shouldn't think so. I will see that we have Pullman reservations all the way through; that way you may retain some semblance of privacy for most of the trip, but I warn you, it will be considerably less spacious than the captain's quarters on the *Lucky Chance*. I am not going to leave you alone while I find other accommodations, so you must put up with my company for three entire days and nights."

"At least, it will be proper this time and of my own choosing, so I think I might tolerate it." Jennifer braved a small smile which he returned with gravity. "Will we see Indians?" Jennifer couldn't resist the temptation to ask. Now that the decision was made, there were so many things to think of. It was too unbelievable to imagine that she would actually be going West to a place she had previously only read about.

Her ingenuous question brought a merrier grin to his face. "They ride free, so you may expect them as fellow passengers, but I doubt if you will meet with any wild types. You aren't frightened, are you?"

"No, no—I just want to know what to expect. What about buffalo? Do they still have buffalo?"

"You'll more likely see steers than buffalo; the railroad has civilized too much of the land. The best you can expect to see are miles of prairie and desert until we reach the mountains, does that disappoint you?"

"San Francisco, you did say that was where we are going? Is that near the ocean?" She could tell he was laughing at her again, but she felt more comfortable with that than the feelings he had disturbed in her moments before.

"It is near the ocean, and I promise to take you to see it one day, but right now I had better go break the news to Jo so she will start speaking to me again. You had better start seeing to your and Stuart's trunks. I will send a message to your dressmaker to hurry with her alterations; you can't arrive in San Francisco as bereft of clothing as you did here." He took her hand and helped her to her feet, hesitating a moment before opening the door. "You will not change your mind between now and Friday, will you?"

Jennifer stood on her toes and kissed his cheek. "Not unless you do."

Marcus grinned and caught her up in his arms. "You can do better than that." He captured her lips with his, enjoying their surprised response and warm pressure.

Caught off guard, Jennifer responded eagerly to these heated sensations. There was no denying his hold over her, it had been there from the start, but the sudden intensity of his tightening embrace shot signals of alarm up her spine. She knew now where this led, and she struggled from his grip.

Marcus returned her to the floor and opened the library door with a mocking bow. "After you, madam. In the future, you'd best be careful when you bestow your kisses. I won't settle for second best."

Jennifer raised her eyebrows archly. "Then consider

yourself lucky to get any at all." She swept past him, gathering her skirts into her hands as she ascended the stairs, hiding her rapidly pounding heartbeat.

Eight

The train ride was hellish and exhilarating, sometimes both at the same time. The magnificence of the open plain, extending to the horizon in undulating waves as far as the eye could see, the ghostly desolation of the arid alkali deserts, the fascination of Salt Lake City and its extraordinary inhabitants—Jennifer stared at the strangely garbed men with their retinue of women and children after Marcus explained the basic tenets of their religion, amazed that any woman could be so subservient, but secretly wondering how they organized their sleeping arrangements, and Marcus laughed at the questions in her eyes—kept Jennifer captivated from the moment the train left the station.

The ride itself was exhausting; their privacy, despite Pullman's extravagant declarations, was minimal, and above all, it was incredibly filthy, the billows of sooty black smoke combining with the dust of the tracks into an impermeable second skin, but Jennifer loved it all. During the day, with their curtains pulled back and their bunks converted to seats, her excited chatter was as much an attraction to the mostly male passengers as was the scenery to Jennifer. At night, with the curtains drawn, and Marcus' bunk only a few feet from hers, the excitement was of a different sort, but in the darkness, it lay unrevealed to anyone but herself, an unassuaged hunger she carefully hid.

But the mountains, the mountains were a separate creation, terrifyingly magnificent, and Jennifer could feel God's hand upon them as they clattered across horrifying divides, sluggishly rising to the peaks only to fly mindlessly, breathlessly to death-defying bottoms. She clung to Marcus in terror, trying to protect Stuart with her body while gripping for dear life to her husband, amusing the more travel-weary occupants of the car while causing Marcus second thoughts about the whole affair. It was with relief and gratefulness for the hand of God that she heard Marcus tell her Sacramento was just ahead, and the remainder of the trip would be by steamer. The familiar laziness of river travel would give her the time needed to calm her nerves and collect her thoughts before arriving in the lion's den, as she had come to consider the home of the formidable woman Marcus had described as his mother.

The closer they came to their destination, the moodier Marcus became. The stony grayness returned to his expression as he drew away from her, once more becoming the cold stranger who awed and intimidated her. On the train, he had been the image of a considerate husband, and Jennifer had grown used to his thoughtful explanations and affectionate caresses, accustomed even to his presence near her at night. But she would never grow used to this icy armor he donned when his temper frayed or when that invisible hand clutched at his heart, because she had learned by now that the anger wasn't directed just at her, but at something beyond his control. She could only wait for the mood to pass, avoiding him if at all possible so as not to be the spark that set fire to his fuel of rage.

They floated downriver into the bay at night, the myriad stars above descending to land by means of the tall hill that was San Francisco. It was breathtakingly beautiful, and Jennifer ached to take the lighted pathway to the heavens, forgetting herself in her longing and moving closer to her

husband's side as they stood at the rail, watching the re-
flections in the water. Marcus drew her closer, pulling her
head to his side as his arm enclosed her. They were encircled by the bonds of understanding, united in their knowledge that they were arriving in this new life as a pair.

It was too late to make a decent arrival at the Clay Street
house, and Marcus took them to the city's newest hotel, a
marvel in ostentation and a far cry from the weary inn
that Jennifer knew. She was relieved at his decision to wait
until morning, feeling bedraggled and filthy after the long
journey, eager for a long night's rest on a bed that didn't
move and a bath that didn't include the company of
strangers on the other side of a flimsy curtain. With disappointment, she observed he took two rooms and realized they were back on contract terms again—familiarity
between employer and hired help strictly forbidden. Jennifer suddenly realized it had been pleasant playing wife
for a little while; certainly not more odious than her present nonexistent position. If only Marcus would continue
playing the part of agreeable husband, she could almost
accept it as a rewarding life. Fine chance there would be
of that, she grumbled to herself as they climbed the stairs
to their apartments.

Marcus entered the bedroom with her, directing the
placement of trunks and tipping the young boy carrying
them, discreetly closing the door after him before addressing Jennifer.

"I have the room on the other side of that door, if you
should need anything." He nodded toward a door in the
back of the room. "Will you be all right alone?" There
was concern in his eyes.

Jennifer looked at the floor. It seemed she had been
alone most of her life, what did it matter if she were alone
in a strange hotel room? At least, she had Stuart—there
was some human warmth to comfort her; it might be all
she had for a long time to come. She almost regretted
leaving St. Louis and Josephine.

Not raising her eyes, she replied, "I will be fine; a good night's rest is all I need."

Marc's gaze swept over her thoughtfully. It was true, she had slept little on their journey. Between tending to the infant and starting up at every strange noise from the other compartments, she could not have slept more than a few hours each night. He should know, he had slept even less, lying there listening to her soft breathing and knowing that tempting body was within arm's reach of him had not been conducive to rest. Their constant proximity for three days and nights had been harder on him than on her, he reflected wryly.

"Sleep late then. I will be up early to see to the rest of our baggage, we can breakfast after I return." He made his way to the adjoining door, checking on the sleeping infant in his progress.

Jennifer prayed silently that he would leave while she still had the strength to control her tongue. If he delayed longer she would cry out her despair and desolation, throw herself on his mercy and the comfort of loved arms, and regret it forever after. She kept her head bent as her husband's tall figure hesitated at the door, clenching her hands together as he glanced back. For a moment, Marcus almost changed his mind, desiring only to take her in his arms and comfort her somehow—and comfort himself in the process, he thought grimly, grasping the knob. Neither of them was prepared for the consequences of such an action.

Gratefully, Jennifer listened to the door closing softly behind him.

The next morning, with Stuart fed and sleeping—Jennifer wondered what she would have done if he had been a colicky, disagreeable baby—she bathed, then dressed her hair, watching as the sun climbed slowly to its zenith. The sun didn't look any different here than in St. Louis, but the city she could see from her window bustled with a brisk energy that had been lacking in the Mississippi River town. Beyond the busy street of hills she could glimpse the sparkle of blue water in the bay. She wished she could see it all, wished she could be anywhere but here, waiting for this encounter she dreaded.

The gown she had chosen for this meeting was of a daring style, and she smoothed the slim line of the yellow crepe de chine. The dressmaker had claimed it was the latest style from Paris, and Josephine called it the style of the future, saying they would soon do away with petticoats altogether and then banish the corset. Jennifer just hoped Marcus would approve of this one with its one petticoat and slim skirt that showed the more natural curve of her hips instead of the bouffant skirt and crinolines that most women were still wearing. It was cooler than wearing the half dozen petticoats, and she prayed Josephine was right, once stripped of all these undergarments, women might truly be as free as men.

But right now she couldn't even finish lacing the hidden closure at her back, and she wondered what she would do when it came time to feed Stuart again. Maybe she had been foolish to try something new on a day like this; she paced nervously, almost stopping to reconsider the contents of her trunk when there was a knock at the door.

Not waiting for an answer, as usual, Marcus strode in, well-dressed in a light three-piece suit with top hat to match, an accessory he promptly threw on the bed as his eyes scanned Jennifer's costume. He had lost none of his tan since leaving the river life, and his dark coloring set off the gleam of white teeth as he smiled delightedly, running his fingers through the curls that fell to his forehead.

"I should have known if there were any way you could get out of wearing some of that frippery, you would find it." He circled her while Jennifer stood stiffly under his gaze, tightening as she felt his fingers at her neck. But he was only completing the lacing, and she relaxed.

"Do you like it? Will your mother be too shocked?"

He put a reassuring hand on her shoulder. "It's ideal. She'll be so fascinated by the dress she won't think of anything else. You're learning faster than I've given you credit

for." Marc's hand slid down her arm, and his head bent
to brush heated lips against her nape.

Jennifer stepped swiftly away, clutching her elbows nervously as she looked out the window, avoiding his gaze and
the tingling sensation rippling up and down her spine. "I
don't want you to be ashamed of me since you are forced
to present me as your wife. Since she knows nothing of
me, perhaps you should just say I'm the child's governess;
then you wouldn't have to worry about my doing something foolish." She had rehearsed this speech all morning,
not certain if she would give it, but it was better to remind
herself, and him, of their contract before she gave in to
any of the foolish dreams his touch stirred in her.

The smile left Marc's face, and his eyes hardened. "I
sent a wire before we left St. Louis, notifying her of our
arrival. Whatever our private opinions of the situation, we
are man and wife in the eyes of the world; I have no intention of denying my claim to you. Do you have any other
stimulating suggestions?"

Jennifer's spirits plummeted to new depths at the coldness in his voice; there seemed to be no happy medium
between them.

Her mood had not eased by the time she entered the
darkened foyer of her husband's former home. Bonnet
tied securely with matching yellow ribbons, one gloved
hand clutching Marcus' arm too tightly, she held the basket with her sleeping son and glanced around. Little light
entered the stained glass fanlight to lift the oppressive
gloom of darkened mahogany paneling. The staircase to
the second floor and the balustrade were of a similar dark
wood, sturdily built with no hint of the graceful proportions of their St. Louis home. This was a modern house,
built only a few years earlier with the no-nonsense pioneer
spirit and the wealth to include only the very best. Jennifer
gazed at it with dismay.

A uniformed maid scurried off to announce their arrival, but Marcus waited on no ceremony, following close on
the maid's heels as she entered the back parlor. Heavily

curtained and furnished, this room was equally dark despite its southern exposure, and Jennifer blinked at its dusty remoteness, trying to focus on the waiting figure lost in the gloom. In the wing-backed chair by the fireplace sat a middle-aged woman who still held herself with youthful grace, the dim outline of her figure suggesting slender height. She set aside a teacup as they entered, turning a face lined with permanent disapproval to study them, cold features registering no welcome as Marcus greeted her.

"You certainly were in no hurry to get here; your father's been dead nearly six months now—the least you could have done was to come and pay your respects. And I take it this is the bride of whom you failed to inform us?" Piercing blue eyes took in Jennifer's appearance with one stony glare, catching momentarily on the basket at her arm before returning to Marcus.

"This is my wife, Jennifer Lee. Jenny, the charming woman before you is my mother, Clare Armstrong."

"Maria!" Instead of acknowledging the introduction, Clare commanded the waiting maid, "Go make up their suite. I take it that is a baby you are carrying there?" Without waiting for an affirmative reply, she continued, "Better send someone to the attics for a cradle and whatever else they can find." She dismissed the maid with a wave of her hand.

Upset by this cold greeting, Jennifer turned her gaze up to Marcus, but his jaw was clenched as he glared at the stiff figure of his mother.

"I can see the years have not changed you much, madam. We will endeavor not to abuse your hospitality for long. As soon as I have concluded the business of my father's estate, I will begin searching for an establishment of our own."

"Nonsense. I take it that means you intend to finally settle down here. You know as well as I do that this house and everything in it is yours, left to me only on a temporary basis." Her voice was bitter as she looked away from them.

"And you have obviously changed little yourself—I am your mother, call me so."

Jennifer felt ignored and confused. Marcus had been gone ten years, returning home with wife and child; shouldn't he be greeted with open arms and cries of joy? What kind of woman was this who could not welcome her son or even ask to see her grandchild? Suddenly weary, she leaned lightly against Marcus, wishing they were anywhere else but here.

He felt her weight against him and relaxed his angry stance enough to encompass her shoulders with a reassuring arm. "We have had a tiring journey . . . Mother," the slight emphasis was almost, but not quite, sarcastic. "And my wife is little recovered from the birth of our child. If you have no further need of her, perhaps she could retire while we continue our argument alone?"

"Of course. She looks barely older than a child herself. I shouldn't have thought your taste would have run to youth." Clare pulled a velvet rope, and there was a sudden scurrying on the far side of the door, as if someone waited there already. The door swung open, but she ignored it. "And the child, is it boy or girl? You could not have wasted much time having it unless you married her at an extremely indecent age." The words were biting, but the woman failed to even look at him, speaking more out of habit than actual malice.

Jennifer heard a sharp intake of breath behind her and sneaked a quick peek over her shoulder. A young maid was standing in the opened door, her dark eyes reflecting uncertainty as to whether she should enter or not. Jennifer could not take the woman in the chair seriously, and a streak of wayward mischief made her wink at the maid in the door before returning her solemn mask to the speaker. Neither Marcus nor his mother noticed the exchange, both lost in their separate angers.

"The child is a boy, we call him Stuart, and if you must insult my wife, I prefer you not do it in her presence."

Startled to hear her own voice speaking, Jennifer interrupted. "Actually, if I'm being insulted, I prefer it to be done in my presence rather than behind my back."

Clare looked up quickly, her raised eyebrows taking on startling familiarity as her gaze once more studied Jennifer. "Sensible child. Now go on with Lucia, she'll show you your room." Her wave of dismissal was regal and meant to be obeyed.

Marcus squeezed Jennifer's shoulder and released it. "I will be up shortly, little one; there are business matters to be discussed of no interest to you. Henry will be here with the trunks later, so get some rest while you can."

She followed the maid out, closing the door gently behind her before daring to meet the laughing black eyes of the olive-skinned maid, but as their eyes clashed, they each emitted a slight giggle that threatened to become a roar at their mutual understanding, and they dashed for the stairway before the sound could be heard behind them.

Upstairs, their gales of giggles woke Stuart, and Lucia insisted on scooping him from his basket while Jennifer untied her bonnet ribbons, surveying her new room. Spoiled by the well-lit spaciousness of the St. Louis country home, this one seemed drab and crowded in comparison, but a far cry from the attic dormer where she had spent the majority of her life. The appointments were elegant and of the best quality from the heavy walnut bedroom suite to the thick velvet draperies, but the sheer weight and number of them made the room oppressive. Staring at the magnificent four poster bed, Jennifer wondered if she were meant to share it with Marcus, or if he were already making other arrangements.

Quickly dismissing such stray thoughts, she turned her attention to the foreign-looking maid. She had never seen a Spaniard or Mexican before, but she guessed the girl must at least be of Latin descent. Her hair was thick and black, braided into heavy ropes and wrapped neatly about her well-shaped head. Black eyes dominated a proportionately small face, round cheeks and chin creating an almost perfect oval. Her eyes were serious now as she changed the infant, soothing his angry cries, but small lines about her eyes spoke not only of exposure to the sun, but of laughter, and it seemed to bubble merrily just below the surface as she looked up to find Jennifer studying her.

"I am the oldest of *doce niños,*" she stated proudly, amending at Jennifer's puzzled expression, "twelve children. I am a very good nursemaid and an excellent house maid. You will be needing someone like me if you and the *señor* are to set up a new establishment. I have worked for *Señora* Armstrong eight years now and I know everything about running a household. You will let me be your personal maid and take me with you when you go to your new home?" Her black eyes were sparkling and eager as she rocked the now mollified infant in her arms, confident of her acceptance.

Jennifer laughed, holding out her arms to claim her son. "Right now, I need a friend more than a maid." Then she accused her, "You were listening at the door, weren't you?"

"*Sí,* that way I am always ready when someone needs me." Her mischievous smile gave her away, and they broke into laughter again at her blatant opportunism.

"I must warn you, my husband has an ugly temper, and I do not dare ask too much of him, so don't count on anything until it is done. You may not wish to leave here after you've worked around him for a while." Jennifer settled in an overstuffed chair, one finger entwined in a tiny fist.

Lucia grinned, and Jennifer felt a tie of friendship for this presumptuous young maid. San Francisco couldn't be too dreary if she could be allowed one friend, but Marcus' ominous warnings about making pets of the servants made her hesitant. How could she ever show him she was capable of running a household full of servants when she felt more at one with them than with him? Dejected and weary, she leaned her head against the back of the chair and closed her eyes, unable to respond to Lucia's enthusiasm. Hearing Stuart's whimpers, she knew it would soon be feeding time, and this foolish gown wasn't designed for the demands of hungry infants. Her trunks hadn't arrived yet, and try as she might, she couldn't think of this monstrous room as home. How could she ever fit in here? It was so cold and artificial, just like the woman below; Marcus must have inherited his coldness from her, and the thought of her husband depressed her more. To live with this coldness was one thing, but to long for the warmth hidden underneath was pure torment. She should have stayed in St. Louis and allowed distance to put an end to her torture.

"This little one, he is hungry, no?" Lucia hovered anxiously beside the chair, uncertain of what she should do to please the bride so she would remain happy with her.

Jennifer opened her eyes and saw the maid's anxiety, smiling lightly to dismiss her fears. "He is hungry, yes. But my trunks have not arrived and I . . ."

Her words were interrupted by a flash of understanding. "*Señora* Armstrong has many robes, let me get one for you. Then when the little one is asleep, you may lie down and rest, also. You must be very tired, and I have worn you out with my silly chattering. I will go, I will be right back." With this stream of words, she departed, her heels clicking rapidly against the uncarpeted floor.

Accepting the robe Lucia brought her and changing with the maid's help before dismissing her, Jennifer curled up in a chair and gave in to her son's demands. It was senseless to bemoan her fate as long as she had Stuart; it was something she must continually remind herself of when things looked worst.

Still, she wondered what explanation Marcus was giving his mother of their marriage. It was impossible to imagine that formidable woman understanding her plight as Josephine had done. For a moment, she longed for the happy companionship of the older woman, but it was a weak substitute for what she felt for Marcus, and Jennifer knew it. In one way or another she owed her husband her life and her son; it was only natural that she feel strongly about him. If she could only remember her place in his

life so she wasn't tempted to think there could be more
than that between them. It would be so easy to convince
herself that those feelings he had stirred that first night
could be renewed, that they meant more than just this
physical attraction between them. But she knew now that
what they had done was not out of love. It was hard to
separate the two, but Marcus had told her there was a
difference, and although she couldn't see it, it was obvious
he could, and it wasn't love he felt for her.

She shook her head to rid it of such nonsense. It was
doubtful if Marcus even thought of her, much less felt anything for her. She was simply a minor obstruction in his
well-laid plans, an object to be moved around and used as
necessary. She had best remember the next time he looked
at her with those deceitful blue-gray eyes that the only
thing they held for her was lust and nothing more.

Stuart had drunk his fill but was still looking around
with eager eyes, ready to play. Jennifer lay him on the bed
and lay beside him, crooning nonsense and letting him
toy with her ribbons until he drifted off to sleep, and she
with him.

When Marcus returned, the afternoon sun burned behind the window hangings, illuminating the room with a
surreal dusk. Entering, he knocked lightly at the open
door, and Jennifer smiled lazily up at him, awakening
slowly.

He held out a hand to help her to her feet. "The men
are outside with your trunks, if you would care to cover
yourself, I will call them in."

The masked hunger of his gaze drew Jennifer's attention
to the loosened robe, its front gaping to reveal milk-taut
breasts pushing against a dainty chemise. Blushing, she
secured the robe more tightly and brushed a loose strand
of hair from her face before raising her eyes to his stern
visage.

"It was meant for a smaller woman," she apologized
shyly.

"I can see that." His gaze fell from the tight bodice to

trim ankles exposed by the short length of skirt. "It doesn't seem to suit you."

He beckoned in the men carrying the heavy trunks, directing their disposal in a corner not totally filled with furniture. Henry carried the first one, and Jennifer smiled in greeting at his familiar grin.

"Henry, why don't you tell the captain he no longer has a boat and should help tote his own bales from now on?" she asked teasingly.

"Cap'n loaded and unloaded most of 'em hisself; we just carried 'em in." The old man dropped his burden in place and slipped off his cap, giving Marcus a surreptitious glance as he spoke, his employer's ominous frown warning him his chatter wasn't appreciated. Leaving a broad wink for Jennifer, Henry hurriedly left the room.

While the trunks were being placed, Jennifer's thoughts swung to the formidable man beside her, as Henry had meant them to do. There were so many things she didn't know about him, so many things needing to be asked, so many questions spinning around in her head, it was hard to reach out and grab one and put it properly, but if she said nothing, he would slip away and leave them all unanswered. When the last man left, she ventured to open the conversation.

"Your mother, was she very upset?" She clutched the edges of her robe closed as she raised her eyes to her husband's, too aware of their warmth when they rested on her.

"I didn't notice your being too concerned after you left the room. Do you think giggling with the maids a dignified response?" Marc's eyes were half closed and hidden as he gazed down at her.

Jennifer flared up at the rebuke in his voice. "And do you consider your mother's behavior ladylike? I may as well not have existed, or been no more than a piece of furniture to be examined and discarded as unsuitable. I only asked for your sake; for my own, I care not what the woman thinks."

"It's just as well you don't, because you'll never win her approval with your present behavior. I warned you she would be difficult, and I will not be here much of the time to protect you from her tongue, so you better learn to be a little less rebellious or develop a leather hide."

His mild manner put a lid on Jennifer's anger, but she vowed silently to develop a leather hide before she gave in to either him or his mother. There were other matters she wished discussed, but she knew not how to raise them without also raising his ire, and she wished to avoid that as much as possible.

"Marcus . . ." She raised her eyes to him again with a silent plea for understanding. He waited patiently for her to continue, the hollow curve of his jaw shadowing his face in darkness. "How much have you told your mother . . ." she gestured helplessly, "about . . . about us? Does she know . . . ?"

The ridge of muscle along his jaw tightened as Marcus jammed his hands into his pockets to prevent their straying elsewhere. "I have told her no more than you heard this morning, that you are my wife and Stuart our son. That is all anyone needs to know." His eyes darkened more at her hesitation, sensing further inquiry.

"I just thought it might make it easier on you . . ." It was so difficult to get the words out with his black stare on her, but she had to have some understanding of her position. She clasped her hands and stared at them as she forced the words out. "If she understood *why* you made such an unsuitable match. I do not wish to harm your relationship with her . . ."

His laugh was cold and bitter. "Do not worry yourself on my account. You are providing me with just the service I asked of you. My mother's attempts at matchmaking were quickly thwarted with your arrival, which makes her exceedingly angry, but not nearly as angry as I would be at having to escort the greedy little nitwits she would consider suitable. I can assure you, my little waif, that riches and position are the only things she considers for suitability. If you wish, I'll let her know you are the daughter of a respected businessman and landowner in Kentucky, which is the truth so far as I have gathered. That will settle any question of suitability in her eyes as far as you are concerned. Or was there some ulterior motive in these questions?"

Jennifer looked up at him with surprise, ignoring his final question. "What do you know of my parents? I cannot remember ever telling you anything of them, and I certainly wouldn't have drawn that picture of them. You can tell your mother whatever you wish of me, I am not ashamed to admit what I am."

There was a nearly imperceptible relaxation of tension in his stance. "The picture is my own, yours was a rather sinister portrayal if I recollect rightly." His words came out in a drawl as he watched her reactions. "But what I know or do not know isn't the question. If you are not ashamed of what you are, then why worry over what I have told my mother? Are you ashamed of our marriage?"

"It would not have mattered to me if we had not married at all; I cannot believe that what I did was wrong, and I am not ashamed of Stuart." Jennifer swung her hands wide in a nervous gesture, then paced about the room. "It is *why* you had to marry me that preys on my mind, I would have no one know of . . ."

She swung around and stared at him, not able to say the words. Shame and degradation still swept through her at the thought of what she had almost come to, a feeling of pure horror shaking her at the memory. She had experienced only one night in a man's arms, and its result was nearly the torment of hell. The fact that the same man had rescued her from that fate was twisted insecurely into the picture. She was not quite certain that he wouldn't cast her off in the same manner once again, leaving no chance of rescue the next time.

"There is no need to worry, madam. I can assure you no one will know of the circumstances of our marriage; they are something I would prefer to forget myself since they scarcely reflect well on my character, either. Now, I still have other business to conduct this afternoon. Do you have any further questions before I go?''

She swirled around to face him, the girlish robe flaring like a candle in the gloom, hiding the womanliness of her figure and accentuating her youth as she gazed at him with innocent eyes. He need only pull a few pins from her hair so it flowed loosely about her shoulders to bring back the angel who had lightened his life at a moment of black despair. And in gratitude, he had brought her pain and degradation. The thought still darkened his conscience, and Marcus had found no means yet of lightening it.

She drifted toward him, the light fragrance of her perfume wafting through the air between them as she drew closer. "Your trunks, sir," a pale hand indicated the collected baggage behind her, "where are they?"

It cost Jennifer some effort to ask, but he had made no attempt to reassure her of what was uppermost in her mind. If they were to be looked on as man and wife, how would he explain separate rooms?

Marcus answered the question more gently than she expected, a strange look in his eyes as they rested on her upturned face. "I have not forgotten our agreement, Jennifer. I have explained you are still convalescing after the birth of our son, and it would be better for your health if we slept apart. The sitting room in the adjoining chamber is being converted for my use, unless you have some objection?" His eyebrows rose questioningly.

She shook her head and looked away, her glance falling on the enormous bed that filled the room. She had never shared a bed with anyone before, but suddenly, it felt wrong to sleep alone. A blush colored her cheeks at the memory of waking up beside this man in the morning darkness, his heat warming the bed beside her.

"No, Marcus, of course not. I . . . I just wondered. I'd better unpack then. Do you think your mother would mind if I did something with these draperies? It is so oppressively dark in here . . ." her voice trailed off as she surveyed the room, avoiding his look.

"As far as I am concerned, you may take the dreadful things and burn them; anything would be an improvement. Furnish the room in any way you wish. It may be a long time before you have another. You are satisfied with these arrangements, then?" His voice was flat and cold and distant.

"There isn't much room for choice, is there?" she asked dismally, aware that once more she had somehow said the wrong thing.

"No, madam, there is not. Now, if you will excuse me . . ." He spun around and strode out, leaving Jennifer to listen wistfully to his retreating footsteps on the hall stair.

Before she could turn to the task of unpacking, her husband's deep voice caught her attention. Thinking he was calling her, she entered the hallway, only to hear him answered by a stranger.

"C'mon, Marc, you can't expect me to wait until dinner time. If you don't, I'll introduce myself. I've got to see the girl that finally captured the city's most elusive bachelor; she should be given a medal for saving the virtue of the world's remaining women."

The argument faded out with her husband's rumbling response as Jennifer dashed back to her room, well aware she wasn't properly attired for receiving male company. There wasn't time to don corset and petticoats, but she could at least find a more suitable robe. Throwing back the lid of a trunk, she rummaged within, drawing out the green velvet that so ably covered her from head to toe. Swiftly arranging the folds around her, she had time to tuck a few stray locks of hair away before approaching heavy footsteps told her who had won the argument.

Marcus' eyebrows rose again as he surveyed her change of garments, but he said nothing, moving aside to allow his companion to enter the room.

"Jenny, I would like you to meet my cousin, Stephen

Duquesne; Josephine sent him out here some time back in hopes he would either grow up or get lost, but apparently he has failed to do either. Stephen, this is my wife, Jennifer Lee."

Blatantly disregarding the sarcasm, the slim, blond youth stepped from behind Marcus, hand outstretched in greeting, and Jennifer found herself looking up into the now familiar Armstrong gray eyes, this time accompanied by an engaging smile. Next to Marcus, he appeared slightly built, but as he took her hand, she could see he was nearly a head taller than herself, his lean frame not as muscular as her husband's, but still well proportioned. He could barely be more than twenty-two or three but she decided his laughing charm was nearly as dangerous as his cousin's.

"Jennifer Lee, I cannot believe the dragon has captured a maiden as fair as yourself; if you should need rescuing from his lair, I am here to offer my services." His hand was warm as it enclosed hers, the gray eyes light and dancing.

"Sir Stephen, the dragon is more formidable than he appears, and I fear you are not properly armored. I'd suggest a strategic retreat for the moment." She laughed and disengaged her hand from his eager hold. She glanced at Marcus, but he remained aloof from their nonsense, waiting patiently for the pleasantries to cease so he might depart.

Stephen followed her glance and grinned at his cousin's austere visage. "I will retreat after I express my delight in your choice of brides, Marc." His eyes returned to Jennifer's fair face. "Up until now, my cousin's choice in women left much to be desired. I was greatly concerned that our peaceful existence might be ending when I heard of his marriage. I am relieved to find his taste so vastly improved."

Jennifer chuckled as her gaze strayed to Marcus. "Having met some of the ladies to whom I assume you refer, I can well understand your concern; I trust I won't be a disappointment."

A quirk of his lip greeted her riposte, but Marcus kept his silence, reaching a hand out to take possession of her shoulder as he leaned against the door frame.

Hands in pockets, Stephen studied the pair thoughtfully, catching the silent thrust and parry between them. "I'm not so certain that the beast might not need rescuing from the beauty. It's hard to believe a baby like you has been able to keep this character in line for—how long has it been now?" he asked casually with a twinkle of mischievous curiosity.

"Long enough," Marcus rumbled at this impertinence. "Now if you don't mind, I have business to see to . . ."

Stephen shook his head in slow motion. "I fail to understand why my mother would neglect to inform me of such a momentous event—unless to prevent my coming home to get a better look at the bride," he amended quickly as Marcus made a threatening motion in his direction.

"Jo has the sense to know when to hold her tongue, something you would do well to learn." Marcus straightened, and grabbing his cousin by the elbow, bowed politely to Jennifer. "If you'll excuse us, my dear, we really must be going." Then he steered the grinning youth out the door.

"A temporary setback, milady," Stephen called over his shoulder, "I'll return by dinner with better armor, never fear!" Then turning to his impressive gaoler, Jennifer heard him remonstrate as they went down the stairs, "Glad to have you back, Marcus. I'd forgotten what it's like to have a bully around the house." She giggled as she closed the door, deciding this house might not be so gloomy after all.

The day was still warm as dinner time neared, and Lucia chose a white piqué for Jennifer to wear, its elbow length sleeves and low neckline elaborately trimmed with layers of fine lace and pink ribbon to match the pink inserts of the full skirt, the combination of girlish color and daring cut effectively pairing Jennifer's youth with her womanly charms.

The results of her labors were immediately apparent as Jennifer descended the staircase under the admiring eyes of husband and cousin. Their ongoing argument halted in mid-sentence while they turned to watch her descent, and Marcus met her at the bottom step, slipping her fingers possessively into the crook of his arm.

Shyly, Jennifer brushed a hair from the lapel of her husband's tan linen coat, hesitantly looking to his eyes for some sign of approval, finding it in their softening gray and warm approbation. The smile that touched his lips smoothed the stern lines and returned the handsomeness to his bronzed countenance, and Jennifer returned it happily, well rewarded for her efforts.

Blinded by the effect of her radiant smile, Marcus failed to notice the advance of his cousin until Stephen was ensconced at Jennifer's other side, his bright eyes absorbing with pleasure the beauty revealed by her decolletage.

"Mrs. Armstrong, I do declare you look like the icing on a cake, and I hunger to have a taste." Before she could stop him, he'd brought her fingers to his lips, kissing them one by one.

Blushing profusely, she drew her hand away before he could finish. "Mr. Duquesne, has no one ever taught you not to drool over your sweets?"

Marcus made a slight choking sound at her side, but Stephen ignored him, his wide grin taking in only the beauty before him. "A little tart beneath the sweet improves the flavor. I think I'll enjoy having you around, Jennifer Lee."

"Not if you intend to devour her every time she comes within reach. You'll soon discover she more nearly resembles the bourbon balls they favor where she comes from; underneath the sweet is a very heady liquor, not to be sampled lightly. An empty head like yours would soon be fuddled." Marcus drew Jennifer closer to him and moved away from the stairs and Stephen.

Clare Armstrong was already seated at the large dining table when they entered. The distant glow of gas lamps, softened by the table's candlelight, bathed her smooth face in a pale hue. Her classic features still held their beauty, but the hard lines of pain and bitterness detracted from their grace. For the first time, Jennifer noticed the carved handle of a wooden walking stick hooked over the back of her chair, and with better insight, understood some of the woman's morning rudeness.

Silently, she accepted the seat Marcus held for her, aware that she was on display as she had never been before. The glittering candles danced patterns of light across the polished silver and crystal, the ever-present velvet draperies creating a hushed atmosphere within the enormous cavern of the room, and she felt as if she were one of the shining ornaments in a jeweler's case, not meant to be touched but admired against the glass enclosed background. Hands clasped in her lap, she kept her head bowed until the others were seated: Mrs. Armstrong at the head of the table, Marcus and Stephen on either side, and Jennifer next to her husband. The table stretched out beyond them, but places had only been set at one end. Jennifer was grateful she had been allowed to remain close to Marcus' sturdy presence.

While the meal was being served, Marcus occupied his mother with murmured news from St. Louis, but before long Jennifer felt the piercing scrutiny of cold, blue eyes.

"My taciturn son has told us nothing about you, Jennifer, perhaps you would care to enlighten us somewhat." On someone else's lips the words could have been a gentle quip, but from this woman they became a cold command.

Jennifer could feel her heart beat nervously, but conscious of Marc's intent interest, she held her head high and gazed calmly to the head of the table.

"I am from a small town on the Ohio River in Kentucky. I have two parents like everyone else, I grew up, met Marcus, married, and here I am. I've led a very uneventful life."

Several voices intervened on this ingenuous speech, but Clare's prevailed. "If you were not part of St. Louis society, I fail to see how you met Marcus unless your parents were in the habit of letting you associate with riverboat captains." She spat the last words out with a black look at Marcus who met the stare impassively.

"Not everyone has your antipathy for men of the river," he replied calmly. "Her parents entertained me graciously one evening, and I made Jenny's acquaintance." With a glimmer of amusement, Marcus glanced down at his child-wife, his hand under the table squeezing her thigh warningly to prevent her from protesting or laughing at his carefree handling of their highly improper meeting. "Over a period of time, we became attached to each other's company." His amusement grew as Jenny bit her lip at this embellishment. "Rather than take a chance at losing her, I married her." And that was no lie, either, although the quivers of silent laughter beside him bespoke his bride's opinion of this version of the truth.

Clare refused to be put off. "I still fail to see where either of you have anything in common other than the obvious."

Her scornful glance at Jennifer's lightly covered bosom caused the muscle in Marcus' jaw to jump, but he controlled his temper before replying. "Jennifer's age has little to do with her understanding; with a little effort you would discover we have a great deal in common, and I would thank you to treat her with the respect she deserves."

It was Jennifer's turn to rest her hand on her husband's muscular thigh, a familiarity she would never have dared under other circumstances, but she could not be angry at Clare's practicality, and the ardor of his defense gave her courage. His warmth caught her by surprise, and she would have quickly withdrawn this daring touch, but Marcus captured her hand and held it there.

Jennifer's slow blush and the sudden twinkle in her son's eye didn't escape Clare's sharp notice, and it wasn't difficult to guess their meaning. Focusing on Jennifer's flushed face, she resumed her interrogation.

"What is your opinion, Jennifer? What do you have in common with this obstinate son of mine other than the fact that he likes good-looking women?"

Jennifer felt the gentle squeeze of Marc's hand as he released her fingers, a slow smile on his face boding trouble if his wrath were further aroused.

"We have our son," she replied quietly, her grave dignity startling her audience.

The snort of disapproval from the end of the table was covered up by Stephen's infectious laugh. "That won't do; I strongly suspect Stuart is a direct result of Marc's partiality to good-looking women." He ignored his aunt's shocked gasp, concentrating on returning the smile to Jennifer's eyes. "Besides women, Marc also has a partiality for gambling, boats, and books, not necessarily in that order. Do you have an inordinate fondness for any of these pastimes?"

"Sir Stephen, you will certainly lose your knighthood if you continue to offend ladies' sensibilities in that cavalier way. And yes, I have an inordinate fondness for at least some of those pastimes, but I am afraid gambling is something at which I will never excel." She calmly returned to her meal, enjoying Stephen's attention and avoiding Clare's.

"Yes, and if I remember correctly, you are still in debt to me for that last little wager you made. I must agree, your gambling often has drastic results."

She didn't dare look at Marcus, wishing she had never mentioned the subject, knowing there was no reply she could make without bringing a barrage of questions from the others down on her head. Marcus was enjoying her plight; she could feel the amusement in his glance as he looked at her. The memory of that last minute wager burned in her mind. If he should ever be dastardly enough to demand payment—twenty-four hours at his beck and call—the possibility didn't bear thinking.

"Next time I will select a more reputable opponent," she murmured as the tide of conversation swept around them, leaving the words to fall in his ears alone.

"If I catch you making another wager like that with any other man, he will be a dead opponent." Marcus spun his wineglass slowly, drawing his words out with emphatic intent, his brow drawn down with the intensity of his stare.

"You have no need to worry about that; the one debt hanging over my head is more than I care to think about. I will not be making any others," Jennifer said coldly, angry that he would speak to her in such a way, convinced he had no right to tell her what she might or might not do.

Marcus only raised a quizzical eyebrow at her tone before returning his attention to the conversation. Jennifer smothered her anger and concentrated on the food.

When the last plate was cleared, Clare ordered coffee sent to the parlor and permitted Marcus to assist her to her feet, shaking off his offered arm as she moved from the table. Leaning heavily on the cane, blue eyes flashing, she held herself as proudly as her disability allowed.

The gas lamps were lit, making the parlor brighter than it had been in daylight, but the dark draperies and heavy furniture eclipsed their effect. Jennifer chose a chair near the piano and Marcus stopped behind it, resting a heavy hand on her shoulder.

He was so close, Jennifer could sniff the scent of cigars lingering on his clothes, the odor reminding her of dark nights on the river when they strolled hand in hand in total innocence of past or future. He was caressing the smooth skin of her cheek now, one finger rubbing aimlessly as he spoke to his mother, the words drifting by unheard as the pain knotted inside her. He touched her so casually, so thoughtlessly, unaware of the torment that twisted inside at his indifference. She bent over her needlework and allowed the discussion to flow on around her.

Feeling the heat of someone's intense gaze diverting her concentration, Jennifer looked up to find Stephen watching with sympathy. She looked away, but it was too late;

the pain wasn't so easily hidden. He crossed his arms and leaned against the wall, his study shifting to Marcus.

"Cousin, you're in the lady's light. Why don't you find your own chair?" Stephen didn't move from his position as he waited for the effect of his words.

A faint smile crossed Jennifer's face; she didn't have to see Marcus to know the irritation with which he was impaling this nagging gnat. She sensed the off-hand shrug of his broad shoulders under the tailored coat as he moved from behind her to settle himself on the arm of her chair, out of her light. This proximity was even more disquieting than his former position, and Stephen frowned, but Marcus' words were pacifying.

"It seems the tyke has grown thoughtful. I apologize, my dear, if I'm in your way." The faint trace of amusement belied his meaning, but his next words were more sincere. "Why don't you persuade Jenny to sing, and we'll all be quiet?"

Stephen's expression brightened considerably. "You sing?" he asked Jennifer. "This gets better and better. We'll leave Marcus to argue with Aunt Clare and you and I can run through our repertoires."

He moved into the lamplight, swinging himself onto the piano seat with lazy grace as he reached for the music. Jennifer gave Marcus a beseeching look, but his expression remained implacable, and when even Clare showed signs of interest, she resigned herself to the embarrassment.

"I know mainly hymns, Stephen," she replied quietly, still hoping for some reprieve.

"Nonsense. If you were raised on the river, you surely must know some of the showboat tunes. Let me see what I have." He began rummaging through the leaflets. Finding the music he sought, Stephen spread it on the holder. "Surely you know this tune, everybody in St. Louis was doing it when I was there last." Then he looked at her with a pucker of wry curiosity. "Hymns?"

Jennifer ignored his comment, staring at the music he had chosen, whispering in dismay, "Oh, no, Stephen, not this one. Find a livelier tune, please." Meeting his eyes with reluctance, she saw the surprise in them, but with alacrity, he began to withdraw the music.

A bronzed hand reached over Jennifer's shoulder to halt the withdrawal, its mate resting possessively on the nape of her neck as Marcus studied the piece chosen. "I want to hear this one," he stated firmly.

The first slow chords of the familiar love ballad flowed from the keyboard, reverberating through Jennifer's memory. She was two thousand miles from the Mississippi, but she heard the paddle wheels lapping, an unseen guitar strumming in time, the darkness warm with the man beside her. Unconsciously, the music formed in her heart, and the words slipped from her throat with a will of their own.

The notes soared through the air above them, blending with the music in a perfect shell enclosing all within hearing, drawing them together in a fleeting moment of perfect harmony—until the last note faded away, leaving only the current from now smoky blue eyes to sustain her. Jennifer was ensnared by the desire she found there, unable and unwilling to free herself from her husband's binding gaze.

Entranced by the electricity generated by Jennifer's passion, the stirring words and melody brought to life by the clarity of her emotion, the room fell into silence, until, simultaneously, Marcus took his young wife by the hand and lifted her to his side, Stephen broke into a round of applause, and Clare spoke to break the spell.

"You have an excellent voice, child. You should have it properly trained instead of wasting it on silly love songs."

The words broke Jennifer's reverie. Tearing her gaze from her husband's hypnotic hold, Jennifer was acutely aware of the overpowering virility of the man standing so close to her. She bowed her head to Stephen, unable to meet his eyes, then turned to Clare. In hushed tones, she replied, "Thank you. If I might be excused, I would like to go up to my room now."

There was a flurry of protests, good-nights, knowing looks—she passed through them all, oblivious to everything but the hand still gripping hers, its tension sending signals through her fingers and up her arm until it ached with the stiffness necessary to keep it from quivering. Nervousness swept over her at the sudden realization Marc intended to accompany her from the room. The determination with which he held her sent her into a whirl of anticipation and fear, and her heart pounded so loudly she felt certain all could hear as they hurried from the lighted sanctuary into the darkness of the unknown.

The memories of nights past, of moments of tenderness and love, held them spellbound until they reached the darkened entrance of their bed chamber. With searching fingers, Marcus grasped Jennifer's shoulders, turning her to face him, unable to see her expression in the gloom, but reading her hesitation clearly. Torn between twin desires of his own, he groaned at the impossibility of resolving them, and gathered her against his chest, his lips swooping down to encompass the sweetness of hers.

With astounding willingness, Jennifer's arms flew about his neck, and her lips met his with an eager hunger that should have shocked had she been in her right senses. Instead, safe within the concealing darkness, she fell victim to her passion, and her fingers ran greedily through thick curls while her lips parted to his kiss. Thinly clad breasts pushed against his waistcoat, and she strained to be closer, heart pounding erratically at the ravishing thrust of his tongue.

Then the bedroom door opened and dimmed lights revealed Lucia, finished with the unpacking. At Jennifer's sudden nervous start, Marcus released her, freeing her from his spell even as he dismissed the maid for the night.

Shutting the door after the maid, he barred the door by leaning against it. In unconscious imitation of Stephen's earlier stance, Marcus stood with arms crossed, watching the slender back of his wife as she hurried away to bend over their sleeping son. The delusion of domesticity slapped him in the face. After an evening acting as husband for a roomful of believers, he had almost made a believer of himself. Now he was shoved abruptly back into the role he had agreed to play.

"Jenny." Marcus could see her back stiffen at the sound of his voice, but she didn't turn from her task of removing the infant's toys from the cradle. "Do you regret choosing to come with me?"

Jennifer tucked the last stuffed animal in its place and turned, velvet eyes blurred and indistinct in the half light as she contemplated his question. "No, not yet," she finally replied.

"Not yet? Are you anticipating it? Has my mother frightened you that much?" Marcus asked with concern, unable to concentrate on anything but the vision on the other side of the room.

"No, she does not frighten me. She is in pain, and I think that frightens her; I cannot be afraid of anyone who suffers so. Do they know what is wrong with her?" Jennifer remained stationary.

"It has grown worse since I saw her last. Stephen's letters never mentioned the cane, and I had no idea the condition worsened. It is a crippling of the joints, and the doctors have found no real cure for it, but you must not think that is the cause of her rudeness. She has ever been this way; it has only grown more pronounced with the disease." Marcus regarded her thoughtfully, thinking how like a deer prepared to bolt she looked, wondering how best to tame her fears.

"There must be a deep sorrow to hide such bitterness. I will do my best to remember that so I won't say anything to anger her."

"Then if my mother did not give you cause for alarm, was there some other reason that might cause you to regret your decision?" Marcus asked carefully.

The reason was right there between them, so palpable Jennifer was certain he already felt it and was only waiting for her to say it aloud, but there were limits to her frankness, and this was one of them. If he couldn't tell how she felt, hadn't seen it in her eyes, felt it on her lips, perhaps she had only dreamed his response, and he was better off not knowing. But the warmth and intensity of his gaze made her doubt her thoughts even as she formed them, and desire sprang anew.

"I just cannot see how I can be very useful to you here," she answered cautiously. "You have a houseful of servants to wait on you, just the news of your marriage should be sufficient to drive away your 'scheming women,' what is there for me to do? Could I help in any way with your business?" Restlessly, Jennifer smoothed the nightgown Lucia had laid out for her, observing the covers turned down invitingly. Marc's gaze burned against her skin, and she was aware of his proximity, but she did not dare betray the path of her emotions.

He studied her, his mind whirling at the juxtaposition of woman and bed, fogged by the soft willingness of earlier. He had wanted to wait until she was ready to accept this marriage of convenience. He realized she did not trust him fully yet, had every reason to despise him for his careless abandonment and destruction of all her hopes and dreams, but he could not believe it was hatred hiding beneath the shadows of her eyes tonight. His body ached to seek that soft respite she offered.

"There is only one other thing I know you can do for me," Marcus replied tentatively, eyeing her with speculation.

Jennifer looked up eagerly, until she saw the smoldering hunger of his gaze. Clutching the tall post of the bed for support, she asked, "Within our contract?"

Marcus stepped forward into the pool of light beside the bed, hoping to draw her closer, to decrease the distance between them until it returned to the stage they had reached outside the bedroom door when she had not flinched from his touch. "The contract can be amended."

The bed stood between them, and she didn't release her grip on the post. The fear in her eyes sent him searching for other arguments. "You asked in what way you could be of use to me, I can think of no better." He spoke coaxingly, his memory stirring him to a hopefulness that renounced common sense.

Moist brown eyes peered at him from under a fringe of lashes as Jennifer slumped against the post, hugging it to her breast. "Why didn't you leave me with Delaney if that is all you think of me? It would have been cheaper," she replied, looking away. To be of use to him by being a willing whore was not how she had interpreted his kiss or question. She had misunderstood his intention again. Would she never learn?

"Goddamn it, Jennifer!" Marcus shouted, making her jump with terror. The words had been wrung from him in anguish more than anger. He couldn't be angry at that bent head, the coppery curls begging to be crushed, the slump of shoulders betraying her youth. He had known in his heart what her reply would be, but he had been driven by the desperation of his need to try it.

Containing his pain, Marcus circled the bed and pulled Jennifer gently from the post, his hands resting on bare shoulders. "We are man and wife, little one, there is nothing immoral or illegal about it any longer," he reminded her, willing the passion hiding beneath her surface to rise at his touch as it had before, driving her into his arms where she belonged. But still she strained to pull away, and after some hesitation, he let her go.

Jennifer backed out of his reach, knowing how close she had come to surrendering. She countered his spell with anger. "I do not know about the legalities, but it is definitely immoral to sell my body, and you can never convince me otherwise! I thought I made that perfectly clear from the very beginning. If that is the only way I can pay back the debt I owe, then you have made a whore of me as surely as Delaney would."

Sparks of anger flew with her words, but her eyes were wells of sadness, and Marcus fell before them. "Very well, my beautiful Jenny, I do not wish to hurt you any more than I already have. Come here." He sat on the edge of the bed, bracing one boot on the frame as he beckoned to her.

She came hesitantly, and he gestured for her to turn around, strong hands guiding her into position. He began unhooking her bodice with deft sureness. She stirred beneath his touch, and he assured her, "I am only trying to help since your maid has probably long since gone to bed. Now hold still." The unmanageable little hooks fell open, and he loosed the corset strings.

Jennifer gripped the bodice of her gown and turned around to confront his warm gaze with wonder. "You are not angry with me?" She was puzzled by his reaction, he was neither laughing at her or foaming with rage, either of which she could have understood.

"No, Jenny, we made a deal, and I have some honor, although you try it sorely." Marcus stood up and pulled the ribbons from her hair, running his fingers through the curls until they fell apart about her shoulders. Smiling wryly, he said, "Anytime you change your mind, Jenny Lee, just let me know, I'll be glad to rewrite that contract."

His hands brushed her shoulders, then abruptly pulled away. With his hand on the knob of their adjoining door, he turned around to add, "You're a woman now, love, you'd best learn to use your charms wisely lest I forget honor and agreement and take you as you were meant to be taken. For both our sakes, I will try to be more careful in the future."

Jennifer watched the door close and let the dress fall of its own weight. Corset, petticoat, and undergarments fell after them, and she stood naked before a mirror, fingers tracing remembered paths over full breasts and now firm, taut belly. The river man had branded her skin with his heated touch, and she burned now for his searing possession. Yet, she could not see the man who had just left as the same one who had taken her earlier, and she could not surrender to his cold aloofness so easily.

Still, she had almost given herself up to the muscled embrace of the gentlemanly stranger, allowed him to take her to his bed as wife, and for the same foolish reasons as that first time. Only this time he had made the mistake of spearing her illusion first, offering payment for what she had wanted to give, and the memory of three gold coins burned hotly on her cheeks. Hastily donning nightgown and dimming lights, she climbed into her cold bed, vowing never to give in to foolish dreams again. Only as the first clouds of sleep penetrated her hurting rage did she remember—he had called her a woman tonight, he no longer saw her as a child.

With a smile of relief, Jennifer allowed the clouds to billow around her, closing out all consciousness of everything but a smoldering pair of smoky blue eyes.

Chapter Nine

Marcus sat up and crossed the floor to the washroom as Stuart's cries first disturbed Jennifer's sleep. Chucking the infant under the chin, picking him up to whisper words of mock anger in his ear, he handed him to Jenny. Shaving and washing before his wife had time to feed and change their son, he was dressed and ready to go before Lucia arrived. In dark suit and cravat, he was all business once more, kissing Jennifer lightly on the forehead before departing for the day.

Breakfast was shared with Stephen, and he welcomed Jennifer's company with delight. He was in full form, his light-hearted banter and engaging grin keeping her entertained with no cold stares of disapproval to daunt their laughter. Being a stranger to all his old jokes, Jennifer soon became a favorite target for his witticisms, and the refreshment of laughter brightened her surroundings.

With Marcus gone much of each day, and Clare scarcely a congenial companion, Jennifer was left alone to amuse herself. Deciding to fill her time by refurbishing her dreary bedroom, she obtained Marc's disinterested approval, and she and Lucia became frequent visitors to the shops up and down Montgomery Street. Searching for materials and papers to lighten the constant gloom, she made few purchases, hesitant to spend too great an amount of money, afraid it would only come back to her as a greater debt than she already owed. With some decision, she concluded the work should be done, but only at the best possible prices. This necessitated much shopping and haggling, but left her confident of her new prowess as an expert shopper.

She rode the new trolley cars on Clark Street for the sheer joy of riding and persuaded Stephen one day to take her to the cliffs overlooking the bay just to see the view. For Jennifer, it was the first step in an unknown world on her own. The excitement of making her own decisions, meeting the stares of the world, going where she chose without relying on anyone but herself was a heady experience to be absorbed and mulled over when left alone in her room.

It was on one of these excursions that Jennifer learned a little more of her laughing companion and felt a closer bond for Marc's entertaining cousin. Coming upon a group of street musicians on their return from the cliffs, Stephen gave a crooked grin and flipped a large coin into their bucket.

At Jennifer's questioning glance, he shrugged lightly. "There, but for the grace of riches, go I." At her look of incomprehension, he explained.

"Did my close-mouthed cousin tell you nothing of my

disgrace? I ran away from home once to join a band of roving musicians. We did well for a while, until winter came and the others drifted off one by one. I woke up one morning to find myself alone and broke and with no offers of employment for a one man band. So I went home again. That's how I ended up here. Marcus and my mother agreed it was high time I learned the family business. The Armstrongs are a hard family to argue with."

In silent agreement, Jennifer slipped her hand into his, and the bond of friendship between them grew stronger.

The afternoons were more frightening excursions into the world, this time into the world of society, and under the constant scrutiny of Clare, a task Jennifer found abhorrent to her basically honest nature. She had nothing in common with Clare's friends, but she was expected to entertain and dance attendance to the steady flow of visitors parading through the parlor at designated hours each afternoon.

It soon became apparent that Marcus created the greatest reason for woe. For the first week of their stay, he appeared at dinner time in a futile attempt to put a civilized front on their relationship. But Stephen quickly saw through the masquerade, drawing Jennifer out with quips and questions, baiting Marcus with ambiguous remarks, replacing the ill humor of Marcus and Clare with laughter. After a week of this badgering, Marc's temper exploded, his caustic comments equaling those of Clare's. In retaliation, Stephen removed himself to the far end of the table. After some cajoling, he persuaded Jennifer to join him, leaving Marcus and Clare to steam in silence. The duo at the far end soon had the room rippling with laughter, and the rift between the two ends loomed ever larger. After several nights of this rearranging of tableware, the servants learned to separate them automatically, and after Marcus assured himself his young wife was in no danger of Clare's tongue, he took to missing meals altogether.

The first night her husband failed to return for dinner, Jennifer watched anxiously for his return, unable to participate in the spirit of gaiety Stephen wove about them, replying absently to his teasing jibes, until her silence served to quiet his nonsense. After dinner, Stephen joined them in the parlor instead of waiting for the usual brandy and cigar he shared with Marcus. But his attempts to liven the atmosphere failed as Jennifer refused to join in his music-making, preferring to do her needlework and listen for the first footsteps that would indicate her husband's return.

The hushed atmosphere of the elegant men's club was not the environment most suited to Marc's nature, but it was a valuable source of contacts as well as providing relief from the complicated tangle he had woven at home. The gaming rooms provided sufficient entertainment, the meals were good, and one could choose one's company.

Marc strode through the high-ceilinged rooms with confidence, renewing old acquaintances, accepting condolences from his father's old cronies, making careful note of who was there and their apparent status. Many years of fighting his way through the world had taught him the wisdom of knowing his surroundings, and his relatively secure position now had not lessened his caution.

Choosing the game and the companions most suited to his mood of the moment, Marcus joined the onlookers at a high-stakes poker game, waiting for his opportunity to join in, studying the men who would be his opponents. Lost in his observations, he was caught by surprise when a hand clapped him on the shoulder.

"Glad to see you back, boy. Your mother's been needing you around. Almost took it in my head to write you myself."

At the sound of that remembered voice, Marc's eyes narrowed, and he turned to greet the older man.

"There were complications preventing my prompt return, sir. No letter would have brought me sooner." Marcus kept his tone formal and respectful. Michael O'Hara was a prominent man in the community; there was no point in antagonizing him over old sores.

The older man watched Marcus wrestling with his temper and nodded at the formal tones. The young Armstrong he had once known would have exploded without thought to caution or respect. The boy had grown up. Too bad his father had not lived to see it, though the Armstrong temperament would have put them at odds no matter how much caution was wielded.

"I suspected that. I knew you would not deliberately ignore your mother, despite your differences. Have you come to stay, then, lad?"

Though he had lived in this country the major part of his life, Michael O'Hara still affected a hint of brogue as a form of familiarity. He had known Marcus Armstrong since the younger man was a lad in short pants. There was no reason on his part to pretend formality.

"That remains to be seen, Mr. O'Hara."

"Come now, Marcus. The past is dead and gone. You're a man now, with a man's understanding. Would you let that old talk come between us now? Call me Michael and let us be friends, for your mother's sake."

"Though my father and I had our differences, we were in agreement on one point, Mr. O'Hara. My opinion has not changed, but as you say, the past is dead, I will not speak of it again." There was no need to mention the point in question, both men knew to what he referred, and no gentleman would question his mother's virtue in public.

O'Hara nodded his respect for young Armstrong's opinion. Marcus was still young enough yet to believe in ideals, his mother's adultery would not be forgiven easily, but it brought to mind another topic.

"My son tells me you brought home a new bride, a real beauty, I understand. When will you give society the pleasure of meeting her?"

"Your son?" Something clicked in Marc's memory, and he turned to survey the group at the poker table again.

At the same time, a pair of jaded green eyes looked up from the cards, and their gazes met. The younger man at the table tipped an imaginary hat in salute to Marc's stare, then returned to his game.

"Back home, just like you," O'Hara stated proudly. "I'll admit, he's been a bit of a rapscallion, but he seems to have settled down a shade. Maybe you ran into him in St. Louis? He just came from there."

"No, can't say that I have," but Marc's eyes narrowed as he continued to watch the game at the table, only half listening.

"We'll come by soon to pay our respects to your new bride, if that's all right with you. She'll be wanting to meet some girls her own age, I expect. Darlene's been dying to meet her."

"Darlene? Of course." Absently, Marcus remembered the spoiled little girl in smocks he had last known as O'Hara's daughter, and wondered what the child would have in common with Jennifer. Then it struck him. Darlene O'Hara would be the same age as Jennifer now, just coming of age and probably society's darling. The thought struck him forcefully somehow, and he scarcely heard the remainder of O'Hara's conversation.

Not until he found himself facing Cameron O'Hara at the poker table did Marcus recover his senses, and only then after he had lost the first round and Cameron began raking in the winnings.

Losing was not something to which Marcus was accustomed, and he came to attention immediately. Cameron's appraising gaze met his as the next hand was dealt.

"Did dear old dad fill you in on all the details of the prodigal son's return?"

Marcus glanced around to notice Michael O'Hara was not within hearing distance.

"He mentioned you had just returned from St. Louis. You should have looked me up while you were there," Marcus answered calmly, studying his cards. Something about this young scoundrel struck him as peculiar, but he could not put his finger on it. Instead, he played the disinterested party.

"We didn't exactly travel in the same circles. Besides, I understand you had your hands quite full these last months."

The taunting undertone warned Marcus, but none of the other men at the table were following the conversation and took little notice of it.

"I keep busy, wherever I am." Marcus avoided the subject coolly, testing his adversary.

"Heard a lot about your new bride. Can't wait to meet her."

The sly implication produced an angry tic in Marc's jaw, but Cameron's gaze was blank as their eyes met. His last statement had finally attracted the attention of the other players, and the rest of the conversation dwindled into an exchange of insights on the wedded state, but the underlying anger simmered, baited by Cameron's knowing smirk.

When Marcus hadn't returned by the time they usually retired, Stephen persuaded Jennifer to join him in one duet before they quit for the night. Clare had already retired to her room, and he played softly, encouraging her by choosing a haunting melody of lost love. In *sotto voce,* they harmonized, Jennifer sitting next to Stephen on the bench and following his lead, concentrating on the blending of their voices with the music and losing themselves to the sound until Stephen grabbed her waist for the grand finale, the mocking passion of their last few notes dying together with dramatic grace and ripples of laughter. Their pleasure was quickly extinguished at a warning cough from behind, and they spun around to find Marcus lounging in the open doorway.

"Your talents never cease to amaze me, cousin," he commented drily as he entered the room, bringing with him the scent of night air and stale cigars. It was bad enough to have his wife's reputation openly slighted over a gaming table, but to come home to proof of it was more than a man should have to bear. Marcus stoically held his temper and waited for explanations.

Wishing to run to her husband's side with joy at his safe return, Jennifer refrained, holding herself aloof and distant until he gave some indication of his mood. She could smell the whiskey on his breath as he approached, but he was not drunk. The cold glitter in his eyes told her anger was not far beneath his wry smile.

"Well, Jenny, I came home to see you to your room, but perhaps you would like to stay and play a while longer?" The light mocking tone of his question held a hint of steel, and with dismay, she saw the gray of his eyes harden.

Stephen leaned his elbows back against the piano, his long, graceful body relaxing into a leisurely stance as he surveyed his darker cousin, commenting cynically, "It appears you're the one who's been doing the playing; marriage certainly hasn't improved your habits for the better."

Jennifer's eyes widened at this intimation of the cause of Marc's nocturnal wanderings. What other habits would Stephen be referring to but women? She caught her breath as the realization sent her mind reeling. Of course he would have other women! He was coming home to her from the arms of some lover! He had just stepped from some other woman's bed and dared question her activities!

Sudden fury left her shaken, but common sense prevailed. Sharp words would not relieve the mounting tension between Marcus and his cousin. Stephen had no place in this argument, and she hastened to end his involvement.

"Stephen and I have not been doing anything more than we have done every night in your presence. I don't know why you're behaving so abominably." With set lips, Jennifer forced herself to lay a hand on Marc's arm, preventing him from advancing any farther on Stephen. "It's late, I would like to retire now."

Raising a dubious eyebrow, Marcus glanced from wife to cousin and back before deciding she had logic on her side. With a sardonic bow to Stephen, he trapped his wife's hand with his own. "We'll continue this discussion at a more opportune moment, cousin. Don't count on being let off so easily next time."

Swinging Jennifer around, Marcus stalked out of the room in silence, not releasing her from his furious hold.

Gaining the privacy of their bedroom, Jennifer jerked loose, quickly putting the width of the room between them as she checked on the sleeping infant.

Marcus watched her retreat with growing wrath. She had time to dally with his cousin, showed no fear of Stephen's embrace, yet bolted like a wild deer whenever her husband sought her company. The newly recognized fact that she was more nearly Stephen's age and the two had much in common did little to alleviate his anger.

"Damn it, Jennifer! Do you have no notion of what you do to men when you lead them on as you do Stephen?"

Jennifer tucked the blanket more securely around her sleeping son, then straightened, eyes flashing.

"Of course, Marcus! I am so enamored of men that I must fling myself at every available male and grovel at his feet in my desire to please his every need. Flaunting myself before men is second nature to me, have you not noticed that before?" Jennifer replied scornfully.

A corner of Marc's mouth bent at this description of his prim and proper wife, but the righteousness of her cause in no way reduced the facts. With Cameron to spread them, the rumors of their scandalous marriage would soon hit the streets of San Francisco, and both their reputations were at stake. It would not do to worry her with what had not yet occurred, but it would pay to shake a little sense into that obstinate head.

"I will not tolerate an unfaithful wife, even if she be wife in name only. Do you understand that? You will at all times behave as if I am standing right at your side."

With deliberate cruelty, Marcus took advantage of the

magnetic current passing between them, bringing their bodies together almost against their wills. His lips came down hard and slanting across hers, his hands trapping her into contact with his arousal.

Jennifer shuddered and tried to jerk away, but his lips pressured hers, forcing them to part. Her breasts were crushed against his waistcoat and he could feel the strong pounding of her heart as his mouth plundered hers, taking with a vengeance what she once had given freely. With her hand beating against his chest, she tried to push away, but he bent her backwards until their hips met and the pressing urgency of his need made all struggle useless. There would be no stopping him from taking what he wanted, when he wanted it; the point was clear.

With a quiver of unleashed passion, Jennifer surrendered to his onslaught, no longer capable of active protest. Curving into his embrace, she melted at the intrusion of his tongue.

With a rapid movement, Marcus threw her away, tossing her to the bed.

"Remember that when you next feel the need for a man. You have a husband now to satisfy you; you have no need to look any farther than that door." Glancing disdainfully at Jennifer's disheveled figure huddled against the mattress, Marcus gestured toward his adjoining room. "You will rue the day you look elsewhere."

And with that threatening farewell, Marcus stalked out, ignoring the sound of a glass object shattering against the door behind him.

Chapter Ten

With heavy eyelids, Jennifer dragged through the monotony of the following day, unable to concentrate on any one thought or accomplishment. All roads of thought led to Marcus and the picture of his naked body lying in another woman's arms. It was easier to let her mind blot out all thought.

As promised, Michael O'Hara appeared during afternoon calling hours, bearing his daughter as a peace offering. Jennifer greeted the pair politely, just as she had the endless line of friends and acquaintances Clare had introduced these past weeks. It wasn't until she noticed Clare's sudden, uncharacteristic animation that she became aware of any difference in these visitors.

Needing any distraction, Jennifer studied the older man and his unprepossessing daughter. There was nothing distinguished or outstanding about him. He could not be much taller than herself, and his figure tended toward the portly, his hairline receding to the point of baldness. Yet Clare came alive when he looked upon her, and for the first time in weeks, a hint of warmth touched her voice and a smile bent her lips.

Darlene O'Hara looked up with a smile when Jennifer's gaze turned her way. She was nearly as tall as her father, and equally stout, but a dancing glint of green in her eyes spoke of wit and a sense of humor. Her dour Scots mother had obviously passed on her looks, but not her nature.

"I am so glad to meet you at last. Your name has been on everyone's tongue since Marcus brought you home, and I could not believe such a paragon of virtue existed. Do you have wings and a halo hidden somewhere?"

The words were whispered with impish glee, and Jennifer grinned.

"I got them soiled and Marcus sent them out for cleaning," she whispered back, under the indulgent gaze of the older couple who were safely out of hearing. Until now, the simpering females she had met in this salon had been without humor, wisdom, or candor, and she had despaired of finding a sympathetic companion beyond Lucia. Hope rose anew.

Darlene giggled. "Good. While they're at the laundry, will you go shopping with me tomorrow? I'm not allowed out without a chaperone, but my father cannot object to a married woman as my companion, can he? Am I being too bold? My brother tells me I am."

Her girlish chatter was just the remedy needed to shake Jennifer's failing spirits. A shopping date was swiftly settled upon, and when the visit ended, both girls parted with an air of satisfaction.

Marcus only dined at home twice that week, and each time he remained in the dining room long after the others had adjourned to the parlor. He only stirred himself from his lonely vigil with brandy and cigar when they reached their final songs, materializing in their midst as some phantom to offer his protection for the short walk to the second floor, then retiring to his own chamber with taciturn dignity. There were no further demands for Jennifer's time or attentions, and with stoicism, Jennifer accepted the position of nonexistence he placed her in. The rift between them was opening wider, there for all to see, but understood by no one, least of all the two participants.

But on the morning of the eighteenth day of June, Marcus broke his self-imposed restraint, arriving in Jennifer's bedroom before either she or Stuart awoke, and sitting on the edge of her bed as she slept. Still in dressing gown and unshaven, he hesitated, wondering if he should take the time to wash first, but the first flicker of Jennifer's lashes entranced him, holding him in place. She no longer wore her hair in a braid at night, and now the first rays of dawn played against the strands of red and gold that nestled against her cheek and spilled across the pillow. Fair skin translucent in the morning light blushed pink with warmth in the first heat of the day, and her lips wore a deeper shade of the same color. Fascinated, he watched as they parted slightly with a small exhalation of breath just as her lashes fluttered against her cheek and opened to reveal the sleepy depth of her surprise.

Without thinking, Marcus placed his hands on either side of her head as he bent to touch those tantalizing lips with his own, the contact passing an electrifying thrill through both their bodies. Gently, Marcus pressed for response until he felt her lips awaken under his touch. Then they clung to him, parting as he traced their outline with his tongue, and with a surge of relief, he knew the sweetness of her surrender.

With a low growl of pleasure, Marcus deepened his kiss. His fingers stroked the auburn tresses spread across the pillow, twisting through sensuous silkiness while his lips fell victim to his wife's response. All reasoning dissolved beneath his shattering desire to hold and possess the delicate female beneath him.

His palm slipped from hair to shoulder, caressing the smoothness of ivory skin before seeking lower. Beneath his lips, Jennifer gasped with surprise as the cover separating them fell away and his hand touched her bare breast.

In astonishment at this unanticipated touch of flesh upon flesh, Marcus raised himself to gaze down upon the length of his wife's uncovered figure. The roundness of young curves bared to his gaze brought a smile of pleasure. Sleeping nude was not a habit Jennifer had exhibited previously, but one he heartily approved.

"You are so lovely like this, sweet Jenny," he murmured,

lowering his mouth to taste the delights thus exposed, sampling a rosy crest with his lips and the tip of his tongue.

Coming fully awake at this searing touch, Jennifer regretted her impulsive decision to shed her night clothes, but her protests were quickly swallowed. Marc's lips sucked her aching nipples into the heat of his mouth, releasing a rush of relief followed by an overwhelming sensation of need, a need so great she strained against him for more. Marcus obliged, devouring her softness with decreasing restraint.

Marcus dropped his robe and lowered his weight to the bed, covering his wife's nakedness with his own.

The startling hardness of his male body pressed against hers shot a tremor down Jennifer's spine, and she hastily attempted retreat, but his weight held her imprisoned.

Shocked that he had once more taken advantage of her weakness, Jennifer pushed at the heavy male weight pressing her into the mattress. Instead of moving away, Marcus gathered her tighter against his chest and rolled over, holding his bride in place with powerful arms. Trapped by his strength, Jennifer beat fists of frustration against his muscled chest.

"Stop that." Calmly, Marcus crushed her closer, refusing to release her until her rage relented. When Jennifer collapsed, exhausted, against his side, Marcus stroked the silken hair cascading down her back. "Ladies who sleep in the nude get no more than they deserve."

Outraged, Jennifer pushed from his side and stared down into sparkling pools of blue. The maddening pirate captain was back, making jokes at her expense.

"If you had left me alone, you would not have known what I wore. What gives you the right to invade my privacy?"

Chuckling, Marcus traced a finger along the shapely underside of a breast dancing enticingly over him. Jennifer's swift intake of breath and the hardening of rosy crests told him much, and with regret, he let her edge away.

"I only sought to bring you a birthday surprise and demand a kiss in payment. The rest was inevitable, my love."

Offended more with the truth of his words than their content, Jennifer snatched the sheet around her and prepared to escape the shared prison of their bed. A strong hand on her shoulder prevented freedom, and she swung around with a cry of despair.

"You promised, Marcus! You said I could be my own person, that there would be no more between us than our contract stated. If this is what you do to all your hired help, I'd best send Lucia away!"

Marc's brow blackened with a scowl. "Don't be such a damned child, Jennifer. You are eighteen today, are you not?" When she made no denial, he continued, "You are a woman grown, with a woman's needs. You cannot keep denying there is more between us than this thrice-damned contract. We are married, we have a son, and though neither of us had a choice in the matter, we must make the best of what we have. If we enjoy the one advantage of being married, why should we shun it?"

"Why!" Jennifer stared at him, incredulous, but her pirate captain would never understand without being told—frequently. "Because I have no wish to be your mistress or to be left barefoot and pregnant whenever another woman catches your eye! I will not go through that hell again for any amount of pleasure. Take your hands off me, Marcus. Leave me alone."

The scowl was replaced by a look of pain. "You will never believe differently of me, will you?" he asked bitterly. Releasing her, he rolled over and left the bed, picking up his robe and donning it in one swift gesture. From the contents of one pocket, he produced a long, finely wrapped package. "This is what I came in here for. Happy birthday." He flipped the package on the bed and jammed his fists into his robe pockets, the puzzled frown between his eyes a small measure of the perplexity in his soul.

Jennifer lifted the package gingerly. His abrupt departure from the bed had left her shivering with a chill she did not dare admit to herself. "How did you know it was my birthday?" she asked quietly, searching for some grounds on which to meet.

"That was the date you gave on our marriage papers. You were conscious enough to get the date right, weren't you?"

"I suppose so." A small crease formed at the bridge of her nose as she thought about it. "I was conscious enough to get the date right, apparently, but I can't remember writing it or much of anything else that day. Are you certain we're married?"

Marc's anger eased at the sight of the slender, sheet-clad figure puzzling over a memory all too well engraved in his mind. He was moving much too fast for a young girl just out of the country who had never been courted and didn't feel married. He must learn patience.

"There is no doubt as to the legality of our marriage and I have the papers to prove it, if you wish to see them. It wasn't much of a wedding day for you, was it?" he questioned softly. The tilt of her bent head gave his answer. It was incredible how this child-woman could generate such a spectrum of emotions in him where no one else could. It wasn't wise to allow her such power, but this was a special occasion and for once, he indulged her. "Open the gift, Jenny. There can be nothing wrong in accepting a birthday token, can there?"

Jennifer didn't answer. The soft persuasion of his voice left her fingers trembling as she tugged at the bow. The promise in his voice melted her anger; the promise in his eyes would destroy all sensibility. Shakily, she tore open the package.

The velvet-wrapped jeweler's box inside snapped open, and with a look of awe, Jennifer ran a finger over the polished surface of a beautifully matched string of pearls, circling the diamond encrusted clasp with a fingertip.

"I have no idea what an eighteen-year-old would want for her birthday, but these cried out for a perfect setting, and I could think of none finer." Marcus lifted the strands from the box and held them against her skin, its lustrous pallor reflecting the soft glow of the pearls. "See? I was right. You are too young yet for diamonds, but these are perfect."

His hands were brown and hard against the paleness of her skin as they lingered at her throat, and Jennifer was more conscious of them than the jewelry as she looked up into his chiseled face. "They are beautiful, Marcus, but how can I accept them?" She sighed as she took them from his hands, laying them lovingly in the box while she added, "My father remembered my last birthday with a satin ribbon for my hair; I am not accustomed to gifts so magnificent as this."

Having denied himself much this morning, Marcus was in no humor to accept further refusals. With a hard finger against the soft underpart of Jennifer's chin, he tilted her face up until their eyes met and frowned sternly. "They are yours, and as my wife you will wear them. I want to see them on you tonight when we go out."

His face hovered just above hers, each dark feature distinct in the clarity of its angles and planes, his eyes alone shining with amazing light, and Jennifer had no further thought of argument.

"Go out? You are taking me with you?" she asked incredulously as she read the answer in his expression.

Marcus smiled in satisfaction. "Yes, I think you are ready for full-scale social warfare. Even Clare admits you have handled yourself well these last few weeks, and she was convinced you weren't old enough to wear your hair up no less commune with your elders. So in celebration of your official coming out, we will attend the theater this evening, and I expect you to dress accordingly and be ready when I arrive."

Jennifer wasn't inhibited by nature, but she had learned the folly of taking this man too lightly, and stifled her natural response to hug his neck. His gaze on her was too warm to misunderstand the direction of his thoughts, despite the warning of his words. She lowered her eyes and clasped his hand, contenting herself with the strength she found there.

"I won't disappoint you, Marcus . . ." Her voice ended on a questioning note, and she couldn't resist looking up. "Thank you."

A slow smile turned up the corners of his mouth. "I collected my payment in advance, you need give no other thanks." He squeezed the small hand that enclosed his large brown one. "I think our son hungers for his breakfast and in a few minutes will let the whole house know his complaint."

He rose from her side to rescue the wailing infant from his cradle, holding him gingerly as he presented the soggy bundle to Jennifer. "I will be grateful when the little brat learns to mind his manners and hold his tongue. The next one will have to be a girl who looks like her mother so I can learn to tolerate her bad habits easier." He stood back to watch his wife's efficiency at setting the infant right.

At his words, Jennifer gave Marcus a sidelong glance, but he seemed thoroughly absorbed in the process of diapering and totally unaware that what he had said should give cause for any reaction at all. Accustomed now to Marcus' presence at feeding time, Jennifer wrapped the baby in a dry blanket and threw a nearby shawl over her shoulder as she placed the baby at her breast. "He is not a brat, he is beautiful and better behaved than his father."

Hands deep in the pockets of his dressing gown, Marcus gazed down at the tableau made by mother and son, assailed again by a mixture of emotions at the sight. He had once vowed never to love again, to marry only when he found a woman useful to him, but here he was with wife and child and neither of any use whatsoever, not even to warm his bed, yet he stood staring at them as one entranced. It was hard to accept what this child was doing to him without even trying.

"If I were in his place, I'd be better behaved, too." He spoke gruffly. He caught her glance and a wicked grin crossed his face, causing her to blush and look away.

"Ahhh, Jenny, your modesty is very becoming, but sooner or later you know I will divest you of it, so you'd better get used to the idea." His expression grew serious, then disappeared altogether as he left before she had time to respond.

The day could never pass swiftly enough, and it seemed like eternity must arrive before the last copper coil of her hair was patted in place by the patient Lucia, and Jennifer was allowed to gaze at the results of hours' work in the glass of her mirror. The transformation from the backward, plainly dressed girl with the severe hairstyle in the cracked looking-glass, to this butterfly of fashion, shocked her. Yards of sumptuous satin were drawn up in cascades of golden material, exposing exquisitely embroidered lace underskirts to match the lace undersleeves. The image needed only Marc's gift of pearls to break the smooth expanse of ivory flesh from throat to low cut bodice.

Jennifer gazed long and hard at the reflection she found there, not seeing liquid brown eyes or dusky pink cheeks or shining copper curls, but a person she didn't know and wasn't sure she liked. As Lucia added the final touch, smoothing the elegant pearls into their perfect setting, Jennifer wondered what had happened to the plain spoken working girl who had once been reflected there.

Painful questions glittered in her eyes as Marcus came to claim her, striking him with the impact of an oncoming train. Stunned, he stared down into the depths of twin wells knowing there was no way out once he lost himself in them. She was a beautiful woman, he had known many such, but the depths of her soul were revealed tonight in that sad expression, and he knew he had never seen her equal.

With the care one uses with priceless porcelain, he took her hand, murmuring senseless phrases as Lucia hastily departed, leaving him staring, enraptured. Under his stare, the wondering eyes glazed over with the usual courtesy with which Jennifer maintained her distance, and he felt cheated of a precious gift.

"You were so pensive just then, angel, has something upset you?" Marcus asked in gentle tones, searching her face for further enlightenment.

"No, I have only upset myself," she answered almost to herself, instantly diverting him by dropping his hand and making a sweeping curtsy. "How do I look, milord? Will I make a suitable companion for you this evening?"

He remained serious, ignoring her frivolity. Dressed formally in frock coat tailored to his broad shoulders and trim figure, the white satin brocade of his vest an eccentricity that looked well on him and contrasted with the dark four-in-hand that he preferred, he presented a dashing image of elegance, only his beaver hat and walking stick necessary to complete the picture.

"You need never worry about that, little one. You would make a suitable companion for me at any time. Now what have you done to upset yourself?"

"This is neither the time nor the occasion to discuss it, we will be late." She slipped her fingers about his arm.

He covered them with his hand and inquired no further.

To Jennifer, the theater seemed enormous, its incredibly ornate embellishments carried from floor level to towering heights where they would have been lost to sight if not for the tremendous chandeliers that tinkled above their heads with every sudden gust of wind. Despite the spectacular size of the lobby, it was packed with theatergoers, the dark suits of the men contrasting splendidly with the brilliant diamonds and festooned gowns of the women. It was a display of extravagance that could only leave Jennifer speechless as she clung to her husband's arm, not wishing to be parted from him when they were caught up in the crush of strangers.

There were hurried cries of greetings from familiar faces in the crowd as they pushed they way to their box, but Jennifer was at a loss to put names to faces—the dreary parlor where she placed them could not compare with their present setting, and they all became a blur. She followed Marc's example and simply nodded acknowl-

edgment to their cries, making no attempt to return their
familiarity. This response apparently suited Marcus, whose
somber visage soon developed an appreciative twinkle
when he glanced down at her.

They were joined in the lobby by Darlene O'Hara and
Stephen, an unexpected delight to Jennifer, but a well-
planned gesture on Marc's part. Jennifer's cry of excitement outweighed his doubts. She preferred the company
of others to his alone, and for her birthday, he generously
accommodated her wishes.

Their next encounter was neither planned nor pleasant.
A shriek of recognition echoed over the heads of the crowd
as the small party made their way to their box, and all eyes
involuntarily turned to the source of the sound. They were
promptly accosted by an elaborately gowned woman of
more than Marc's age, although she attempted to hide
that fact with artfully applied paint and an overly youthful
style of dress.

With a knowing grin, Stephen took Darlene's arm, and
they were carried off in the eddy of people, leaving Jennifer and Marcus and the newcomer to form a small island
in the current of humanity.

"Marcus Armstrong! As I live and breathe!" The spectacle raised a beringed hand to her well-displayed bosom
in an attitude of breathless amazement. "They told me
you were back in town but I just couldn't believe it. Why
haven't you called on me?"

Jennifer watched Marc's jaw tighten and the hard look
return to his eyes and knew at once this must be a San
Francisco version of Gwendolyn. She turned suspicious
eyes to their captor, who caught the look and gushed, maliciously. "Why this must be your new bride everybody's
talking about, she can't hardly be older than Melissa when
you . . ."

Marcus abruptly interrupted her speech. "Jennifer, this
is Madelyn Worthinger. Madelyn, my wife, Jennifer. You
must excuse us, there are people waiting." And with hur-

ried rudeness, he pushed into the crowd, leaving the startled woman to stare open-mouthed after them.

It was impossible to talk while shoving through the throng of people, but once they entered the comparative safety of their box and joined their companions, Jennifer appealed for explanation.

"Marcus, why were you so rude to that woman? Is she someone I shouldn't know?"

While Marc's jaw tightened, Stephen yelped with laughter beside her.

"Madelyn! If Aunt Clare heard you were associating with Madelyn, she'd have you banned from the house."

"Stephen, that's not nice!" Darlene exclaimed, but her suppressed giggle gave her true opinion. "The lady is simply enjoying her new-found freedom."

"No one ever called her the Black Widow, that's for certain. Hubby Number One must have left her in dire straits if she's already searching for Number Two," Stephen commented irreverently. "Where do you fit in, Marcus? Hasn't anyone informed the lady you're already taken? Or have you joined the growing numbers of her 'gentlemen callers'?"

Stephen's wicked tone made the implication clear, but Marcus silenced him with a crushing scowl. "I would suggest you hold your tongue while there are ladies present, cousin." Turning to Jennifer, he replied, "Suffice it to say there is no need for you to know Madelyn further."

Curiosity aroused, Jennifer couldn't resist a further question. "Who is Melissa? Should I avoid her, too?"

Silence greeted her inquiry, and Marcus looked down at her with ill-concealed temper. "She's dead." He returned his attention to the stage where the curtain was going up.

Absorbed in the first performance she had ever seen in her life, Jennifer quickly forgot the incident. She had read Shakespeare when very young and again, more recently, in St. Louis, but it had never had the full effect on her that this enactment of his words did, and she sat, captivated, totally unaware of the hand holding hers or the amused glances she attracted from the men on either side.

When the curtain went down at intermission, she emerged from the trance slowly. It was moments before she realized she was being spoken to and that Marcus was bending over her chair with laughter again in his eyes.

"Are you back yet, little one? Would you care for some refreshment?"

"No, no, I couldn't," she answered absently.

Slipping back into his seat beside her, he kept his hand on her chair back. "I have never seen anyone become so immersed in an activity as you do; you give yourself totally, don't you?"

Jennifer looked to see if he was laughing at her again, but he seemed completely serious and talking to himself as much as to her. "It would be easier if I could give myself totally, instead of enduring the frustration of being an inactive observer," she admitted candidly.

"I can appreciate that," Marcus remarked wryly, leaving Jennifer to feel they were talking about two entirely different subjects.

But before she could consider the possibility, her thoughts were interrupted by the arrival of a stranger. He was not tall as Stephen and Marcus were tall, but he carried himself with a sense of height. Green eyes dominated his features as he draped himself over a chair back.

"My, my, what have we here? Dear sister, you failed to inform me you have been accepted into the exalted presence of the Armstrongs." Insolent eyes swept to Marcus, then over the feminine figure at his side. "Now I understand why you're so quick to go home early, Armstrong. What I fail to understand is why you ever leave at all," he drawled.

"Cameron!" Darlene admonished, "can you not manage to act with some degree of sensibility for a change?"

"I thought I was, fair sister. Do I not deserve introductions for my efforts?" His gaze strayed from his sister's doting amusement, past Stephen's lifted eyebrow, to Jennifer's bewilderment. Casually ignoring Marc's glare, he took Jennifer's hand and bowed over it. "You must be the lovely Jennifer of whom I have heard so much. My name is Cameron O'Hara, since none of these loutish knaves have presence of mind to introduce us."

Marc's ominous silence served as warning, and Jennifer hesitated, not certain how to react to such presumption. Warm fingers held hers, and unabashed emerald eyes roamed appreciatively over the curves displayed by Jennifer's low cut gown.

"Pleased to meet you, *Mr.* O'Hara," she murmured pointedly, attempting to disentangle her fingers before her husband's frown could grow blacker.

"I'd suggest you put your eyes back in their sockets where they belong before Marc removes them permanently," Stephen commented with a touch of irony, having already noted his cousin's unnatural calm, a certain warning of the coming storm.

Cameron smiled leisurely, kissed Jennifer's fingers and let her go. "Sorry, my lady, I could not resist. That's what comes of being the black sheep of the family, though, dear sister," he shifted his gaze to Darlene. "The company you keep is questionable." His insolent gaze indicated Stephen before returning to Marcus. "Just stopped by to see if you'll be at the club later this evening."

"No, I won't be there this evening. I will have to get my revenge some other night," Marc replied evenly, disregarding Jennifer's questioning glance while his fingers played possessively at a dangling curl on her neck.

Cameron took the hint, dropping a wink. "Then I shall bid you adieu. It's been lovely meeting you, Jenny, I hope we may meet again soon." He was gone as swiftly as he came.

Jennifer's attention swung back to Marcus who studiously avoided her gaze by examining the other occupants of the theater with a pair of opera glasses. If she were not such a coward, she would question him of this talk of clubs and revenge, but it did not seem her place to do so. She could not claim the privileges of a wife as part of their contract without paying the price. All the questions the evening had raised clamored for answers, but she would have to remain silent.

The rest of the evening was pure magic. The ending of the play left Jennifer completely satisfied. Combined with the heady sensation of Marcus' company, and the knowledge that he wanted to be with her tonight, it became the most enjoyable birthday she could ever remember. Floating out of the theater, she clasped Marc's arm in pure giddiness, a precaution to keep her feet on the ground.

Not until they reached her room did her head come down from the clouds, and then only gradually.

Indulgently, Marcus settled into one of the few good chairs Jennifer had not banished to the attic and allowed the tide of her excitement to flow around him, receiving as much pleasure from her enjoyment as she did. Tired eyes admired the youthful figure of his wife as she flitted about the room, setting things in place and responding enthusiastically to his questions concerning the play. She moved as if there were no earth beneath her feet and even in this dim light there was an incandescence about her that lit whatever corner of the room she graced. Never had she looked more like an angel than she did tonight, and the devil within him stayed out of sight.

Jennifer tucked her gloves away in their drawer and came to Marcus for help with the unfastening of her necklace.

As he gravely undid the necklace for her, she asked, "What kind of revenge are you seeking from Mr. O'Hara? He does not seem the type who would cause a need for revenge."

Marcus quirked a sardonic eyebrow. "He's an idle fellow with little better to do than gamble his evenings away." He chose his words cautiously, not wishing to arouse the curiosity of his overimaginative young wife. It was enough that his own suspicions had been aroused by the rogue.

Jennifer folded the pearls back into their case, as she

daringly questioned him further. "Is that how you've been spending your evenings, then? Gambling? I hope he can afford to lose."

Marcus smiled at the guilelessness of her questioning. Her concern lay more with his activities than Cameron's, and he relaxed.

"Do not worry, angel. I can well afford to lose whatever stakes we play, and so can Cameron. Do you have an objection to my whiling away an evening or two in this manner?" He knew it was his time concerning her, and not his money, but if she ever learned the amount that had exchanged hands in these last weeks, she would be horrified. It was not a subject he intended indulging in. Gambling had once been his livelihood, and he was accustomed to coming out ahead, but the pattern had changed recently. He had yet to prove Cameron the culprit, but time was on his side. There were ways of dealing with cheats.

Jennifer turned to him with a wide-eyed expression of innocence that amused him greatly.

"It's not my place to object to what you do with your time, I was simply curious. I try hard not to be inquisitive, but it goes against my nature. I know as little about you now as the day we were married, and I find it hard to curb my curiosity."

"Am I all that mysterious? What is there left to know? Speak now, for you might never have a better chance."

"I know you are laughing at me as usual, but shouldn't a wife know something of her husband's business? I only know you came here to settle your father's estate and look for a situation of your own. Do you think me so ignorant of such matters you cannot divulge whether you have accomplished this or not? I would like to know what you do, what you want to do, what hopes you have, so many things! If I am a partner to this contract of ours, does that mean we cannot be friends?"

"You are not ignorant, my little one, but if I have neglected you, it has been for good reason and has nothing to do with your lack of understanding. Be assured that I am doing just what I told you I would do. I am disposing of my father's estate so that my mother will be comfortably provided for without needing my assistance, and in the process, I am watching out for opportunities for myself." He did not mention the fact that income from his father's estate was so great it could provide for his mother for twenty lifetimes and that the excess was being carefully invested for his wife and child. He did not question Jennifer's understanding of his investments, but her understanding of the reasons for these investments, and he had no wish to endure a show of moral indignation at this point.

"After all I have heard of this golden land, there must be many opportunities for a man of your ability. If I cannot participate, will you not at least try to tell me of them so I can feel I share some small part of your life?" Big, brown eyes were lifted wistfully to his, the long lashes tilting upward in dark fringes.

Marcus contemplated her serious expression, wondering how he had found the only woman in the world who refused to use her more than ample charms to make her fortune, but preferred to use her head. She was not vain of her looks, but surely she must know she could have all the opportunities she wanted in exchange for full access to her body? But it was up to her now to make that decision; he would not be classified in the same category with Delaney again.

"All right, angel, that seems fair enough. If I have robbed you of your chance to make your own way in this world, you may have the dubious experience of sharing mine. But it is getting late, and you'd better be getting yourself to bed unless you've trained that greedy little monster to wake up later."

"If you continue to need my companionship in the evening, I might seriously contemplate doing just that," she answered impishly, turning her back to him for unbuttoning.

Marcus made quick work of the row of tiny buttons, then

rested his hands against the satin curve of her shoulder. Without her heeled slippers, her head scarcely reached his chin, and he drank of the heady fragrance of her hair. Her soft surrender of the morning scorched his memory, and even as her back stiffened under his caress, he sought words to return her willingness. He had taken advantage of her vulnerability before, but now that she had become fully aware of the attraction between them, he knew it would not be so easy again.

"You know I desire more than just your companionship," he whispered against her ear. Drunk with the headiness of desire, he hesitated, unable to find the phrases that came so glibly with others.

His hands were hard and strong against her shoulders, his masculine body close and exuding a powerful attraction, but Jennifer sensed his hesitation and drew strength from it. He was not offering what she wanted, and he knew it. He was offering her a place in his bed, but not in his heart, and she shook him off.

Turning to face him, holding her bodice in place as she studied the uncertainty of those deceptive blue-gray eyes, Jennifer offered the only gesture of understanding she dared spare. Beckoning him to lower his head, she pressed a warm kiss against his cheek and murmured a hurried thank you in his ear before retreating.

It was not what Marcus wanted, but it gave him room for thought. If she could not be won by passion, reason, or wealth, perhaps gentle courting would bring her around. Lightly caressing her blushing cheek, he uttered his good-nights, and with the air of a man well-satisfied with his decision, he went whistling from the room.

Chapter Eleven

Jennifer lost no time the next day in tackling Stephen on the subject of gambling and clubs, and he was only too delighted to act the part of informant. Marcus had taken his father's place in the stylish Pacific Club, an elite men's club modeled after those in London allowing gentlemen to be undisturbed by the opposite sex while engaging in the pleasant pastimes of eating, drinking, and gambling.

Stephen didn't mention that old Mr. Armstrong had used it nightly as an escape from an increasingly irritating wife. He still hadn't formed any clear theory on the nature of the relationship between his arrogant cousin and his country bride, but it seemed strange to desert a young and charming wife for the smoky gaming tables of a men's club, and he had no wish to make the comparison. It was hard to believe that Marc's roving eye did not fancy Jennifer, yet he completely abandoned her to her own pursuits. It was the next best thing to unnatural and in total contradiction to his jealous behavior when his wife appeared in the presence of any other man. Stephen vowed to get to the bottom of the mystery.

Jennifer wasn't fooled by Stephen's reticence. She knew why men would wish to frequent an all male club; she had learned that much from Marcus. It was painful to think he classed her in the category of women to be avoided, but at least she had learned he was holding to his plan and not out searching for the company of other women as she had feared. She had lived in dread of the day he began seriously looking for a more suitable wife.

With the object of finding a watch fob for which Marcus had expressed a desire, Jennifer persuaded Darlene the next day to accompany her to Montgomery Street before afternoon visiting hours began. Last night's outing had reawakened her hopes and spirits, and they couldn't be contained by quietly sitting at home tending to her sewing; she needed activity to salve her restless energy.

To her surprise and consternation, Darlene arrived with Cameron in tow. Noting Jennifer's expression, he swept off his hat and bowed low, but when he lifted his eyes to hers, they crinkled with amusement.

"My pardon for intruding, Mrs. Armstrong. Having business of my own downtown, I thought to escort my sister and her charming companion. But if I am in any way imposing . . ."

The glib phrases rolled off his tongue with an insincerity even Darlene noticed, and she gave him a sharp glance. Jennifer's answering grin erased her worries.

"Mr. O'Hara, you may be a lying rogue, but the pompous role does not become you. Behave, and Darlene and I will not deny you our company."

He laughed at her quickness and offered his arm. Despite the day's heat and humidity, Jennifer stepped lightly down the hill, too exhilarated to pay any heed to the heat. She was learning the ways of Marc's world. Maybe, someday soon, even he would recognize it.

Between jewelry stores they dawdled, stopping to watch a man make cigars in the window of a tobacco shop, choosing between the temptations of the sweet shop, admiring the latest shipment of bonnets in the milliner's window. The steep slope of the street and the warmth of the sun made any faster pace unappealing.

Cameron suggested a jeweler's they had not yet seen, and once inside, showed a surprising adeptness at bargaining over the price of Jennifer's choice of fobs. As they left the shop triumphantly, jewelry box in hand, he suggested

a stop for lemonade and guided them down a side street
Jennifer had not traversed before.

Occupied with her own happy thoughts, Jennifer was
caught unaware by Cameron's sudden halt in the midst of
a bustling crowd. Darlene, too, turned to question him.

Staring straight ahead, he shifted his attention to the
two girls, and hastily attempted to turn them around.

"I was mistaken. The sweet shoppe is on another block.
Let us go back this way."

But Jennifer's gaze had already found what Cameron
sought to hide. In the crowd of pedestrians ahead of them,
Marc's well-tailored, erect figure stood out above all others,
even as it bent intimately to hear the words of the woman
on his arm, her eloquent gesticulations emphasizing the
gush of speech she was pouring into his ear.

For a brief moment, Jennifer's stricken gaze met Cameron's sympathetic one, and then quickly, she hid it. Marcus
owed her no loyalty, but the O'Haras had no understanding
of that. Their suspicions would have to be diverted while
her own would have to wait until she was alone. She should
have known better than to write off a hussy like Madelyn
so easily.

"It must be a business appointment; it's best not to intrude. Let's go back now, it's dreadfully hot out here."
Jennifer composed herself as she redirected the O'Haras,
but no amount of outward composure could calm inner
turmoil.

All the way back to the house Jennifer chastised herself
for this feeling of outrage burning in her soul. Whatever
Marcus was doing with that woman, she had no right to
complain; their contract said nothing of how he conducted
his affairs as long as he provided her support. She was
under obligation to avoid compromising his reputation,
but nothing had been said of himself; he was free to do
as he wished.

Returning home, Jennifer longed to retire to her room
with the excuse of a headache to work this out by herself,
but the O'Haras would immediately suspect the cause of

her illness. They were quite capable of complaining to Stephen, or even Marcus, and Jennifer wished no one to know they had witnessed the incident, or that it had upset her in any way. So, reluctantly, she entered the parlor prepared to welcome the day's callers, acting as if nothing had happened.

Jennifer sat there, wrapped in her own thoughts throughout the afternoon while the chatter of idle women spilled on around her. Clare's warning frowns went unheeded as Jennifer drew inside herself, determined to barricade her defenses against any further disturbance of this sort. Stephen's knowing snicker at Madelyn's gentlemen callers left no doubt that this woman was another Gwendolyn, and although, surely, Marcus could not seriously be considering her for wife, he was just as surely capable of using her to satisfy other needs.

Why should this thought disturb her? Had she expected him to remain celibate since they were married? That would be pure idiocy on her part; Marcus was not made for a monk's life as his past so plainly indicated, and if she would not give herself, she must expect him to go elsewhere. She still did not fully understand his contention that there was a difference between love and the physical act of love, and she could not imagine any man but Marcus satisfying the aching need just his presence aroused in her, but obviously what they had done meant nothing to him if he could so easily find others to take her place. Jennifer stirred uneasily at the thought of Madelyn in his arms, but she crushed the ache to the back of her mind. It was no good thinking about it.

But at dinner, she couldn't help avoiding Marcus' offered arm, slipping away at the last minute and allowing Stephen to seat her at the foot of the table as usual. Marcus cast a quizzical glance in her direction, but said nothing, taking his usual place at Clare's right. Stephen chortled at this exchange.

"Well, Cousin Marcus, it seems one night on the town

does not change the lady's opinion of you; she still prefers my company to your boorish society."

"Stephen . . ." Jennifer pleaded to silence the irrepressible idiot, but Marcus didn't give her time to finish.

"That's quite all right, cousin, the lady is entitled to her moments of madness, and I prefer a civilized meal to your abominable chatter. I would only remind you that the lady is my wife, see that you treat her as such."

Stephen snorted with disgust. "From what I can see, I realize that better than you do. In case no one has informed you, wives have more purposes than mannequins to decorate your arm. Would you care for a few lessons?"

Jennifer dropped her fork against the plate, unaware of its clatter as she snapped out in anger. "Stephen! I will hear no more of this nonsense. If I choose to sit here . . ."

Marcus interrupted her a second time, his voice low and soothing. "Enough, little one, you have chosen your seat and need make no excuses for it. If Cousin Stephen here has any complaints to make, he can make them in private." The timbre of his voice slanted warningly, leaving the last words hanging in the air.

"If there are any complaints to be made, *I* will make them." With grim determination, Jennifer stared down Stephen's implacable gaze, bringing the subject to an uneasy close. She refused to acknowledge Marcus.

But Stephen did not give up so easily. Grounded on one objection, he proceeded blithely to the next, determined to ferret out the truth of their relationship.

"I have tickets to the Centennial Ball," he declared with a deceptive grin. "Would you care to accompany me, lovely lady?" Before Jennifer could make an astonished reply, he appealed to the head of the table. "And Aunt Clare, would you do us the honor of acting as chaperon?"

Clare calmly continued sipping her wine. "You're an impertinent twit, Stephen. You're quite old enough to look outside the home for female companionship; might I prevail upon you to do so?"

"And give up the pleasure of escorting the town's two most beautiful women? Certainly not."

"You've failed to ask the lady's opinion of your plan, cousin. Perhaps Jennifer would like to have some say in the matter. Jenny, would you like to accept Stephen's invitation?" Marcus leaned over the table, trying to gauge her reaction.

"I think not," she murmured, not looking up from her plate. It might be easy for Marcus to escort other women, but she was not yet ready to be seen in public with any other man but he.

"Would you care to go with me?" Marcus pursued softly, as if there were no others in the room.

Startled, Jenny raised her eyes to his, feeling the warmth rush to her face at the intimacy they conveyed. "Dancing?"

There was no denying the blue sparkle of his eyes underneath those dark brows and unruly curls as he replied, "That is usually what one does at a ball." His teasing smile told her he remembered well that last night on the river when she decided dancing could easily be sinful. The words burned deep in her memory, but the result of them burned even deeper.

Warmth completely suffused her face as she returned her gaze to her plate. "If you wish," was all she could murmur, without revealing her trembling.

The rest of dinner was an aching blur; there were too many things to think about and the chaos of Jennifer's emotions left it impossible to think of any one of them. How could he court her with soft words and promises as he had last night and this, then make mockery of their marriage by consorting with the notorious likes of Madelyn? It made no sense. She felt as if she were being dashed against rocks with the ocean's unmerciful regularity, and it was with relief that she escaped to the parlor out of the confusing presence of her husband. But there was scarcely time for the throb in her head to subside before the men joined them. Of all the nights Marcus chose to stay home, it had to be this one; now there was no need to pretend a headache, her suffering was real and evident.

Stephen was the first to notice. "Jennifer, are you feeling well?"

"It's just a headache. I think I will retire early, if you don't mind." She set aside her sewing, eager to escape.

Anxiously, Stephen strode to her side, but Marcus was there first, solicitously tucking Jennifer's arm in his. He led her from the room, making no comment until they reached the bedroom. There, Lucia was still hovering attendance, tucking the sleeping infant under his covers and whisking away the remnants of before-dinner dressing rituals.

"Lucia, go fetch cold compresses for Jennifer," he commanded, giving up his attempt to maintain formality with the little maid his wife had befriended, adopting their habit of addressing each other by first name. "Then come back and see that she goes directly to bed. She apparently didn't get enough rest last night."

His peremptory tone left no room for abeyance and Lucia did as commanded, giving Jennifer a quick glance of sympathy and Marcus a quelling look as she swept by.

Oblivious to Lucia's cold attitude toward him, Marcus helped Jennifer into a chair, rubbing her wrist with a rough hand. "I think I know you well enough by now to know you aren't the delicate type who complains of headaches without cause. What is wrong, Jenny?"

The light from the lamp sent a circle of brightness over the midnight blue of the new carpet, its oriental ivory and crimson design twisting into new dimensions of color as it tapered off into darkness. Jennifer found it useless for steadying her thoughts through the throbbing pain in her head, but she focused her vision on it rather than the proximity of her husband.

"It's nothing, Marcus, I simply have a headache. I will be fine in the morning." Her voice trembled, but she couldn't prevent it. She felt as if she were being pushed in two directions at once. The tension mounted the longer she stayed in his vicinity and she prayed for his swift departure.

"There is something troubling you, but I cannot force it from you if you do not wish to tell me." He spoke stiffly.

"You know nothing of me and you probably never will! Just leave me alone. I want some time to myself." Jennifer's words were sharper than she intended, but in her pain she revelled in their viciousness.

Stabbed by her words, pride wounded by the blow of her unexpected rejection, Marcus replied coldly, "I had hoped we put an end to this nonsense some time ago, but if you persist in your little display of independence, you may have your privacy. I am leaving."

With a curt nod to the dumbstruck maid in the doorway, Marcus stalked from the room, cursing the madness that put him at the mercy of this capricious child. His footsteps clattered down the darkened stairway, and the front door slammed as he stormed into the night.

Morning and Lucia's rush of excitement brought back what Jennifer had managed to forget the night before—the Centennial Ball. How could she have been so insane to agree to go? But Lucia's excitement was catching, and Jennifer couldn't help being swept into it, especially after Lucia insisted on her mother making a new gown for Jennifer to wear. Mrs. Lopez was an experienced seamstress, and Jennifer readily gave in to her urging, if only to avoid the thought of an evening in Marc's arms.

Lucia's subtle hints and knowing looks revealed she knew much of the strain between Marcus and Jennifer, and Jennifer carefully avoided the topic. The fact that she and Marcus did not sleep together must be apparent to the entire household, but she rejected the urge to speak of it to her only confidante. Lucia had to be content with the romantic intention of designing the gown that would bring her new employers back together again.

In the meantime, the O'Haras were becoming regular

visitors to the household, distracting Jennifer's thoughts from the coming ball to some degree. The fact that there was some understanding between the elder Irishman and the stricken Clare became more obvious with each passing day. Deciding if Marcus should ever look upon her in the same manner Michael O'Hara looked upon Clare, she would no doubt fall at his feet, Jennifer turned away from the painful observation, only to be met by Cameron's enigmatic stare.

Cameron had taken to accompanying father and sister on these visits, causing no small amount of comment among family and friends alike. He made no attempt to be as entertaining as Stephen, but whenever Jennifer looked up, he was there, always at her side with a word or a phrase to suit her mood.

On the day after the Madelyn fiasco, he attempted to draw her out on the subject, but she refused his sympathy. Since then, he offered only companionship, and Jennifer accepted his friendship without a second thought. He could be cynically irreverent and solicitously kind and the combination appealed to her wayward nature.

Jennifer's anticipation of the Centennial Ball bloomed slowly, but as the days passed, a sparkle of excitement began to glimmer in her eyes whenever someone spoke of the dance. Marcus noticed the change and wondered at it, coming in early from his lonely walks to linger in the shadows of the parlor and watch as the others laughed and played in the lamplight by the piano. Clare looked at him with disgust and left the room soon after he made these appearances, but Stephen and Jennifer seemed hardly aware of his presence, and he was left alone to watch as Jennifer played straight man to Stephen's wit, and the chimes of Jennifer's laughter rang across the room.

Sipping the brandy he brought into the room with him, Marcus tried to remember when she last laughed like that for him, knowing too well that he had offered her no occasion to do so. Instead, they spent their moments together in solemn silence, Jennifer venturing no word of her own until spoken to. The light-hearted gaiety he watched so glumly from his darkened corner disappeared once he took her hand and led her from the room. The gap between them was widening, and although at one time this had been his intention, he was beginning to regret his accursed chivalry. He found it increasingly impossible to be close to the little wretch and remain a gentleman, too, and was rapidly losing sight of all reasons why he should.

It was almost with relief, then, that Marcus discovered the late arrival of a train would delay an important out of town business meeting on the Fourth, and he would be unable to attend the Ball they all eagerly awaited. When he broke the news at dinner, a general wail ensued, but the tear-filled silence of his wife caused him the greatest regret. She made no complaint, though the others scolded him vigorously. Ignoring the chatter from either side, he turned his attention across the table where Jennifer sat with bent head, making a pretense of cutting her food, and his eyes softened at her attempt to hide the disappointment. Knowing he was a fool and would regret his leniency later, he tried to soften the blow.

"Jenny, there is no reason why you can't go without me; it is a charity affair, and there is no harm in your attending with the family. Perhaps I can be back in time to catch a dance or two."

Almond eyes fastened steadily on him, and Marcus plunged into their unfathomable depths, only understanding that the excitement he had anticipated did not appear. But the moment was lost as Stephen demanded her agreement, and her gaze returned to him. A flicker of a smile caressed Jennifer's lips at Stephen's triumph in escorting both Armstrong women by himself, and dinner progressed happily from there with only Marcus aware of the aura of silence encompassing that one slight figure.

Jennifer tried valiantly to conceal her disappointment. Once she had given in to the idea of spending an evening dancing with Marcus with no huge belly to separate them,

her imagination had taken flight, and she had been looking forward to the event. It never occurred to her that she
could dance with anyone else but her husband, and his
casual consigning of her to Stephen's care hurt more than
his forbidding her to go at all. But she could make no
complaint; the terms of their contract certainly didn't specify an obligation to keep her entertained. She was bitterly
regretting that she had ever agreed to such a monstrous
compact; the freedom he granted her was more painful
than the duties.

Jennifer wasn't alone in her hatred of the contract separating them, but as usual, it was for entirely different reasons. While Jennifer vilified the freedom it gave Marcus to
act as an unmarried man, Marcus cursed at the frustration
of being unable to make her either wife or mistress.

Not only could he not bend Jennifer to his desires, but
it seemed she was only too willing to place others in the
same position as he. The news that Cameron had been
added to the list of his wife's admirers was not an observation calculated to cool his simmering temper.

Finding the thought of rape unappealing, Marcus had
deliberately concentrated on his work, avoiding his wife's
tempting company only to discover in his absence she was
courting both cousin and rogue. It was not enough for
Cameron to attempt to make a fool of him at the gaming
table, but he desired to make a cuckold of him, also. It
was past time that this game of chance came to an end.

With that thought in mind, Marcus faced his insolent
opponent over the poker table one last time. He'd had
ample time to study Cameron's methods, knew just which
card was hidden where, what shiny object would appear
on the table at a strategic moment, reflecting a player's
draw, and what distraction would take place when the cards
were dealt. They were old ploys, deftly manipulated by a
cunning cheat and a charming facade. Tonight, the house
of cards would tumble.

As the night wore on and the stacks of chips at Marc's
elbow increased, the young man across the table grew ner-

4 BESTSELLING HISTORICAL ROMANCES BY YOUR FAVORITE AUTHORS CAN BE YOURS, FREE!

Kensington Choice brings you historical romances by your favorite bestselling authors including Janelle Taylor, Shannon Drake, Bertrice Small, Jo Goodman, and Georgina Gentry, just to name a few! Each book is filled with passion, adventure and the excitement of bygone times!

To introduce you to this great club which is part of Zebra Home Subscription Service, we'd like to send you your first 4 bestselling historical romances, absolutely free! And once you get these 4 free books to savor at home, we'll rush you the next 4 brand-new books at the lowest prices available, as soon as they are published.

The way the club works is that after your initial FREE shipment, you will get our 4 newest bestselling historical romances delivered to your doorstep each month at the preferred subscriber's rate of only $4.20 per book, a savings of up to $8.16 per month (since these titles sell in bookstores for $4.99-$6.99)! All books are sent on a 10-day free examination basis and there is no minimum number of books to buy. (And no charge for shipping.) Plus as a regular subscriber, you'll receive our FREE monthly newsletter, *Zebra/Pinnacle Romance News*, which features author profiles, subscriber benefits, book previews and more!

*We have 4 FREE BOOKS for you
as your introduction to
KENSINGTON CHOICE!
To get your FREE BOOKS, worth
up to $24.96, mail the card below.*

FREE BOOK CERTIFICATE

Yes! Please send me 4 Kensington Choice (the best of Zebra and Pinnacle Books) Historical Romances without cost or obligation (worth up to $24.96). As a Kensington Choice subscriber, I will then receive 4 brand-new romances to preview each month for 10 days FREE. I can return any books I decide not to keep and owe nothing. The publisher's prices for Kensington Choice romances range from $4.99-$6.99, but as a preferred subscriber I will get these books for only $4.20 per book or $16.80 for all four titles. There is no minimum number of books to buy and I may cancel my subscription at any time, plus there is no additional charge for postage and handling. No matter what I decide to do, my first 4 books are mine to keep, absolutely FREE!

Name _____

Address _____ Apt. _____

City _____ State _____ Zip _____

Telephone (_____) _____

Signature _____

(If under 18, parent or guardian must sign)

Subscription subject to acceptance. Terms and prices subject to change.

KF1098

4 FREE
Historical Romances

are waiting
for you to
claim them!

(worth up to
$24.96)

See details
inside....

vous. Only Marc's practiced eye caught the watchful look as the silver candy dish was replaced by crystal. Nor did the other players note Cameron's consternation when Marc's hands covered the deck at the first sign of an altercation behind them. As these incidents continued throughout the evening and their meaning became evident, Cameron's confidence slipped.

With a shrug, he eyed his dwindling chips, and announced it was not his night. As he pushed back his chair to depart, Marcus sailed a card to the center of the table.

"Don't go without your ace in the hole," he stated coldly.

Cameron's fingers whitened on the table's edge. "Don't do this, Armstrong," he answered warningly.

"I'm not. You did it to yourself." With a nod of his head, Marcus indicated a tall, distinguished gentleman propped against a sideboard amidst the few remaining onlookers. All heads at the table turned to follow the direction of Marc's gaze, and the man nodded greeting. All the action at tonight's game, and many other night's, had been followed by a trained observer, and the well-known detective's significance was readily apparent.

The other men at the table remained silent, leaving action to the hands of the man who had discovered the cheat. Men had been shot for less in this town, but this was a society of well-bred gentlemen, and they waited for Marc's verdict.

Cameron paled, but his eyes took on a furious fire. "You can't prove anything, Armstrong. You're in no position to call names. What I know about you and that fancy dame of yours would make these stalwart gentlemen blush. Call it off, Marcus, and we'll call it even."

Gray eyes hardened to slivers of steel. "You will leave my wife out of this. If I so much as hear you breathe her name, I'll skewer you so badly you'll never be able to show your face in polite society again. I have my sources, too, and if your father should find out where you've spent this past year, you'll have more than your reputation to consider. Get out of here now, O'Hara. You're no longer welcome at these tables. My suggestion is that you find another rock to crawl under. The law in this town will know your name after tonight."

The icy calmness of Marc's threats was more effective than any more theatrical revenge, and Cameron swallowed the knowledge painfully. Glaring at his antagonist, he gritted out between clenched teeth, "You'll pay for this, Armstrong," before rising to leave the table.

As he shouldered his way out of the tight circle of men that had formed, mutters of ". . . too good for him," and ". . . should have been horse-whipped," followed him out. But it was Marc's threats that sounded a death knell to his hopes, and he knew it.

Marc remained at the table, absently shuffling the cards until the culprit was properly expelled from the club. Amidst the clamoring of a thousand questions, he abruptly rose, and saying good-night, walked out on the scene he had created.

Cameron's threats were not idle, as Marcus well knew. Whereas most of St. Louis society had only heard tales of their last minute wedding, the residents and employees of Magnolia House knew warped portions of the truth. And Cameron, as Marcus now knew, had been the manager of Delaney's gambling operation. With the closing of Magnolia House, Cameron had been thrown out on the streets again.

Marcus wondered what had caused the prodigal son to suddenly return home after all these years, at the same time as he had done. The answer did not bode well. His memory turned to the anguished expression on Jennifer's face when she had learned Marcus was the person responsible for her torment at Delaney's hands. He had thought to protect her from further pain, but it seemed that would not be possible. Wearily, he turned his feet toward home.

Chapter Twelve

Dressed in a shoulderless gown of palest green, the darker green satin underskirt rustling with every movement, only the off the shoulder froth of chiffon sleeves preserving any sense of decorum, Jennifer spun around for Lucia's inspection and approval. The nearer the time came for their departure, the more terrified Jennifer was of meeting this occasion with only Stephen's idle wit and Clare's haughty manner to rely on, but she could not let anyone see her fear. She would meet this occasion with all the pride she could muster and learn to go her own way. She would show Marcus she had no need of him for her pleasures.

"I'm beginning to think Parisians are a little more daring than I am meant to be," Jennifer commented as she glanced down at the dip of the new gown's clinging bodice. Her breasts swelled above the satin decolleté, and she feared to breathe deeply. Her mother would certainly see the fires of hell dancing about her in this gown.

But Lucia only smiled and fastened the string of pearls about her neck.

Not entirely reassured by her maid's knowing smirk, Jennifer tied the green cashmere shawl about her bare shoulders before leaving. It might be old-fashioned, but she was attached to it, and it would serve a good purpose tonight; its warmth enfolded her protectively.

Remembering to slow her pace at the stairway, Jennifer

descended as Josephine had taught her, instead of rushing in her usual headlong manner. Stephen was already waiting below, and with delight, she measured her descent by the changing expression on his mobile features; by the time she reached the last step he was nearly speechless.

With a decided effort, he recovered his breath and brought his eyes back to hers before venturing to speak. "My God, Jenny Lee! I now have a fair understanding why Marcus keeps you home to himself; it would take a man less selfish than he to share your beauty with the greedy eyes of the world."

"I'm not sure if that's a compliment, Stephen, but I'll pretend it is. Lucia has given me explicit instructions to enjoy myself, and I intend to by ignoring your teasing." Jennifer hesitated to take his arm, the warmth of his gaze embarrassing her, but she soon found her gloved hand caught in his.

A smile of pleasure illuminated his face as he gazed down at the impish gleam of her eyes, noticing for the first time the sprinkle of freckles across the bridge of her nose. She was a treasure too rare to neglect and if she had belonged to any other but the man who had long been his hero, he would have long since repaired the lack. Instead, he would have to find some other means of bringing happiness to her smile.

"You are the eighth wonder of the world, Mrs. Armstrong, and I intend to prove it. We will make a rare pair tonight, you and I."

"As far as I'm concerned, you already are a rare pair, but of what, I'm not prepared to say." The caustic voice came from behind them as Clare advanced slowly into the hallway. Black hair caught in a fashionable upsweep, diamonds glittering at ears and throat, black silk setting off still lustrous skin, she was a woman of immense beauty and carried herself accordingly, despite her infirmity.

"Aunt Clare, you are stunning, as always. We will bring the dance to a crashing halt when we enter the room; all others will be forced to bow before us." Gallantly, Stephen took her hand and slipped it into the crook of his arm.

Before she took Stephen's other arm, Jennifer shyly kissed the older woman's cheek. "You are magnificent," she whispered.

Clare gave them a suspicious glare, then pounded her walking stick against the hardwood floor. "I'm not putting up with any shenanigans." Her meaningful stare swept by its blithe recipient.

With single-minded enjoyment, her nephew swung them toward the door. "No fear, dear aunt, we will be ready and waiting to take you home whenever you require, won't we, Jenny?"

Jennifer heard this exchange with some bewilderment, but before she could reply, Clare interrupted.

"And that doesn't mean you can turn around and go back for the fireworks later; Jennifer is still too young to go about unchaperoned."

"What a suspicious mind you have, Aunt Clare," Stephen chided, guiding them to the carriage. "Jennifer is perfectly safe with me, and you know you won't want to leave before the firework show. Now be a good girl and get up there and stop your worrying."

He nearly lifted Clare into the brougham, then turned to Jennifer with a sly wink, swinging her up in the same manner. She was inside before she could protest and got even with him by sitting next to Clare. He accepted his fate with aplomb, and the ride continued without further incident.

The night air was warm as they strolled into the eddying crowd entering the ballroom, their voices deadened by the immensity of the sparkling heavens above. It wasn't until they were washed up like waves upon the shore into the glittering cavern of the ballroom that the sea of humanity broke into individually colored particles, the older, slower ones forming small clusters along walls and halls, the younger ones traveling onward into the dance floor to be swept away in the vortex of music and swirling couples.

With meticulous care, Stephen located a seat and a table
for Clare, leaving Jennifer to keep her company while he
sought refreshments. He was soon lost in the still eddying
currents, and Jennifer tried to reduce the panorama of
color into recognizable portions by picking out familiar
faces and attempting to identify them. The flood of motion
and the pervasive gaiety of the orchestra served only to
sweep them all together again. The dancers swung about
the room with the swirling tempo, and Jennifer cringed
inwardly at the thought of being caught up in this wave
of movement, afraid she would sink like a stone to the
embarrassment of all.

Clare's words cut abruptly into her thoughts. "I suppose
you were at least old enough to have attended a coming
out party or two before you married Marcus, weren't you?"

With surprise, Jennifer shifted her thoughts to this new
attack, replying with only a little hesitation. "No, it was a
small town, and we seldom had social affairs, never anything as grand as this." Perhaps she should add her parents
didn't approve of dancing. That would excuse her from
any attempts to coerce her to join this tumult, but she was
reluctant to reveal any more than necessary.

Clare nodded her head and returned to silence. She
had already formed an opinion on the circumstances of
this marriage. Knowing her son too well to believe that he
was in love with his young bride, she decided there were
only two other possibilities. One was that he married for
wealth or other advantages, and it was obvious from the
start that this was not the case. Although she found it hard
to believe the alternative, the presence of Stuart practically
confirmed it. Marc's amorous adventures had gone one
step too far when he chose an unmarried child for his
attentions. She would like to meet the father that had
forced an unwelcome marriage on her arrogant and headstrong son; no wonder the air practically crackled with tension whenever these two came together. The Armstrongs
certainly weren't fated for happy marriages.

Clare's gloomy thoughts were interrupted by the return

of Stephen and the almost simultaneous arrival of Cameron and Darlene. Clare watched with approval as the two girls admired each other's gowns and the men lavished them with flowery compliments. Jennifer's tall, slender figure compared well with Darlene's less elegant, stouter shape. The gown Jennifer had chosen was daring in its simplicity, its main adornment being ivory shoulders crowned by the glitter of copper curls, whereas Darlene had to resort to girlish ruffles and bows. As fond as Clare was of the O'Hara offspring, she was forced to admit Marc's country bride showed better breeding.

Jennifer sensed none of these thoughts. Her mind was fully occupied by the predicament Marcus had placed her in by sending her off under the dubious protection of his light-headed cousin. She had assumed she would be allowed to sit quietly in Clare's company for the evening, but both Stephen and Cameron were making it plain they would allow no such peace. Only Darlene's presence prevented an open argument over the first dance. To be polite, Stephen was forced to offer his arm to Cameron's sister, leaving Cameron to triumphantly claim the dance.

As she watched Stephen walk off, deserting her, Jennifer attempted to disentangle herself from Cameron's victorious hold. "I'd really rather not, Cameron. I only came to watch and keep Clare company . . ."

"Nonsense. Here comes my father now, that is all the company anyone needs. Correct, Mamita?" he asked teasingly, using his pet name for the formidable Clare.

Clare sniffed and gave him a disparaging frown. "Remove the young pup from my presence, Jennifer."

The royal command was all Cameron needed, and with a gloating laugh, he swept Jennifer into the swirl of dancers.

Laughing green eyes met Jennifer's hesitant ones as his arm encircled her waist and his hand caught hers. "What do you fear, *chiquita*?"

Jennifer didn't notice the shadow behind those eyes as he asked. Her thoughts were more of the last time she had been held like this; Marcus, and not Cameron, was where her fear lay. She shook off the mood and attempted to reply gaily.

"I fear trampling your feet, Mr. O'Hara. I have little experience with this dance."

Easily, he waltzed her into the throng of dancers. "I find it hard to believe that dastardly husband of yours does not take every opportunity to escort such loveliness around the floor. Where is the cad, may I be so bold as to ask?"

"It is business as usual for Marcus. He warned me business would take up much of his time, so I do not expect more," Jennifer explained hastily at Cameron's frown.

"That is overly generous of you, madam," he commented, before swinging her in a wide circle, seemingly absorbed in the intricate steps of the dance.

Jennifer tried to dispel the uneasiness his frown caused but could not. He had kept silent about the incident with Madelyn, but his attentiveness since then had been marked. Now he held her a little more closely than she felt proper, but the concern in his words and expression prevented her protesting. She could think of no way of correcting the picture of neglect Marcus had created in this man's mind.

With relief, she watched Stephen approach at the end of the dance, but Cameron noted it also, and whispered, "You will give me another dance, won't you? There is much I have to say to you, if I can only find the words."

Startled, Jennifer glanced at the serious wrinkle across his brow. She had not thought the idle Cameron capable of extended concern. This new aspect was a trifle frightening. What could he have to say to her?

Before she could do more than bow her head in acknowledgment of his request, Stephen claimed her hand and carried her off.

"What were you two looking so solemn about?" Stephen demanded, swinging into the long strides most natural to his height.

Jennifer felt almost giddy at the rhythmic grace of

Stephen's movement, but she followed him easily, enjoying
the freedom of his protection after the stilted uneasiness
of Cameron's. She smiled up into the familiar Armstrong
gray of his eyes.

"I was concentrating on avoiding his toes and I believe
Cameron was concentrating on avoiding Marcus. You
dance superbly, cousin."

Stephen laughed. "Jenny, you're outrageous! I feared
your argument with Marcus the other night would drive
you to something foolish, but it's we males who are being
the fools. Do you laugh at us behind our backs?"

"It's no fun to laugh at your backs," she replied impishly, then more soberly, she added, "How did you know
we fought?"

"Little innocent," Stephen scoffed. "If loud voices and
slamming doors didn't tell everything, Marc's black scowl
these last days would. When are you going to confide in
me, Jenny? My mother refuses to tell me anything, though
I have pleaded."

"If there is anything to tell, it would have to come from
Marcus. I am quite content to leave things as they are."
An outright lie, but a justified one, Jennifer hoped.

Stephen snorted in disbelief, but he relinquished her
hand at the end of the set with only a word of warning.

"Marcus has a distaste for all the O'Haras, in case you
have not noticed, Jenny. I don't know the reason, but I
would beware Cameron, if I were you. He has a bad reputation and Marcus would think the worst."

Jennifer wrinkled up her nose in dismissal of such
thoughts. "Cameron is Darlene's brother and a friend. He
always behaves a perfect gentleman, which is more than I
can say for some other people I know. Go have fun and
do not worry about me."

Stephen grinned and left her in Clare's company. Michael O'Hara offered his arm for a dance since Clare could
not, but Jennifer refused him, preferring this chance to
rest and praying to be left alone.

It was not destined to be. Cameron was soon at her side

again, and when a fast reel began, she gave in to his persistence, figuring there was no harm in such a melee.

But it was not so easy to escape him once he had her on the dance floor, and when the next waltz began, she found herself being swept into the swirl of dancers once more.

"Mr. O'Hara, surely there must be some other women in this room to catch your eye. Might I prevail upon you to find them?" she asked, a trifle acerbically.

"I should think we are sufficiently acquainted for you to call me Cameron, don't you? I didn't figure you for the pompous sort," he taunted, ignoring her question.

"You may call me any name you wish, Mr. O'Hara, but it is not proper for a single man to escort a married woman on the dance floor so frequently."

"Then I will call you Jenny." A lazy grin spread across his features at her expression. "And if you are so concerned about our appearance on the dance floor, I will gladly escort you to a more private nook. I told you I wished to talk with you."

"There can be nothing of which we need to talk and a private nook is the last place I would follow you. You have a reputation, sir." She said it teasingly, but the fiery flame of his eyes caught her by surprise. He pulled her closer, and she did not protest.

"I am not the only one. That is why I must talk with you. You need never fear me, Jenny, you must know that."

He seemed so sincere, and the look in his eyes was one of concern. Jennifer moved nervously in his arms, uncertain where his words led. Marcus would be furious . . . But what matter was that? Marcus disapproved of everything she did, everything she was. If she were to be her own woman, she must do it without thought to what Marcus would say. What harm could there be in a moment's conversation in a public room?

"I do not fear you, Cameron, I fear Marcus. He will be very angry if I spend too much time with you. Can you not talk to me in Darlene's presence?"

"I would, if you were free to hear my words, but you are not."

The message in his voice and eyes was clear, the gentle pressure of his hand upon her back that of a lover and not an acquaintance. Startled at this sudden change in character, Jennifer searched his face for understanding.

"I am going too swiftly for you, I know, but time is my enemy. You have bewitched me ever since I first lay eyes on you, my charming Jenny, but I thought you happily married and kept my distance. Now I have heard differently, and I cannot keep my hopes from rising. Even if it were not for that, I must let you know what is being said. I want to protect you, Jennifer, will you let me?" His voice was caressing, his hand a gentle persuasion as they guided her around the floor.

Jennifer shook her head in bewilderment. The dance ended, and she found herself following him off the dance floor, away from Clare's protection. A cup of punch miraculously appeared in her hands, and she accepted Cameron's offer of a seat in a small alcove. Events were happening too fast and she felt her head swimming. She sipped at the punch as Cameron's lithe frame usurped the place beside her.

"I wish there were some easy way to begin, some way to ease the pain, some way to make you see my arms are open to you no matter what happens, and that you need look no farther." He claimed her hand and an emerald gaze caressed her in a manner she had longed to find in eyes of a different hue.

Confusion was the only emotion Jennifer registered. "Cameron, I truly believe you have taken leave of your senses. What are you trying to say?" She attempted to ease the stiffness his words had placed between them.

A bitter smile touched his lips. "I am trying to say I love you and Marcus does not, but you already know that, don't you?"

Jennifer's hands trembled as she lowered her cup from her lips. "What does love have to do with the way the world

goes around?" she asked abstractedly. What did he know
of Marcus and herself that he could dare say these things?
She wasn't certain that she wished to know.

"Ahhh, Jenny, you are not such a hard case as that. I
was in St. Louis when I heard the mighty Marcus Armstrong had been forced to wed practically at gunpoint. I
thought it humorous, then, but not since I've met you. It's
not funny any longer. I've watched you carefully. There is
no love lost between you. You fear him, I suspect, and
rightly so. He's a dangerous man, Jennifer. He'll do anything to get what he wants. At the moment, it pleases him
to hide behind the protection of the married state. He
cannot be forced to wed again if his dalliances come to
light, but what happens when he tires of this charade? You
must plan for the future, Jennifer, as I am."

He took the empty cup from her hand and set it aside,
capturing both her hands with his as he pled his case.

Jennifer shivered with a chill of apprehension at the way
her worst fears were placed before her in someone else's
words. She had never thought to classify Marcus as dangerous to herself, but that he was a dangerous man was a
certainty. She could not erase the sight of those steely eyes
the day of their marriage. He would have killed that day
if there had been any way of escaping justice.

What could she say? He spoke of Marc's dalliances as if
they were many. The thought was painful to her. Had he
gone from her bed to another woman's arms? Their marriage would soon become the talk of the town and she, an
object of ridicule and pity; that was what Cameron was
telling her. The pain was so great she could concentrate
on nothing else. Cameron's warm concern meant nothing.
Only Marcus could do this to her. Only Marcus was capable
of turning her entire world upside down over and over
again until she knew not where she stood. She hated him.
She hated his ability to do this to her. She hated him for
the hold he had over her.

In a seething turmoil, Jennifer rose, unseeing, uncaring,
incapable of rational thought. Without a word, she walked

out on the dance floor and held her hand out for Cameron to take. The music carried her away and she followed its call. It was so much easier to flow on the currents of sound and pretend the world did not exist. Almost as good as immersing herself in the river and letting it carry her where it would.

Cameron took what advantage he could of this non-reply. He had expected anything from tears to passionate kisses at his declaration, but this withdrawn state of no reaction at all left him confounded. Holding his executioner's wife as close as he could, he spun her around the dance floor until whispers started to flow and knowing smirks began to appear. If he accomplished nothing else, he confirmed their reputations.

Stephen's unusually stern look as he advanced through the crowd served as warning that this act would shortly end. Taking a chance, Cameron whirled around the dance floor to the curtains draping the French doors to the terrace, and whisked Jennifer out into the night. Kidnapping was not the word he would have used for what he had in mind, but he knew two men who would pay well for Jennifer's return. And when they knew they were bidding against each other, the stakes would get high, indeed. Harm was not his intention, but the thought of bleeding Marcus dry was most pleasant.

Jennifer looked up, startled to find herself in the cool night air away from the heat of the crowd. She shivered, wishing for the protection of her shawl.

"Cameron, I will catch a chill out here. I need to fetch my shawl."

No words of protest, only a plaintive chiding. Cameron smiled at the ease with which this would be carried off. Under the clear night skies with the stars within an arm's grasp, she was more beautiful than he had dared notice. Tendrils of damp auburn hair fell down about her temples, and her skin was smooth and nearly translucent in the moonlight. A tempting morsel, indeed. He could easily understand why she might drive some men to madness.

Though his jaded tastes required more than innocence for his pleasure, she might provide an interesting interlude until her bidders came to terms.

"I will keep you warm, my dear. Come here, and let me show you."

His voice was silky, his eyes, a lambent flame, but Jennifer took no notice. She wandered to the terrace edge, looking out over the parapet to the bay far below.

"It is so beautiful," she whispered, staring out into the fairy tale of lights she had seen that first night with Marcus on the steamer. A man's arm circled her now, too, but it was not the same man, and there was no shared feeling of emotion. She remained cold in his embrace, though his hand assumed an intimacy it had no right to possess.

"Jenny, I love you as Marcus cannot. Let me take you away from this. I will protect you and make you happy. You can have anything you wish. Just say you'll be mine."

Words that she had longed to hear. Words that she lay awake nights imagining. How many times had she waited, listening, for the man who would speak these words to her? As far back as that hot July night when she had swum restlessly in the river, wishing for another life, another world. And now here it was, all she had ever dreamed— love, a handsome man, wealth, travel, anything she desired. But it was the wrong man, the wrong love, and all that he promised was meaningless.

She felt no surprise when Cameron took her in his arms. She felt nothing as their lips met and his played warmly over hers. He pulled her to him, held her tightly, caressed her back and whispered sweet words against her ear as his kisses streamed across her cheek and down her throat.

And then the night exploded in a whirlwind of events that Jennifer could never quite piece together later. Cameron was ripped from her side and tossed like a piece of flotsam against the stone parapet. As he pushed himself up from the flagstone terrace, a large, menacing shape loomed beside Jennifer, and she stifled a scream as she was shoved carelessly aside.

"Marcus!" The sound emerged as a terrified whisper as she caught sight of the chilling gray warning in his eyes. But they rested only momentarily on her, turning back to the trespasser who now stood shakily on his feet.

"You were warned, O'Hara. I'm almost glad you ignored me. It gives me a chance to do what I've been dying to do for some time."

Cornered against the parapet, Cameron had no choice but to throw himself forward, hoping to catch the larger man by surprise and so make his escape. Marcus neatly sidestepped this maneuver, caught the culprit by the shirt collar, and with the force of his entire body behind the blow, brought his fist up against Cameron's jaw.

The lighter man sailed backwards, stumbled on the low parapet, and tumbled over the edge.

The smack of bone against bone joined with Jennifer's terrified scream, both drowning in the explosion of a trial skyrocket bursting into a thousand tiny pinwheels over the bay far below. A devilish glare lit the terrace as Marcus jerked Jennifer against him, crushing her to his chest, his arms wrapping tightly about her back and waist to prevent her struggles.

Impervious to furious fists pounding at his arms and shoulders, bending her backward enough to unbalance her, Marcus drew Jennifer's slim hips against his as she grasped at him for support. His mouth sought hers, hard lips bruising the tender ones beneath until he felt their first involuntary quiver. He pressured them furiously until they parted with a soft sigh, allowing him full access as she gave in to his embrace. Her body curved against the length of his while her arms hugged him tightly, her lips drawing him deeper with their passion.

The bliss of surrender was cut off abruptly with the explosion of a million colored stars against the background of a purple sky. The crowd spilled out of the doorway and onto the terrace, breaking into cheering applause, and awakening the entwined couple to their exposed position. With masterful composure, Marcus held Jennifer's waist, stepping back from the railing to allow the crowd to surge around them.

Marcus and Jennifer stood silently in the dark crowd, watching the glittering display of showering sparks light the heavens, totally aware of every point their bodies touched and every breath the other took. Hemmed in and crushed together by the throng of people, they were forced into acute consciousness of the passions their kiss had aroused.

Every new explosion of light brought a rippling moan of pleasure whispering through the crowd. With Marc's hand stroking the bodice at her waist, sliding provocatively back and forth, climbing higher until it lingered beneath her breasts, then teasing the undersides with exploring fingers, Jennifer's breath exploded from her lungs with a sound duplicating the moans about her. With just the touch of his hand he sent her blood racing, sent shivers of desire through every fiber of her being, and she was helpless to resist; it was a fact of life she would never understand.

Throughout the firework display he held her captive, pressing her bottom against the hardness of his thighs, his fingers playing a sensuous tune against her skin as they dipped and circled the exposed flesh of her breasts. As his hand slid beneath the low bodice to play with a sensitive crest, Jennifer groaned at the intimate touch, melting against him as the aching need opened between her thighs, and hot tears edged her lashes. He was toying with her as if she were some plaything, and she was dying inside with this hunger for his touch. It wasn't fair that he could remain so detached when she could not.

As the display diminished and the sounds of the orchestra drifted through the open doors, the crowd began to thin, making movement possible again. Clasping Jennifer's waist with an iron hand, Marcus steered her trembling figure back into the brilliant light of the ballroom.

"Before we go, we will complete this part of our performance here and leave no doubt in anyone's mind that we are not only married, but lovers. Do you understand?" His voice was grim as he led her relentlessly toward the dance floor.

Slapped by this unwarranted coldness, Jennifer tried to hold back, but it was a wasted struggle against his strength. "No, I don't understand. I want to see if Cameron is all right, you could have killed him! I think you are insane, let go of me!" Her voice rose with angry hysteria. Had everything that happened on the terrace been a performance then? Even the furious hunger of his kiss? She fought against his grip, but she was still weak from the desire his touch aroused in her, and Marcus—curse him— seemed to be in complete control of himself.

"I could have killed him, but I didn't, be satisfied with that. Now we are going out there to rectify the impression the two of you created earlier, and you will not argue with me further."

Pierced by the steel of her husband's eyes, Jennifer allowed herself to be drawn once more into his embrace as they swung onto the dance floor, joining the other couples in a graceful swirl of skirts and feet. But this time there was a startling difference in the manner in which the elegant dance was executed, and it wasn't just in the fact that she had no need to adjust to her husband's movements. They moved easily together, sweeping into the mood of the music with their first steps, but the difference didn't end there. Gone was the respectful distance Stephen had held between them, that had been enforced by the bulge of her pregnancy when last she danced with Marcus. He held her now in tight embrace that rendered her powerless. She could feel every movement of his hips as they circled the floor, her breasts brushing against the front of his coat, his arm circling her waist while his hand teased the satin beneath her breasts, reminding her of its earlier possession. With his breath ruffling her hair and whispering in her ear, they moved fluidly as if with one body, joined together in rhythmic embrace, completely unaware that there was another soul in the room, the music enfold-

ing them in its magic and carrying them away to places
they had never been.

She was his puppet; all he had to do was move his hand,
and she would respond. Jennifer wondered if he were
aware of this, could not see how he could possibly doubt
it, and shuddered at the advantage such knowledge gave
him. If he could use her like this, here, on a public dance
floor, what would keep him from trespassing farther in
private? And she shuddered with the incipient passion this
thought loosed in her.

As the music died, Jennifer found Stephen's knowing
eye on them and blushed deeply when he gave her a cheerful wink, shaking his head with a grin and disappearing
into the crowd. It was more than she could bear, and once
more she tried to pull away from Marc's iron grip.

"Why are you doing this to me?" she cried in frustration
as he pulled her even closer.

Muscles tightened over planed cheeks, Marc's mouth set
obstinately. "Can't you imagine? It wasn't enough for tales
of our marriage to cause snickers behind closed doors in
St. Louis, or our sleeping arrangements to start gossip
among family and servants, but now you must flaunt your
availability in public for all the world to see. I have worked
too hard and given up too much to be made cuckold of
in public or to have Stuart's legitimacy questioned. And if
you raise that hand to slap me, you will regret it forever
after." This last was spoken softly as Marcus caught her
wrist before Jennifer could raise it. "For tonight, we are
lovers, and you will play the part accordingly."

The turmoil his words raised in her had need of some
vent, but he had cut off all avenues but one, and Jennifer
would not be reduced to tears for him or anyone. It wasn't
just anger that seethed in her, but a confusion of emotions
that she would be hard put to describe. The injustice of
his charges, the embarrassment of her position, the mention of her son, the pressure of Marc's arm around her,
and the dizzying pleasures of their dance left her groping

for an adequate response and coming to the conclusion
there was none.

As the music slowly filled the room again, Marcus drew
her back into place, his eyes never leaving hers as their
bodies touched. They were locked into each other's gaze
and arms, the music carrying them off without their will
or knowledge. The flash of a flower green stem topped by
a dark red blossom, held by the tall man in black became
a vision to be watched as they swirled in and out among
the other dancers, oblivious to the world at large. And the
watchers nodded their heads with knowing smiles, remi-
niscing with one another on what it was like to be young
and in love.

Afterwards, Jennifer could never remember having
touched the floor. It was as if they had left time and space
behind while they explored the universe in one another's
arms, only the music holding a tenuous connection between them and earth. When the music stopped, they
floated slowly to earth again, and she found herself looking
up into smoky blue-gray eyes once more. Captured by the
smoldering stare, she lingered in his embrace, aware of
the pressure of his thigh and the rough texture of his coat
against her skin. In disappointment, she watched the gray
glaze over again, and he stepped away from her, catching
her elbow in a cruel grip to lead her from the floor.

"I think it's time we bring the curtain down on this performance and bring it up on the next act. We now have
to convince the family and servants we are a happily married couple."

"And if I refuse?"

His grip tightened as Marcus swung her around to face
him, the blunt cut of his sideburns framing the hollows of
his cheeks as the muscle stretched over them. "Our contract specifies your performance of loving wife in public.
If you break your end of the bargain, I will feel free to
break mine."

Light played across coppery curls and struck a fire in
almond eyes, curving full lips upward with a strange twist

as Jennifer murmured a dazed but vaguely speculative, "Oh."

Marcus gave her a grim look of suspicion. "We can discuss renegotiation later." With controlled fury, he returned her to Clare's corner of the room where they were awaited with angry impatience.

"Good God, Marcus, are you possessed with some need to scandalize society wherever you go? I demand to be taken home at once." Clare stood with the help of Michael O'Hara, his grin of sympathy to the young couple not affecting the solicitousness with which he treated the angry beauty on his arm.

"If you two would care to stay longer, I would be happy to see your mother home, Marcus." The older man's look was that of mutual understanding.

"Thank you, but I think you'd best look to your son. He should be somewhere in the bushes below." Marcus ignored the older man's sudden change of expression, covered Jennifer's bare shoulders with her shawl, and determinedly guided his infuriated mother toward the door.

Outside, their carriage was waiting for them, and as they walked down the steps, a familiar figure uncurled from his lounging position against the carriage side.

"Thought you might be about ready to leave."

Marcus made no acknowledgment of his cousin's foresight, but simply handed the two silent women into the carriage. With a quick glance at Marc's frozen jaw, Stephen clambered in after them, and the interior grew stiff with unspoken words as Marc took his seat, slamming the door as a signal for the carriage to roll on.

"I suppose some explanation of your behavior is not necessary?" Clare's strident words cut the air.

"It's not," Marcus replied calmly.

His hard thigh pressed intimately against Jennifer's, and his hand held hers with a bruising grip she could not escape. Trembling, she dared not speak, but stared out the empty window.

"Did you tell Jenny how you managed to return so early?"

Stephen's attempt to lighten the mood was lost in the concern his tone scarcely concealed. Jennifer stiffened as Marc's arm circled her shoulders, but she gave no other recognition to the question raised.

Just as if she had responded with curiosity, Marcus answered, "I found other transportation which I may sorely regret come morning." His finger bit into her shoulders as he stretched his long legs in the confinement of the cab, reminding her of the role she was meant to play.

Stiffly, Jennifer spoke her part. "Other transportation?"

Stephen snorted derisively. "Being from Kentucky, I should have thought you'd be aware of his prowess with horses. The devil must have come down the mountain on horseback. Rather unsporting, I must say."

"I saw an opportunity to keep my promise and took it. It never occurred to me that my return would be a disappointment to anybody."

With masterful control, Jennifer placed a hand on his leg, forcing herself not to flinch when the tension in the muscle under her hand tightened with her caress. "I would rather you broke your promise than your neck. It was foolhardy to attempt riding down a mountain on horseback at night." She almost meant it. She was playing a part for the benefit of others, just as he, but the awful part was that she meant it, and he did not.

"It was well worth the ride, my dear," Marcus nuzzled lightly at her neck, his hand coming up to cup her breast.

A polite cough and a sharp, incensed intake of breath from across the carriage reminded them there were others present.

"For God's sake, Marcus, you're behaving like a lovesick adolescent tonight. At least have the decency to wait until you're in the privacy of your bedroom before claiming your reward for your misbegotten zeal." Clare's dry sarcasm brought a wry smile to Stephen's lips.

"I apologize, Jenny, if I underestimated the situation

after all. It should be interesting to count the months until
Stuart has a brother."

A warning squeeze cut off Jennifer's sharp retort, and
Marcus replied with surprising amiability, "Sister. We've
already decided the next one will be a girl."

Any further protests or surprises were cut off by the
brougham's arrival at its destination. Marcus jumped out
to assist the women in their descent, aborting any further
effort at conversation.

Lucia had heard the carriage arrive and waited in the
vain hope that Jennifer would tell her about the evening.
One look at Marcus' expression as they came through the
door told her there would be no gossip session that night,
and if she read the signs right, perhaps none in the morning. With a hopeful curve to her lips, she awaited her orders, noticing Jennifer deferred to her husband with
almost an air of docility. That, in itself, was a hopeful sign
that things had returned to the way they should be.

"Jennifer won't be needing you this evening, Lucia.
Thank you for watching after Stuart for us, and sleep late
in the morning, you need your rest as well as we." Marcus
dismissed the maid graciously; her quick curtsy not fast
enough to hide the covert smile on her face, and he guessed
he had made a convert of one of Jennifer's friends.

As the door closed behind them, Marcus released Jennifer and strolled across to the cradle, loosening his tie
and throwing his coat over a nearby chair. The sight of
dark curls and the infant's awkward sleeping position
made him smile as he turned to throw his cravat over his
jacket, finding Jennifer still standing where he left her. His
smile quickly turned to a frown.

"What are you waiting for? There is the wash room, I
grant you first turn. Do you need help with the gown?"

Stunned at his evident intent to remain, Jennifer responded angrily. "Hasn't this farce gone on long enough?
Did I not play the part of loving wife well enough for your
tastes? What more do you want of me?"

Her voice rose to a near-hysterical pitch, but she could

not prevent it. She hated this arrogant, demanding beast who held the strings to every aspect of her life: heart, body, and soul. She only wanted his quick departure so she might begin the task of picking up the shattered pieces this night had left behind.

But the destruction was not yet over. Marcus advanced on her threateningly. "Your loyalty would be nice. Your obedience, a little too much to expect, I suppose. I thought if there was nothing else between us, I could always count on your discretion, but it seems even that is too much for you to pay. Have I entirely misplaced my trust, then?"

Shocked at the intensity of his bitterness, Jennifer took a step backward. A mistake, as she quickly learned. Marcus grabbed her arm and jerked her against him.

"You showed no fear of Cameron's embrace earlier. You never flinch at Stephen's touch. Why is it my closeness that sends you into trembling fear? Guilt, perhaps?"

His grip was harsh, forcing her into contact with his hard length, much as it had on the dance floor. Only now, they were not in the safety of numbers, and the bed lay only a few feet away. The tension in the muscle of his jaw, the angry tic at the corner of his mouth, and the steely coldness of his eyes warned Jennifer of her danger, and her own anger fled on the heels of fear.

"Let me go, Marcus. You're hurting me." She could not think when he held her like that, and she must think clearly if she were to answer his charges. There was a pain and bitterness in his voice that her heart responded to, but she would not let him manipulate her so easily.

"It is not the first time I've caused you pain, is it?" He threw down her arm and retreated a safe distance across the room. "But does that give you some reason to continually stab at me and draw as much blood as your puny weapons will allow?"

"What do you know of pain?" Jennifer asked incredulously. "Your heart is as cold and hard as an anvil! You play the part of a free man, dally with whomsoever you wish, and come home to expect me to welcome you with open arms, though I have made it more than clear I detest what you have done to me. And when some other man dares to treat me as something more than an idle bauble to decorate your bed, you behave as if I am the guilty party! No good can ever come of this arrangement. Let me return to St. Louis."

Her own words surprised her. They were no less of a shock to Marcus. The grim line of his thin lips set harder.

"Go, but it will be without Stuart."

The sudden tense silence between them billowed, causing Jennifer's heart to thump. Even the icy granite of his carved features could not hide the ghastliness lurking behind Marc's eyes. Jennifer stared at him in pain and bewilderment and hatred. What had happened to the laughing riverboat captain? Had something killed the gentle man beneath the hard facade, the man she loved?

Loved! The word hit her with the force of a summer's storm, tearing up all the remaining pieces of her beliefs and tossing them like leaves in the wind, blowing them away, never to be seen again. It was impossible to believe she loved this man who so coldly suggested she get out of his life but leave her son behind. Yet even while denying the possibility, her heart trembled with the recognition awakened that long ago day at the river.

"Never, Marcus." The quiet words broke the silence more forcefully than any amount of angry ones. "You may lead me to the mouth of hell, but you will never separate me from my son."

Was it her imagination, or did she see some flicker of relief lighten that steely gaze? Whatever it was, it was gone in a second, and that same cold voice answered her.

"Then you will stay with me, because I have no intention of losing what I have given up so much to keep. If such is the case, then I suggest you wash as I asked earlier. The farce, as you call it, is not ended."

His tone was chilling. Did this mean he considered their contract terminated? The thought blew like a cold wind through her. Whatever her own feelings, she knew he held no love for her, and she would not be taken like this—coldly, and in anger.

"What more is needed, Marcus? Did I not perform well enough? There is no one to watch the performance here. Let me alone, Marcus."

Marcus moved toward her again. "We have yet the servants and the remainder of the household to convince. All we have done so far will be for naught unless it is known we sleep together tonight."

"How will they know what we do behind closed doors?" Jennifer inched away, avoiding the trap of the bed as he drew closer.

"You still have not learned what it is like to live with servants, have you? Did your mother also protect you from all knowledge of what went on in the rooms above you in the inn? Did you ever notice which rooms were claimed but never slept in? Or which rooms were claimed by men but reeked of a woman's perfume in the morning? The servants know everything that goes on in this house, my dear. They know we never sleep together, just as they know where I spend my evenings and who comes to call on you. They even know what you buy when you go out. Where is the watch fob you bought the day you went out with Cameron?"

At Jennifer's startled reaction, he smiled bitterly, then followed her gaze to the dresser and opened it. The jeweler's case lay just below the folded nightgowns and he found it easily. He examined the jeweler's label on the inside.

"That is not a shop you frequented before, is it? Who told you of it? Cameron?" He didn't even wait for her reply. Lifting the fob, he dangled it carefully between his fingers, watching Jennifer's expression. "You saw me with Madelyn, didn't you? If you had been just a little bit later, you would have seen me in this jeweler's with Madelyn, helping her choose some bauble she insisted she could not decide upon herself. Does that bother you?"

Jennifer could read nothing into his expression. After

that day, she had been unable to give him the gift she had so lovingly selected for him. Now it dangled derisively between his fingers and she could not speak the words of truth to clear herself. He would never believe them.

"There is nothing in our contract that specifies your faithfulness. I never expected it. But I cannot be another one of your Madelyns. That is all I have ever asked of you, leave me to myself, Marcus."

"You do have tendency for the practical, don't you?" Marcus commented sarcastically. "It does not bother you, then, to use my money to buy gifts for your lovers? Why did you not give it to him then? Didn't he earn his reward for showing you how I spend my time?"

Instead of being angry, Jennifer felt a heavy weariness steal over her, and exhausted, she leaned against the massive wardrobe. "You have made up your mind already, Marcus. What good is it for me to protest? Just tell me what you expect of me. I did not wish to go to the dance tonight with Stephen, but you deserted me. I did not wish to dance with anyone, but Clare insisted. I have no need of these fancy gowns or jewels you decorate me in, but you demand it. I am allowed no decisions on my own, no life of my own, and now I see I do not even have the privacy of my own actions. All I have ever asked is that I be left alone, and you cannot even abide by that request. What is it you wish me to say?"

The interrogation was over. The answers no longer mattered. Gently, Marcus replaced the jeweler's box and closed the drawer. Jennifer's wilted figure was a remonstration he could no longer ignore.

"You are tired and this discussion is fruitless. Come here, and I will unfasten your gown."

He left her no choice. Whatever he decided her punishment should be for these imagined wrongs, she was in no position to argue. She presented her back to him for unfastening.

As drained as she was, his nearness still had the ability to excite her, and the touch of his fingers against her skin returned the sensations they had created earlier. Prickles of gooseflesh ran up and down her spine as he slowly worked the fastenings down to her waist, but he did no more than release her when he was done.

By the time Marcus had finished his turn washing, Jennifer had donned her most modest nightgown—not an easy task since Marcus had purchased the majority of them and only a winter one offered any semblance of modesty. The long sleeves of the heavy lawn gown were an irritation in the warmth of a July evening, but the deep "V" formed by the Grecian wrap of the bodice was an even greater irritation since it made moving difficult without exposing a good deal more of her breasts than she was prepared to reveal. She lay still under the sheets and prayed the dimmed lights would not expose her.

But Jennifer quickly forgot her own nakedness in the sight of his. Stripped to the waist, Marcus came from the wash room, his broad chest well furred with a mat of dark hair that narrowed over a firmly muscled waistline. Her eyes riveted on the width of his tanned shoulders, the strength of rippling muscles well apparent as he reached to lower the gas lamp, and the memory of the time she had held him like that crept like a lingering soreness into her thoughts.

When it became apparent he had no intention of respecting her modesty, Jennifer tried to look away, but she could not keep her fascinated gaze from following the narrowing mat of hair to the point where it crept below his belt. In their few brief encounters, she had scarcely been given the opportunity to observe the masculine figure in its entirety, and her curiosity overcame sensibility.

Amusement flickered behind his masked expression as Marcus noted the path of her gaze, but he made no pretense of preserving decorum. His trousers joined the rest of his clothes over the chair back and he entered the bed wearing just his masculine splendor.

The bed sunk beneath his weight, creating a hollow Jennifer had to fight to avoid. Acute awareness of his naked warmth fanned the flames already ignited by the sight of his awakening ardor.

"Is this entirely necessary? Lucia is scarcely going to regale the kitchen with what we wear to bed," she asked sarcastically, covering her immodest thoughts.

"The last time I wore anything to bed was when I entertained a very pregnant young lady in my cabin and thought it necessary to preserve her sensibility. That is hardly the case any longer, is it?"

"Thanks to you," Jennifer answered angrily. Their earlier words prevented any easing of the tension between them; too much pain had scarred her heart to take him lightly.

Marcus shifted to his side, propping himself on one arm to lean over her. "Why argue who is at fault? Why fault me when I seek that same comfort again?" As Jennifer opened her mouth to protest, he covered her lips with his hand. "We cannot agree on anything when we speak, but I think you will not protest long once we stop."

He pushed back the sheet to better gaze on the carved perfection of the form beneath him. Auburn tresses trailed across satin shoulders and the frothy white of her gown, providing accents of color against the ivory of her skin. He drew in a breath at the sight revealed, but the rebellious set of Jennifer's jaw told him surrender would not come easily. He had wished her to come willingly to him again, but he was too far gone to stop now.

Swiftly, Marcus pinned her arms to the bed while his mouth swooped hungrily to cover hers. Their brief kiss of earlier had only whetted his appetite for more, and his simmering anger prevented any regard to the niceties.

The suddenness of his kiss left Jennifer stunned. She strained against the confining strength of his hold, shaking her head back and forth to avoid the paralysis of his kiss. He caught his hand in her hair, forcing her to stillness while his lips ravaged the length of her cheeks and her throat, driving her to a frenzy of longing that she fought

with all the strength she possessed. She would not let him
win again.

When his lips finally rested against hers, she clenched
her teeth and prevented his invasion. In retaliation, he
released her hair and slid his fingers beneath the neckline
of her gown. Jennifer gasped as he filled his hands with
her flesh. She strained to catch his head and hold it back
as he bent to taste what he'd uncovered, but his left hand
still pinned her wrists to the bed.

With deliberate slowness, he suckled her breasts, teasing
them to a tautness that betrayed her weakness. Jennifer's
whimpers of protest mixed with sighs of pleasure, but still
she fought him when his lips returned to hers. Cursing,
he plied her mouth with urgent messages, until his persistence finally decimated her restraint. Jennifer shook her
head, feebly fighting against this rape of his tongue, fighting her own weakening response as she felt her body go
limp beneath his.

His hard body spanned the length of her, bringing her
to sudden awareness of the extent of his desire, and another
rapidly developing problem. While his tongue invaded the
confines of her lips, the boldness of his manhood probed
at the aching emptiness between her thighs, tempting her
with the need for his filling thrust. She kept her legs tightly
closed, but she sensed he had no intention of letting her
win this battle. He was enjoying the struggle too much.

Feeling her weakening restraint, he released her hands
to better hold her hips, but Jennifer twisted away, striving
for the edge of the bed.

Marcus allowed her to move away, but held her waist to
prevent her escaping entirely.

Jennifer tugged at her gown, but there was no protection
from the hard arm holding her firmly in place. With controlled fury, she jerked the sheet back over her breasts and
turned to face him.

"You are no better than Delaney! Do you think me truly
your whore because you can take me as you will?"

"Jennifer, I . . ." Marcus moved to caress her cheek, but she slapped him away.

"Don't touch me again! Don't ever touch me again! So help me, Marcus, if you ever do this again you will have to bind and gag me to keep me and my son here."

Their gazes met and clashed. Marc's fingers bit into her waist as he searched her face, and then with a vicious curse, he jerked his hand away. Coldness invaded her where his warmth had been, but Jennifer remained defiant.

Silence reigned as they lay stiffly apart, gathering their defenses for renewed attack. It was Marcus who broke the quiet, muttering bitterly, "You use your weapons well. What will it take to convince you there is no sin in enjoying what is between us?"

Jennifer closed her eyes and breathed deeply, trying to ignore the fires left by his fingers still burning on her skin. "The sin is in your using me for whore. You do not even *like* me, Marcus, you hold no respect for me, you have just told me so. I am merely a nuisance you find convenient to appease your appetites. I do not wish to be taken in that way."

Woodenly, Marcus asked, "Were you planning on remaining a virgin all your life?" Then musingly, he answered himself, "I think not. You respond too readily to my caresses to call yourself satisfied with a virtuous life. There can only be one thing a romantic eighteen-year-old would hold out for in exchange for her body and that is Love, with a capital L." He sighed, "It's my own fault for getting mixed up with the last of the world's moral women." His tone was no longer bitter, but resigned.

"You act as if I'm asking too much to expect love in a life that has so far been dismal and bleak. Your riches do not make me any happier than my poverty did before." Jennifer pulled the sheet tightly around her, turning on her side to admire his profile, fighting the continuing urge to touch. The anger had gone out of them, leaving only the lingering sadness of their harsh words.

"Nor will love necessarily bring you happiness, but I suppose you have the right to demand it," Marcus replied wearily. "With all your beauty, charm, and intelligence, it would be unfair to expect less. Unfortunately, it is the one thing I cannot give you, though I would treat you better and with more respect than any dozen lovers you might find. Couldn't that be enough, Jenny?"

The coldness that came over her at Marc's words left her numb and weak; she was stunned by their impact, though she had no right to be. Had she really expected that he would love her? He had made it only too obvious he wouldn't—his fancy society women, his distaste for marriage, his avoidance of family life, that blasted contract— what other warnings could she ask for? Yet she was still left feeling cold and alone and surprised.

Haltingly, she replied, "I think I need some explanation first." Then, more hurriedly before he could guess the extent of her feelings, she added, "I never expected you to love me, we are far too different, and I can never be the sophisticated, obedient wife you need, although I've tried hard to please you. But am I that distasteful that you can swear you'll never have any love for me?" The hurt was all too evident, deeper than she had guessed and difficult to disguise.

Marcus unbent one arm from beneath his head to lean over and stroke the bridge of her nose. "Your active mind conjures up strange fancies, my little one. If anything, I would say we are far too much alike, pride and obstinacy being among those traits we have in common. If it is of any relief to you, I would not love that dutiful wife you would pair me with either."

"Then there is someone else already? Madelyn . . . ?"

Marcus gave her a look of disgust. "You fell for that, just like Cameron wanted you to do. Can you give me no credit at all? Madelyn is simply another in a long line of scheming women, just like her sister."

"That would be Melissa?" Jennifer grabbed at his explanation, hoping it was true, but wanting proof.

Marcus examined the innocent brown eyes staring back

at him and came to a sudden decision. If he could only make her understand . . . Perhaps there was hope somewhere for the burning fires raging inside him.

"You not only have an excellent memory, but an uncanny perception." He took a firm hold on her hand, feeling the fragility of small bones snuggled against his fingers. "Would you care to hear a sorry story? Perhaps it will put you to sleep and we can both get some rest."

Silently, Jennifer nodded acquiescence, watching his eyes as he spoke.

Marcus leaned back and stared at the blot of darkness above them, frowning as he searched for the missing threads of his thoughts, looking for their beginnings. He had never told the whole story to anyone, though several knew bits and pieces of it. Why he believed it would mean anything to this obstinate little fool was beyond his knowledge, but he wanted to do it and he would.

His words came haltingly, as if read from some ancient and unreadable parchment: "Once upon a time, when you were still a little girl in smocks, there was a young man who fell madly in love with a beautiful woman about the age you are now. His mother encouraged the match for the woman was not only beautiful, but wealthy and of a good family. The young man was old enough to know better, but he believed the woman returned his feelings, and confident there would be no objection to the match, he asked for her hand in marriage. The woman agreed, and in the way of young love, gave herself to him in full knowledge that they would soon be wed.

"Alas, when presented with these plans, the young man's father went into a terrible rage and forbade the marriage. Now the father was extremely wealthy and provided his son with a large allowance and a position in the family firm which he fully intended to turn over to his only son one day. So when the young man threatened to carry out his plans, his father threatened to disinherit him.

"This did not disturb the young man greatly, for being

young and foolish, he was confident of earning his own wealth with his young love beside him. Unfortunately, his love had other ideas. Upon learning of the father's action, the woman scorned the offer of marriage, and in great anguish, the young man set out to prove himself by making his own way in the world.

"But the country had just come through a long war, money was scarce, and after several months the young man still had more prospects than cash. Determined to try once more to win his love, he returned to friends and family and further disillusion.

"In his absence, the woman had quickly found and wed another man, a wealthy nobleman from across the seas, and they had left to return to his home. The woman left no word, but her married sister inadvertently gave him her final message: his love was with child at the time of her marriage, and he knew the child could only be his."

Jennifer clutched her husband's hand tightly, her heart torn with the depth of despair and anguish he must have suffered and that she could understand so well, but Marcus took no notice. The story wasn't over yet, and she waited patiently for him to continue as he stared absently in the direction of the ceiling. She understood now his insistence on not parting with Stuart regardless of the consequences; he had lost one child, he would not lose another. Marcus began to speak again, interrupting her thoughts.

"Just as the young man thought he would surely die of grief, word came that should certainly have killed him. The ship in which his love and her husband were sailing had gone down at sea, leaving no survivors. But before grief could take its final toll, he learned the full extent of his love's perfidy.

"Her father applied to mine for aid, aid that the Englishman had promised him in exchange for his daughter's hand, aid that he had expected to obtain from me if I had claimed his daughter. His fortune had been a myth for months, wiped out in mining speculation. Without financial assistance, he would be bankrupt, and his daughter had willingly complied with his plans to obtain it rather than face certain poverty. She had deliberately sold herself to the highest bidder to maintain her position, and for a time, I had the high card, until my father withdrew the stakes. When he refused the man's request for aid a second time, the man committed suicide.''

Marc's gaze was thoughtful now as his story ended, and he realized the black despair that had once been associated with his tale was gone without a trace. It happened too long ago, to another man than the one he was now, and the wound no longer festered but was healed and closed. It was a relief to be rid of it, but the scar would never be erased.

He turned in time to see Jennifer rub a hand across her eyes, and he reached over to trace a finger across wet cheeks.

"Those aren't tears I feel, are they, Jenny?" he asked in astonishment. He had only wanted her to understand his harsh words; he had never meant to transfer his pain to her.

She shook her head and turned her face away from his inquiring look. "No, of course not, I never cry."

"Now that's a lie, I know; I heard you cry once before." It was strange what she did to him, instead of feeling sorry for himself, he wanted to comfort her, but he knew too well what the result of that would be.

Jennifer sniffed and turned back to him, her voice bristling with irritation. "If you're looking for accuracy, then make that twice. The first time I vowed never to cry again; the time you heard was an understandable lapse."

That was a quick change, and Marcus grinned at her challenging tone; he would be better off comforting a prickly pear. "What was the first time to make you swear such a terrible vow?"

"The same day I gave up dreaming and decided to make my own way in the world, just as your fairy-tale character did," she said bluntly, irritated at the emotions he stirred in her and aggravated by his mockery.

He thought about that, understanding too well what she meant, and his chuckle had a hollow sound to it. "A lovely couple we make, little one, neither of us prepared to give what the other wants most. I think we've reached an impasse."

"That may very well be," she replied thoughtfully. "Marcus, I . . ." but the thought hadn't been a conscious one and the words fell back, unformed, into her subconscious before she could utter them. Lamely, she finished, "I'm sorry."

He raised her fingers to his lips and kissed them lightly. "So am I, sweetheart, so am I."

Chapter Thirteen

Marcus woke with the first rays of sun to find Jennifer curled at his side, one fist flung limply across his chest. The long, flowing hair cascading over her gown enhanced the impression of childishness, although the soft push of her breasts against his side belied her appearance. He could feel the length of a silken leg pressed against his, and his tormented body responded to these pressures, aching for the release he dared not seek. But if she did not move soon, he would have her ravished before she could fully wake.

Stuart's whimpering cries saved him, bringing him back to harsh reality as Jennifer stirred at the noise. Making love to a reluctant wife while a baby wailed and brought the house to the door was not the way he wished to start this day. He would have her again when the time was right, and she was willing, but he would have her, Marcus vowed silently. Tightening his arm around Jenny, he whispered her name softly to waken her.

She stretched lazily in his embrace, not quite awake. Her lashes flickered, and the beginning of a long, slow smile spread across her face, remnant of pleasant dreams as she nestled closer. Lashes closing again, she sighed deeply, and slender fingers curled tighter into the mat of hairs on his chest.

"Darling Jenny," Marcus laughingly drawled, running a finger down the length of her arm, "unless you have changed your mind since last night, you had best scoot back to your side of the bed before I change it for you." He watched her through half-closed eyes, his blood racing hot and eager at the soft pressures of her touch, but the trusting brown of sleep-filled eyes held him back. She hadn't moved from him in fear, that was some progress, and it would be unfair to take advantage of her sleepy vulnerability.

Stuart's cries pierced her consciousness and reluctantly, Jennifer rolled from her husband's side, but not out of his embrace. His hand caressed her, stroking the side of her breast and the uncorseted curve of waistline. She responded with a rapturous smile, not yet awake enough to register the intensity of his need.

The hoarse thickness of Marc's voice brought an abrupt end to her ignorance. "Jenny Lee, I suggest you go rescue our son from his misery or put me out of mine; I fear I am in no condition to do either without offending your maidenly modesty."

Her questioning glance followed his gaze to the sheets over his hips and with sudden comprehension, her cheeks flushed bright with color, and she scampered quickly from the bed. With pained amusement, Marcus watched the slight figure of his wife bend over the cradle, the clinging folds of her hastily donned robe molding to her figure, the hot color of her cheeks still evident. She was still nearly as innocent as the day he met her; there was so much she needed to learn, and he firmly intended to be the one who did the teaching.

Shy now, Jennifer slipped back under the covers with her whimpering bundle. As she prepared to fling the concealing shawl over her shoulders, Marcus caught it and pulled it away.

"There is no need to hide yourself from me. Surely, by now, I have proved myself worthy of that small concession."

Even if she could trust him, she doubted herself. Well-muscled, bronzed shoulders outlined against the pillows propped at his back, Marcus vibrated with such virility and strength in his nakedness, she feared being swallowed up without the strength to fight it. But, obediently, she snuggled under his welcoming arm, her lashes lowered to conceal her nervousness as she bared her breast for the hungry babe. It was one of the more exhilarating experiences of her short life: nestled in the security of her husband's presence while their son greedily drank his fill, small fingers flailing at being disturbed, then grasping his father's finger where it rested against her breast. She settled contentedly into this embrace.

"I thought you were going to train Junior to wake later. Will we ever have this interruption to our sleep?"

A soft smile curved Jennifer's lips as she looked up at him. "Actually, he did remarkably well considering how early he dined last night. Were you planning on making this a habit that you are worried about your sleep?"

Marcus smiled with a tantalizing glimpse of white teeth, leaning back against the pillow with an air of self-satisfaction. "No, it's a habit I can ill afford under the circumstances. However, I have decided on an equally effective, although not as pleasant alternative."

"Not as pleasant for whom? If you were a cat, I'd say the canary was in trouble." Worry wrinkled the bridge of her nose despite her attempt at nonchalance. What was he planning now?

Marcus grinned. "How would you like an extended vacation to the mountains?"

She eyed him suspiciously. Was that how he intended to get rid of her, ship her off to some distant outpost? It was impossible to know what to expect of him, he seemed to make a habit of loving her and raising her hopes only to turn around and dash them to the ground. His temper was too volatile to trust.

"With you?" she asked.

He glanced at her in surprise. "Of course, with me, you goose. Do you think I'd send you off alone after last night? You're too much a simpleton to be trusted on your own; that's why I've decided to take you with me. There will be no servants to gossip or neighbors to listen, and we can do as we please without these charades."

Jennifer's indignation flared, but was quelled by suspicion and curiosity. "I may be naive, but I'm no simpleton. Just what are you planning to do?"

"My naive little simpleton," Marcus grinned at her glare, "I have some mining interests I would like to see further developed. The city is hot and boring this time of year, I mean to take you and Stuart to a more suitable climate to keep me company as any good husband would do. Unfortunately, the attractions of a mining town are few and far between, but this one has a fairly comfortable hotel run by a respectable widowed lady, and I will be able to see you at the end of every week instead of leaving you to Stephen's care for months. Have you any objections?"

There was no point arguing, he had already made up his mind. Although his reasoning was based upon a flaw, Jennifer knew she would not object. Stephen was a friend and nothing more, but Marcus was everything she had. She would go willingly wherever he did.

"You know I will do whatever you wish." She ignored the wry twist of his brow. "But may I ask a favor?"

"Whatever you wish, madam," he echoed her words mockingly, a teasing light in his eyes.

"May I ask Clare to come with us? I think it would be healthier for her to get away from this house." She searched his face anxiously, hoping she hadn't presumed too far on his good humor.

Marcus frowned and played idly with Stuart's tiny fists. "You may be right, but I wouldn't think my mother's companionship would be what you would choose." His mother's presence might put a crimp in his plans for seduction, but Jennifer had reminded him of a responsibility he had too long neglected. She was right, and he would just have to work around this new obstacle. "If anybody can bring her back to health and sanity, it will be you."

"I'm scarcely one to advise on an unhappy love life," Jennifer sniffed derisively.

Marcus raised an eyebrow at this remarkable perceptivity, but at her wry look, he grinned. "Do you think any of us are? This is a sorry household you have entered, little one, if you have not already guessed."

Jennifer eyed him thoughtfully. "I have done some speculating, but a few facts might be helpful; you're not a very communicative family."

"Which is why I cannot give you many facts, only more informed speculations. My mother does not confide in me any more than I do her." Marcus studied his wife's face with her wide, trusting eyes and eager responsiveness. Jennifer was meant to be a giver; her warm, generous nature blossomed easily under love and sympathy, returning it many times over. He'd certainly had evidence of that the first night he spent with her, but he had seen it over and over again since then: Helping Josephine, befriending Lucia, worrying about Stephen, and now with Clare. But she was beginning to hold back part of herself from him, and it wasn't just physically. Was the family malaise spreading to envelop his warm-hearted Jenny with it coldness, or was it just from him that she retreated?

"Your mother has retired from the world for a reason, and it cannot be entirely physical."

Marcus shrugged. "As far as I know, my mother and father had separate bedrooms from the time we arrived in California. They fought continually over the move. My father spent most of his time away from home while establishing his new enterprise. I was only a lad of ten at the time and it meant nothing to me, but I remember Michael O'Hara being a frequent visitor. It's only since then that I began to put two and two together."

Jennifer turned in shocked surprise to stare at him, much to Stuart's disgruntlement. With amusement, Marcus leaned over and cradled the infant's head in proper position until the greedy mouth found Jennifer's breast again, giving Jennifer time to register the meaning of his words. Looking into her eyes, Marcus could see the confusion and consternation there, and realized she wasn't yet ready to accept the concept of marital infidelity, despite her show of bravura last night. For some reason, this relieved him.

Stuart was tired of the effort of eating, finding his mother's hair more to his liking as he entangled it in his chubby little fists. Jennifer patiently extracted it. "Now I see why your father left everything to you, but if he didn't intend to acknowledge his wife, why did he allow her to stay on in his home?"

He shouldn't have doubted her compassion; brown eyes brimmed with sympathy for a problem not even hers. Nothing would ever affect her loving nature, not even the torments he put her through. Reassured, Marcus took his mischievous son from her arms.

"My father would never turn his back on his family, and Clare is my mother, he couldn't deny that. They had married for convenience, not love, and as long as the convenience remained, there was no reason to end it." Stuart grabbed his father's nose, and Marcus shook himself free, tickling the infant's belly.

Jennifer curled up beside them, entranced by this aspect

of Marcus as father, and she basked in the glow of the
warmth they radiated. He had given her so much to think
about, so much to tear apart and scrutinize for every shred
of hope she could find, but that was for the times when
he wasn't with her. Right now, all she wanted was to be by
his side.

Marcus pulled her into the curve of his arm and kissed
her forehead. "Will you use your angel's charms to make
things right again?"

Sighing with contentment, Jennifer leaned against his
brawny shoulder, no longer shy of his nudity. "If you promise not to use your devil's brew to contradict them, there
may be hope for Clare once she comes to her senses."

"Sometimes, my dear, I think you were put on this earth
specifically to keep me in hell and that is a hellish thing
for an angel to do. When are you going to learn I'm not
the devil you think I am?"

"When you stop behaving like one."

Lucia's knock went unheard in their laughing banter
and according to custom, she entered the room, coming
to an immediate halt, struck dumb by the sight which
greeted her. The cold, correct pair who had little to say
to each other beyond mutually respectful exchanges of
news were now cavorting and laughing in bed like a pair
of newlyweds, their differences apparently overcome if
their state of dress or undress were to be believed. Lucia
debated departure, but not in time to prevent Marcus seeing her standing there.

"Lucia! Go have that man of mine find my robe and
bring it back here so you can help Jennifer get dressed.
I'm starving."

The little maid grinned and dropped a quick curtsy before speeding from the room. Marcus grinned wickedly
after her.

Jennifer slammed a fist against his chest. "You beast!
You stayed here on purpose just to conduct that little
scene, didn't you? Admit it!"

He turned the devilish look back to her. "And loved

every minute of it!'' He buried his unshaven face at the
nape of her neck, nuzzling the soft skin there.

Jennifer squealed and pulled away. "Well, it won't do
you any good. Lucia would never tell anyone anything that
happens in here. I'm certain of it."

"She doesn't have to, my love. All she has to do is smile
knowingly when the others start their gossip, it's a dead
giveaway." He whispered dramatically in her ear as Lucia
returned with the robe, "Your reputation is ruined, my
dear!"

The next few days were spent in hectic excitement,
packing and repacking, and a constant chatter of female
voices. Clare refused to accompany them on the trip but
the maids were given full rein to aid as requested, and
Lucia was given official permission to attend Jennifer. Lucia was beside herself with equal amounts of fear and
eagerness at the prospect of leaving home and family for
the first time, and her near hysteria threatened to bubble
over until almost nothing was accomplished. On the
other hand, Jennifer was rapidly becoming an experienced traveler thanks to Marcus, and her calm directions
kept things moving in proper order, if not at a proper
pace. She had come a long way from the girl who had
packed her trunk with two muslin dresses and said good-
bye to home and family forever.

Jennifer's only concern was raised by Darlene's frantic
visit the day before they were scheduled to depart. A maid
led her to the parlor where Darlene waited, pacing the
floor. At Jennifer's entrance, the distressed girl ran to grab
her hands, her eyes tear-stained and red from crying.

"Oh, Jennifer, please do something! You've got to talk
to Marcus, make him see. Cameron isn't bad, he's just a
little wild, but he'll settle down, I know he will. He just
came back to us, he can't go now. Won't you say something
to him?"

Jennifer attempted to soothe the frantic girl, leading

her to a sofa and making her talk slowly. Darlene just shook her head, tears welling up in the corners of her eyes again.

"Darlene, you'll have to tell me what you are talking about. Where is Cameron going? What can Marcus do about it?" Jennifer tried to collect her thoughts. She had been assured Cameron had survived the short fall over the parapet the other night, but she had heard nothing else. Surely Marcus had not gone out of his way to make trouble for something so silly as a foolish kiss? But Marcus had been irrationally furious, and she knew he was capable of almost anything. She pressured Darlene for the whole story.

"I don't know where he's going," Darlene wailed in reply. "Father just ordered him out and he's packing his bags. I don't know what Marcus said to him, but Father was furious, said Cameron would never be any good. Then he ordered Cameron to leave until he could prove he could make an honest living. It was horrible, Jennifer. You should have seen the look on Cameron's face! I know he was terribly hurt. Please, Jennifer, make Marcus talk to Father again."

Jennifer stood and crossed to the mantel, fiddling with the pieces of bric-a-brac and keeping her back to the weeping girl. What could she tell her? That if she should argue Cameron's case with Marcus, it would only make matters worse? How could she tell her friend Marcus suspected her of infidelity and that Cameron was taking the blame? It was a hard punishment for so small an infraction of the rules.

"I am certain there must be some reason for your father's harsh judgment, Darlene. I cannot promise anything, but I will ask Marcus for explanation. Perhaps you can persuade Cameron to stay in town until your father cools off. With a little time, things might improve."

But Jennifer doubted it. She remembered Cameron declaring time was his enemy. What had he meant by that? Did it mean more than she had thought? His declaration of love had seemed impetuous at the time and Jennifer had thought little of it. Was there some other motive to his actions that had made him wish to hurry the process? Marcus would know, but would he tell her?

Stephen walked in, and before he could apologize for intruding and back out, Darlene threw herself in his arms and the whole story tumbled out again. He and Jennifer exchanged worried glances over Darlene's bent head. What madness possessed Marcus?

He placated Darlene until she regained her composure enough to be embarrassed at the scene she had created, and departed. Then he held out his arm and prevented Jennifer from doing the same.

"I know Cameron played fast and free with you the other night, but there is no danger of your leaving Marcus, is there?" Warm gray eyes searched her face with concern.

"No, Stephen, you know there is not," Jennifer answered quietly, reading all the questions in his eyes and unable to face them. She attempted to get around him, but he held her fast.

"Jenny, I wish you would talk to me. I've been hearing rumors for weeks, and Cameron had some pretty vicious things to say when I saw him last. I think I know some of the truth, but I do not understand what is happening. Even if the rumors are true and your wedding was an afterthought, at best, I am not wrong in thinking that you love him, am I?"

Heat spread across her cheeks under Stephen's steady gaze. So most of San Francisco knew of their forced marriage. What must they think of her? Yet there was only concern in Stephen's eyes, none of the scorn and ridicule she had feared. She prayed no one knew more than that; Marcus had promised that they wouldn't.

"What does it matter, Stephen? Marcus does as he pleases. Direct your questions to him. I have things to do, let me by, please." Again, she tried to avoid him, but he was not ready to accept her excuses.

"No, Jenny, that is not enough. Marc and I have our differences of opinion, but I respect the man. He would not deliberately harm you, but he is stubborn and a little too accustomed to having his own way. If I thought you were truly unhappy with this marriage, I would bend over backwards to help you. I want to know, do you love him?" He stated the words firmly and clearly, his gaze burning through to her soul as he held her with both hands.

"Oh, Stephen, how can I say it to you when I cannot even say it to myself? Do not make me dream dreams that can never come true."

Jennifer's words ended with a sob, and the suspicion of moisture in her eyes was enough to cause Stephen to regret his persistence. With gentleness, he folded her into his embrace and held her securely until she could regain control. The anguish in those wounded eyes told him much, and his jaw tightened in the same manner as Marc's, but before he could say what he thought, he sensed another presence in the room, and glanced over Jennifer's shoulder.

Marcus stood in the open doorway, his cold gaze taking in the intimate scene with disturbing calmness.

Feeling Stephen tense, Jennifer pulled away and turned to find her husband's gaze resting on her with icy stillness. There was no reproach, no anger, no pain, just that icy calm, and she was forced to wonder how much he had overheard, or understood. She stepped away from Stephen's embrace.

"I have packing to complete. Marcus, I believe Stephen would like to have a word with you."

That hit a nerve, and she watched him flinch. But the pain was so brief, she wasn't certain if she had not imagined it. Whatever the case, there were no protests from either man as she swept from the room, head held high. If Stephen wished to know their true story, let Marcus explain it. It was all she could do to hide it from herself.

It was some time later before Marcus joined her in the bedroom where she bent over their trunks, packing the last of her garments. Lucia had fluttered off earlier, and

Stuart slept. Marcus closed the door and waited for Jennifer to rise and meet his gaze.

Almond eyes were as cool as his when she turned to greet him. "Did you clear up Stephen's worries?"

"I doubt if that is possible. I simply set the record straight."

Jennifer nodded. Whatever anger he held stored, she knew Marcus would still remain honorable in his explanations. Stephen would at least understand that her unmarried pregnancy was due more to ignorance than immorality. She trusted Marcus to reveal little more than that.

"Darlene was here. She said her father has thrown Cameron from the house after some discussion with you. Am I entitled to explanations?" she asked coolly.

"Do you need them? If I tell you what he really is, would you believe me?"

Marcus watched her carefully. The scene with Stephen had shaken him more than he cared to admit. He had never really feared Cameron's hold over her, knowing she had too much practicality to fall for Cameron's evasions and half-truths, but Stephen could be a different problem entirely. What was it that she could not admit to herself? What dreams did she harbor? And why should it matter so much to him?

"I have no reason to think you would lie to me, Marcus. I hope you have not overreacted, but I will believe whatever you tell me. Darlene is heart-broken. I hope the cause is justified."

Their words remained unnaturally calm and controlled. Neither dared probe too deeply behind the other's thoughts.

There was no sense in opening up a wound only partially healed, stirring fears best left unfaced. Delaney was a nightmare he hoped they had left behind, and Cameron's connection with him was best left unmentioned. Marcus gave her only half of the tale he had given Michael O'Hara.

"Cameron is a compulsive gambler and a cheat. He has

swindled half the men at the club and countless others unknown to me. He is wanted by the law in several places. He has no other choice but to leave." Marcus searched her face to be certain she was satisfied with this explanation.

"I see." Jennifer bent over the infant's cradle as he stirred restlessly in his sleep. Marc's intense gaze told her he still held no trust for her or any other woman. Melissa had scarred him well. She stood and faced him with what she hoped was composure. "Then I suggest it is better that Darlene not know the truth of Cameron's departure. She blames it on you, you know."

"And so did you."

Jennifer tilted her head quizzically. "Would you have told Mr. O'Hara if Cameron had not made that scene the other night?"

With a wry twist of his lips, Marcus acknowledged her perceptivity. "Most likely not. I am sorry, Jennifer, but a young girl who can imagine herself in love after one night with a man is capable of worse stretches of the imagination. I could not trust you with him."

"Thank you for your honesty," Jennifer replied with irony. "Then there is nothing further to discuss, is there?"

"Not unless there is something you wish to tell me."

If he thought her foolish for imagining love after their first night together, how much more foolish would he think her if she expressed love after all they had said to each other since? No, he had no wish to hear her emotional imaginings; she would keep this secret to herself.

"No, there is nothing, Marcus." And she returned to packing, effectively dismissing him.

But that night, alone in bed once more, Jennifer tried to piece together all these new revelations, straining to find some hope or comfort somewhere. Marcus claimed there was a difference between love and physical desire, but in her case he was wrong, dreadfully, terribly wrong; she knew that now. She loved him and would never be happy without him. That was the reason for following him

clear across the continent when she could have had a
home and friends in St. Louis. That was the reason she
was going with him to some God-forsaken mining camp
just as she was learning to enjoy the benefits of a social
life. A person didn't uproot themselves like that just for
the sake of physical desire that could be quenched by any
available male. She was irrevocably his, and he didn't want
her.

That wasn't quite right. He wanted her, but in the same
way he wanted Gwendolyn and all the other women in all
the ports up and down the Mississippi. And because she
wasn't available, maybe he wanted her a little more. But
he had left her once after having her, and he could do it
again, and this time she would not be able to bear the loss.
If she could only keep herself from him, she would at least
have her pride left this time when he left; it was small
consolation but better than total self-destruction.

Would he leave her? If he couldn't love anyone, was
there any reason to leave her? Of course there was, she
thought sadly, knowing it would be her own fault when he
did. He wanted a grand lady to run a houseful of servants,
to be gracious hostess, and reflect well on his family; he
wanted more children and a proper mother to bring them
up. Jennifer knew herself too well to believe she could ever
fill that description, however hard she might try out of
love for him. She was miserable here, she didn't belong
in drawing rooms making pleasant conversation, and although she would gladly be mother of his children, she
would want them wild and free and not cooped up in some
sterile nursery overlooked by a stern governess. Already
Marcus had indicated his disapproval at keeping Stuart by
her side, disapproved of her friendship with Lucia, disapproved of almost everything she did. But she was more at
home with Lucia than Clare, would be more comfortable
in the kitchen than the parlor, would find more delight
in grubbing in the garden than making neat stitches in an
embroidered handkerchief, and she couldn't live her life
pretending otherwise.

If he could only love her, she could make him see that. He understood her better than anyone realized, he understood her need to be doing things herself, he understood her goals and ambitions, and he could respect her for it, otherwise he would never have agreed to their contract, but he would never willingly have married her for it unless he loved her. And he didn't. And he never would. And so someday, he would have to leave her for the wife he should have had, and it would all be her own fault.

The months of torment and anxiety and uncertainty she had suffered through were pent up in a deep well inside. Until now, she had kept a stern hold on them, but once the lid was removed, they were free to tumble out all at once in a grief stricken torrent of hot tears that flooded her pillow and drowned what few hopes she had left. She was lost, her dreams of independence vanished in her need for Marcus beside her, knowing she could never be happy without him. And she sobbed helplessly, heart-wrenching sobs that shook the very foundations of her soul and left her empty and lifeless in their futility.

In the silence of his lonely room, Marcus heard her muffled sobs and remembered another night when he had allowed them to continue uncomforted. He knew now what he didn't know then, that he had the power to comfort her whatever the reason for this sudden outbreak of long abandoned tears, but in using that power he would be promising her something he couldn't give, and he had to weigh her sorrow now against the pain of that discovery later. As much as he ached to hold her in his arms and kiss away the tears, he steeled himself against his softening thoughts. He wanted her more than any other woman he had ever known, more than he had desired the traitorous Melissa, but he couldn't let his need muddy his thinking, couldn't take advantage of her unhappiness to press his cause. He would have to wait until she was ready to accept him on his terms; until then, the best thing he could do for her was to keep his distance.

He wondered what could possibly have broken down

that formidable reserve enough to reduce her to tears? He would give up everything he had to be able to go in there with open heart and find out. Instead, he lay long after she finally quieted, staring at the ceiling.

Chapter Fourteen

Their leave-taking the next morning did not disturb Clare's rest, but disrupted the routine of the remainder of the household. A wagon load of trunks was sent ahead to be loaded on the train while the two women raced about rounding up last minute articles, sending servants scurrying in every direction. Stephen lounged about uselessly, underfoot at every turn, but his expression was so doleful they took mercy on him and let him be. Marcus simply stayed out of the way, only appearing when it was time to leave for the station. Stuart blissfully slept through it all.

The train destined to take them on their brief journey was a smaller, noisier, dirtier version of the one they had traveled cross-country on, but Lucia was ecstatic, appropriating the window seat and exclaiming over the passing countryside as if never having seen it before. Marcus and Jennifer exchanged looks of amusement, but said nothing to discourage her ebullience.

As Jennifer tended the infant and answered excited questions, Marcus surreptitiously studied her for any signs of last night's tears. Her lovely dark eyes were dry and clear, expressing a lively interest in everything about her;

there was nothing in her manner to indicate she was anything other than a happy traveler. But Marcus sensed a
difference, an inner stillness as of decisions made and accepted, or perhaps just a new maturity he hadn't noticed
before; there was no way of telling until she told him. He
crossed his arms across his chest, leaned his head back
against the seat, and tilted his broad brimmed hat over his
eyes. It would be a long time before she trusted him
enough to tell her secrets; perhaps she was justified in her
reticence.

These mountains were not as steep as the ones they
crossed a month and a half before, but their gasping uphill
route succeeded in silencing some of the excitement while
the wide-eyed observers peered down tumbled rockslides
to flower studded valleys far below. A rolling hillside covered in a blanket of brilliant red blooms dipping their
heavy heads to a mountain breeze left Jennifer totally
awestruck. Even the carefully cultivated gardens of St.
Louis couldn't compare with the mountain's natural abun-
dance, and Jennifer sighed wistfully.

"What it must be like to get up every morning and look
out over a view such as that! You couldn't forget God's
presence with such constant reminders."

Marc's eyes gleamed from under half-open lids as he
watched his wife's wistful expression. "Is that what it would
take to make you happy, a field of flowers?"

Jennifer looked up in surprise, unaware he had even
noticed. She returned his stare, replying evenly, "Among
other things, I suppose."

He continued his gaze a moment longer, then closed
his eyes with a nod of his head, retreating once more beneath the brim of his hat, one more piece of knowledge
tucked discreetly away in an obscure corner of his mind.

Lucia became fascinated by a dialogue carried on behind her, a tale of robbery and murder on a mountain
line similar to this one where boulders were easily tumbled
from the cliffs to the tracks below, leaving the train passengers trapped and defenseless. In horrified whispers, she

repeated it to Jennifer, but when they dared question Marcus further, his scornful grimace relieved the maid's worries. But Jennifer had seen the flash of holstered guns on his hips, hidden by the long tail of his coat, and understood their presence. She traveled the remainder of the trip in tight-lipped silence.

Fortunately for Henry and the men he found to help him carry the parade of luggage, their hotel was directly across from the railroad station. Stepping into the dust filled streets, Jennifer took a quick look around at what would be their home for the next months.

Town apparently consisted of one unpaved main street, its billows of dust now promising acres of mud during the rainy season, a promise verified by the high wooden sidewalks bordering the street. Besides the hotel and railroad station, a multitude of wooden edifices adorned this dust basin, ranging from windowless shacks to the three-story colonial of the hotel. There appeared to be no planning or arrangement in the construction: whenever a new building was needed, it was thrown up in the next available space. Marcus had informed them that with the recent advent of the railroad and reopening of the mines, this would soon become a thriving little town, but so far there was little evidence of it. It was hot and dirty and deserted.

The hotel lobby was cooler, a slight breeze from the mountain behind circulating gently through the dim interior. A sprinkle of men lounged about on wooden chairs, occasionally aiming at, and usually missing, the brass spitoons put there for the protection of the rough plank flooring. The front windows were shuttered against the afternoon sun, trapping lazily buzzing flies against the heated glass, leaving it speckled and spotted with their remains.

Marcus strode briskly to the battered wooden desk, leaving the women to trail behind, the heat having melted their enthusiasm and their surroundings dampening their spirits. Jennifer shrugged and smiled grimly at her companion; the inn she had lived in for most of her life probably looked worse than this to unsuspecting travelers. Who was she to complain?

Behind the desk rested an elderly and extremely stout woman whose black bombazine attire must have been made twenty years earlier and added to the red flush of heat on her sweating face. But behind her spectacles beamed pleasantly faded blue eyes, and a cherubic smile welcomed them as she pulled herself to her feet.

"Mr. Armstrong, you're back already! You don't waste no time, and you've brought your wife like you promised." She turned to Jennifer with welcoming arms. "The captain's told me all about you. It'll be so good to have another woman about the place again." She came out from behind the counter and hugged Jennifer with enthusiasm.

"Jennifer, this is Mrs. Thompson, sole proprietor of the Grand Hotel." Marcus leaned against the counter and watched their confrontation with amusement. "Mrs. Thompson, my wife Jennifer and our maid, Lucia. They thought a brief vacation to your lovely resort would bring some relief from summer boredom in the city." He spoke with amusement but the woman heard his sarcasm.

"Now you mind your manners and don't be scaring off these ladies. I'm too happy to have someone to talk to besides these loud-mouthed swearing miners of yours for you to spoil our fun."

"Now, Emma Jane, are you counting me along with the rest of that motley crew?"

Turning, Jennifer saw a lively, dark complected man with brilliant white teeth and a dazzling smile, his thin figure draped in an immaculate white shirt with billowing sleeves and a pair of loose fitting denim trousers. He held his finely boned hand out to welcome Marcus.

"Well, Mr. Armstrong, are you going to introduce me to your harem?" Glittering black eyes swept over their entourage and his smile broadened.

"Charlie, the last thing in the world I want to do is introduce you to my women, but I know you'd spend your time moving heaven and hell instead of my mountain to get your introduction some other way, so I may as well save some time."

As chief engineer, Charles Mangione was young, ambitious, and far from his New York City home where he'd left behind a large family and a dozen weeping girlfriends in order to make his fortune in a desolate, womanless mining town. His delight at these new arrivals was immediate, regardless of their relationship to his boss.

"Ladies, I am delighted to make your lovely acquaintance." He lingered over Jennifer's hand and smiled deeply into Lucia's eyes. "Marcus, you are a man of rare insight. Your men will be quite content to work their fool heads off all week if they know they'll have a sight of such beauty at the end of every shift."

"Mr. Mangione, your flattery is impressive but we have just left an army of such flatterers behind. If you wish our company, simple friendship would be sufficient." Jennifer spoke firmly, before Marcus had time to be irritated, and he raised his eyebrows in salute to her quickness.

"I stand corrected, Mrs. Armstrong, but you must call me Charlie because I answer to no other name. If you should ever be in need of assistance, feel free to call on me." He bowed over her hand with a charmingly puckish grin.

"Thank you, Charlie. Mrs. Thompson, are our rooms ready? It's been a tedious journey . . ."

At Jennifer's words, the room erupted into motion. Baggage began disappearing upstairs, Mrs. Thompson shepherded them through the lobby, Marcus and Charlie were lost in the bustle. Even the idle men along the walls seemed to rise and add their presence to the occasion, although, in truth, they did little more than admire the swaying hips of the town's latest guests as they ascended the stairs.

Upstairs, Jennifer found herself alone in a spacious but sparsely furnished sitting room while Mrs. Thompson's voice carried down the hallway, ushering her other charges to their rooms. A large cupboardlike cabinet filled most of the space on the back wall, the rest of the room contained only a chest of drawers, a few occasional chairs, and a pedestal table. A few of their trunks lay scattered about, but there was no sign of the remainder.

"I'll have them bring Stuart's cradle up in a minute."

Jennifer started at the sound of his voice; engrossed in her inspection, she hadn't heard him enter. She swung around as Marcus flung his hat onto the nearest chair and came toward her, his tousled curls giving him a boyish look as he grinned at her.

"A bit different from my mother's palace, wouldn't you say? Are you ready to turn around and go back?"

She scarcely heard his words for all awareness was swept away in the clarity of dancing blue eyes, and her heart jumped at this unexpected return of her riverboat captain. Forcing herself to look away, she replied, "No, of course not. This room is even larger than the bridal suite at home."

"The bridal suite?"

"The room where we met. My mother called it the bridal suite because of its size and privacy," Jennifer explained.

"How appropriate, but haven't we done things a little backward? Started with the honeymoon and worked our way back to . . . what? Good friends? Familiar strangers? Isn't it time we went forward again?"

Long lashes swept upward as she studied him with surprise. "Forward to what? I thought good friends and business partners were all you wanted."

"You know better than that, Jenny," Marcus replied patiently.

"Is that why there's no bed in here? I suppose I'll find the rest of my trunks next door with yours?" The scorn in her voice held a hint of tears, and she quickly turned away, stalking to the far side of the room to investigate the curious cabinet.

He came up behind her and rested a hand on her shoulder. "Of course, I would prefer you share my bed, but if you insist, there is always this one you can use when I am here." He pulled a latch at the top of the cabinet and lowered the door, revealing mattress and bed attached to its inner surface. "Your trunks are in my room because that's where the wardrobe and dressers are."

Jennifer stared at the fold-up bed with amazement, a hideous piece of furniture, but highly convenient. She smiled her apology. "Very ingenious, sir, you've thought of everything."

His arms circled her waist from behind, one hand brushing against her breast, seeking its sensitive tip. "I'm hoping you won't find much use for it," he whispered against her ear.

A now familiar melting sensation weakened Jennifer's resistance. If she continued to allow his embrace, she would be consumed by this fire inside her, but she couldn't summon the strength to step away. Taking advantage of her nonresistance, Marcus pressed the length of his body against hers, narrow hips and broad chest pressing seductively against her as his lips drifted down her throat. Jennifer weakened rapidly, waiting nervously and impatiently for the moment when he raised his lips to hers.

The moment never came. Stuart's hungry wail filled the empty room, and Marcus dropped his arms.

"You have that child well trained; I believe he is jealous of my attempt to share your attentions."

Jennifer stiffened, wrapping her arms about herself to preserve the warmth he had aroused and to prevent total disintegration. The devil had done his work well again.

"It's been a long trip, he has a right to complain, and you don't." She crossed the room and lifted the infant from his basket, kissing the dark head she held in her arms.

Marcus watched with glum interest as she bestowed the affections she denied him on the helpless infant, well satisfied with herself, he thought. Next time he would time his attentions better.

"I have some work to do, I'll be in my room if you need

me. You might want to come in later and appropriate the space you need in the wardrobe so Henry can start unpacking my bags," he said brusquely, retrieving his hat and turning toward their connecting door.

"I'd like to take a bath if I have a chance, is there a place in here to wash?" Jennifer thought dismally of the flights of stairs she used to carry water up; marriage to Marcus had certainly made her appreciate the luxuries of life.

"It's better appointed than the bridal suite, if that's what you mean. There's a tub in here with running water; I wouldn't subject you to any inconvenience." He gestured toward the door he held in his hand, then left the room.

She had irritated him again without having done a thing. She should be the one who was angry at his holding her like that, teasing her into an act he very well knew she would regret, but she wasn't. Even as Jennifer put Stuart to her breast, her body cried out to be held again, to feel his touch on her, and when she had that, she knew she wouldn't be satisfied until she had more. His touch was fatal to her willpower, she would have to avoid it in the future.

With Stuart fed and returned to the cradle Henry brought up, Jennifer prepared to beard the lion in his den. It would be extremely inconvenient to be forced into her husband's chambers every time she needed an article of clothing, and she strongly suspected he had planned it that way. She would have to find some way to outwit him at his own game if she valued her self-respect at all.

The bath provided a gloomy connection between the two rooms, with no window and only a single gas lamp to light the darkness. She knocked lightly on the far door and entered at his call. He was poring over sheets of drawings at a desk under the room's one large window and barely acknowledged her presence. It was the first time she had ever entered a room of his and only now because he intended it for both of them; she was beginning to have some feeling of what it really meant to be married. By sharing the same bed, they would of necessity be sharing the same life to an extent she had not yet fully comprehended. But seeing her things thrown together in confusion with his began to open her eyes. The large bed with its heavy walnut canopy filled the room and across it lay her clean gown and petticoats, jumbled together with her husband's coat and the unpackings of his trunk. Henry and Lucia had already been at work, and Jennifer wondered if they'd been chased away by her arrival. Giving Marc's back a cautious glance, she gathered up her clothing and prepared to leave the room.

"I'm going out to find Charlie in a few minutes, so you may take your bath in peace." Marcus turned around in his chair and caught the furtive look of relief on her face. He had figured as much when she came tippy-toeing into the room without saying a word; he had frightened her away again.

"I will get my things out of your way as soon as possible. Is Lucia with Henry?" Jennifer held the gown crushed against her, avoiding his gaze.

"Probably. I will tell her you need her on my way out." He turned back to his desk in curt dismissal.

Jennifer fled gratefully.

Rolling up the drawing he was working on, Marcus ignored the sound of bath water running, shutting out the images that formed, unbidden, before his mind's eye. If he did not have that girl soon, he would be driven to other sources of relief, he thought, it was either that or rape. She was making it impossible to think of anything else; even the distance from the mining camp to town wouldn't be sufficient to banish the thought of her nearness. He had to keep busy, keep occupied to put a curb on his thoughts. Marcus pulled on his coat and jammed his hat back on his head, striding out the door with the drawings under his arm.

Halfway down the stairs, he remembered his promise to find Lucia. He hesitated, then swung around and began the climb back up, muttering irritated curses until the stillness was broken by an ear-piercing scream, followed by another and another in an increasingly higher crescendo, reaching the shrill frequency of a shriek just as his foot hit the top step, and he flew into a run back in the direction from which he had just come.

The scream was too intensely familiar to be anyone else, and Marcus flung open the door to his room as a clatter of footsteps hit the stairs behind him and heads peered out from other doorways up and down the hall. Marcus never noticed them, crossing the room in fewer strides than humanly possible until he stood before the door from which the screams emanated. It was impossible to know the cause of the screams, but instinct told him caution was necessary, and he eased the door open slowly, his hand already reaching for his gun, easing off the safety as he drew it from its harness.

Jennifer was in the tub, bubbles covering the water nearly up to her shoulders, hair wet and streaming down her back. Her screams had ceased but she remained transfixed, hand over mouth and terrified eyes staring at a sight somewhere above her head. Marcus followed the path of her gaze, his breathing stopping as he found the source of her terror.

Wrapped around the water pipe directly over Jennifer's head was a lengthy viper, its bright coloration providing the only target in the darkness of the ceiling, its rattle shivering out a deadly warning as it held its precarious perch. Slowly exhaling and clenching his teeth, Marcus raised his gun arm, holding it steady as he sighted along the barrel, looking for the creature's head, aware that if he missed, the snake would very likely dive for the tub below. As the head came into his sight, he squeezed the trigger, the explosion creating deafening echoes in the small room as the snake uncoiled.

Before it could hit the water, Marcus dragged Jennifer from the tub, pulling her shivering body close to him while pieces of the dead reptile hit the floor. Hugging her close, he was unable to hold her slender body tight enough as

Jennifer wrapped her arms around him and buried her face against his chest, water running off her nakedness and dripping in puddles about his feet, drowning his vest and shirt. Marcus never noticed the wet, only knowing he had nearly lost a precious treasure before he had a chance to really possess her. He caressed her quivering body with an emotion akin to awe.

Noises from the other rooms intruded, terrified murmurs of women, the wail of a baby, and a low mutter of male questions. There wasn't time to contemplate or enjoy his wife's tantalizing nakedness. With regret, Marcus grabbed a towel from the wash stand and gently wrapped it around her lovely figure, tucking the corners in over her breasts. Jennifer trembled as his hand brushed against the soft satin of her skin, but she didn't resist.

"I never thought I'd see the day when I would have you in my arms like this and set you aside, but I guess that's what I'm going to have to do." The whole episode had taken only minutes, but the sight and feel of her were permanently embedded in his mind, and his body was already responding. Marcus courteously wished the roomful of people outside to hell.

Jennifer didn't move from Marc's arms. Shivering uncontrollably, she buried her face against his chest, unaware of the effect she was having on her husband, seeking only the comfort of his protection. His touch, instead of warming her set off a new series of tremors, and she wanted only to curl up somewhere safe and warm.

"Lucia!" Marcus hollered at the partially opened door knowing the little maid wouldn't be far from it. "Fetch Jenny's robe!" The trembling figure in his arms had grown colder and more silent while the noise outside grew louder. He caressed the fine line of her back in comforting strokes. "It's all right now, Jenny, everything is fine. I'll get you wrapped up in a minute and we'll be out of here," he whispered against her hair.

"Oh, Marcus," she clung to his coat, still sobbing brokenly.

Lucia appeared with the green velvet robe, her eyes wide and curious, but unafraid. Marcus took the robe from her and gestured her out. "Have Henry get those men out of here, tell them to hang around a while, we're going to have a snake hunt." Lucia closed the door quietly behind her.

Tenderly, Marcus dried the fair, smooth skin of his wife. She was too weak from terror to protest, and obediently, she stood still as the towel rubbed gently over her body, erasing the fear of moments before. Lovingly, he circled a nipple with his fingertip before helping her on with the robe, his hands touching her reverently, his eyes reflecting only a gentle light.

"You're a lovely sight, Jenny Lee. If I keep a supply of snakes on hand, will you let me rescue you again?" he asked lightly, any trace of bitterness his words might hold well hidden.

Out of his embrace, with the robe pulled tightly about her, Jennifer looked at him with a bemused gaze, total confusion rendering her momentarily speechless. How could he be so violent and cold and then touch her as he did then, with all the respect of a connoisseur to a piece of priceless porcelain?

"Why a snake hunt?" Her gaze never left his face.

"Where there's one snake, there's usually two. And where there's two, there usually is a nest of little ones. Unless you want a repeat of this performance, we'll have to get rid of them."

Her eyes darkened with fear, and she grabbed his arm. "Marcus, that's dangerous, you could be hurt . . ."

She was pleading with him, and his heart skipped a beat at her concern. "Have no fear, little one, I'm not about to make a wealthy widow of you yet." He lifted a hand to stroke her long, damp hair.

"I have no wish to be a widow of any sort, but those guns scare me. Are snakes the only reason for carrying them?"

He laughed and slipped an arm about her waist. "First

you say you have no wish to marry me, now you say you don't want to be rid of me. Sooner or later you must decide which it is." Carefully avoiding the subject of guns, he opened the door, guiding her into the bedroom where the others fell upon them with questions.

Jennifer took the crying infant from Lucia's arms and looked to her husband, but Marcus was already halfway to the door, his shoulders set with determination. Before going out, he turned, and his eyes found Jennifer's.

"Lie down and rest; I will be back when we're done." Without breaking his gaze, he added to Lucia, "See that Jennifer gets some rest; she's been chilled and badly frightened, and I won't have her getting ill on us." Then he swung around and was gone.

Jennifer curled up in a chair and comforted Stuart, taking comfort herself from his warmth while she gave a vividly detailed account of Marc's heroism, bringing a merry twinkle to Lucia's eyes. Whatever his faults might be, for the moment, he was excused them all. The tale ended with Mrs. Thompson's arrival and the memory of duties to be performed.

Lucia took the quieted infant back to the sitting room while Mrs. Thompson poured a torrent of apologies into Jennifer's ears, until Lucia came back to lead her away, leaving Jennifer in peace. Jennifer could hear them in the other room, cleaning up the gore created by Marc's gun, but her senses were tuned for other sounds. She closed her eyes and strained to trace the sounds of footsteps overhead, trying to determine what was happening now, until Lucia returned and scolded her into bed. Jennifer didn't have the heart to explain this wasn't her bed, and meekly she obeyed, but when the room was empty once more, she returned to listening.

It took over an hour to locate and capture the nest between the floorboards and ceiling and once the snakes were disposed of, Marcus sent his men to board up any holes they might enter. Satisfied he had done all he could, he returned to his room, anxious about Jennifer's welfare and eager to see her welcoming smile. He had not known what an enticement that smile could be, and he regretted all the causes he had given her for withholding it. If he only knew he could be greeted with that warmth every evening upon his arrival, he could almost see himself in the role of faithful husband. But both their temperaments seemed destined to rebel against such complacency, and he knew his welcome would last only until they crossed swords again. Until she agreed to be the wife he thought he wanted, there would be no permanent peace.

As he entered the room, her back was to him, the emerald robe flaring out across the covers of the bed, her hair, dried, and softly curling, tumbling about her shoulders and down her back as she lay on her side. His gaze swept along the length of that tempting outline, the slenderness of her long legs beneath the clinging folds of the robe, the rounded swell of her hip and the deep dip to tiny waistline, the curve of her breast just barely noticeable from this angle. It was a heady sight to find lying so familiarly in his bed, and leisurely, with his imagination, he stripped the robe from her and savored again the sight of ivory satin flesh accented with the hues of rose and the silk of auburn. The thought inflamed his already simmering passion, and he approached the bed with purposeful tread.

His steps penetrating her sleep, Jennifer turned over, opening her eyes to find him hovering above her, the smoky blue she remembered so well kindling a flickering flame inside. It was all over, all her vows and promises and threats, all gone the instant he reached out to touch her, and she was powerless to move, aching for his touch but terrified of its results.

Her fears were groundless. The moment Marcus saw the frightened little girl in her eyes, his protective instincts were aroused and his passion died. All the obstacles between them were still there, solid as before, and not swept away in a grand gesture of gratitude as he'd secretly hoped.

Marcus lowered himself to Jennifer's side, leaning across her and resting his weight on one arm as he searched her face. Her lips quivered, then relaxed into a smile when he made no other move to touch her.

Perversely, now that he had refrained, she wanted to reach out and stroke the hard angle of his face, reassure herself of his reality, but that would be an incredible folly while she lay in this position, vulnerable to his every whim. She struggled to sit up, and courteously he helped her, averting his eyes from the loosely wrapped bodice of the robe until she tightened it.

"They're all gone?" Jennifer sat cross-legged in front of him, still clutching his callused hand, the waist length tresses and large eyes making her look more than ever a twelve-year-old.

"All gone, my love, you may bathe as you wish now, unless you're still frightened of the room, in which case I'd be more than happy to stand shotgun while you wash." He leered convincingly, and she laughed, a clear, musical peal that brought him pleasure.

"Then I would not only have to watch for the snake over my head, but the one behind my back, and I'm not sure which would be the most dangerous." She played with his hand, entwining her slender fingers with his large ones.

He captured her hand with both of his. "I don't understand why you consider me dangerous, Jenny."

"Don't you?" She peered at him through a thick fringe of lashes, considering her reply. "Then perhaps it is myself who is dangerous."

"That I can well believe. Since you walked up the plank of my boat I have found myself in one predicament after another. You're a walking disaster area, but that is hardly any reason to avoid me."

"If you'll recall, even our first meeting had disastrous results, so don't scoff. Just accept it that I can never be the wife you want and don't tempt fate by pretending otherwise."

"Jennifer, you're a first-class, grade-A fool, and I intend

to prove you wrong. But right now, Mrs. Thompson would like to know if you would like a little supper sent up. That's a major concession on her part. She has no help downstairs and never serves meals in rooms for anyone else." He released her hand and rested his casually on her knee, wondering what insane fantasies she had cooked up this time to classify herself and their marriage as dangerous. Dangerous to whom?

"No, I don't want her going to any trouble for me. I will dress and go down with you. Would it be all right if Lucia ate with us, also? I hate to leave her here by herself."

"I'll never make a snob out of you, will I? Bring her along. We'll set Junior in the middle of the table and we can all admire him while we eat." Marcus gave up on her and stood.

"I told you I would be better as governess than wife, but you wouldn't believe me." Jennifer swung her legs over the edge of the bed and let them dangle while she studied his irritated expression. "To me, children are to be enjoyed and not shut away behind closed doors until they are grown."

His eyes softened as he conceded the point. "You are right; I was being selfish in expecting your company as much to myself as possible. We will allow it now while you are adjusting to life here, but when I come back after spending the entire week away, I will expect a little more time alone with you. Is that too much to ask?"

Jennifer looked at him with surprise; he had never shown much interest in her company before; what new tactic was this? But he seemed deadly serious, and she lowered her gaze. "No, of course not, Marcus. I will miss you while you're gone."

"Will you now? Well, we'll see when I return, but I haven't left yet. So run get yourself dressed while I get rid of these clothes you've so nicely ruined." He pulled her to her feet and stood holding her hand for a moment, amazed at her slightness next to him now that she was bereft of bulky petticoats and bustles.

Timidly, she rubbed a finger over the watermarked silk of his vest. "I did rather drown it, didn't I?"

"I would gladly repeat the performance—without the snake—if you wish, but I make no guarantee that the result will be so innocent the next time I catch you like that," he replied with a rakish lift of his brow.

Jennifer flashed a quick grin, then scampered out of reach. "Your suits are safe from me; I'll not give you the opportunity again." With an impudent grin, she departed, leaving Marcus to stare after her as one would an elusive will-o'-the-wisp.

The hubbub diminished to a whisper as they entered the crowded dining room, Jennifer clinging to Marc's arm, Lucia following with Stuart. All eyes turned to their entrance, watching as Marcus guided them to their table and saw them seated, the murmur growing louder and warmer as the women shyly surveyed the room. Their all male audience watched in appreciation; it had been a long time since they had been in the company of respectable young women; what women were here were either old or far from respectable.

The room was obviously intended for both saloon and dining, but the long mahogany bar that ran the width of the rear was deserted despite the lateness of the hour. Most of the tables displayed a bottle or two and few of the men were eating at this hour, but there was no bartender to serve them, and the only waitress in evidence was Mrs. Thompson herself. She hurried to their table the moment her guests were seated.

"I've set aside a pot of stew for you, and I've got some fresh biscuits in the oven, would you like something to drink?" The woman looked questioningly to Marcus. She appeared exhausted and harassed, her fine, gray hair escaping in wisps from the neat bun at her neck, but she smiled cheerfully at their greetings.

After Marcus made his request, Jennifer asked, "Do you do all the cooking *and* wait on tables?"

The old lady smiled wearily. "I used to have some help

but the respectable girls couldn't take their pinching and lewd remarks," she made a rude gesture at the men behind her, "and the ones who enjoyed their attention found better paying jobs elsewhere." Her tone was expressive. "It's been a while since I've been able to get any help at all; I can't afford pay that competes with the mines." Without waiting for further comment, she hurried off to the kitchen.

Charlie appeared with a bottle of wine and lavish compliments and tried to finagle a seat, but Marcus declined to offer one. They had shared meals together when Marcus was here alone, but he had no wish to establish a precedent while the women were here or trouble could arise with the rest of the men. He watched the disappointed young man walk off and ignored the disapproval in Jennifer's eyes; he had offended her southern hospitality and there was no use in explaining why. She'd already made up her own reasons. Marcus sighed and took a long drink.

The unnatural quiet that possessed the room dissipated immediately upon their departure, and loud cries and raucous laughter followed them up the stairs. The miners were out of practice in good behavior, particularly on payday, and the strain of exercising it in the women's presence was broken with relief when they left. Marcus smiled to himself; at least, they'd had the sense to restrain themselves, whether in fear of him or awe of the women he might never know.

Marcus entered the sitting room behind Jennifer, and stood silently watching her tend to his son. Only one lamp had been lit and in the dim light, her hair took on a subdued gleam of its own. Caught in an unfashionable net, it threatened to spill over as she moved about in pursuit of her tasks. Her ivory eyelet gown was simple and demure but couldn't disguise the seductive grace of her movements. If he had to have a wife, he couldn't have found a woman whose looks were more to his liking than this one, and he had already whetted his taste with the passion of her response in bed. With a little experience, she could easily satisfy this need that had burned inside him since that first night, but she was a stubborn little brat and would fight every halter he would use to ensnare her. He had no wish to break her like a wild horse, but gentle her like a young one, only his patience was rapidly wearing thin.

Jennifer set the cradle to gently rocking and turned to meet her husband's gaze with an outward composure she did not feel. She knew the path of his thoughts, but she could not guess their final direction. To all purposes he had forgotten their contract in his single-minded efforts to persuade her into his bed. Her continual reminders would not hold him much longer, but a fraction of an idea had begun to form at supper tonight, and with a little more time it might develop into an obstacle he would not care to hurdle. She smiled at his serious expression.

"Come, give me a good-night kiss and I will not bother you more tonight. You look worn out." He advanced into the room, holding out his hand to her.

Reluctantly, Jennifer took it, wary of his embrace even as he drew her into it. Close to him, she could feel the hard leanness of his body, the iron strength of his arms around her, and she steeled herself to resist. Marcus made no effort to pull her closer, but bent to taste the sweetness of her lips. He warmed them gently with his kisses, plying her with his tenderness, not arousing passion but allowing it to simmer. Sighing softly, she rested her head against his shoulder when their lips parted.

"You are teasing me, Marcus, but I won't give in. I'm stronger than you think," she whispered against the roughness of his coat.

His hand stroked the curve of her back. "I will woo you, little one, and change your mind. Do not underestimate your opponent."

"Do not underestimate yours." She stepped back from his arms, amazed at her ability to do so. Knowledge of her love for him had given her a strength she had not known she possessed. It was for his happiness as well as hers that she fought.

Marcus smiled gravely at the young face before him, her eyes darting sparks of fire in the lamplight. His Jenny had a character and will of her own, but he would not be denied.

"Good-night, little one." He stroked her cheek with a lingering caress and left her to herself.

Chapter Fifteen

The weekend passed swiftly in Marc's almost constant company as he acquainted Jennifer with the town and its inhabitants. He had lived here for months once, on that ill-fated attempt to make his fortune with these same mines, and the town had not changed greatly, only growing larger with the advent of the railroad. His reopening of the mines made him a popular and respected man about town, and his lady was treated accordingly. Jennifer had to confine her smiles as the roughly clad, bearded miners attempted gentlemanly gallantry whenever they were in her presence.

Marcus made no further demands on her person other than his request for a good-night kiss, and she meekly acquiesced to that request in hopes it would satisfy him temporarily. The pattern didn't change from the first night: he remained gentle and undemanding, leaving her hungering for more, a fact she felt he was counting on. Her husband was no fool, and Jennifer fully believed his declaration to woo her into submissiveness, and he would succeed too, unless she successfully launched a counter-attack.

That was a difficult thing to do, knowing its result might be to drive him away forever. But if he were going to leave her, it would be better now than after he had breached all her defenses. No, it was better that he realize now what kind of person she was, that she could not give up her dreams to be his dutiful society wife, and that he choose to accept or reject her on this knowledge. They were painful thoughts, but on Monday, after her husband's departure, Jennifer began laying the groundwork for her strategy.

With the miners returned to camp, there was little activity in the town, and left to themselves, there was little to occupy the women's time but talk. Mrs. Thompson was more than happy to oblige, and under Jennifer's skillful questioning, she soon revealed the dismal state of the hotel business.

Mr. Thompson had died a few years back leaving no debts and no savings, only the monstrously empty hotel in a nearly deserted town. With the promise of the railroad's arrival and eventual hope of the mine's reopening, his wife had been able to borrow the money to update the building, installing plumbing and gas lighting at a time when the rest of the area was bathing in creeks and eating over campfires. The luxuries were a sensation that eventually wore off, particularly when it became apparent the service was less than excellent.

In her sixties and with a history of heart trouble, Emma Jane Thompson was no match for the hotel. Unable to find or keep good help, the majority of the workload eventually fell on her already overtaxed shoulders. As the burden grew heavier, she was forced to close down the popular bar, eliminate room services, open the dining room only on weekends, and leave the more difficult cleaning to those times when help was available. A newly built tavern down the road soon made large inroads on her whiskey

profits and now threatened to open its own inn. She had
retaliated by reopening the dining room, but few people
came. First visitors to the town were her main source of
income, and they soon left town or found lodging elsewhere. Only Marcus remained loyal; he and his miners on
the weekends provided enough profit to barely cover expenses.

Lucia listened to this tale with sympathy, but Jennifer
heard it with interest and firm resolve. Her talents had
gone begging too long, now was the time to reestablish
her priorities. It would be a delicate task: Mrs. Thompson
was a proud woman and wouldn't accept help easily, and
if Marcus ever suspected her intentions, he would be scandalized, but if there were a way to do it, Jennifer would
find it.

It was a gradual process. Out of seemingly restless boredom, Jennifer followed the old woman about her chores,
occasionally giving a helping hand when needed while allowing the woman to pour out a lifetime of talk. While
Lucia watched Stuart, Jennifer would appear in the cav-
ernous kitchen and idly peel vegetables for that night's
supper while exchanging gossip with her garrulous hostess.

By Thursday, Jennifer had persuaded Emma to let her
bake a pie for Marc's expected arrival the next day, and
she spent a joyous few hours covered in flour and well-
steamed with the kitchen heat, a sure cure for homesick-
ness as well as being a soul-satisfying pastime. Lucia
watched with interest as Jennifer explained her techniques
and together they proudly presented the twin results of
their efforts to Mrs. Thompson for approval.

"We baked two, one for our supper tonight and one
for Marcus. You don't mind, do you? Lucia said she
wanted to learn, and that's the best way I know to teach
her." Jennifer's happy face was flushed with heat, hair
hanging in moist tendrils about her neck, muslin gown
well-decorated with flour, but the excitement in her eyes
prevented criticism.

Emma smiled her approval. "Of course, I don't mind. It's been a long time since I had the time to mess about with such nonsense. It's all I can do to get the meat and potatoes cooked. You are going to let me have a taste, aren't you?"

"You don't think we could eat it all by ourselves, now, do you?" Jennifer laughed. "Let me set them out on the buffet to cool, and we'll get out of your way."

She backed through the swinging doors and into the cooler dining room, arranging the pies carefully on tiles at the serving counter.

"Those wouldn't be fresh baked pies you're hiding from me over there, would they?"

The voice came from behind her, and Jennifer swung around, startled to find anyone in the room at all at this hour. Charlie stood with legs apart, hands in pockets, and grin spreading across his face, eyeing first Jennifer, then the pies, hungrily. His little-boy look of starvation was too blatant to be ignored, and Jennifer laughed at his expression.

"Charlie, you look like you haven't been fed in a week. What are you doing here today?"

"Hungering for a taste of those pies. Do you have any idea at all how long it's been since I've had a fresh baked pie? Do you have any idea how much I'd *give* for one of those pies right now?"

"Judging from the fact that you've scarcely looked at me since you spotted the wretched things and that I haven't heard one flowery compliment out of you for a record two minutes, I guess you must want them pretty badly. But they're already promised. One's for Marcus and I've already told Mrs. T. and Lucia we'd have the other."

His grin broadened. "Then you can let me have the one for Marcus; he won't be here to enjoy it."

"Charlie! Don't say that. Why shouldn't he?" Jennifer quit smiling and searched his face, certain nothing could have happened to Marcus. Why shouldn't he return as promised?

Charlie stopped laughing and patted her hand. "I'm sorry, that ain't no way to tell you, but I was too tickled to be polite. We got a new pump in to drain one of the mines, and he wanted to stay around and see that it's working. That's why I'm here. I came by to pick up some parts and give you the message. He said to tell you he was sorry, and he'd make it in first chance he gets."

Jennifer withdrew her hand and nodded her head. That was like Marcus, his work came first, and she had no right to complain, but she could feel the disappointment well up inside here. She had not been separated from him for so long a time since they'd been married, and although he often irritated her and frequently frightened her, she missed him heartily. It was lonely enough at night in bed, knowing he was only a few steps away, but when he wasn't there at all, it became a terrifying experience.

"Gee, Mrs. Armstrong, I didn't mean to upset you." Charlie watched with alarm the change from gay excitement to disappointment in the girl's face. It hadn't occurred to him before that his boss was leaving the dirty work to him.

"The name's Jenny, Charlie." She smiled crookedly. "And I guess you're right, we won't be needing the extra pie. I'll ask Mrs. Thompson what she wants to charge for it."

His face lit with expectation. "I'll give you everything I've got on me." He started dumping the change from his pockets on the counter. "It will be worth every cent of it."

"Charlie! That's way too much! Put some of it back!" Jennifer tried to push the money back, but he refused to take it.

"Supply and demand, my dear. This is a precious commodity, and you should expect to charge dearly for it. I thank you kindly, and I will think of you with every bite." He swept up the pie, devouring it with his eyes while contentedly thinking of his boss' reaction when he found out what he was missing. That would pay him back for this expedition, and give his missus a chance to get even, too.

Charlie smiled with satisfaction, until Jennifer interrupted his reverie with a warning.

"You're not to tell Marcus about that pie, Charlie; I never saw it before in my life, understand?"

Charlie looked at her in surprise, "Nope, I don't, but if that's the way you want it . . ." He shrugged.

"I do and I'm holding you to it," she admonished firmly.

When he left, Jennifer's overactive mind began to churn, and as she jingled the change in her pocket on the way back to Emma, a plan gradually took shape. It might take weeks or months to turn the hotel into a profitable business, but there was no reason the dining room couldn't start paying for itself.

With a self-satisfied grin, she dumped the money into Emma's apron pocket. "I have just earned my first honest dollar," she declared, causing Emma and Lucia to look up at her, startled, to see if the heat had addled her wits. "Marcus isn't coming, so I sold his pie to Charlie; the poor boy was desperate, what else could I do?" Her laughter tinkled merrily through the kitchen, and the other two smiled at her delight.

"I'm sorry Mr. Armstrong won't be able to make it, but should you have sold that pie to young Charlie? It's one thing to be down here baking pies for your husband, but to go selling them is another." Emma wore a worried frown between her eyes.

Jennifer waved away the objection. "It was fun and Charlie was thrilled. We ought to make some more and make everybody happy." She planted the idea casually.

"Well, I ain't got the time, and you certainly can't be doing it, so be off with you. We'll be eating in a little while." Emma shooed them away.

Jennifer smiled mischievously and waited for Lucia to join her so they could ascend the stairs together. Lucia watched her employer with suspicion, perceiving that Jennifer was too pleased with herself for someone whose husband wouldn't be home as expected. There might be some deep grievance between husband and wife, but there was a good deal of affection, also, and she knew Jennifer had looked forward to her husband's return. Jennifer was definitely up to something.

The first hint of what it might be came as they finished supper that evening. During the week, the dining room was nearly empty of anyone but the two women and Emma. This night two more engineers from the mines showed up, and their first request was for pie. Jennifer's lips twitched as Lucia caught her eye; the way to a man's heart, not to mention his pocketbook, was surely through his stomach.

Emma was forced to turn them away disappointed, but when several more men trickled in late that night and began arriving early next morning, even her limited business acumen became excited. With a show of reluctance, she acceded to Jennifer's eager offer to bake a few more pies, just to keep the men happy.

At first, Lucia was horrified at the idea of Jennifer's actually working in the kitchen like a scullery maid, but as she began to realize what fun her employer was having, she slowly changed her opinion. She had to admit there was not a lot for an active person to do around here, and surely Jennifer couldn't get into any trouble making a few pies out of sight in the kitchen. It was a charitable proposition even Marcus must approve. So, against her better judgment, Lucia joined in the scheme, sitting at a table and inexpertly paring the fruit while Jennifer worked up to her elbows in flour and pastry and Stuart slept contentedly nearby.

As fast as they could remove the pies from the oven, they sold them. The men had no interest in buying a single piece and genteelly consuming it on the premises, but bought pans and all to take back with them to camp. This practice quickly depleted their supply of baking pans, and they ran to purchase the entire supply at the hardware store. By the end of the afternoon they were out of pans again, and the room was filling with miners with pay in their pockets and an entire weekend in which to spend it.

They had to surrender their efforts to Emma's whiskey and stew.

Upstairs, Jennifer washed and changed from her heat sodden, flour laden clothes, and faced another problem. With Marcus in attendance, they had casually dined in the same room with a hundred carousing miners and thought nothing of it. They had been slightly embarrassed by the attention they had drawn, but the men were polite and respectful, and they soon learned to live with it. But daring those same men without Marc's protection caused even Jennifer to hesitate. They would be trapped in their rooms the entire weekend while the streets and hotel filled with shouting, laughing, drunken miners. How could Marcus be so thick as to leave them to such a fate?

Marcus had had no intention of leaving them to that fate, but his original plans quickly dissolved when he discovered the reason for the early disappearance of so many of his men. Instead of sending Henry in alone as planned, he located an engineer to take his place with the pump. His expression was not pleased when he rode out of camp that evening.

But when Marcus knocked on the sitting room door a few hours later, he had assumed a more affable expression, apologizing for his delay and offering Jennifer his arm to take her to dinner. He made no mention of his sudden change in plans. Jennifer was wary of his unusual solicitousness. The ice gray of his eyes was fair warning, and she knew a storm to be brewing. It was in uneasy silence that she accompanied him to the dining room.

By the end of the meal, Jennifer's stomach was tied in knots waiting for the explosion that was sure to come, wondering what form it would take. She had taken care to avoid the men knowing she was the source of the pies; Mrs. Thompson had done all the selling but the first one to Charlie and she had stayed out of sight in the kitchen. But some sixth sense told her the pies were the reason for Marcus' unexpected appearance, and it would be the pie that would bring his judgment down upon her head. She prayed Emma had sold the last one.

Luck was against her. Mrs. Thompson came bustling out proudly bearing the one remaining pie she had scrupulously set aside for her favored guests, congratulating herself on her foresight now that Marcus was here. She set the pie in the center of the table and began distributing clean dishes, chattering merrily.

"The girls were so upset when young Charlie told them you weren't coming. I sure am glad you changed your mind. You wouldn't believe the excitement we've had in here over these pies; you'd think those men of yours had never seen one before. I sure am glad I had one saved, Mr. Armstrong, you can have a taste and tell me if it's worth all this carrying on."

Jennifer frowned warningly at the old woman; she had made her promise not to let anyone know who made the pies, but Emma might not think it applied to Marcus. But it was specifically for Marcus she had wanted the promise; she wasn't ready yet to let him know her plans; they were still in their formative stage. The old woman took no notice of her frown, but smiled cheerfully and hurried on to wait on another table.

"So this is the famous pie I've been hearing about; I hadn't realized Emma was such a celebrated cook." These were the first words Marcus had voluntarily uttered since they sat down, and he drew the immediate attention of both women. They watched expectantly as he helped himself to a large piece and handed the server to Jennifer. There was no sparkle of amusement in his eyes as his gaze met hers. "You do realize my mines were half empty today while the men rode down here to get one before the supply was gone, and those who remained could talk of nothing else? Charlie did a fine job of spreading the news."

Jennifer lowered her gaze from his and passed the server to Lucia without touching the pastry. He had already made up his mind that the fault was hers, whatever it might be, and nothing would save her from his wrath. Stuart sucked on a piece of dry bread, while she wiped his hands with her napkin. "He was told that pie was intended for you; there was no way of knowing he would broadcast it."

Marcus took a bite of pie and all eyes once more centered on him. He chewed slowly, savoring the taste before setting his fork down and turning to Jennifer. "If Charlie ate the pie intended for me, then why does this one taste the same as the one Henrí baked from *your* recipe? Better than Henrí's, actually," he amended, but the hard set of his chiseled jaw made it clear he intended no compliment.

"Henrí probably figured he could improve on any recipe from a mere woman," Jennifer replied, purposely misconstruing his question.

"That is not what I asked." Marcus glared at the uncontrollable imp who purposely went out of her way to overthrow his plans. "It was out of place for you to enter a public kitchen to bake a pie for me, but excusable. But to make a spectacle of yourself by baking pies for every man in town is downright incredible. No wife of mine will act as serving wench for a camp full of miners! If you must cook, you will wait until we have a kitchen of our own; I won't have you setting foot in this one again!"

Jennifer waited for his tirade to end, her chin rising higher with each word and her eyes smoldering. Satisfied he was finished, she casually lifted his dish of pie, and as Lucia watched in horror, deliberately dumped the contents in his lap, the juicy fruit running down the leg of his trousers in rivulets of sticky syrup.

"And I won't have you telling me what I can or cannot do," she spat out, snatching Stuart from his seat and stalking from the room.

The incident had gone virtually unnoticed by all except the horrified occupants of a nearby table, but Jennifer's precipitate departure and the resulting loud slam of a door overhead caused heads to turn all about the room. Marcus stoically removed the pie from his lap and rejected Lucia's offer of assistance, ineffectively swiping at the juice with his napkin, then drying his hands.

Jennifer had taken advantage of her head start to bolt the hall door to her room, but the connecting door posed a problem. With the fury of anger to give her strength, she lowered the bed cabinet and shoved it until one massive corner rested against the door while the head braced itself against a wall. He would have to break the door down to get through that, she decided.

Her exertions were done none too soon. A rattle at the hall door told her Marcus was already upstairs. No one else would consider walking in without knocking. Finding the door bolted, he stomped away, but a minute later he attempted the door from the wash room. Jennifer held her breath and bit her lower lip as the door hit against the bed and went no farther, not even creating a crack he could speak through. His fury must have multiplied a thousandfold at this unexpected obstruction, but the only sound she caught was a muffled curse and retreating footsteps. He wasn't going to attempt more, and she released her breath in a sigh of relief. There was no telling what Marcus would have done in a fit of temper, and she wasn't eager to find out. By tomorrow, perhaps he would be more reasonable, although she had her doubts.

Now another problem struck her. By barring the connecting door, she had shut herself from both bath and wardrobe. She could not keep the door barred forever, or much longer than morning at best. Her sigh this time was a depressed one. There was no winning a battle when the other side held all the weapons. She could only hold out as long as possible. Carefully hanging her gown over a chair, she checked to see if Stuart slept, then removed all but her chemise and retired to her solitary bed. It had finally become more than a symbol in their strange war, it was now a weapon.

Chapter Sixteen

Stuart's cry woke Jennifer early next morning, and she had time to dress in yesterday's gown before the first knock came at the hall door. It wasn't light like a woman's, but hesitant, and obviously not Marc's. Cautiously, Jennifer unbolted the door.

"Henry! It's just like old times, isn't it?" She swung the door wider and allowed the old man to enter with his large tray. "Does he have one of his miners stationed at the stairs to keep me from going down?"

Henry managed a small grin as he set the tray down. "No, ma'am, but he says you and the maid better keep to your rooms until the men are gone. I can bring up whatever you need. I'll just be outside somewheres any time you need me." He eyed the strange position of the bed, then dared ask, "Want me to move that thing so's you can get in there? Cap'n done gone back to the mines this mornin'."

Jennifer couldn't decide whether or not it was a relief she received this news, but she nodded acquiescence. "I guess you better, Henry. I'll have to turn this place back into a sitting room if we're to live up here for two days. Captain didn't mention what we're supposed to do with ourselves during that time, did he?" she asked, not really expecting an answer. Anything Marcus said would have been too impolite for the old man to repeat.

"No, ma'am. Cap'n was in a foul mood when he left,

but you know he's only worried about you, you won't be disobeying him, will you?" Henry pushed the bed back in position and looked at her through worried eyes.

"No, Henry, I shall be the dutiful wife for two whole days, so you won't get in trouble with the boss man. You can report back Monday that I was a paragon of virtue," she replied bitterly and dismissed the servant.

Lucia soon joined her, and they breakfasted together in the sitting room. Jennifer could feel the little maid's sympathy, tempered with a cross current of curiosity. Both their rages had seemed out of proportion to the cause, and Jennifer knew Lucia was waiting for some explanation, but the story was too long and not hers to tell, so Lucia waited in vain.

Emma interrupted while they were still drinking coffee. She looked more harassed than ever, the heat in the kitchen having reached furnace proportions judging by her flushed coloring and uneven breathing. Jennifer watched her with concern.

"Come in, Emma, and have a seat. Those men will wear you out if you let them." Jennifer got up and ushered the elderly woman into a chair.

" 'Tain't nothin' new. I just come up to see if everything's all right. I'm afraid Mr. Armstrong is awful mad at me, and I had to promise I'd see that you stay out of the kitchen, Jennifer," she admitted abjectly.

"If Mr. Armstrong is mad at anybody, it's me. Have some coffee, Emma, and don't fret about it. I promise I won't set foot in your kitchen again, that's what he said, wasn't it?" Jennifer grinned as she carefully worded her question.

"That's what he said. I'm so sorry if I caused you any trouble, I didn't mean for him to get so mad," Emma mourned.

"You didn't cause anything, Emma. I did. And if he makes any more trouble, I'll be responsible for that, too. You just don't worry about a thing."

Lucia had already seen the warning sparkle in Jennifer's eyes, and in light of that, her words sounded more like a battle cry than a pacification attempt, but there wasn't much she could do to stop Jennifer once she made up her mind and that determined gleam meant she had. At least, life would never be too dull with this one around, and remembering Marc's face as the pie trickled down his leg, Lucia grinned.

Saturday night was the grand finale of the miners' weekend and Jennifer lay into the early morning darkness listening to the rumble and laughter of male voices below. She stirred uneasily with any footstep that lingered overlong outside her door, wondering with each one if it might be Marcus returned. But she knew he wouldn't, that it was only this aching midnight loneliness that raised her hopes, and she wondered what he was doing now. She hadn't meant for this struggle for freedom to get off to such a bad start; she had wanted to ease him gently into it until—possibly, hopefully—it had become an accepted routine, but now it looked like a long and bitter fight to the end.

Lord, but she loved him with every pore and cell of her body, would always love him whatever happened. She yearned to nestle closely to him, to kiss and coax him into loving her back, to wake up by his side and know she was his and his alone, to bear his children and grow old together, sharing their lives in everything they did. Excitement flooded her body at the memory of his hands against her skin, and the desire for the incident to be repeated was strong.

But she would fight him tooth and nail, every minute of every day until he freed her from this slavery, until he recognized her independence and gave up the idea that he had complete control of her life. She had spent seventeen years under the control of others, a repressive, destructive constraint that had almost ruined her life; she would not allow it to happen again, not for all the love in this world.

When she slept, she slept badly, dreaming of smoky blue

eyes hovering over her, pressing her down into a suffocating pillow of softness.

Sunday passed uneventfully and with it went the miners. Monday, and they dared venture from their rooms again, lingering over coffee with Emma and listening to the latest gossip in the safety of the empty dining room. When Emma expressed a need to do some shopping, Jennifer offered to do it for her, assuring her she was an experienced bargain hunter. When Lucia offered to accompany her, Emma accepted the proposal. The town was not a large one and the stores were few, but it was a burdensome task of which she was well rid.

But when Jennifer returned with the knowledge of local prices for simple staples, she was brimming over with money saving ideas and insisted Emma let her go over the books to see if they would work. Her excitement was contagious as she outlined plans for bulk purchases based on regular supplies needed, of ordering direct from the city and saving money even over transportation costs, and all she needed was access to the books to determine amounts, and she could show Emma the savings. Emma gave in to her urgings, figuring it a good, safe occupation for her restless boarder.

Eagerly, Jennifer buried herself in the boxes of receipts and scraps of papers that Emma euphemistically called her books. When she had worked with these figures at home, suggestions for improvements had come readily but were generally rejected in favor of "the way things were always done." A child wasn't expected to correct her parents, but as the wife of a rich man, her suggestions might hold a little more weight. Gleefully, Jennifer went to work.

It was a tedious, time consuming task bringing order out of chaos, and Jennifer had scarcely skimmed the surface by the end of the first day. Emma complained about her positioning herself at a public counter in the lobby, but since visitors were few and far between, and that was where the majority of the records were kept, she didn't make an issue of it. With no desk clerk, it gave Jennifer

an opportunity to meet anyone who did come in and relieved Emma of running up and down stairs every time
the bell over the door rang. Jennifer knew she was acting
in deliberate defiance of Marc's wishes, but she wasn't
backing down now. This was something she could do and
do well, if he would only give her time to show him. She
worked feverishly on it all Monday afternoon, starting in
on it again Tuesday. If only no one informed him of her
project, she could have most of it organized by Friday.
Then if he protested, she could show him her results.

Luck ran out on Wednesday with the appearance of
Charlie. She was so engrossed in a list of figures she was
attempting to add in her head that she ignored the ringing
of the bell until a shadow bent over her papers and removed the pen from her hand.

"Charlie!" She looked up in surprise to find his jolly
grin hovering over her and had to return his smile, though
her heart sank at his presence. Marcus would most certainly find out now. "What are you doing here? We have
no more pies. Is Marcus making an errand boy of you
again?"

"No, *ma'am,*" he stated firmly. "He's been in a fine temper all week and I'm not getting nowhere near the man.
If you two don't kiss and make up, I'm not taking any
responsibility for what happens to that gentleman." He
shook his head in solemn dismay, then smiled winningly
as he changed the subject. "I'm here on my own business,
and I just couldn't help stopping by to inquire if we'll be
getting any more of those pies this week." He crossed his
arms and leaned on the counter, his black eyes twinkling
merrily.

Jennifer made a face at him. "You're after getting me
killed, aren't you? Go away with you if you've just come
here to pester, I'm busy."

"I see that. Has Emma hired you as chief bookkeeper
or are you really that bored you can't find anything else
to read?"

"I happen to be an excellent bookkeeper and don't

laugh at me like that. If you tell Marcus a word of this, I'll have your head in the next pie we bake."

"Bake me another pie and I promise I'll never say another word."

"If I could rely on that, I'd be off to the kitchen this minute," she commented sarcastically.

"Ouch. Now I know you two better make up, you're as prickly as he is. What's Emma up to if she's got you out here?"

Jennifer bit the tip of her pen thoughtfully and studied Charlie for a minute before answering. "She's upstairs cleaning; she has to do everything for herself, you know."

"I know. So why are you looking at me like that? I feel like a side of beef that's just been marked, labeled, and hung in the butcher's window."

"That's probably because of the flies buzzing around your head. You told me once you'd do just about anything to have one of those pies, didn't you?"

Charlie watched her warily. "Except get myself killed. What did you have in mind?"

"I can't go into the kitchen anymore, and Emma is too busy to do all the work herself. What I had in mind was some kitchen help. You wouldn't know where we could find some, would you?"

"Well, not right off hand. Is that what it takes to get those pies on a regular basis?" He looked skeptical.

"That would be a fair start. Do you think you can do it?"

"I'll sure as hell try, ma'am, if you'll pardon my French." His skepticism was gone, replaced by a wicked grin.

"I'll pardon most anything if you find that help. Now, if you have nothing better to do, go away with you." Jennifer flicked her hand at him, shooing him from the counter.

"I'm going, but I'll be back, lovely lady. Just start practicing some of that well-known charm so I can live long enough to find that help for you." He went out the door, paused, then stuck his head back in. "You wouldn't want to send a loving message to that husband of yours to soften him up a mite, would you?"

"Tell him I'm planning cream pie this weekend and my aim has improved," she retorted, causing Charlie to shake his head in dismay again and disappear.

Thursday, against the objections of all and sundry, Jennifer sent Lucia to the kitchens to start pastry for the pies. If Jennifer couldn't do it, nothing had been said about Lucia, and the money made last week had been nearly all clear profit. As Jennifer now knew, it was cash Emma badly needed to meet upcoming debts, and she wouldn't abandon this project readily. With Stuart at her feet, she sat in the deserted dining room, peeling fruit by the bowlful. She peeled rapidly, entertaining herself with a varied repertoire of songs as she worked, until her selections broke down noisily into the bawdy ballads she'd heard from the miners, bringing Emma and Lucia out to see if she'd taken leave of her senses and leaving them all giggling.

Friday, Emma refused to let Jennifer near the dining room or kitchen and only major persuasion convinced her the lobby wouldn't be dangerous grounds in the morning hours. Jennifer had almost all the figures she needed together and once that was done, she could draw up an overall budget that should surely convince both Emma and Marcus that she could serve some useful function besides ornamentation. She tackled the task with fervor, ignoring the fragrant smell of baking pies drifting in from the kitchen, unaware of the heat, or the buzzing of flies, conscious only of the pattern of figures that formed beneath her fingers.

Not until a strong hand gripped her wrist, cruel fingers jerking her to her feet did Jennifer realize anyone had come in. Frightened, she looked up into the stormy gray of her husband's eyes. He hadn't bothered to change into formal clothes, but wore an open neck loose shirt and wrinkled denims similar to his men's, only the broad brim hat remaining familiar attire. He appeared tired and dusty and furiously angry, and Jennifer had visions of another fiasco like last week's, and all her hopes swiftly crumbled.

"What in hell do you think you're doing now? This town will be crawling with men in a few hours. Were you planning on personally greeting every one of them as they come in? Get out from behind there and get upstairs where you belong. Where's Emma?"

Jennifer attempted to snatch her wrist from his grip, but he only held it tighter, drawing her out from behind the counter. Fruitlessly, she smacked the hand that held her, replying through clenched teeth, "Unless you want to entertain the entire town with my screams, I suggest you let me go and we carry on this discussion in a more private place."

Glaring at her, Marcus flung her arm down and bowed sarcastically toward the staircase. "After you, then, by all means, madam." His dark face held no hint of respite.

They ascended the staircase in furious silence, Jennifer's heels tapping out an angry tattoo on the hardwood floor. Marcus slammed the sitting room door behind them and leaned against it, glaring at the infuriating figure of his wife as she whirled around to face him. To take her over his knee and whip some sense into her was his first and only thought as her tongue lashed out at him.

"You're a bully, Marcus Armstrong, and I'm tired of being told what I can or cannot do! I wasn't hurting a soul sitting out there, and you know it!"

"Damn it, Jennifer, how many times do I have to tell you! You're my wife! Look at you—you've got dirt smeared across your face, ink staining your hands, and you were sitting out in a public lobby just like some kind of . . ."

"Clerk, maybe? Servant? Working class lackey? Or were you searching for stronger terms? You've got the grounds to call me every name in the book, why don't you? Look at where I come from! What do you think I *am*, Marcus?"

"My *wife*, and a damned fool! What happened to our contract? Have you decided to rescind it in my absence?" Marcus stepped closer, his first irrational desire to spank sense into her rapidly disintegrating into an altogether different desire.

"That's a joke, you reminding *me* of our contract when you've done everything but tear it up and throw it away in your lust to get me to bed! Now that I'm trying to do something I want, you remember its existence. Just keep away from me, Marcus." Jennifer backed away.

"And what is it you want, madam? To make a fool of me in public? To reduce yourself to the status of servant as you once suggested? Just what did you have in mind?"

"I have in mind doing what comes naturally to me, working. I am no knickknack you can set on the shelf and take down and admire when the spirit hits you."

"And being my wife doesn't come naturally to you, is that it? Climbing into my bed certainly seemed natural enough the first time, perhaps you prefer it without the ties of matrimony," Marcus sneered, reaching out to catch her wrist.

Jennifer smacked his face, but Marcus didn't flinch. Snatching her arm, he jerked her against him to prevent further repetition of that maneuver.

"By God, lady, you will pay for that." Pinning her arms with his, he crushed his lips against hers.

Jennifer had forgotten how strong and hard his body felt. She was literally crushed against him, her breasts pressing against his well-muscled chest, her heart drumming an erratic beat against his masculine solidity. With deliberate pressure, Marc slid his hand from the small of her back to her buttocks, bringing Jennifer's hips into startling contact with his hardening need, stirring her own aching desires. His tongue gave a fair imitation of his intentions, ravishing the recesses of her lips with heated thrusts. Her fingers curled in the soft material of his shirt, catching in the hairs on his chest as she resisted his onslaught, even as her hips rubbed against his arousal.

Tearing her lips from the scorching reminder of his, Jennifer shoved at Marc's chest, catching him by surprise with her vehemence. She had never openly rejected him before, and he hesitated, but the still burning brand of her hand against his cheek inflamed his anger. In retaliation, he dipped his hand into the hollow between her breasts. With satisfaction, Marcus noted her shuddering intake of breath as his hand closed around sensitive tips.

"You are my wife, Jennifer, and it is past time you learned it," he stated steadily.

Firmly pushing her bodice from ivory shoulders, Marcus savored the sight before him. Copper curls tumbled about a fragile throat, and he could watch the pulse of her heart beat in the shadowed hollow of her collarbone. The full swell of her ripe breasts lay exposed to his touch, and the thought of any other hand but his on their softness filled him with irrational rage. She was his now, for better or worse, and it was well past time not only that she recognize that fact, but that he derive some benefit from it. Not until he possessed her again would he be entirely certain of her surrender.

The heat of Marc's gaze as it raked over her was almost as scorching as the path of his hand, and Jennifer arched instinctively to meet his caress, savoring the sensation of rough fingers plucking at tender nipples. Once again, it seemed too right to be wrong, and she lingered in his embrace, longing for a return of that gentle lover who would teach her body what it meant to be loved.

Instead, she looked into the icy eyes of the murderous stranger she had seen once before, the hard lines of his dark jaw clenched and angry as he lifted her from the floor and carried her toward the bed, and fear swept through her veins. A life of whoredom was what Delaney had intended for her; to submit to Marc now would be no different.

As his mouth once again covered hers, Jennifer sank her teeth into his lower lip and wrenched free of his hold with the slackening of his embrace.

Jennifer met her husband's fury with a madness of her own. "I will *never* be your wife, sir, not if it means my only purpose in life is submitting to your devilish lusts. I may not be the lady you desire for wife, but I sure as hell won't be your whore! And your claim to the title of gentleman is sadly tarnished!"

Whipping from his grip, Jennifer fled to the wash room, locking both doors and breathing heavily as she awaited his onslaught, raging sobs choking her throat.

Marcus heard the click of the keys and swore vividly. Twice now, she had locked him out. It would become a habit if he did not take measures soon, but conditions between them had deteriorated so swiftly, he was left bewildered. In pursuit of some solace for his frustrations, Marcus stormed from the room, slamming the door behind him with ear-shattering fury. Emma's bottles of whiskey beckoned.

Jennifer lay awake late that evening, alternately debating barring the doors and listening for Marc's arrival. She had tried to hide her fears from Lucia, but she couldn't hide it from herself any longer. If Marcus had decided their contract was void, he was capable of anything, and she wondered how much of a fight she dared wage the next time he attacked her. Whatever she did, she would lose, not only because of his superior strength, but because she had no desire to win. She wanted him with every aching inch of her body. Desire as much as anger kept her awake now, wondering and dreading the direction his lust would take next. If this was how he decided to take her, she would accept it, but how much better it would be if he could accept her, instead. Jennifer clamped her eyes closed and willed her body to stillness, but her blood raced and sleep proved elusive.

The night edged toward dawn's grayness before Jennifer heard unsteady footsteps in the room next door, and she waited with bated breath to hear the direction they would take. He walked softly, as if to keep from disturbing her, hesitating before entering the connecting room. There he stopped, and she wondered if he had just decided to wash and go to bed, but no, his hand touched the knob and it turned gently, the door easing open until he decided it wasn't blocked.

Her bed was close by, but Jennifer could make out Marc's outline in the dim light as he leaned against the door frame. He didn't move except to fold his arms across his chest, and Jennifer wondered if she dare call out to him. If she didn't, perhaps he would go away, but somehow, she knew he was waiting for her to show she was awake.

Shaking her fear, she called softly. "Marcus?"

He came forward then, jamming his hands into his pockets. "You do not fear the devil, then?" he asked, his voice only slightly slurred as he halted before he reached the bed.

"The devil is but a man, I do not fear him," she whispered in return.

"A man, but not a gentleman. And you are not a lady." He spoke slowly, as if repeating a lesson.

"Nor an angel."

There was a movement, as if he were nodding agreement. "Nor an angel." He started forward again, then restrained himself. "We will discuss it in the morning." The words obviously took an effort to speak, but before she could answer, he was gone.

Chapter Seventeen

Dressing carefully in a summer silk, tying her hair back with matching ribbons, Jennifer tried to dispel the image of the unadorned muslin and untidiness Marcus had found her in yesterday. While waiting for him to wake, she

made neat copies of the budgets and figures she had com-
piled, sending Henry to prepare the hangover tonic. If
Marcus truly wanted a wife and not a whore, perhaps she
could show him she was capable of being a wife and working, too. There was no reason she couldn't do both, if he
was ready to listen to reason. She prayed silently and impatiently while she paced the room.

She shared a late breakfast with Lucia, then sent her off
with Stuart. If Marcus wanted her alone, she would be
alone. Her strategy didn't go beyond that. If she wanted
their agreement to expand to working, how far in his direction was she willing to go to get what she wanted? She
hadn't decided, and indecision and impatience kept her
pacing the room until she heard the first stirring from the
other side of the wall.

Grabbing up a book, she did her best to concentrate on
it and not the noises of awakening from her husband's
room. He would be in no hurry if he had a hangover if
she remembered correctly, and it might be a long time
before he was ready to meet her again. Perhaps he was
still angry and would leave without remembering last
night's promise. She would not think of that.

So it was with relief that she watched the opening of the
connecting door and the entrance of Marcus, clad in smoking jacket and carrying his drink, his face still unshaven
and hair disheveled, but smiling.

"I am glad to find the door unbarred for I fear I am in
no condition to break it down." He rubbed his head ruefully.

"Is that what you were planning to do? Mrs. Thompson
wouldn't approve." Jennifer allowed herself a cautious
smile while scanning his face for some sign to give her
hope.

Marcus pulled up a chair and straddled it as he sipped
his drink. "I considered it last night, but you were one
jump ahead of me."

"You forget. I was raised surrounded by drunkards, I

know how they think. It may be the only time I know how you think."

"I did not think I was so hard to understand. Have you eaten?"

"Breakfast. Shall I send Henry or Lucia to find you anything?" Jennifer began to rise, but he waved for her to stay seated.

"Henry will come up with something eventually. Let me look at you for a while, it eases my eyes. I am sorry if I insulted you yesterday; you were beautiful in spite of ink and dust, but I was too angry to admit it. I doubt if you could ever be anything but beautiful, even when you are angry and dumping pie in my lap." He did not smile, but there was no coldness in his eyes, either, only a steady thoughtfulness.

"You do not need to apologize for speaking the truth, just as I have no intention of apologizing for my behavior. You deserved what you got, and I will do it again if the occasion calls for it." That was not a speech determined to appease him, Jennifer knew, but she had to stand firm if he were to hear her at all.

Rolling his glass between his palms, Marcus contemplated his young bride. This was the girl from the riverboat, the fighter, striking back at any who dared stand in her way. But the wistful little girl underneath was gone now, replaced by the woman he had known she could become, the woman he had desired to make his mistress. She was more than ready for him now, as mistress, but not as wife. She was still rebelling against the title of wife and for that matter, he wasn't leaning too favorably in the direction of husband. Perhaps she sensed that, and that was the reason for her rebellion. He would have to find out somehow.

"All right, Jennifer, no apologies. You told me before you were not the obedient, wifely type but I had hoped our agreement would temper your behavior to some degree. Instead, you are still fighting me every inch of the way and perhaps, if we are speaking truths, I have given you some cause. I will admit that I should have known better. However, we are stuck with this situation and must make the best of it, so we'd better start looking for some new solutions. We can't continue fighting for the amusement of our waiting public. I realize it must be boring for you here, perhaps you would prefer to return to San Francisco?"

Jennifer listened to this speech with growing qualms. He was giving her the opportunity she was looking for, did she dare take it? Hesitantly, she tried to frame her reply in mild terms to avoid antagonizing him before she finished. "If I am an embarrassment to you or you wish me to go away, I would prefer being sent back to St. Louis. San Francisco is not less boring than here if I must return to the routine I endured there." She hurried on before he could voice his objections. "If it is not your wish to send me away, I would like to propose some other suggestions."

"I did not realize you found San Francisco so objectionable; I thought you found the company there to your liking." Marcus watched her steadily.

"Most of that company is here with me now and under more pleasant circumstances," she reminded him gently. "It is the boring routine I find unendurable."

"And you think Josephine leads a more enlightened social life. That is possible, but I'm afraid St. Louis still may not be safe for you. Until Delaney is behind bars, I would not rest easy with you in his vicinity. Besides, I have no wish to send you away. If there is some way to keep you here without this constant bickering, let me hear it."

Jennifer took a deep breath; it was now or never, and she would need all her persuasive talent. "You said we are partners, but our contract only specifies where I am to fit into your life, it does not say anything about having a life of my own. Partners should have lives of their own outside their business arrangements, shouldn't they?"

Marcus frowned. "I should think being my wife should be sufficient. What other life would you have?"

"You said my spare time was my own," she reminded him. "You didn't place any restrictions on it."

"I said you were at all times to act in a manner fitting my wife."

"Then that is where our dispute is. We need to clarify that clause; my idea of what is suitable and yours are entirely different things, it seems. You said to pattern my behavior after Josephine's, and I thought I had, only my knowledge is in hotels, not shipyards."

Standing up abruptly, Marcus threw aside his chair and slammed his empty glass down on a dresser. "Damn it, woman, you cannot run a hotel in your spare time!"

It was time for action. She must make him listen and listen willingly; their future together depended on it. Her whole life depended on it. Jennifer rose to stand in front of him, reaching out to make him look at her.

Instantly wary at her touch, Marc stiffened. His eyes narrowed, but he waited.

Being this close to him was distracting, and she had to concentrate. Her words now could decide her fate. Her need to be held by these same arms she touched must wait. "I only wish to help, Marcus, and I think I can if you will only give me half a chance. I have some figures worked out—just rough ones, I haven't had time for more—but they will give you some idea of what I mean." Reluctantly, Jennifer moved away from him to find the papers in the drawer. He took them without looking, watching her questioningly. "Emma is going to lose the hotel if something isn't done soon. With my ideas, she might be able to get enough operating cash to put the place back into business. But it will take some work, and she'll need our help. If she thinks the ideas come from you, or that you approve them, I think she will go along with them. All I'm asking is that you look at the figures and my suggestions, nothing more. I will do nothing until you've had time to go over them."

Marcus sifted through the painstakingly neat pages of writing, then returned his gaze to Jennifer. "You will not bake pies or entertain my engineers in the lobby or scrub floors or whatever else you've been up to until I read this?"

"Within reason, of course. I ask that Lucia be allowed to help if she wishes; those pies represent an awfully large amount of income, as you'll see."

"Then after I read it, what happens if I disapprove?" He stared at her now, waiting for an answer. It was obvious this meant a lot to her, but he would like to know just how much. From her serious expression, it might mean more than he was willing to accept, and a cold draft of emptiness blew through him.

"We will have to discuss it then. As I said, that one clause of our contract needs clarification. I am trying to show you what I would like that interpretation to include, but it is open for discussion."

"Personally, I would like to tear that damned contract to shreds, but I suppose that would lead to more violent confrontations?" He smiled crookedly at her. She had kept her distance from him after giving him the papers.

"Under present circumstances, most likely." She bowed her head.

"All right, my little brat. I will read your papers, but it may take some time before I come to any decision. I have your word you will do nothing until then?"

"I will try, but it is hard for me to know what you object to. So the sooner you decide, the easier it will be for me to understand my position. I haven't made you angry, have I?"

"That hasn't bothered you before, why should it now?" He put his arm around her and kissed the top of her head. "I better go wash up. Run tell your friends you have not been eaten alive by the ogre and ask if they would care to join us later for a walk. I am tired of looking at the ugly mugs of miners all week and desire a little feminine companionship for a change."

Impulsively, Jennifer stood on her toes and kissed his wiry cheek. "Sometimes, you are almost a reasonable man. I hope the headache's better." Before he could reach for more, she darted under his arm and dashed from the room, leaving a trail of rippling laughter behind.

Tensions returned to normal and everyone breathed collective sighs of relief after Marcus was spotted romping through a field in pursuit of his elusive wife, and when the couple entered the dining room that evening, they were greeted by brief cheers and grins. Abashed, Marcus doffed his hat to his crew and ordered a round of beer for them all while privately resolving to keep any further quarrels to more private places. But the good humor around the table that evening drove away all thoughts but those of a certain impudent grin and glowing eyes.

Still, for his two remaining nights, he did no more than claim his good-night kiss, although it was becoming more difficult for either of them to keep it under control. Whatever their argument might be, it did not decrease their physical desire for each other, and Marcus began to wonder if it might not be the simplest solution after all. Once bedded, would she truly be as eager to run off as she claimed? He dared not take the chance while any other alternative remained.

Chapter Eighteen

Monday, Marcus returned to the mines content that things were beginning to move in his direction. He had Jennifer's promise of obedience, and her willing kiss still quivering against his lips, and the only problem on the horizon was the packet of papers he carried in his coat pocket. He had already glanced through them and been surprised by the understanding of monetary matters they reflected, but Jennifer was a constant surprise to him and he expected no less. The problem lay in her solutions and the amount of work on her part they conveyed. It could get very sticky indeed if he refused to accept any of them; he would have to go over them more thoroughly when he had time.

Jennifer, on the other hand, resigned herself to at least a week of boredom. She knew Marcus too well to expect him to return early just to release her from her promise. In fact, he would drag it out as long as he could, and she was already working on ways to circumnavigate the promise as well as speed his reply. But there was still the week to be trudged through without the anticipation of any exciting interludes to relieve it.

Practicing her best behavior, Jennifer was in her room mending one of Stuart's gowns when Lucia entered with an odd expression on her usually open face. At Jennifer's inquiring look, she produced a small, folded sheet of paper.

"The man from the train station brought this. Said to give it to you." She waited as Jennifer unfolded the message.

After perusing it once, Jennifer started at the beginning and read it again, not certain she had understood it correctly. At Lucia's impatient movement, Jennifer waved her away.

"Tend Stuart for me for a while, would you, Lucia? I must see what this is about."

Not giving further explanation to the disappointed maid, Jennifer drifted from the room, still puzzling over the odd note. Why would Cameron be in this God-forsaken place and why would he wish to see her? His reason for not wishing to be seen in the hotel was obvious. If Marcus learned of his whereabouts, he was quite likely to turn him over to the sheriff.

Perhaps it wasn't even wise to meet him. Jennifer hesitated, contemplating other alternatives. Cameron was her friend, she could not ignore the message entirely. Darlene would never forgive her if anything happened to her brother. She could send someone else to ascertain what Cameron wanted, but who would she send? She couldn't send her young, unmarried maid to meet with a man of Cameron's reputation. Henry was with Marcus. She could not ask Emma. Whoever she sent, it would raise too many questions. He'd certainly chosen a strange meeting place.

If Marcus discovered her whereabouts, his distrust would multiply a thousandfold, but there was little chance of his learning anything if she were careful. She would simply meet Cameron, find out what he needed, and send him on his way.

The narrow mountain trail was hot and dusty as she clambered along its rocky path, out of sight of town and travelers. No one had seen her leave. No one knew where she was going. Marcus would never know the difference.

When she came upon the stretch of evergreen forest referred to in Cameron's note, Jennifer feared she had misunderstood the location. No one waited at the road's edge and the place was quiet except for the melodious note of some song bird.

She ventured off the rocky path into the cool green shade of the overhanging trees. The forest floor was pine-scented and soft with layers of centuries of evergreen needles. It was a beautiful spot, and Jennifer drank deeply of the free mountain air, glad she had made the journey, even if it were for naught.

Cameron stepped from the shadows like some apparition from the forest's past, startling Jennifer from her reverie. He looked little the worse for wear, not as she had imagined an outlaw should look. He was clean-shaven and well-dressed as usual, his tan linen suit dappled with the little sunlight allowed through the ceiling of branches. Heavy-lidded emerald eyes raked over her as he approached.

"I knew you would come," he murmured, his hand

grasping hers with surprising strength. "It took me weeks to find you. Marcus has hid you well. I didn't think he would be so cruel as to bury you alive out of society's reach."

The gleam in his eye was unmistakable as his hand came up to caress her hair, but there was only affection and concern in his expression.

His words and look left Jennifer somewhat disconcerted, and she attempted to remove her hand from his grasp. Surely he did not intend to continue his ballroom flirting here, under these conditions?

"Marcus has business in the area and thought we would enjoy the vacation. What has brought you here, Cameron? Is Darlene well? Is there something I can do for you?"

Emerald eyes dimmed with assumed hurt at the coolness of her tone. "Darlene was extremely unhappy at my departure, but otherwise well. What has that dastardly husband of yours told you about me to make you speak so coldly? I came running to find you, fearful he would do you some harm after that last episode, and you greet me as a stranger. Do I not rate a kiss for all that I have suffered in your name?"

Instead of waiting for a reply, Cameron pulled her into his embrace, his arms surrounding her and holding her captive while his kisses marked her brow. Jennifer felt the warmth of his breath against her forehead, and the litheness of his masculine body pressed to hers, but she could summon no desire to remain there. She twisted in his grip, seeking some escape.

"Cameron, stop it. I came to offer help if you needed it. I am ashamed of the part Marcus played in your departure, but do not accuse me of being the cause."

"What did he tell you?" The demand was an angry one, and Cameron's grip tightened.

"Only that you cheated some men at cards and the law is after you. What else could he tell me? Please, Cameron, you're hurting me." Jennifer shoved her fists against his chest. He was not nearly so large as Marcus; surely she could break free.

"And you believed him? Ahhh, Jenny, you are cruel. How can I persuade you that I have been badly wronged? Look at me, Jenny. Do I look like a card shark? Marcus only fears I will make a fool of him. He is a greedy man who will not share his possessions. Do you want to be another of his possessions?"

Jennifer quit struggling, mesmerized by the charming candor of his words. He knew Marcus so well, could there possibly be some fragment of truth to his speech? There was no doubting Marc's possessiveness, and the rest made some sort of twisted sense. Had she truly wronged Cameron and been the cause of his downfall? The thought was shattering.

Cameron took advantage of her momentary stillness to press his case. His mouth covered hers with a gentle plea Marcus had never used. With tender care he pressed for response, his lips plying hers with butterfly caresses. His hands circled her waist, holding her like some fragile object of porcelain too delicate to crush.

It was an entirely new experience to Jennifer. Marcus had taken her with passion, with anger, with near-cruelty, but never with delicacy. She allowed Cameron's lips to play against hers, then gave in to his pressure to part them, taking his tongue as lover. It was mildly exhilarating, and she made no immediate protest as he clasped her triumphantly in his embrace.

"Ahhh, Jenny, you are my heart, my soul. With you by my side, I can be anything." His kisses trailed across her cheek and burned against her ear and throat. "Come with me now, my love. I will make you happy as Marcus never will. Let me show you what love can be."

His hand came up between them, fumbling at the tiny ebony buttons of Jennifer's bodice. The pressure of his palm against her breast drove curiosity into flight, and Jennifer shoved away.

"Cameron, don't be a fool. Marcus would kill us. Go and find someone who is free to love you. I am not."

She almost accomplished her goal, but Cameron quickly captured her wrist.

"You need not worry about Marcus. I have already made arrangements to take care of him. He will not follow you. You must be mine now, Jennifer; it is too late to turn back now."

There was nothing in his tone to strike fear in Jennifer's heart. Green eyes were warm and gentle as they looked upon her, but terror quaked her insides. Cameron suddenly seemed to be two people at once: Darlene's beloved and charming brother, and a treacherous liar. What plans had he made without her knowledge and consent? And why?

The hand not holding her wrist began removing the pins from her hair, freeing it to the forest breeze. Jennifer slapped him away and tugged at the wrist he held.

"Cameron, I have no earthly idea what you are talking about. I am married. I think of you as a friend, nothing more. Let me go!"

Simple statements even simple minds could absorb, but Cameron ignored them. Freeing her hair, he returned to the task of loosening her bodice. As his warm fingers brushed against her bare flesh, a shiver of revulsion shook Jennifer, and she shoved free of his inquisitive fingers. His arm snaked about her waist to hold her firmly imprisoned.

"A friend and lover, my dear. You will not fight me so foolishly after I show you what lovemaking can be. Then we can go away together where we will be safe until the time comes when we can wed. There will be enough money to support us comfortably for many lifetimes. I will show you what it means to live. A woman as beautiful as you should be dressed in silks and satins and live in fine houses. Marcus and his tight-fisted ways do you wrong, Jenny. I can protect you as well as he, better, perhaps."

As he talked, he carried her to a soft patch of turf, and kneeling, deposited her struggling form on the bed of mossy grass. Jennifer instantly turned to flee, but Cameron grabbed her arm and dropped down beside her, pinning her against the ground.

"I would rather this were done properly on satin sheets and behind velvet curtains, but you seem to need persuasion. I don't wish to carry you off, kicking and screaming. I want you to walk out of here on my arm, as lovers. Lie still. There is no need to be afraid; I will not harm you, only love you. Don't you want to be loved, Jenny?"

His words were soothing, caressing, as if his victim were not fighting him with every ounce of her strength, but lying complacently in his arms. Madness flickered briefly behind green eyes, and Jennifer watched him warily.

If only she could respond to Cameron as she did to Marcus. Was there something wrong with her that she could not? Marcus had told her that what was between them was no more than the physical desire between man and woman but she felt none of it now for this man above her. It would be easier if she could, easier if she could believe Cameron's promises of a better life, but she could not. Therefore, she must find some means of halting Cameron's intention before it was too late and he destroyed her.

When Jennifer finally fell silent and ceased her struggles, Cameron's gaze returned to her face with surprise. He had captured her flailing gown and petticoats with his leg, but it took both of his hands to hold hers as he watched her carefully.

"It will be better if you do not fight me. It is not as if you were a virgin and need protect your virtue." His look became one of curiosity. "I had heard you and Marcus slept apart, but surely he has not failed to take advantage of his rights as husband?"

Jennifer attempted to focus her attention on the concerned lines of Cameron's handsome face and not the pressure of his heavy weight above her. He had not yet succeeded in unfastening her clothing, and for this, she was grateful. Marcus would have had her stripped and mounted by this time. Cameron was evidently not a man of so violent a passion as her husband.

She prayed her lies would be convincing. Her earlier acceptance of his kiss had apparently disarmed him into thinking she was his for the taking. She used this knowledge shrewdly.

"He has taken me cruelly, and you are no better than he!" she spat out with petulance. "If you must do this thing to me, do it quickly, but I will be no better off with you than with him."

Cameron considered this new angle, his gaze wandering over Jennifer's slender figure trapped beneath him, his to do with as he would. It would be pleasant to ride astride so beautiful a steed, to feel her buck at the thrust of his spur, but it would be more pleasant to do it at his leisure, when she was fully within his power and he could take her in any manner he wished. His main intent now was to get her away from here quietly. He would have to judge the best means carefully.

"Darling Jenny, I admit the surroundings are a bit crude, but if you would relax, I could show you how pleasant this can be. I don't ever wish to use you cruelly."

One hand caressed the roundness of her bosom, but his eyes searched her face questioningly.

Jennifer bit back a sigh of relief. She was not yet out of danger, but she felt almost in control of the situation now.

It was easy to produce tears at this point. Her eyes were already moist with real tears of terror. She let her voice tremble slightly as she replied. "I don't want it like this, Cameron. Marcus took me like this and then refused to wed me. How do I know you are not the same?"

Frustrated, Cameron eased his length atop hers, his hard male weight crushing against her hips. "I would never do that to you, my love. You have been like a sister to Darlene, I would make you one in truth. Unlike the haughty Armstrongs, my family will welcome you with open arms. We will be wed as soon as we are rid of Marcus."

Again, that mention of removing Marcus. How did he intend to go about accomplishing the impossible? She could not risk suspicion by questioning him too carefully.

"If you truly mean that, can't we wait to do this on our honeymoon? I have never had a honeymoon. We could have champagne and stay someplace extravagant. Cameron, please, could we not do this properly? I want to feel like a respectable lady."

Marcus would have laughed aloud at this blatant foolery, but Jennifer knew she was appealing to Cameron's idea of femininity, and he did not see through her transparent ruse. Instead, he closed his eyes as if in pain, then with rueful grace, eased from his compromising position.

Jennifer's fingers shook as she attempted to rebutton her bodice and Cameron's clumsy assistance only made matters worse. The intimacy this gesture suggested was nerve-racking, but she dared not rebuff him until they reached the safety of town.

Together, they arranged their clothing into some measure of respectability. As Cameron offered his arm for the return journey, Jennifer hesitated, searching for some way to avoid his company altogether. She was still not quite certain what the motives behind Cameron's lovemaking were, but passion was the least of them. Not knowing motive and unable to appeal to passion, she must continue to apply to his fixed notion of femininity.

Tentatively, she tested her theory. "I must return to the hotel for my things. If I am seen with you, I fear I will be stopped by one of Marc's men. If you wait at the train station, they will never know you're here. That will make it easier to get away, won't it?"

Cameron glanced at his watch and gave her an impatient look. "We haven't time for packing if we're to get off this wretched mountain tonight. We'll buy what you need later."

Jennifer pouted her lower lip and looked up at him through trembling lashes. "This gown is ruined and I have no night clothes or jewelry. And what of Stuart? He is only a babe. I will be quick. The train is always late."

"Damn." Cameron gritted his teeth together and glared down the mountain trail as if that would tell him the train's location. He had not planned this far ahead. Getting her on the train and out of Marc's reach had been his only consideration. Now he would be saddled with infant and baggage. He ran his hand through his hair, glanced at tear-stained almond eyes, and gave in.

"All right. Get your things together and have your maid carry them to the station. I will see they are loaded. As soon as you hear the whistle blow, get Stuart and yourself over to the station, without being seen, if possible. Can you manage that?"

Jennifer beamed with a delight not entirely feigned. "Isn't this exciting? Like an elopement! Of course, I can do that. Just watch me!"

And with the blithe recklessness of a young girl, she lifted her skirts and raced off down the mountain path, leaving Cameron standing on the forest's edge with a slightly perplexed look on his face.

Jennifer's heart beat wildly as she rounded the curve out of his sight. She did not know what Cameron would do when she did not appear as arranged, but it was far better to find out when she was in the safety of the hotel. There would be time to contemplate the next step when she was safe. At the moment, rejoicing at the miracle of her escape filled every ounce of her soul.

She burst through the hotel door at a wild speed that made the lobby's lone occupant look up with astonishment.

"Jennifer, what's wrong?" Charlie jumped to his feet and dashed toward her, his gaze going to the door as if expecting a band of wild Indians to follow.

Jennifer gasped with relief. Charlie! He could get Marcus and she would be safe. Then she came to an abrupt halt, assailed by second thoughts. It would take hours for Marcus to reach her and only minutes for Cameron to discover her perfidy. And Marcus would demand explanations, explanations that would surely lead to Marcus and Cameron killing each other. Cameron had already made statements that sounded suspiciously like threats and Marcus had made his opinion clear from the first. If there were any way to avert such a catastrophic showdown, she must locate it.

Nervously brushing disheveled hair back from her face, she contemplated Charlie's anxious expression. "Charlie, can you do me a favor and keep it a secret?" As she spoke, she hurried to the desk and searched for pen and paper.

Charlie followed her, dark eyes questioning. "You can trust me, you know that. Just tell me what to do."

Jennifer scribbled hastily across the paper. One lie led easily to another and it worked even better in black and white. The words formed faster than she could write them: *Marcus knows you're here and has gone for the sheriff. I'm trapped. For Darlene's sake and mine, catch the train and go!"*

Hands shaking, she sealed the note. "Take this to the station master. Have him give it to the man with the green eyes and tan linen suit who will be waiting on the platform. Don't, on any account, let the man see you, Charlie. Just watch and make certain he gets the note and gets on the train. Can you do that for me, please?"

He took the note reluctantly. "Marcus is not just my boss, but a friend, Jennifer. If you're doing anything . . ."

Jennifer shook her head. The sound of the train's whistle echoed up the valley, announcing its approach. There were only minutes left.

"Nothing like that, Charlie, I promise. The man is the brother of a friend of mine and I think he's in some kind of trouble. I don't dare speak to him because Marcus has threatened to kill him if he ever comes near us again. I can't let my friend down, but I can't endanger Marcus like that, either. Please, Charlie, this is the only way."

Charlie still looked dubious, but his weakness for women left him unable to say no. He took the note and left the hotel at a brisk pace.

Jennifer paced the worn wooden floor of the lobby. Instinct told her Cameron was not the kind of man to risk all to come back for her. He would save his own hide first and ask after her later. But if she were wrong, she had left herself little protection. She did not understand his motives in coming after her, but she had the sinking feeling his rage would know no bounds should he discover he had been duped.

Ears alert to any sound, Jennifer listened to the rumble and roar of the gasping steam engine as it pulled into the station and held her breath until the rhythmic clickety-clack of the metal wheels told her it was moving out again. Then she flew to the window to watch for Charlie's approach.

He appeared within minutes, his normally cheerful expression pulled tight and grim as he confronted Jennifer.

"It's done. The man looked as if he'd been hit alongside the head with a pick ax when he read your note, but he wasted no time jumping on that train. I could see him through the window. He was still on it when the train pulled out. I hope I did the right thing."

He didn't sound at all certain that he had, and guiltily, Jennifer couldn't swear to it, either. Had Cameron for once in his life been sincere? Had she, perhaps, heaped one load of hurt on to another, added her guilt to Marc's? She set her chin determinedly, refusing to consider the possibility. Cameron had got what he deserved and that was that.

"Charlie, I would never do anything to hurt Marcus, or anybody else, if it could be avoided, you know that. This time it couldn't. The man's gone now and won't be back, so there's no more harm done than what you saw, thanks to you, Charlie."

"You're sure there's been no harm done?" Charlie remained dubious.

"No harm, Charlie," she assured him. Looking him square in the face, she changed the subject abruptly. "Now, tell me, what are you doing here in mid-week?"

Charlie cast aside his doubts and returned to the project that had brought him here.

"I was looking for Emma, but actually, you'll do just fine. You commissioned me to find some kitchen help, and I think I have, providing Mrs. T. approves."

"Providing they'll accept next to no wages, just room and board until things start picking up around here, you mean," Jennifer sniffed disparagingly. She would have been elated at the news earlier, but her thoughts were too distracted to show proper appreciation of it now.

"I kind of figured that, but he's agreeable. Said he don't need anything anyway but a roof over his head and something solid in his belly."

That caught Jennifer's attention. "He?" It was one possibility that had never occurred to her, a man in the kitchen. But Henrí had done it, maybe it wasn't so incredible after all.

Charlie grinned as her face fell. "You didn't specify any qualifications but a willingness to do kitchen work. Old Harry's been cooking for himself and cattle drives most all his life. Guess he ought to know his way around potato peelings by now. Says he's getting too old to be moving on anymore and he might as well stay here as anywhere. Harry's not too fond of mining, he's not."

"Sweet, Charlie," Jennifer mocked him, "if I didn't have a wicked husband, I would hug your neck. How soon can he start? We'll have to find Emma and tell her." Jennifer moved toward the dining room, trailing Charlie behind. It was time to distract Charlie's attention and her own. The danger was over, she must act as if nothing had happened, as if she hadn't come face to face with the truth of Marc's cautions. Could that really be all men thought of her? She refused to think of it.

"Your wicked husband seems to have recovered his temper this week, madam. Let me express our heartfelt thanks to you for his speedy recovery," Charlie remarked from behind her.

Jennifer threw a grin over her shoulder. "Don't count

on it lasting long. Get what you want out of him while you have the chance. We seldom let a week go by without a major disagreement."

"Well, next time you throw a pie at him, let me know in advance. I missed all the fun last time and suffered all the consequences," he replied with a hint of laughter.

Not finding Emma in the dining room, Jennifer continued on to the kitchen, pushing open the swinging door and calling Emma's name as she entered. She stopped in mid-stride, Charlie nearly walking into her as her call turned into a shriek.

"Emma!" Hastily kneeling on the floor beside the older woman's fallen form, Jennifer moaned, "Oh, Lord, Emma," and tried ineffectively to turn the bulky form over to search for signs of life.

Charlie shoved Jennifer aside and bent over Emma, expertly holding her wrist with his fingers to locate a pulse. "She's alive. We'd better not move her until we get the doc. Stay here, I'll holler for Lucia to join you, and I'll go find Doc Adams."

All other thought flew from Jennifer's head. "What's wrong with her, Charlie? What can I do?" She lifted the woman's unconscious head into her lap, stroking her clammy brow.

"I don't have any idea, sugar. Just hang in there till I get back."

Lucia raced down at Charlie's call, and the two women alternated turns bathing the cold face in Jennifer's lap until some signs of consciousness appeared. Then they did what they could to make the older woman comfortable, but the cold, stone floor was not a bed.

Doc Adams was an elderly, patient man who had seen too many serious accidents in his time to allow flustered females to hurry his progress. He examined the softly moaning woman, nodding his head in agreement with his own thoughts, then called for Charlie to help move the patient to her room. Jennifer scampered ahead to prepare the way.

When Emma was settled and pronounced comfortably resting, the doctor cleared the room and the others gathered in Jennifer's sitting room.

The doctor's first words shattered their silence. "I think we're going to have to close the hotel. Lad, you'd better get word back to your boss to come take his family home; Emma's not going to be in any shape to take care of them."

Voices instantly erupted around the room, and the doctor shook his head, raising his hand for silence. "Emma's had a bad heart for a long time; she knew this was coming if she continued operating the hotel. It will be months before she recovers sufficiently to take care of herself. She has no other relatives that I know of. I'll have to find someone willing to nurse her until she's able to do it herself. Running this place is out of the question."

Jennifer stepped in before anyone else could speak. "Dr. Adams, this place is her life. If you make her give it up, she'll have no reason to go on living. And how will she pay a nurse with no income? Don't be so hasty about sending us home, maybe we can help."

The doctor peered over the top of his unrimmed glasses. "You have some other suggestion, Mrs. Armstrong?"

"I've had experience running hotels, Doctor. I'd like to keep it going until Emma is well enough to decide what she wants to do. One of us could keep an eye on her at all times so she wouldn't need to hire a nurse, and I think she'd recover faster if she thought she was still needed. Surely, she'll be able to give us advice in a week or two, won't she?"

The doctor's gray head nodded thoughtfully a time or two. "Advice is all she can give. I'll agree, she would respond better under those conditions, but taking on this place by yourselves is a hopeless task. No matter what your background, Mrs. Armstrong, you can hardly be expected to run a place this size by yourself. This is no genteel ladies' salon."

Jennifer thought of the drunken river men she had been accustomed to for clientele and wondered how far from a ladies' salon that could be considered, but she made no reference to it. Lucia and Charlie were shocked enough at Marc's ladylike wife admitting to experience of any kind. The doctor was right though, without Emma, it was nearly a hopeless task.

"We'll need your help. Charlie, how soon can your friend come to work?"

"Soon as he can get himself down here, I reckon. He's up at the camp right now."

"All right. When you go back up, tell Marcus what has happened and ask him if he can spare Henry. Tell him we'll be nursing Emma and not to worry about us, but we'll feel better having Henry around." She gave him a wry smile. If he said any more than that, they would be in San Francisco tomorrow.

Charlie got the drift and frowned. Leaving two young girls to the care of one old man wasn't a particularly sound idea, especially if they continued to keep the hotel open. On the other hand, the town would lose Emma, the hotel, and the company of these entertaining women if he disagreed. He was taking a chance, but if Emma could do it, surely this strong-minded little brat could, and no one would willingly harm the boss's lady. The captain would handle it soon enough when he found out.

Jennifer waited for Charlie's nod of agreement before returning to the doctor. "Dr. Adams, could you not suggest anyone in this town who could help us out? There is little cash for pay, but there is always a good meal on the stove and a spare room . . ." She gestured helplessly. She was doing the unthinkable and would need all the allies she could get; she could not afford to alienate the good doctor with her high-handedness.

"Young Ned Tackett might be what you want. Not old enough for the mines but too old to be hanging about underfoot; about time that young man found some useful work. His father won't have any objections to your feeding him, of that you can be sure. I'll talk to him soon as I chase him out of whatever woodpile he's hiding in."

"Thank you, Doctor. Now you better explain to us what needs to be done for Emma. Charlie, you'd better get back to camp, remember, we're counting on you." Jennifer's eyes flickered warningly at the bemused engineer.

With a mocking look, he bowed extravagantly from the waist. "Madam, your wish is my command." Then he winked and spoiled the effect. "I trust you'll save my head when they begin to roll."

"Off with you or I'll see yours is the first." She chased him out before the doctor grew suspicious of his words. If he should learn of her husband's objections, she would never get this chance again. Her fate lay in Charlie's hands now; she prayed she had chosen wisely.

After the doctor left, Jennifer waited for the usual string of protests, but none were forthcoming. Instead, Lucia waited patiently for instructions.

"You aren't mad at me?" Jennifer asked incredulously.

"Will *Señor* Armstrong understand?" was all Lucia asked.

"I doubt it, Lucia," Jennifer sighed. All her hopes of gradually introducing Marcus to her plans were dashed now. He would be hit broadside with them and come up hollering. Any idea of warning him of Cameron's visit was completely dashed. She would have her hands full with this new problem. "But this is something I have to do for myself as well as Emma. I don't expect you to understand that, so please feel free to go, if you like. This isn't going to be much of a vacation."

"You will need someone with experience to clean rooms and help in the kitchen and wait on tables. I can do all of these," Lucia answered determinedly.

Tears formed in her eyes as Jennifer looked at her loyal friend and maid. Marcus would rant and rave, but he couldn't physically carry both of them out. There was hope yet.

Harry arrived that evening and young Ned the next morning. Jennifer introduced the new cook and his helper to their tasks and let them settle in to become used to their chores before the hectic rush of the weekend. Henry appeared as she finished seeing to the rooms in the servants' quarters, and she approached him nervously. Charlie had apparently got part of the message through; how much more had Marcus guessed? Henry would be the one to know.

"Hello, Henry. Have you come to help us or lock us up?"

"Cap'n just said to see you keep out of trouble and to let him know if you need anything. He's kind of busy right now, and I don't think he rightly understood what Charlie was telling him." The older man eyed Jennifer's apron dubiously. Once out of Marc's hearing, Charlie had made it all too clear what was happening back in town, but Henry hadn't entirely believed it until now. Marcus was under the impression Emma was only down for a day or two and had sent messages of concern that were highly inappropriate if what Charlie said was true. The concern was going to have to be for this ferociously independent young woman when Marcus found out what was really happening.

"He'd only worry if he knew, Henry. There's no point troubling him if he's busy. By the time he finds out, everything will be under control, and there won't be a thing he can complain about." Jennifer spoke these words more to reassure herself than Henry; she was dangling dangerously at the end of a long rope, afraid it would break before she could climb up. She had to make this work, she was risking everything she had on it. Cameron had forced her to look at herself from another point of view. If all men saw her only as an object to be bedded, as her mother had warned and Marcus had stated, then she must do everything in her power to prove otherwise. Marcus must see her as a person if she were ever to be a wife in truth.

"If you say so, ma'am. But what are you gonna do when the men come in payday? Cap'n said he's not sure he'll be able to make it lessen you need him for somethin'. How you goin' to feed and room all them men?"

"We've got someone to do the cooking, and we can see to the rooms ourselves if we go in pairs and make sure the rooms are empty before we clean them. It's just a matter of getting the tables waited on. We only have one little boy to help out and Marcus would hear about that for certain if we tried to do it ourselves."

Henry bunched his brow together in a frown. "Cap'n ain't gonna like any of it one bit. I'll take care of them tables this once, but you and the maid gonna have to stay out of sight while I do. I can't take care of you and them tables at the same time."

"Thank you, Henry. We'll be on our best behavior. I've written to some friends to ask about getting some help up here, so maybe you won't have to worry about us for long." That was reaching pretty far, but Henry didn't have to know that. There was no money yet to pay salaries for help, so there was no use asking for it. She had written one letter, though, a feeble hope in a moment of desperation, and she expected little else to come of it. By the time next payday came around, maybe she could think of something else.

Emma was scarcely aware of what was happening around her. Teetering on the border of consciousness, she was a docile patient, presenting less trouble than the activity around her. They took turns nursing her willingly, eager to escape whatever problems were cropping up outside the bedroom door. Even Jennifer used the time in Emma's room to relax and set aside worries while she tended Emma and nursed Stuart. They deserved her full attention while she was there, and they got it in generous portions; it was only after she left the room that all the problems fell back into their torturous patterns.

The day-to-day hectic activity of the hotel forced Jennifer to drive out all remembrances of her humiliating ordeal, but the empty nights became hours of torment. She felt herself held prisoner in her dreams, Cameron's laughing eyes quickly turning to Marc's stormy gray, accusing and angry. She could almost feel his hard body against hers, and she strained to take him in her arms, make him understand, but then with the unreality of nightmares, the

form above her dissolved into Delaney's cruel grip, and
she would wake, stifling hysterical screams.

The stormy gray of Marc's eyes in her sleep frightened
her, but not so much as the pervading sense of loss the
dreams conveyed. His anger worried her, but the thought
of losing him entirely was even more terrifying. Yet every
day she got up and deliberately set about the tasks that
would drive him farther away. It was a situation with which
even her dreams couldn't cope, and she tossed and turned
in the depths of the mattress, hugging her pillow for comfort.

A sense of doom enveloped Jennifer even as the weekend passed without major incident. Marcus didn't come,
but sent a loving note instead of a cold message. Still, she
couldn't escape this feeling of impending disaster. He
would know soon enough the seriousness of Emma's illness, learn that Jennifer had checked in and accepted payments for rooms, that the hotel was operated by a skeleton
crew including his wife and maid, not even the fact that
they hadn't managed the pies or that they had stayed clear
of the kitchen would control his anger. But somehow, she
thought she could talk him out of it by playing on his sense
of decency in a time of trouble. This sense of doom was
more pervasive than that, all encompassing, threatening
her and Marcus alike. And she prayed for his return, knowing it would only be in anger.

Harry's cooking was not the fare Henrí had provided
for the steamboat trade, but it was familiar to the miners
and no worse than Emma's, so Jennifer suffered it without
complaint. If she could only have access to the kitchen,
she could find some way of improving the menu, but she
had to draw the line somewhere and her promise to Marcus tugged at her conscience. Surely he would understand
she couldn't keep it as well as she had planned now that
Emma was ill; he couldn't possibly expect her to. But guilt
nagged at her just the same.

It was tickling the edges of her conscience the next morning while she sat with Emma and nursed Stuart. Emma was dozing, so Jennifer redirected her guilty thoughts and concentrated her attention on the hungry infant at her breast. He was intent on filling his stomach with little inclination to amuse his mother, and Jennifer marked the resemblance to his father, not just in looks but in their determination to get things done in the proper order without distraction, especially from Jennifer. She giggled softly at her own nonsense in assigning adult qualities to such a tiny babe, but it was better than worrying about Marc's reaction to her broken promises. For a certainty, it would not be a pleasant one. She was only surprised that it had not come yet.

So it was with a guilty start that she heard the knock on the bedroom door, recognizing it at once and not bothering to answer it. Emma's eyes flickered as the door opened and Marcus walked in, his eyes finding Jennifer first, warm with approval as they rested on his son, then switching back to the awakening figure on the bed.

"Good morning, Emma. How are you feeling?"

Buttoning the front of her dress and rocking Stuart over her shoulder, Jennifer watched the ramrod straight figure of her husband while he conversed with the patient. His head was in profile so she could not read his eyes, and she could tell nothing from his posture; he seemed relaxed and confident as always. His cream colored linen shirt fell open casually at the neck, revealing the dark hairs curled against the deepening bronze of his chest. She could tell he had been working outside without his shirt these last few weeks; the river tan that had begun to fade with months of office work and enforced idleness was returning darker than ever. Her gaze swept over tight denims and polished boots and she blushed at her thoughts. She remembered well the hard body and rippling muscles beneath those clothes and the sensation of his nudity in the bed next to her. Would she ever know it again?

With a quirk of his eyebrow, Marcus commanded her attention, and Jennifer returned to the conversation.

"Do you think you could spare my wife a few minutes, Emma? We have a few things we need to discuss."

The fleshy white face peered suspiciously from the pillows. "She and the others been mighty kind to me, Mr. Armstrong. I don't know what I would have done without them." There was a warning behind her whispered statements, but she stood too much in awe of her arrogant guest to put it into words.

"I wish we could do more, Emma. Let me call Lucia." Jennifer touched the old woman's hand tenderly, avoiding Marc's gaze, and went to the hallway.

Already waiting, hesitant to enter after hearing her employer's voice, Lucia met Jennifer's eyes with a worried question, but Jennifer only shrugged. Marcus had made no indication of his mood; with any luck, that was a good sign.

Marcus took in the maid's appearance with a look of disapproval. Hair pulled into an untidy bun, old cotton dress covered by a dust smudged apron, she flashed defiance at Marc's appraising glance.

"What have you been doing?" he asked, almost too casually.

Lucia took the baby from Jennifer's arms, deliberately delaying her reply. "I am cleaning the rooms as *Señora* Armstrong says," she muttered, almost defiantly. Whatever she thought of the situation between man and wife, her loyalty lay entirely with Jennifer.

Marc's eyebrows nearly touched his hairline at this display, but he said nothing, gesturing to Jennifer to join him. "If you'll excuse us, Emma, I think my wife has some explaining to do." Bowing politely, he guided Jennifer from the room with a firm hand at the small of her back, leaving worried stares behind him.

"I expected you to make an impression on our one and only servant, but this isn't exactly what I had in mind," Marcus remarked, continuing to steer his errant wife down the hallway. He had already discovered she had discarded her stiff corset, and he could feel the sway of her hips beneath his hand, a glance revealing the soft molding of her slender figure beneath the muslin dress. He could appreciate the difference as his hand rode the curve of her waist, except for the thought that she must have lost weight to allow the dress to fit so readily. His brow puckered further with this new worry, and he almost missed Jennifer's reply.

"I have asked nothing of Lucia; everything she does is at her own suggestion. She is rapidly becoming an excellent nurse, and she has done Emma a world of good."

Jennifer's quiet remarks dampened the fire of Marc's anger further. He had come prepared to do royal battle with his obstreperous wife only to find her dutifully nursing her patient and son as promised, completely disarming him. He led her into the sitting room and closed the door, eyeing the gracefulness with which she walked away from him. His anger was so easily replaced with lust, it was difficult to remember his argument.

"You made a promise to me before I left here last time. Are you prepared to tell me you've kept it?"

Jennifer swung around to face her opponent. She could find no sign of anger in his face as he leaned against the door, hands in pockets, watching her with curiosity. Puzzled at this lack of reaction, Jennifer kept her reply unemotional.

"No, I'm sorry. I have not. Circumstances made it impossible."

"So, in deliberate defiance of my wishes, you have taken over operation of the hotel, made a nurse of our maid, publicly collected money for rooms, and exposed yourself and others to untold dangers. Am I supposed to be pleased?" His eyes raked over her uninhibited figure and settled hungrily on the rise and fall of her bosom.

Jennifer turned away to pace the room and stare out the window at the sun-drenched mountain. "What would you have me do? Pack my bags and go back to San Francisco, leaving a dying woman to her dead hotel?"

Conflicting emotions rampaged through Marc's breast, unsettling his equilibrium as the little scamp had managed to do ever since he first laid hands on her. He had always prided himself on being a rational man, wise to the wiles of women, unmoved by their elaborate displays of passion. There was no reason to believe that this one was any different, but he had continually allowed her to divert and turn upside down all his carefully guarded thoughts and schemes until he no longer knew what he wanted or why. It was maddening, and only one immediate solution came to mind: he had to have her again, relieve this craving he had developed for her and her alone, and then he would be free to return to rationality. There was a stirring in his loins as he contemplated this thought. He would say anything, do anything to obtain this objective, then once freed, things could return to their normal state. Why hadn't he thought of this before?

Coming up behind her, Marcus put his hands about Jennifer's waist, enjoying the sensation of pliant softness under his fingers. There wasn't time for what he wanted now, but he could pave the way for later. "Emma's illness is that serious?"

Jennifer tensed at his touch, but relaxed with the concern of his words. "If the hotel is closed, and she is left with nothing to do but stare at the ceiling and worry about money, yes. You cannot take away someone's livelihood and expect them to survive easily."

The fresh scent of her hair filled the air he breathed, and Marc's hands wandered farther over his wife's uncorseted figure, finally cupping the fullness of her breasts. They weighed more heavily in his hands now than they had that first night, filled with the milk that fed his son. Tenderly, he caressed them and felt her quiver in his arms.

"I see," he replied thoughtfully. "And how long will it be necessary to keep this place operating to ensure Emma's recovery?"

The combination of calm voice and passionate caresses

was destroying Jennifer's composure. His fingers located and manipulated the rising hardness of her nipples beneath the thin material of her dress, and she felt herself weakening, succumbing to the heat that spread through her like wildfire. If he continued his thoughtless handling, she would lose all sense of their conversation and throw herself upon his mercy. She could make no resistance.

"I have no idea, Marcus . . ." She gasped as his fingers loosed the buttons of her bodice and slipped under the thin chemise to rub against the bareness of her skin. The sensation loosened a torrent of pent-up desire, and tears flowed freely down her cheeks as his caresses destroyed all her defenses, leaving her aching for more. She wanted to turn and throw herself into the comfort of his arms, to feel his strength crushing her, but a strange lethargy prevented movement.

Cupping a breast in his bare hand, feeling the tempting curve of soft buttocks pressed against the hardening in his groin, the light scent of perfume filling his nostrils, Marc felt his own composure rapidly retreating. He could have her right now, he could feel her surrender, but it wouldn't be enough. He had to leave shortly, and the minute he turned his back, she would be gone. No, he needed more time than that to dissolve this weakness. His lips brushed longingly against scented curls.

"I have read your notes, little one, and your suggestions are sound. If I give you permission to try them for these next weeks, will you promise to keep out of sight of the men on paydays? Unless accompanied by me, of course." Reluctantly, Marcus withdrew his hand from her bodice and with maddening slowness, fastened the buttons, his fingers wandering occasionally to fondle the stiffened points pressing through thin fabric.

Weakly, Jennifer leaned against his chest and helped him, well aware of the state of his arousal as she pressed against him. Too confused by his abrupt withdrawal to think coherently, she nodded her agreement. Her body screamed objections at this callous rejection, but she could only hang on weakly, wiping her eyes and consoling herself that he must suffer as much as she.

Marcus grasped her shoulders and turned her around to face him. Seeing the tear-streaked cheeks and wet lashes, he drew her into his arms and kissed her with all the tenderness and passion he had denied her before, giving her the warmth and closeness she so desperately craved. The artificial wall between them began to crack and crumble and Jennifer responded with a rush of love and passion that left Marcus astounded and almost ended his resolve in his desire to possess her. Carefully, he set her down.

"Angel, I've got to get back to camp, there are men waiting for me. Will you reconsider our contract while I'm gone?" Gently, he brushed a tear from the corner of her eye and cupped her chin with his palm.

She searched his chiseled face longingly, not finding what she sought. The smoke of desire still burned in overcast eyes, but anything else was hidden or did not exist. Disappointed, she lowered her lashes, and Marcus released her.

"You are playing with me again," she said sadly.

Marc's heart lurched, and he began to doubt the truth of her words. Her bent head and sorrowful tones affected him in ways he could not describe; he would have to steel himself masterfully to prevent her outmaneuvering him again.

"That would be akin to playing with fire, Jenny Lee; I haven't quite taken leave of my senses yet. I have tried to be honest with you, Jenny, and I will tell you now that the celibate life is not for me. You must come to some decision soon."

Jennifer's heart pounded erratically at the warning his words conveyed, but she was still too shaken to think clearly, the only images coming to mind were those of Marcus in another woman's arms, and she shoved them violently from her thoughts.

She glanced up at his squared jaw and angular cheekbones, his eyes gray as a winter's sky now. He had just given her everything she wanted but the one thing he did not have to give, yet she still could not admit defeat, not without more time to think.

"Are you coming back Friday?"

"I fully intend to try." His grim expression softened a little as he saw her uncertainty. She was wavering and needed only a little more persuasion to bring her to him. This was no time to frighten her.

"And you mean it about my suggestions? You will really let me try to turn this place around, even if it means my being in the kitchen and waiting tables?"

Marcus dug his hands into his denim pockets and contemplated her fragile figure from the disheveled auburn of her hair to the still flushed coloring of her cheeks, over soft ripe curves to slipper shod feet. She was a tempting morsel, easily snatched up by bigger fish than she, but she seemed totally innocent of this fact, even now, after he had shown her how easily it was done. Maybe her innocence protected her, he didn't know, but he was jealous of anyone's attempt to share what was his. But to get what he wanted he would have to meet her at least partway.

"I do not like it, but if that's what it takes, you may try for a few weeks, until we see what comes of it. I'll leave Henry here to keep an eye on things, but if anyone so much as *tries* to get fresh with you, I'll have his head blown off before he knows what hit him. So I suggest you dress yourself a little more modestly and stay out of sight as much as possible, or you will seriously endanger men's lives." There was no smile on his face as he spoke.

Seeing the direction his eyes had taken, Jennifer blushed and smoothed the bodice of her dress. With no one to notice, it had been easy to slip back into the habit of wearing the absolute minimum to combat heat, but it hadn't taken Marcus long to discover it. She would have to be more careful in the future.

"Your men respect you too much to insult me or Lucia.

I am not worried about them, and I shall be extremely wary of strangers. I think I am well protected here; you really needn't worry. If it makes you feel better, I will keep to the kitchen as much as possible, but your restriction on the men is going to be a difficult one. Henry is not over-fond of waiting tables."

"There will be no discussion on that point. I will not have you waiting tables in a room full of drunken miners. Set Henry on guard duty and you can do the cooking and send your cook out to do the tables if that makes you feel better, but you are not to set foot in that dining room over the weekend unless it is with me."

The tender love had disappeared once more, leaving the authoritative stranger in his place, but he was no longer really a stranger. Jennifer felt like a child every time he spoke to her thus, but she knew all she had to do was reach out and touch him and the distance between them diminished. It was a strange feeling, having this power over him, but to exercise it willfully was courting danger. Though she longed to touch him again, she curbed the impulse and hid behind her businesslike composure.

"Of course, Marcus. Thank you for understanding."

It was as if he had been hit by an icy draft, and the coldness settled around his heart. Marcus cursed himself for a fool. She had been right at the tips of his fingers, willing and eager, and he had jerked his hand away instead of reaching out to pull her closer. Had it become a habit he couldn't break? Now he would have to spend the week wondering what reception awaited him when he returned when only a moment ago, he had been almost assured of success. There was no time to correct the problem now.

He tipped her chin upwards and planted a light kiss on her lips. "Be good, little one, don't disappoint me," and he left.

Jennifer raised a wondering finger to the spot where his lips had left their firm impression, and she rubbed it thoughtfully. Was she mistaken, or had he actually softened there at the last? One thing was certain, he had been nowhere near as angry as she had expected, and she feared to find out the reason. Her breast still burned where he had held it, and she suspected the truth behind his lack of anger, but she was still too confused by her own reaction to study it closer. There was too much work to be done and too many lonely nights between now and Friday to waste time worrying over it now.

Chapter Nineteen

Jennifer returned to reassure Lucia and Emma that everything was fine, that Marcus approved what they were doing, happy to lighten their worries but secretly wondering what price she would have to pay for this unhoped-for cooperation. For there was a price attached, she became more certain of it with every passing moment. Marcus was a man of action, and he had made it all too obvious that a good-night kiss would no longer be satisfactory.

Greeting their first outside guests with the train's arrival, preparing the evening's menu with Harry, supervising the cleaning of the lobby and repairing of the back rooms, the problem remained in the back of Jennifer's mind. It lodged firmly and refused to budge, gnawing a niche in her thoughts that she could not work around. She took it to bed with her and tried to wipe it out with sleep, but when morning broke, the problem still lay unresolved.

Throughout the week as she tackled the problems of feeding and housing paying guests and overworked staff, meeting bills and ordering goods, nursing patient and infant, Jennifer wrestled with her conscience, often throwing herself into a task to avoid further confrontation with her thoughts. But at night, lying in the empty bed in her lonely room, there was no escape.

For months, she had been holding Marcus off, afraid of being hurt, afraid of being left again, not wanting to surrender herself to anyone, let alone the man who had torn her so rudely from her protected existence. She had argued that he laughed at her and mocked her, ignored and avoided her, then tried to buy her with baubles and charm. He had admitted he didn't love her and made no effort to reassure her he wouldn't leave. But despite all her fears and arguments, he had made her love him, and that was the crux of the matter.

If she loved Marcus, why should she continue to deny him? He didn't love her, and he had made it plain it would be easy to leave her behind, but he could do that whether or not she gave herself to him. He hadn't run when she told him she would never be a lady, he seemed to understand when she told him about the hotel, whatever new problem she tackled him with, he accepted and stood by her side. It was only pride separating them, no longer fear; she had grown strong under his care, and it was time she gave him something in return, whatever the consequences.

Jennifer reached this cataclysmic conclusion Thursday evening. Friday morning she woke with a shiver of fear and anticipation as she faced the day and the prospect of her husband's arrival and the night to come. She had known the feel of a man's body joined with hers only once. She was eager to relive the experience, learn more, yet the chasm between them was so enormous, it was a giant step just to admit it could be bridged. She didn't know where to start or how to go about it, but she was willing to try. It was much like finally making the decision to be his wife: a tremendous relief followed by even more enormous anxieties. It would be best not to think about it.

So she threw herself into the production of making a weekend's worth of pies and supervising the preparation of a special Friday night supper. Now that she was allowed access to the kitchen, she could show Harry there was more to a meal than beef and potatoes. When Marcus arrived, he would be presented with a dinner unmatched by any of his fancy French chef's.

Jennifer's excitement was contagious, and friends and staff rallied around her to make it a celebratory weekend, though they had no idea what was being celebrated. Their new guests luxuriated in polished cleanliness and prompt, smiling service, and the first shift of miners became almost subdued in their awe at the changes made. What ones didn't notice the scrubbed floors and shining windows, couldn't miss the array of foods and tempting odors from the kitchen, and even the most hardened cases fell before the appearance of Lucia as waitress.

In the commotion of their preparations, Lucia had made the offer to continue her table waiting over the weekend. There had been no trouble through the week, but the guests had been few and orderly. To send her out into the Friday night melee, despite Jennifer's assurances to Marcus, was a step that made even Jennifer pause. It wasn't until Charlie volunteered to stay and keep an eye on her that Jennifer gave in.

The miners' response was instantaneous approval, and the matter of respect was quickly handled when the first few men to make unwelcome overtures were bodily thrown from the room by their irate comrades. That matter soon settled, the rest of the evening sailed smoothly, but for one thing.

Marcus didn't arrive. Jennifer bathed and changed and waited in the kitchen, tearing lettuce for salads and waiting for Lucia to bring news of his arrival. As the hour grew late and the revelry more rowdy, they withdrew upstairs, leaving their guests in the capable hands of Harry and Henry. The two women dined in the peace of their sitting room, but Jennifer's restlessness was worse than the turmoil below.

Jennifer slept in Marc's bed that night, wondering if he would appear, afraid that he would and terrified he wouldn't. He had sent no word, but he had promised to come. Had she been wrong about what he wanted? Had she imagined those few minutes together? Was it only wishful thinking to think he desired her? She knew she was being foolish, but he had destroyed her confidence in him before, and it was not easily rebuilt; it was still a thing of great fragility.

But it was still strong enough to keep her going the next day. He had promised to come that weekend and had sent no word otherwise; Jennifer was convinced he would be there tonight at the latest. He could show up any time today and try to surprise her, but she would be ready for him. Wearing one of her new silk dresses with the narrow skirt and no bustle, her hair carefully combed into a cascade of ribbons and curls, she spent the entire day upstairs, out of sight of the men as much as possible. He would find nothing to complain of when he arrived.

By dinner time, Marcus still had not put in an appearance, although the second shift of miners reported he was alive and well and doing fine. Giving up all her fine plans with disgust, Jennifer pulled on an apron and returned to the kitchen. As the evening became more hectic, Henry joined her, and they prepared salads and peeled potatoes in silence, the tension of the last two days beginning to tell on their nerves. They ate what they had time for, when they had time for it, avoiding last night's restless peace.

Exhausted and worried, Jennifer finally gave in to Henry's urging and prepared to retire to her room. Sending word to Lucia to join them, they were surprised when she came back to the kitchen with Charlie in tow.

"Ladies, before you leave, I'd like to ask a favor. The men would like to show you some appreciation for all you've done these last few weeks." Placing an arm around

Lucia's waist as he spoke, Charlie grinned, unperturbed, when she moved away. "Henry, do you think it would be all right if the ladies stepped out here a minute and listened to what the men have to say?" His eyes twinkled as they encountered Jennifer's and swept back to Lucia, but he kept a respectful distance from the object of his affections while he addressed the older man.

"Don't 'spect it would hurt anything so long as they're polite." Henry picked up the rifle he had taken to carrying with him when escorting the women through the dining hall. "It be all right with you, Miz Jennifer?"

Jennifer wearily removed her apron and nodded. "We have to go through there to get upstairs, anyway. It won't hurt to stop a minute."

Charlie beamed with delight and appropriated the place next to a suddenly demure Lucia as they entered the dining room.

With much hemming and hawing, it was made clear they were expected to sit at a table set up in their honor while a few of the more talented miners brought out their instruments and proposed a little entertainment in lieu of speech making. Touched at this tribute, Jennifer smiled agreement after getting Henry's guarded approval. They settled into their chairs and watched as the odd assortment of guitars, banjos, jugs, and mouth organs assembled into a group and began to scratch out a cacophony that eventually smoothed into recognizable patterns.

The men tapped their feet to the rhythm as two of the guitar players sung a familiar Western ballad, then swung into a more foot-stomping tune involving a rowdy chorus the audience joined in. As the song went on from one elaborate verse to another, punctuated by the noisy repetition of the chorus, the women entered into the fun—first humming the tune, then softly repeating the lines until they could no longer resist and roared out the final call with the rest of the singers. Elated with their success, the singers urged them to stay for one more round, and Henry shrugged his approval.

So Jennifer and Lucia sang along with the next ballad, their clear, light voices ringing out over the rumbling baritones. A hush came over the room when the song was done, and it was Charlie's turn to persuade them to linger and sing a final song by themselves. He had finally succeeded in capturing Lucia's hand, and Jennifer grinned in sympathy when he winked at her. To Lucia's embarrassment, Jennifer and the guitar player put their heads together and came up with an old Mexican love song they both knew, and the first haunting notes silenced the room.

Jennifer could feel her spirits lift with the notes of the song. She could ask for no more appreciative audience than this room full of rowdy, hardened miners. It was as if she had gained an army of friends, and her voice lifted with her mood, enthralling old and young alike. That she was heartbreakingly lovely in the lowered light of the gas lamps did not occur to her, nor did the image she might be creating in the minds of others, and she accepted the cheering applause at the song's end as a fitting end to the evening and not a personal tribute.

In the ensuing confusion, Henry hustled the women from the room and upstairs, leaving the miners to finish off their evening with a bawdier repertoire lasting late into the night. Jennifer listened to their noise as she retired alone to the bedroom, tired, upset, and in an emotional turmoil she could not analyze.

Soaking in a hot tub, she tried to organize her thoughts, but they were in a hopeless muddle, one leading to half a dozen others. It was late and there was still no sign of Marcus, he had done it to her again: trampling all her hopes just when she was most vulnerable. She was angry and worried and unsure how to react. Sadly, Jennifer tied the ribbons of her lace nightgown, smoothing its filmy folds over scented skin. She had wanted to please him, but now she wasn't so certain she had made the right decision. Perhaps it would be better to return to her own room in case, by some slight chance, he should show up.

Instead, she sat down at the dressing table in the bedroom and began to remove the pins from her hair, unfurling the long tresses and pensively brushing them. Lost in her thoughts, she didn't hear the key turn in the lock and was unaware of her husband's entrance until he closed the door, locking it behind him and dropping the key into his pocket.

Marcus advanced across the room, and to her horror, Jennifer could see he was furiously angry, the muscle at the angle of his jaw twitching, eyes sparkling icily in a manner she knew too well. She rose and backed away in alarm, hair tumbling about nearly bare shoulders. This wasn't the mood she had hoped to find him in, but it was rapidly beginning to match her own, and she narrowed her eyes warningly.

"What excuse would you care to give for breaking your promise this time? Are you so totally incapable of keeping your word you cannot obey one simple command?" Flinging his hat into the corner, Marcus stalked across the floor, tearing at his cravat as he approached.

"You are due no explanation at all when you talk to me like that. Try again when you are prepared to be more reasonable!" Jennifer withdrew toward her door and freedom, only to find retreat barred by her husband's towering form.

Marcus threw his cravat across a chair and began to shed his coat, forcing Jennifer's bemused gaze to travel from the threatening breadth of his muscular chest up to the icy gray of his eyes.

He never once raised his voice as he replied, ominously, "You're not escaping me this time, Jenny Lee. You've had your way too long, and my patience has worn thin with your antics. I am not amused to come home to find you've been entertaining the entire camp as well as half the town with your performance, and that after promising me you would stay out of the dining room when the men were there. I have been entirely too lenient, and this is where the indulgence ends. You are a woman, a child no longer, it is time you learn what it means. I'm calling in your debts."

Jennifer stared in astonishment as Marc's coat joined his tie and he tugged at the fastenings of his shirt. The dim lamp light traced shadows across his face, but the iciness of his gaze was clearly evident. She was too amazed at his actions to hear all his words, but the last few rang clear, and she searched his face for their meaning.

"My debts? I think you have gone mad. If you come one step nearer, I'll scream the house down."

More calmly now, Marcus pulled the studs from his cuffs while he observed the trembling figure before him, noticing for the first time the filmy gown that did little to conceal the slender form beneath, the soft glow of ivory skin in the flickering light, the shimmering tresses that had bewitched him so easily. Somewhere, in the back of his fury, he began to realize his error, but it was too late to back down now. His eager anticipation earlier had been set back by the drunken reports from below, and he was too angry at the tales of his wife being bandied about to think rationally now.

"I have no intention of harming you. I've just decided to call in the debt owed me. You do remember our little wager, don't you?" He dropped the studs on the dressing table and pulled off his shirt.

Jennifer stared at the broad expanse of her husband's chest covered with its thick mat of dark curls that so neatly matched the ones tumbling over his forehead, and her eyes widened as they wandered back to meet his. Their gazes locked, and her body tensed at the answering gleam she found there.

"Twenty-four hours, Jennifer, starting now. Go run the bath water for me, I've had a long, hot day." His gaze never left hers as his words lingered in the air, waiting for her objections.

His eyes held Jennifer spellbound while his words put an end to her breathing. Her mind froze in remembrance of the night the wager was made: there was no escaping her own foolishness, even if she had the power or desire to combat him, and she did not. Trancelike, she started around him, only to find her path blocked again as he stepped back into the connecting room to lock the exit, appropriating that key, also.

"Just a precaution, in case you decide to skip out on your debts. I've left word we're not to be disturbed by anyone but Stuart, so there's no one to come to your rescue this time." Marcus slid the keys onto a high rafter out of sight and well out of Jennifer's reach.

Anger prickled up the back of her neck, and she bit her tongue to prevent a sharp retort she might regret later, but he had already left the room and failed to appreciate her self-control. Running the bath water, she wished the foul thing would run scalding hot, knowing it never became more than lukewarm. Her insides churned with resentment, disguising the chasm of fear his words had set in motion.

When Marcus returned and began to remove his trousers, Jennifer hurried to depart, but he grabbed her waist and forced her to face him.

"You're going to have a very busy twenty-four hours, madam. I know how you hate to be bored. We'll start with the bath. I want to be bathed—by you," he added, in case there was any doubt.

Speechless, Jennifer glared at him, but his gaze was unwavering. He dared defiance with his stare.

Anger and incredulity surged through Jennifer's veins, leaving behind any fear she might have known. As Marcus released her hand and proceeded to remove the remainder of his clothing, she clenched her fists in frustration and swung around, averting his eyes until she heard the lapping of water as he entered the tub. Then, taking up soap and cloth, she knelt beside the bath, fastening her gaze on the cloth while her thoughts whirled faster than she could grasp them.

Marcus rested his elbows on the edge of the tub and

grimaced when Jennifer vigorously applied the lather to one powerful shoulder.

"I see we're right back where we started, and I'll have to do all the talking again," he commented drily.

"You never listen to anyone else, so you may as well," she replied bitterly, bearing down harder as she scrubbed at the rock hard muscles of his chest. Maybe she could scrape the skin right off, or at least, a few hairs, but it was difficult to concentrate on revenge when her eyes kept straying lower. Her hands sketched lingering whorls across his broad chest as her gaze involuntarily followed the narrowing line of curls to their natural destination. She blushed at the path of her thoughts, and jerked her hand back from where it had strayed.

"You never could keep silent very long," Marcus observed wryly. He traced a wet finger down her arm, leaving a soapy trail trickling across bare skin.

Jennifer smacked his hand away, but irritatingly, he only moved it to the other arm. In the ensuing tussle, her hand hit the water, sending a showering spray of water and suds into his face, and Marcus roared, his hand reaching blindly to grasp her shoulder. Capturing it, he pulled her down closer until their lips met, and their anger flared into a sudden rush of passion at the contact.

Jennifer bent eagerly to his wet embrace, her heart clamoring at the possessiveness of his mouth, so unlike the passionless embrace of Cameron.

She could feel his heart beating next to hers, and there was no question of resistance as his tongue demanded entrance. She was his to command and he knew it, taking full advantage of his position by invading her mouth. Roughly, he drew her closer to explore more freely, soaking Jennifer's flimsy gown.

"Now, you won't repeat that maneuver again or you'll be joining me in the tub," he warned, releasing her lips to nibble at a tempting earlobe instead.

"I may as well, for you've ruined my gown. Are you getting even with me for your suit?" Jennifer couldn't face him, but returned to lathering the cloth, her cold words belying the wild confusion inside. He was toying with her and she should be furiously angry, yet she melted at his slightest caress. Her fingers rubbed against the bare skin of his back as she scrubbed, sending a delicious shiver up her arm at the intimate contact. She was aware of the masculine virility harbored so dangerously beneath her fingertips, but it was excitement and not fear causing her to shiver.

The wet lace of Jennifer's gown molded to high curves, and Marcus traced their outline. "I doubt if my ruined suit ever looked so well on me as that gown does on you," he muttered appreciatively, before taking the cloth from her hand. "I'll have a worn spot there if you continue much longer. Fetch me a towel, and I will finish washing myself."

Jennifer drew away in relief, eagerly seeking a towel, and averting her eyes as she brought it to him.

Marcus watched with amusement as she politely stared at the closed door, still the modest maiden. That situation would soon be rectified, he vowed. Taking her offering, he stood up, wrapping the towel around his waist and climbing from the tub.

"It's time you learned about men, my little innocent, if you're going to make a practice of entertaining them." With firmness, he pulled her around to face him, drawing her into his arms. She was warm and trembling against him, the wet material of her gown providing no protection. Allowing his hands to wander down her back and across soft buttocks, Marcus pulled her close enough to feel his rising ardor. Jennifer shrank away at first, but with his calm insistence, relaxed, and leaned against him. His lips brushed her hair and nibbled at her ears while his hands stroked and calmed her trembling.

"It was only a song, Marcus. Why are you doing this to me?" Jennifer whispered, clinging to him for support, her knees too weak to stand. She could feel the rough mat of hair beneath her cheek and her fingers dug into muscular shoulders as a flood of heat swept through her.

"Doing what?" he chuckled softly. "Showing you what it feels like to be a woman? Is that so bad?"

"You know that isn't what I mean." She tried to pull away, only to be halted by the strong hands on her shoulders.

"I intend to show you what every man thinks of when you put on a performance as you did tonight. Now take that gown off," he commanded.

Jennifer's eyes widened as she looked into his face, finding only stern resolution in the set of his square jaw and a smoky gray in his eyes. Instinctively, her hands covered the ribbons holding her clothes in place.

"Marcus, no, not like this," she whispered, fearful now of his intentions, her hopes crying out from the ruins as he trod implacably over them. Could he show her no affection, no love at all?

"Take it off or I'll take it off for you, and none too gently. You will not get away this time; I will have you, whatever the consequences." His bronzed shoulders still glistened with moisture as he held her relentlessly, his eyes piercing the fragile fabric covering her. "In any case, it is too wet to do more than give you a chill."

Hypnotized by the intensity of his gaze, Jennifer fumbled at the ribbons, unable to draw her eyes away from his masculine nudity as the bows knotted beneath nervous fingers. With a quick jerk, Marcus parted the frail strips, allowing the gown to fall to the floor, revealing her nakedness to his avid gaze. Resolutely, Jennifer made no effort to clutch the gown to her, but let it fall. This was what she had wanted for too long a time to quibble over the manner in which it was given. This time there would be no retreat. She stood proudly as his smoldering gaze raked over her and flickering fires of desire crept through her veins, ignited by the heat of his stare.

Almost reverently, Marcus lifted a hand to stroke fair skin shimmering in the lamplight, his thumb caressing the taut crest of her breast before running down the curve of her waist and flare of hip. Months of pent-up desires surfaced, and he groaned softly as he finally captured that slender waist in his hands, bringing her into the circle of his arms so he might bury his lips in the curve of her throat, leaving a flaming trail of kisses across silken skin.

"You are mine, Jenny Lee," he whispered hoarsely, "and I do not intend to share you with any man. The judge said 'to have and to hold, for better or worse,' and whichever it may be, I will have you."

Jennifer quivered as his head dipped and his mouth fastened on the sensitive tip of her breast, and she nearly screamed with the ecstatic sensation of his tongue teasing the already hard points into readiness. As his lips worked their magic, her knees weakened until Marcus alone was supporting her, pulling her hips hard against his, the rough cloth of the towel the only barrier between them.

She cried out as Marcus swung her from the floor and carried her toward the bed, but whether it was a cry of fear or anticipation, neither knew nor cared. Waist length copper tresses tumbled freely toward the floor as Jennifer clung to his shoulders, unable and unwilling to fight his hold. Marcus was like a man demented, but the same madness surged through her veins, and no power under the sun could stop them now. The same moonlight that had enchanted their first tryst danced wildly across this union, and Jennifer gave herself up to its magic.

Laying her gently against the cool sheets, Marcus half kneeled on the bed bedside her. The towel had fallen from his loins and in the moonlight, he hovered as some Grecian god above her, the full extent of his manhood unveiled at last.

As he recognized the direction of her gaze and the sudden flare of questioning fear, Marcus bent to nuzzle at her throat, releasing his relentless grip so she might be free to use her hands.

"I am but a man, my love. Let me show you I am not the devil you fear."

His lips found hers then, his tongue making quick, searching explorations of her mouth as the lean length of his male body covered hers with nothing between them. Jennifer quivered at this naked contact, but as she grew accustomed to the feel of his heat pressing her down into the mattress, she grew brave, and her hands slid over the rippling muscles of his back, entranced by their powerful surge at her touch.

The days and weeks of the last year slipped away, and Jennifer was back in the bridal suite with the man who had taught her love, and nothing else mattered. Her body arched naturally to meet his, and her hands clung to his shoulders, pulling him down to meet her kiss and crying out with the joy of his fingers playing, unhampered, across her breasts.

Marcus groaned his eagerness and tugged her to him, his manhood searing her thigh and sending another tremor throughout Jennifer's body. Her nails raked down the bronzed smoothness of his back, urging him closer, aching for the joining that would make them one again, but Marcus refused to hurry.

His lips and teeth tugged at a tender nipple while his hands sought all the secret places of her body. With deliberateness, he stroked and caressed, fighting his rising need until he could arouse in her a hunger as great as his own.

Jennifer cried out her frustration as he moved away, only his hand tracing burning paths across her skin. When his fingers found the softness between her thighs, she rose against them and Marcus smiled his triumph. Penetrating that dark warmth, he stroked and caressed until he felt her urgent grip and knew success was at hand.

Slowly withdrawing his hand, he traced the curve of her hip to cup a buttock before lowering himself within reach. His lips traveled upward again, past the temptations of twin peaks to a delicate earlobe, while his knees gently parted her thighs.

Jennifer clung to him, feeling naked and defenseless as

her body opened to meet his, fearful of his violent thrust. Instead, he hovered there, brushing against the gates of her womanhood and caressing the vulnerable length of her body, while he whispered reassuringly in her ear.

"It will be better this time, my love. I take you as husband, you have nothing to fear."

With those words, he carefully lowered himself, penetrating the moist recesses of her body with his hardness. Jennifer gave a moan of satisfaction and arched eagerly upwards, completing his impalement, finally eliciting Marc's first uncontrolled response. He gasped in mixed relief and impatience, then cupping her buttocks in both hands, repeated the maneuver. His thrust filled her totally, and crying out her joy, Jennifer clung to muscular shoulders and surrendered to his wild passion.

Desires dammed up too long cannot be held back forever. Their bodies joined with earth-shattering impact, and as Jennifer quickly learned his rhythm, they moved obliviously, in time to their needs, losing all sense of space and time in their driving desire to merge into one being. The tensions of their needs built, winding them tighter, closer, entwining them in a circle of heightening passion until it seemed they would surely pass into oblivion before finally exploding in a climax of fiery proportions that drained the flood of passion and melted them into one, leaving their bodies racked and exhausted and tingling with awareness of every nuance of the other's.

Shuddering with the hot tremors of their passions, Marcus rolled over and pulled Jennifer with him, holding her close to his side, her head resting on his shoulder while copper hair streamed across the pillow. Soft brown eyes met his, and he searched her face, brushing her hair back from her cheeks and wiping away the trace of a salty tear. There was a sadness behind the sparkle of her eyes that he could feel in the pit of his stomach, but her full lips curved with pleasure.

"Well, Jenny, do you still find yourself possessed by a demon?"

Tracing his lips with a fingertip, Jennifer smiled slowly, aware of the contact between their bodies, her breast pressed against his side and her leg entwined with his. If this were sin, she was guilty, and would probably burn eternally in the fires of hell, but she felt no guilt or shame. She was bought and paid for and entirely his.

"Possessed, most certainly, but this time I know the demon and that destroys his power. You are but a man, now, my love." She raised up on an elbow and brushed his lips with hers, fastening more tightly at his insistence. Her tongue flicked over his and then, reluctantly, departed.

Marc's hand wandered down her side, and he knew he would soon have to have her again, but he held back, savoring the moment. "And I thank God that you are a woman and no lady or angel. You must thank your parents for keeping you ignorant. You are as natural and responsive as the day you were born."

Wonderingly, she watched his eyes, their smoky blue smiling at her questioning expression. "I thought my ignorance was a handicap and that you preferred a lady for wife?"

"Your ignorance prevents you from finding this part of married life as distasteful as most ladies do. You are refreshingly innocent of their inhibitions, little one."

A small frown puckered the bridge of her nose. "I don't understand. You said you and Melissa were lovers, and Gwendolyn, and others, I'm sure, and they were all ladies. They could not think of this as distasteful . . ." Her voice trailed off in puzzlement, unable to phrase her question.

Marcus kissed the tip of her nose. "With Melissa, I was ignorant and thought all women felt as she did, that only men enjoyed the physical act of love. With a little experience I learned the difference, and from then on I confined my pleasures to more unladylike ladies. You told me yourself, Gwen was no lady, despite her appearance. But those women made better mistresses than wives. Can you imagine Gwen raising a house full of children?" He laughed at her expression and tugged her closer.

"Then I have been behaving most ladylike in keeping you from my bed and caring for your son. You should have nothing to complain of."

"No lady every kissed me the way you do, minx." And he tipped her chin upward to press his lips against hers, capturing her breath and sending her blood racing. *"No one has ever kissed me the way you do,"* he whispered as he rolled her back against the mattress, his hands taking familiar possession of her body once more.

Jennifer smiled with pleasure as his hands rode over her. She would consider the consequences of his words and actions later, after this burning fire inside was satiated. There could be no logical thought while this need raged between them; he destroyed all thought with his touch. She returned his caress with a startling passion and before long, they blended together again, two hearts beating as one while desire took possession of their bodies.

Afterward, spent and exhausted, they lay curled together in the security of each other's arms, drifting in the direction of contented sleep. Marcus brushed a finger across the flushed cheek of his sleepy wife, admiring the sooty curve of her lashes against the clear skin before they slowly lifted.

"Jenny Lee, you're well worth waiting for," he whispered, kissing her forehead lightly.

The lashes lowered again, and she smiled, nestling closer into his embrace. "If you had to wait as long as I have . . ." Her mumbled words trailed off incomprehensively as sleep overtook her.

He smiled and hugged her sleeping form. "I have, Jenny, I have," he whispered to himself. It had been a long year . . . And he hoped he hadn't destroyed all his efforts tonight. His smile faded as he remembered her excited expectancy when he entered this evening, the lace gown she wore as she waited in his room—waiting for him? If she had already made the decision to come willingly to his bed, had he ruined his chances by his performance tonight? He groaned inwardly as he recalled the shock and fear in her eyes when he approached her with his rage, months of patience gone to naught because he could not control his anger, his jealousy.

Jealousy. That word hadn't occurred to him before, but it fit. And why shouldn't it? She was his wife, and he was jealous of her attentions. They belonged to him and not a pack of strangers; he had a right to be jealous. Sadly, he hoped she understood that, but the words she had spoken after they made their wager echoed in his thoughts: "The twenty-four hours you collect the debt will be the last peaceful twenty-four hours of your life, Captain." With these words ringing through his dreams, Marcus slept fitfully.

Chapter Twenty

From years of habit, Marcus woke early next morning, the rays of sun just beginning to cast their rosy hues across the planked floor. Beneath the covers, Jennifer lay curled at his side, her supple body pressed temptingly within reach. Experimentally, he circled one rounded breast, and she unconsciously snuggled closer, not retreating from his touch. Deciding to take this as an encouraging sign, Marcus brushed her forehead with a kiss and rose from the bed, donning his robe and padding to the wash room.

When he returned, she was awake, watching him as she pulled the covers up to her neck. Marcus smiled at this belated gesture of modesty and acknowledged her unspoken question.

"Your son is stirring, and I expect we will soon have company. I didn't think Lucia would appreciate it if she found herself locked out."

As if to provide evidence for his words, a timid knock sounded at the far door. Warned of Marc's presence and ill humor of the night before, Lucia was uncertain of her reception in disturbing them.

Turning his attention to lighting a cigar, Marcus called for the maid and ignored her guarded glance as she carried in the whimpering babe. Lucia's gaze swept from his robed figure to Jennifer's, a worried frown crossing her face.

Jennifer accepted the warm bundle gratefully, nervous in the presence of a husband who seemed so aloof after last night's intimacy, uncertain of his mood or what to expect next. Stroking the infant's hair, she murmured her thanks, but didn't meet Lucia's look again, allowing Marcus to take command of the situation.

"Lucia, see if you can rustle up some breakfast for us and have Henry bring it up here. You are on your own today; perhaps Charlie can keep you entertained." At the maid's startled blush, he added, "Of course, Stuart will be in your charge, so I don't expect you to wander far." He spoke with amusement, smoke curling from his cigar as he surveyed the two women.

Exchanging a glance with Jennifer, Lucia departed hastily, reassured by Jennifer's nod.

Marcus stared out the window, smoking his cigar while Jennifer fed his son. They exchanged no words until Jennifer, detaching the sleeping babe from her breast, asked for her robe. Then he swung around and eyed her suspiciously, finally shaking his head.

"There is no one here to see you but me, and I prefer you the way you are. Besides, you will not be able to get far without clothes if you should decide to make a run for it."

Jennifer glared at him without comment, then securing her sleeping son amidst the covers, she rose from the bed, striding unashamedly to the wash room, her fair skin gleaming with the first rays of sun.

Marcus watched her progress appreciatively, admiring the sway of rounded buttocks and soft breasts as she moved, her youthful figure draped only in the copper curtain of hair. She held herself proudly, and he recognized the stubborn set of her chin and sighed. Success would not come easily.

When Jennifer returned to the room, she found breakfast waiting and Stuart gone. Marcus smiled benignly at her approach and put out his cigar.

"Shall I serve you breakfast in bed, my love?" His look hinted of amusement as he observed her confusion in longing for the protection of the bedcovers and knowing the danger of placing herself conveniently in its confines.

Stoically, Jennifer resigned herself to her fate and slid between the covers. Although he seemed determined to provoke her, she had already decided not to fight. Beyond that, she had no desire to anticipate. The table was moved next to the bed, and Marcus sat beside her, pinning the covers over her legs with his weight.

Sipping her coffee, Jennifer avoided looking at her husband's virile figure as he rested one arm across her legs. Just the sight of him stirred her, his offhand proximity disturbed her worse. To distract her thoughts from images of last night, she attempted conversation.

"I suppose you have given the servants some reasonable explanation for your behavior," she murmured, her emphasis implying she had received none.

Marcus regarded her steadily. "I was wondering when you would loosen your tongue, but you would have done better to hold it. I owe no one any explanation." His tanned features were set in a stubborn line.

"But you intend to give me one, anyway, don't you?" she asked.

"When I came in last night, I expected nothing more

than to find you long since gone to bed." He finished his juice and massaged her thigh with his other hand while he spoke. "So I stopped downstairs for a quick drink and to see if things were staying well in hand. You have other guests this week besides my men?"

"Salesmen from 'Frisco. They came in yesterday."

"Then they'll be going out on the first train tomorrow and be lucky they're leaving alive," he stated firmly, lips set in a thin line. At her bewildered look, he relented. "Jenny, you are going to have to understand what goes through men's minds when they see you. Your innocence does you a disservice when you present yourself as you did last night. If you behaved as a lady, you would be treated as such, but when you start singing suggestive songs in a public place, you expose yourself to the lascivious desires of all and sundry."

Marcus searched her face for some sign of understanding, but found her usually open expression closed to him. So far, only he knew the sensuous nature lurking beneath that innocent exterior, and he preferred to keep it that way, but she wasn't making it easy.

"I sat next to your salesmen last night and listened to them describe your many talents and attributes in no uncertain terms," he paused, waiting for the implication to sink in. Her eyes widened, but she said nothing, so he continued. "When they began discussing the possibility of locating your room and the reception they expected to find there, I believe I rather lost control. If it weren't for the interference of Henry and some of my men, you would have had to scrape the bastards off the floor this morning. As it is, Doc Adams only had to patch one of them together, and they all have agreed to leave town on the first train. Now do you have any understanding of what I'm telling you?"

Jennifer bit her lip and looked away. She understood her rash behavior had led to unexpected complications and possibly endangered Marc's life, not to mention those of the unfortunate salesmen, but there was more to his story than that, more than he realized himself. She was well protected here and was confident the drunken ramblings of a few men were no danger to her, or not enough to prevent her from doing the same thing again if the occasion arose. Why couldn't Marcus see this as rationally as she did? He was not given to irrational behavior except where she was concerned, and the only answer she could find to explain this phenomenon was complete and total distrust of her. Had Melissa made him so vulnerable, or was she responsible for this lack of confidence? The memory of Cameron preyed uneasily on her mind.

Aware that he was awaiting some reply and unwilling to voice her thoughts, Jennifer took his hand and raised it to her cheek, caressing his palm with a light kiss before meeting his eyes.

"That was not the kind of homecoming I had intended to prepare for you. I am sorry."

Marcus stroked her cheek, pushing the fine hairs from her face as he studied her. "Is that all you have to say? Have you no understanding of what I'm trying to tell you?"

She searched his face, but could find nothing more than his words revealed. The grim angle of his jaw showed none of the boyishness she so loved; the frown between his eyes as he gazed at her could only be understood one way. She nodded her head and felt his hand tighten at the back of her neck.

"I understand that I have again caused you trouble when I already owe you more than I can ever repay. I deeply regret that my foolishness has been such a torment to you." She lowered her eyes, not seeing the pain in his.

"Any torment I suffer is strictly of my own making, and this is no subject to start a day of pleasure with. If that debt so burdens you, you can begin repaying it now."

Marcus bent to kiss her, but Jennifer jerked her head away as if she'd been slapped. Annoyed, he caught her chin with his hand and forced her to face him again.

"We have both admitted there is little chance for love between us, but we are sensible people. This marriage is suitable and convenient for both of us, whatever our personal opinions of marriage may be, so let us make the best of it. As a practical businesswoman, you must see that it is to your advantage to do so."

His arm encircled her waist and pulled her closer, until she sought refuge in the safety of his shoulder, burying her face against it to prevent his seeing the tears welling up there.

His words had frozen Jennifer's spirits, but his caresses warmed her flesh, and her body responded with a will of its own. With tears still trickling down her cheeks, she clasped his neck with a wild abandon while his lips traced paths of fire across her throat and breasts, the heat increasing her frenzy as he applied them to rosy crests. If he understood nothing else at all about her, he understood well the needs of her body, and he made the most of his knowledge.

Soon, she had the robe from his shoulders, and he shrugged it off, pressing her back against the pillows and taking advantage of this display of her desire. Breakfast forgotten, Jennifer ran her hands over the muscled body she had known only in darkness, and with amazing gentleness, Marcus directed her explorations, teaching her the secrets of his pleasure. She responded shyly at first, but his encouragement and their mounting ardor soon swept away all restraint, and they joined together in complete abandon, his final thrusts bringing her to a peak of satisfaction she had not yet experienced.

Their passions temporarily spent, they lay entwined amongst the sadly rumpled bedcovers, safe in the security of silence and each other's arms. Marcus idly drew paths across Jennifer's skin, emphasizing points with a quick kiss to the place marked, occasionally testing the plumpness of a firm breast or popping a grape from their breakfast tray between her lips. In turn, she fed him morsels of toast or bacon accompanied by a wine red grape and denied him nothing. In silence, they were in harmony, and Jennifer reveled in the tranquility of his eyes, wishing she could hold this moment forever.

She wrapped her fingers in the curls on his chest, and he clasped her tighter, kissing her forehead.

"Would it be possible to ask that we spend this one day without further argument, little one?" he asked fervently.

Jennifer turned to rest her elbows on his chest, staring directly into the clear blue of his eyes and kissing him to soften her words. "No, my love, it is not. As long as I am held here against my will, I cannot help but be resentful and rebellious. Put yourself in my place, if I had locked the doors and kept you here against your will, how would you feel?"

Marcus laughed and hugged her to him. "Elated! I shall give you the keys and you may throw them away and keep me here as long as you like."

Punching him in mock anger, she replied, "I said 'against your will,' idiot. You take too many liberties, now let me go." She struggled to free herself, but he rolled over, pinning her beneath his weight.

"All right, I'll bargain with you. I will tell you the doors are already unlocked, and you are free to come and go as you wish, in exchange for your promise to honor your gambling debt."

"Imbecile. If that is the way you always do business, you will need me to save you from bankruptcy." Her arms locked about his neck as he leisurely ran a line of kisses down her cheek. "Twenty-four hours, then, no more, no less," she warned before succumbing to his ardency.

Twenty-four hours. If in twenty-four hours of lovemaking he could not make her love him, he could at least bring to full blossom the desires she had, until now, barely tasted. He had no doubt of her loyalty; if he could bring her needs to the depth of his, she would turn only to him for their satisfaction. Of that, he was confident. Fidelity of the heart was an entirely different matter and not one he was inclined to linger on for long. Love was an ephemeral thing at best, not to be counted on as much as he counted on her physical faithfulness. She was a baffling little wench, but until he freed her, she was his; he knew this as surely as he knew Stuart was his son. As difficult as Jennifer might be, she was invariably honest; there was never any question in his mind about that.

Satisfied with their bargain, they made gentle love: their passions overridden by their desire to pleasure each other. They took longer this time, their driving need to possess one another diminished by the knowledge that for the rest of the day their possession was complete. It was a time of mutual satisfaction in sensual pleasures, leaving them relaxed and content.

It was an enlightening experience for Jennifer, her body radiating with the warmth of his caresses, her heart swelling with the love hidden there. To keep it from him seemed almost sinful and increasingly more difficult, but still, she held back. If he had not guessed her feelings by now, it was because he didn't want to know them, and there was danger in giving herself away. It was all too new, there was too much to think over, and she needed more time to consider it. Maybe, sometime, she could tell him, and it would be all right, but not now.

Instead, they rose and put on their robes, picking at the remains of their breakfast tray before setting it out in the hall, leisurely embracing, while waiting for the inevitable interruption to come. To touch and be touched without restraint or recrimination was too novel an experience to be slighted, and their lips found each other frequently.

Marcus caught her and held her before the window, the sun-drenched mountain behind them indicating the lateness of the hour, the red-gold of Jennifer's newly brushed hair catching fire in the light. For the first time in months, Marcus felt light-hearted and light-headed, and it was only this little slip of a girl who could do it to him.

The knock at the door startled them, and Marcus made a wry grin at Jennifer's expression, kissing her nose but refusing to release her from his embrace.

"Your maid will have to get used to us in compromising

positions because I'll be damned if I let you go now that I've got you." Before she could protest, he raised his voice and hollered for Lucia to enter.

With babe in arms, Lucia entered and stopped short, taken aback at finding them still in robes and obviously exchanging more than their usual pleasantries. With astonishment, she consulted Jennifer for confirmation, the glowing smile she received in return satisfying her curiosity.

"Well, come in, Lucia, and don't stand there gawking. Has the little brat behaved himself this morning?" Holding Jennifer to his side while she took the infant in her arms, Marcus spoke gruffly, but the twinkle in his eye belied his words.

"Un poquito behaved well, but I cannot say as much for others," Lucia replied with a disdainful lift of her shoulders.

Jennifer grinned knowledgeably, "And how is Charlie today?"

Marcus looked baffled at the change in topic, but Lucia returned the grin in apparent understanding. "The same as ever; he does not learn quickly."

"Then tell him I not only taught you how to make my pies, but your aim is now better than mine. Perhaps then he will take the hint."

Marcus chuckled with sudden understanding, and Jennifer looked up in time to catch the quirk of his lips as he spoke. "You might also tell him from me that they taste better than they feel. Why don't you run down and see if you can come up with a cold luncheon for us and warn young Charles I'll have a bone to pick with him in the morning if he doesn't behave."

Lucia couldn't conceal her grin as she curtsied, but she wasn't ready to be dismissed yet. "There is a man from the bank would like to speak to *Señor* Armstrong and *Señor* Harry would like to talk with you, *Señora,* about tomorrow's menus. They ask when you will be down?" Lucia attempted her best formality but the curious speculation in her eyes ruined the effect.

"Tell them neither of us is available today, they will have to postpone all business until tomorrow. If they get huffy, remind them Sunday is a day of rest." Marcus dismissed the topic immediately, and Lucia took the hint this time.

After the maid left, Jennifer settled in an easy chair to feed the crying infant, gazing at Marcus quizzically. "Do you really intend to keep me in here for the entire twenty-four hours?"

He shrugged and sat down on the arm of the chair beside her. "The time is more than half gone, can you think of a better way to spend it? After all, I have more than a year to catch up on, and if I cannot possibly accomplish it in the time allotted, I can certainly make a start." He grinned and kissed the top of her head.

The warmth in his eyes when she looked into them caused the muscles of Jennifer's stomach to tighten, sending a shiver of delight through her.

"You exaggerate, sir. You scarcely knew of my existence until five months ago, and then I was in no condition to be desirable in any way. I am sure the women of your acquaintance have kept you well-occupied since then, and it is only your fastidious nature that has kept you celibate these last few weeks. Your self-control is shockingly lacking if a few weeks can reduce you to such a state." Jennifer attempted to maintain a tone of scorn, but the laughter in her eyes kept his temper abated.

Marcus grinned in reply, but the smile did not reach his eyes as he reproached her. "Your thoughts are scandalous, my dear. Do you accuse me of adultery?" he asked, stroking the bared breast that fed his son. "Do you place so little faith in me as to doubt my integrity or my truthfulness?"

Astonished at this reply to her scornful joke, Jennifer searched for some sign of anger in her husband's face, finding only melancholy behind the clear blue of his eyes. "I have never accused you of anything, Marcus, though I never expected you to be faithful under the circumstances. I have little reason to believe in your constancy, but otherwise, I have never doubted you," she replied in all sincerity, anxious to restore his good humor. Surely he would not think her so innocent as to believe that a man of his nature would deny himself for so many months when it was not expected? What reason would there be to think such a thing? He had certainly made it plain enough that she was wife in name only.

The openness of Jennifer's expression twisted a knife in his heart, and he smiled ruefully. He had done his work too well and certainly made a believer out of the little brat; there didn't seem to be a trace of jealousy in her heart anywhere. He had the evidence to make an unbeliever out of her, but it was his final card. If he didn't win with this one, he was out of the game.

Twisting a strand of auburn hair about his finger, Marcus delayed the decision. "Thank you for the vote of confidence, I beg you to remember it in the future."

Fear and alarm chased each other across Jennifer's pale features, but he smoothed her brow with kisses and reassuring phrases. There would be time enough to explain later, when he was more sure of her affections. For now, he had need to possess her once again. As soon as Lucia left with the sleeping infant, Marcus made his demands clear, and Jennifer submitted willingly, encouraging his eagerness with needs of her own. They were insatiable in their long-denied desires, and afternoon and evening passed swiftly in the search for satisfaction.

Twilight dimmed the room and with it went their passion as it marked the passage of time and the nearness of the twenty-four hours' end. Marcus assisted his well-ravished bride from the bed and wrapped her in his warm embrace before scooping her from her feet and carrying her, laughing, into the wash room.

Dropping her into the tub, he adjusted faucets and lathered soap and cloth, much to Jennifer's delight. His tall form bending awkwardly over the tub, he gently soaped her skin, his dark curls brushing temptingly near her cheek. Jennifer relaxed under the soothing massage, feeling the aching soreness left from the day's lovemaking seep away. With nimble fingers, he stroked the softness between her thighs, erasing the ache, then applying gentle pressures until Jennifer thought she would explode with the joy of it, pulling his head down to hers and covering his face with rapturous kisses even as wave after wave of ecstasy burst through her.

Well satisfied with his success, Marcus allowed her to return the favor, relaxing in the tub under her tender administrations while admiring the delicate curve of cheek above him. In not quite twenty-four hours he had replaced the shy maiden with this affectionate lover. Would she remain so after tonight? Or would she turn on him with bitterness for stripping away the last vestige of her pride?

For a moment, her face pinkened with the return of modesty as his manhood stirred and stiffened at her touch, and he rejoiced that he had not completely changed her. She was no longer innocent, but she could never be the shameless wanton of his other lovers. Her embarrassment was swiftly resolved by repairing to the much abused bed for one last tumble before time ran out.

Weary, but content, they lay wrapped in each other's embrace, listening to the clock downstairs chime the last minute of the day while the gas light guttered low. Neither moved from their position as the last low bong echoed up the stairwell and resounded through darkened hallways. As the sound drifted away on the night air, Marcus raised a finger to the delicate chin resting on his shoulder, lifting it until darkened eyes met his. Where there should have been glittering tears or uncertainty, he encountered a soft radiance that lit her face, curving her lips with a welcoming smile, and his heart leapt with a ferocious gladness.

"You're not going to leave, are you?" It was more a statement than a question as he caressed her cheek, brushing aside a stray hair and devouring with his eyes the look she could not hide.

"I should," she murmured.

"We'll sleep, and wake together in the morning. There is no harm in that." Kissing her brow, Marcus pulled her closer into the curve of his arm. "I have work that must be done and appointments to keep tomorrow, so I must go at my usual time."

"You are not afraid I will pack my bags and be gone before you get back?"

"If you could not leave Emma and the hotel to ruin before, you will not do so now," he answered confidently.

"Did you think of that before you barged in here last night or just make it up now to shame me?"

Marcus laughed and caught a strand of hair in his fist, wrapping it about his hand. "I have thought about it every day and night for weeks. Last night I was incapable of thought."

"You are a wicked man, Marcus Armstrong. Now I suppose you will expect me to fall into your bed whenever you return." Her anger was in mockery, but her curiosity was real. How long would physical desire last? He had easily lost interest in all his other mistresses, would he as easily lose interest in her when they returned to the city?

"Jenny Lee, I have long since given up hope of your ever doing what I expect you to do. I will be satisfied to find you still here, safe and sound, when I return."

Jennifer relaxed against his shoulder, relief sweeping over her. He was making no demands or threats, no attempts to force her before she could make any decision. Was it possible he had learned to accept her the way she was? Or was he just being polite now that he'd had his way? How could she possibly love him so much and not trust him in the slightest? It seemed a contradiction in terms.

As if sensing her disquieting thoughts, Marcus added, "Jenny, I can read your expression like a book, but I cannot read your mind. Have I so reprehensible a character that you cannot confide in me?"

His gaze was warm and understanding, and suddenly Jennifer recognized what was standing between her and total trust. Without thought of how foolish it would make her seem, she blurted out her pride-torn fear, "You deserted me once, Marcus, why should I trust you again? How am I to know you won't repeat the performance? Everything you do is stained by the knowledge that you left me to cope alone." Bitterness, long simmering, now bubbled over, and nine months of terrified desperation swept through her as if it had only been yesterday, leaving her shaking with its intensity. She pulled away from his sheltering arms and buried her sobs in the pillow.

"I see," Marcus replied thoughtfully, caught by surprise at the extent of her emotion. He had been aware that she felt betrayed, and in a sense, she had every right to feel that way, but he had no idea she felt so strongly about it. He rubbed her trembling arm but made no other attempt to assuage her fears physically, knowing she would only reject his advances. The day they were married, he had seen the anguish and the fear in her face when he revealed his identity. He had not expected to be forgiven what he had done, so he offered no excuses. But if he could relieve her pain just one little bit, should he not give her the whole story? How much would she understand? It didn't matter now. He played his final card.

"Jenny, you told me today you had no reason to doubt my honesty; will you believe me if I tell you I did not intend to desert you, that I came back for you?" He turned his head to find her face, afraid to read its expression as she lifted her head from the pillow. Bewilderment was the only emotion he could find there.

"You could not have. I watched for you every day. I lay traps to your room so I would not miss you. It was foolish, I know, but I was certain you would return for me and that I would know it was you. Months, I waited, and never any sign. Don't lie to me now; it will only compound the wrong." Grief was reflected in her accusations.

His smile was gentle as he dared to pull her closer. "You were no more foolish than I, a grown man who should have known better. When I woke to find you gone, I waited as long as I dared for your return, but I had a boat full of passengers waiting for their departure and a crew worried about their straying captain. I had to leave. But I was so convinced you would know I would return for you, that I failed to mention that small fact in my note; it seemed superfluous, somehow."

That was no explanation at all, and Jennifer hid her disappointment in the comfort of his shoulder. "It would only have raised my hopes to a more dangerous degree and dashed me farther when you did not come."

"But I did come, goose, that's what I'm telling you. I'll admit, it took much longer than I'd expected, but then, I had no idea you would get yourself pregnant with just one try. I have little experience with virgins and was too far gone to take precautions on my own; it just simply never occurred to me. So I did not realize my delay was anything more than exasperating."

Hope pounded wildly at his words as she raised her head to search his eyes for truth. If he could only make her believe it . . .

He understood and continued. "I had other obligations to meet, shipments to deliver, routes to complete. Then, when I reached New Orleans, a boiler burst, leaving me stranded for months. I could have caught another steamer, but I had no way of knowing if you would connect me with the *Lucky Chance* or not; it might have been your only way of knowing I was in town. It was insane, I grant you, imagining a girl I had never seen and knew nothing about would have any reason to wait for me, but I spent those months in frustrated delirium. Even Gwen gave up on me; I wanted no one else to sully the image I had formed in my mind. I even went so far as to buy a gown to match the shawl I had given you, choosing one for the young girl

I assumed you to be, gauging your size from the memory of you in my hands."

"The green satin!" she whispered, her eyes growing round as the facts confirmed his story. With uncanny memory, the words of the note that accompanied the gown came back to her: "This was a gift for a faithless lady . . ." Faithless lady! He'd been speaking about her! He had thought her another Melissa, no wonder he had grown so bitter. That explained the black humor Jo complained of when he returned to St. Louis. It all fit.

Trapped by the growing excitement in her eyes, Marcus was forced to complete his story, hoping it would help more than it hurt. "I didn't make it back to Paducah until December, and even then I was risking winter ice by not going directly to St. Louis, but I was obsessed by that time." He shook his head at the memory of his insanity and the pain that followed. He had deserved every minute of it for what he must have put this child through; the thought still made him cringe.

"I went back to your inn, asked for the same room, left the door unlocked, and waited. When you didn't show the first night, I began making discreet inquiries, hoping to turn up your identity so I could go to you if you couldn't come to me. One man told me the innkeeper had a daughter, but he couldn't describe you and I learned nothing further. I waited a second night, hoping by then you'd heard of my arrival. I had even paid my bills with the same type of California gold coin I'd given you, hoping its uncommonness would attract attention. When, again, you didn't appear, I grew desperate. I walked the streets, staring at every pretty girl that crossed my path. I stopped in every bar and tavern along the way and was introduced to half the whores in town; it is impossible to describe someone you have never seen, but I knew you were no whore.

"So I went back to the inn and began questioning every man that walked into the bar until I found out more about the innkeeper's daughter. I grew ecstatic when one fellow mentioned you were a pretty little thing with funny reddish colored hair, but he said he hadn't seen you in some time and maybe his memory was faulty. It got the conversation started, though, and before the night was over I knew more about your parents and heard more rumors than I ever want to hear again in my life. Men are more malicious gossips than you'd ever imagine, my dear."

Marcus hugged her reassuringly, hoping she would understand what came next. To his surprise, she leaned over and kissed him, the sweetness of her lips giving him the encouragement he needed to go on. He sat up against the pillows and pulled her head down against his chest, stroking her hair as he talked.

"Out of all the gossip I heard that night, the rumors that worried me most were the ones that said you'd left some time ago, run off with a salesman from St. Louis in one version, a river man in another. They seemed to be confirmed by the fact that no one had seen you in weeks, and that you no longer attended church on Sundays. I didn't even know for sure that the girl I was seeking and the innkeeper's daughter were one and the same, but just as my hopes had risen so high and fast, they were equally precipitous in their decline. I went to bed that third night with the certainty you would not come."

He did not speak of the black loneliness that had overcome him, an emptiness so despairing he had cried out for her in his sleep, though never knowing her name.

But what was not said in words, Jennifer heard in his intonation and gestures, recalling that one December night when she held her shawl and heard the cry of desolation within her. It could be explained as coincidence, yet she had felt strongly from the first that their fates were joined by some common bond of communication, if they could only open up their hearts and hear it.

She returned her attention to his words.

"But I could not leave without some corroboration, so I attended your church, wheedling a rather idealistic description of you from a lovesick fifteen-year-old, and con-

firming you had suddenly quit attending several weeks before. I managed to have a few words with your mother and
asked after her daughter; it was then that she looked at
me as if I were lower than a toadstool and informed me
she had no daughter." Marcus felt the tightening at the
back of his wife's neck and massaged it lightly, wishing
there had been some other way around this explanation,
but he was fighting for her future and willing to sacrifice
the past.

"So I made one last attempt. By then I was certain the
innkeeper's daughter was the one I sought; it could be no
one else, but I just couldn't believe you had run off with
some two-bit salesman, that you hadn't waited. There was
something wrong with that explanation, but I could get
no other. So I confronted your father."

Jennifer lifted her head and sought his eyes; they were
steady as he met hers, he cupped her chin comfortingly.
What must he have thought of her, coming from such parents and background? How could he not have believed
she had run off with the first man to offer, after she had
so shamelessly thrown herself into his bed? His faith must
have been as great as hers, his disappointment as deep.

"Your father said nothing, but he became very suspicious and started edging toward the shotgun he keeps on
the wall; that was the clincher. I grabbed my bag and left,
convinced you had done the unpardonable. I don't think
I was very pleasant company for a long time after, and I
certainly never made the connection a few months later
when a very pregnant little girl came on board in a different city with completely different parents in tow. I thought
you lost to me forever."

He drew her into his arms and held her close, letting
her warmth exorcise one further painful memory. That
she believed him, he knew, but whether it had helped or
hurt only time could tell. At least, he had been able to
keep one final fact from her attention: that in his first
ecstasy and delirium, and later, in black despair, he had
been unable to look at any other woman but her. He had

thought himself freed when that pregnant little girl had so enchanted him, but he had been too busy to bother finding out until it was too late, and he had found himself married, with no desire whatsoever to possess anyone but his intractable bride. What she would make of that part of his tale, he didn't know, and wasn't prepared to find out. But his words of that afternoon had been accurate, he had been waiting for more than a year, and one day could never be enough to satisfy a year's hunger. Already, he was aroused and ready to take her again, but he had promised to make no further demands that night. He would have to hope he had finally removed her distrust and won her favor so that he had a lifetime of nights to look forward to. He couldn't risk so great a chance for a moment's gratification.

"Marcus . . ."

He looked down into dark eyes swimming with tears, her distress evident in the drawn, pale features, and his heart bled that he had done this to her.

"Hold me, please?" Jennifer's arms crept around his neck, and as he pulled her against his chest, her lips sought comfort in the warmth of his.

Marcus hugged her tight as their mouths met and clung to each other, and he could feel her need growing in the strength of her embrace. His hand covered a quivering breast, and pulling away, he scanned her face for approval.

"Are you sure?" he whispered, not believing the answer he saw in her eyes. Hope had been doused too many times to kindle easily now.

"Please, I need you," she begged, emphasizing her point by seeking his lips once more. There was doubt in her mind no longer; she should have known he would never have deserted her. Now he was all she had, and she needed to hold on to him. If he had gone to all that trouble once to find her, surely, *surely* he would stay this time. She would make him stay, even if she could not make him love her. This was enough: to have him by her as he was now, feeling his strong hands caressing her as if she were a priceless instrument, feeling him inside her, possessing her as she so longed to be possessed . . . the sudden burst of seed flowed in her and she shuddered and lay content.

Marcus lay awake a while longer, trying to attune himself to this fragile body in the bed beside him. Marriage was a concept he had given up more than ten years ago, and when he had contemplated its possibility in some far distant future, it was a more formal arrangement he'd had in mind. But now the idea of separate bedrooms and polite dinner conversation was totally alien to him; this child bride of his had spoiled the whole arrangement without any notion she was doing so. How readily would he be able to change her mind and make her accept their marriage? Marcus smiled down at the sleeping red head on his shoulder—it wouldn't be easy, but she was worth trying.

Chapter Twenty-One

Dawn rose sunny and warm, and Jennifer stretched luxuriously next to her husband's sleeping form, conscious of his size and strength even in his nakedness. She had married a magnificent man, one who could give her everything of which she had ever dreamed, who could satisfy easily the restless discontent of her body, and drive her to distraction just by the look in his eyes. Yet her mind wasn't easy. She lay still, taking comfort in his closeness while she sorted through her thoughts.

She loved him, and last night's revelation had released

her from the black terror of being thrown back upon the world on her own, but it had also made her see how much she had come to depend on him. She had no other family now; they had disowned her. It should be easy to accept Marcus as husband and his family as hers; she had been doing it gradually all along, even knowing he would never love her and might not want her. Now he had made it clear he wanted her, and although she might doubt the duration of his need, she could no longer doubt that he would continue to take care of her. Shouldn't that be enough? It was more than most wives could ever expect.

But she couldn't fool herself into believing she was content with things as they were. How could she love and never hope for its return? How could she give her body completely knowing he only used it for convenience and might someday find another more to his taste? And with these doubts still between them, how could she follow him back to San Francisco and its temptations and sit in a drawing room, waiting for the night he would not return? There were still too many differences to overcome, and she could not expect he would change for her. Could she change for him? And with unexpected insight, Jennifer realized even if she could, she wouldn't. She would never be the dutiful wife and gracious lady he expected of her, and bitter tears rolled down her cheeks at the opposite backgrounds fate had given them.

When Marcus awoke, it was to find his wife up and gone. Muttering curses, pulling on the nearest pair of trousers available, Marcus looked up with visible relief when Jennifer reentered the room. Washed and wrapped in a summer dressing gown, she had rescued their son from the pangs of hunger.

"Damn it, woman, next time would you be so kind as to wake me before disappearing like that? I had all visions of trying to catch up to that train on horseback," he said irritably, cinching his belt before stalking to the wash room, his beard black and unshaven and his hair in a tangled mass of curls.

Despite her husband's irascible demeanor, Jennifer laughed, settling herself comfortably into an easy chair. "Even if you are so lacking in sense, your horse is not. You would soon find yourself on foot."

Marcus reappeared in the doorway, grinning sheepishly as he propped one shoulder against the frame. "You have not only sapped my strength, but my sense, too, I suppose. You could have waited for Lucia and saved my peace of mind."

"I doubt if there is a piece worth saving. Besides, if you remember correctly, Lucia had her hands full yesterday. She deserves a morning's rest."

Marcus threw up his hands in surrender. "I can see my twenty-four hours are up. I'd better get out of here before you find more practical means of wreaking vengeance." He disappeared into the wash room once more.

Clean and shaven, his hair tamed, Marcus returned to the room to find Jennifer still in the chair, staring pensively out the window, the babe asleep in her arms. Removing the infant to the bed, he drew Jennifer into his arms, stroking the long, silky hair hanging down her back.

"I thought we came to an understanding last night. Can you still not trust me enough to confide in me?"

She leaned against his chest, letting the strength of his hands take over momentarily. "It is not a matter of trust this time, Marcus, but a fear of incurring your displeasure again. I would like things to remain the way they were yesterday, but I'm very much afraid we are always destined to be at odds with one another."

Again, that cold gust of wind swept through him, leaving an icy pocket of fear around his heart. "All right, love, let me hear what it is this time and I shall try my best to curb my temper."

"When did you plan to return to San Francisco?"

Puzzled, he looked down into her face, her expression convincing him she was serious. "We could leave this weekend, if you liked. Or in another month or so, whenever

Emma is better. I have more than enough work to keep me busy that long."

"I want to stay here, Marcus, where I'm needed. I don't want to go back to San Francisco." Jennifer tried to pull away from him, but he grabbed her arms and held them tight.

"It will be different this time, Jenny. I will take you to the theaters, dancing, wherever you wish. Or if you feel strongly about it, I'll return now and find a house for us, but I warn you that it will not be nearly as grand as the others. Most of the income from my mines is being reinvested so that one day we can build a mansion of our own, but not yet. I will not compromise my principles on that."

Jennifer shook her head and tried to retrieve her arms from his grasp. "There is no need to compromise anything, none of that means anything to me." On the edge of tears, she bit her lip and ceased her struggles, facing him with pride flaring. "Can't you see what I've been telling you all along? Yes, I love theaters and dancing, I would dearly love a house of our own of *any* size, particularly if I knew you would be coming home to it every evening." She felt his grip relax on her arms, but didn't tug away, unaware of what she was giving away. "You tempt me as you have always tempted me, but I know myself too well to think these temptations will be enough.

"Marcus, I do not fit into your society of friends and associates back there. Your mother chose wealth and position when she married your father and was trapped like a spider in her own web when she finally found love, unable or unwilling to disentangle herself from your father's life. I cannot be like that. I do not want wealth and position. I don't want to live my life through you, and neither you, nor your society back there, will understand that. So it would be better for everyone if I stay here."

"Pardon me if I refuse to believe that. It would not be better for me to have a wife who chooses to live in the mountains like a hermit, and it would not be better for

Stuart to be always separated from one parent or another. What will you do if I pack Lucia off with me next week and return to the city, leaving you here to your own devices?"

"I will continue as I am now. Emma will never be seriously able to work again; she can use me easily as manager. Once the hotel becomes well established, she will not even need your payments to make a profit, and I can support myself. Lucia has been free to go back to the city any time she chose. I would miss her sorely and hope you would allow her to visit, but I do not need her." Not as I need you, Jennifer added glumly to herself. As usual, she spoke bravely, covering up the quivering quicksand underneath. But it was better to face this now before she became entirely dependent on him and unable to extricate herself from her own desires.

With grim determination, Marcus checked his temper. He had not imagined fate would take this turn, but after yesterday he was willing to combat anything that stood between him and keeping Jennifer by his side. Her words of a moment ago had not only given him hope, but strengthened his determination. He was used to having things his way, and this was too important to change for now.

With amazing self-control, he released her. "All right, Jenny, let me think about this. I have more work yet to do here, and Emma still needs your care; we will not have to make any decisions yet." A sudden thought brought a sardonic smile to his lips. "Does this mean you consider our contract terminated?"

Jennifer felt the blood rush to her cheeks, and she shoved her hands in the pockets of her robe and turned away. "I believe we terminated that last night by mutual agreement. Under the circumstances, it might be better if we reinstate it. One child without a father is more than enough."

Understanding dawned and Marcus drew her back into his embrace. "I thought you desired more children. I have watched you with Stuart, you make a wonderful mother."

He brushed her hair with his lips, and he could feel her response. He had not lost yet.

"I would love more children, half a dozen at least, but only with a full-time father to support them. At the moment, you don't qualify, and I'm not having you trap me into returning to the city by making me pregnant now."

Marcus lifted her chin and kissed her lingeringly. "You should have told me sooner that was what you were afraid of, and we could have terminated that contract a long time ago. There are ways of diminishing the possibility of children, you know."

"There are?" Her eyes widened as she looked into his laughing gaze. Was he joking?

"You're still a dunderhead, but we'll discuss this topic the next time I come in. Right now we probably have several impatient people waiting below tossing a coin to see who has the honor of determining if we're still alive. Get yourself dressed, madam, I desire to breakfast with you this morning."

"Aye, aye, Captain." Jennifer escaped gladly, too confused by her emotions and his words to understand anything but his kisses and where they led.

They descended the front staircase together, arm in arm, the glow from yesterday not quite erased with the morning's quarrel, and the little crowd of people below watched them with amazement. Lucia's report of their reconciliation had not been believed, particularly after Henry's recounting of Saturday night's altercation and the rumors that flew at their disappearance on Sunday. Now it was obvious to all observing that there was a rapport between these two that had never been there before, and upon closer observation, a flushed exuberance that explained why.

Charlie winked at Lucia, capturing Jennifer's hand as she stopped in front of them, his merry gaze sweeping wickedly over her from head to foot and back again. "I see you have survived the weekend nicely. You are looking *very* well this morning." Charlie's laughing eyes met hers, and Jennifer blushed, causing Marcus to place his arm possessively around his wife's waist.

"And what are you still doing here, Mr. Mangione? Why aren't you up at the mines this time in the morning?"

"Because, Mr. Armstrong, the ladies prevailed upon me to stay and escort you back to camp. Either they are eager to see you gone or worried you would be unable to sit your horse; although, I must admit, they never expressed either opinion and the latter is entirely my own." Charlie's grin grew broader at the nearly imperceptible twitch of his employer's lips. Marcus of a month ago would have ripped off his head for this audacity; now he only made a disparaging gesture and turned his attention elsewhere.

"Lucia, you will see that this mongrel is fed and sent to see to the horses. I will be ready to leave shortly."

Marcus ignored Charlie's mock outrage as he placed his engineer in his maid's charge, but Jennifer sensed her husband's amusement and wondered at this change in temper. Surely she had given him enough to be angry about, and Charlie wasn't helping any—how could one day make such a difference? She studied his profile, but he only squeezed her tighter.

As the time came for Marcus to leave, they stood momentarily alone in the now pristine lobby. The sun had not yet reached the shining glass windows and the room lay in shadow, the sounds of movement from other rooms muffled and distant in the background. Jennifer's yellow gown shimmered like candlelight as she stood on her toes and stretched her arms about her husband's neck, her supple body molding into the curve of his as he bent and kissed her. Their lips held lingeringly, parting reluctantly.

"You will make no final decisions until I return?" he whispered in her ear, suddenly unwilling to release her, afraid she would once again disappear as a puff of smoke when his back was turned.

"I will not leave, but I make no other promises," she warned him, clinging to his powerful shoulders one last time before he escaped.

A muffled cough at the doorway warned them it was time to part, and they slipped away, Marcus turning to catch one last glimpse of the brightness amidst the gloom, and Jennifer following the dark curls into the sunlight with her eyes, not dreaming how close she was to losing him forever.

Chapter Twenty-Two

The morning swept swiftly by with Jennifer directing the day's activities from the confines of Emma's room. She had neglected her turn at nursing by remaining with Marcus all the previous day; now she freed Lucia to her own devices while she took on the chore. It was not a difficult task, and she enjoyed Emma's cheerful conversation while updating the books from the weekend's receipts. Their economies were beginning to offset new expenses, and for the first time, Jennifer felt sure of their success. All they needed was an increase in clientele to bring in nearly pure profit, and she lay down her pen with a smile.

That afternoon she deserted her napping charges to restore order to the front desk, only to be interrupted at her chore by the portly figure of a mustachioed gentleman she knew to be the town banker. They had been introduced, but the gentleman spent little time in town and less in the vicinity of the hotel, so it was with dubious pleasure that Jennifer greeted him now.

"Mrs. Armstrong." He swept off his hat and made a courtly bow. "It is a pleasure to meet you again. If I had known you planned an extended stay, I would have made it my duty to stop in more often."

"Good afternoon, Mr. Clayton. May I help you with something?" Jennifer had no temper for gushing small talk; she knew better than to believe he was here for any other reason but Emma's overdue mortgage.

Still smiling his best drawing room charm, he inquired, "I understand Mrs. Thompson has been taken ill. Would it be possible to see her for a moment or two?"

"The doctor has recommended Mrs. Thompson not be troubled by any business matters for the next few weeks. If you have come on some financial matter, I would appreciate it if you would discuss it with me."

The man looked vaguely startled. "Why, that is quite kind of you, Mrs. Armstrong, but my dealings have been with Mrs. Thompson. Has your husband taken over her financial affairs since her illness?"

Jennifer saw a glimmer of hope in the banker's eyes and deciphered it immediately in terms of wealth: if Marcus backed the hotel with his money, the banker's worries would be over; the man was in for a large disappointment.

"I am sorry, Mr. Clayton, but Emma has left her affairs in my charge. If you would pull up a seat, I would be happy to answer any questions you may have." She smiled graciously and indicated one of the chairs that lined the wall, knowing what his reaction would be to this invitation from an eighteen-year-old female. She wasn't disappointed.

"Is your husband available, Mrs. Armstrong? I would like to speak with him if I may." Assuming his cloak of authority, the smile left the banker's face, his gruff manner intending to impress her with his importance.

"My husband is at the mine, as usual, Mr. Clayton. I am certain he will be more than happy to talk with you at any time, but if it concerns the hotel, you will have wasted both your time and his, and he will not be pleased. If you are certain I cannot be of any assistance to you, perhaps you would like to call on Mrs. Thompson? She enjoys visitors, but you must promise not to disturb her with business worries." Jennifer stood, giving the banker only two choices: to leave without completing his business or to call on a sick woman and somehow get the information he sought. There was little doubt to his choice.

Outmaneuvered, Mr. Clayton clamped his hat to his head and prepared to follow Jennifer up the stairs.

Lucia looked up with surprise when they entered, raising a finger to her lips to indicate silence, but Emma opened one eye and peered at them.

"Greedy Gus, should have know you'd be pussy-footin' 'round. Don't know what's kept you away this long. Come on in, sit down, I ain't going to die on you, leastways, not yet." Emma pulled a sour face but gave Jennifer a wink behind the banker's back.

Undaunted by this greeting, Clayton stood at the foot of the bed and gave his prepared speech. "Hello, Emma. I was sorry to hear about your illness, just stopped by to see if there was anything I could do for you." Pudgy fingers manipulated the brim of his hat while the banker eyed Jennifer, wondering how far he could go before she raised a hue and cry and had him thrown out. Apparently deciding he could get far enough, he relaxed.

Amused, Jennifer pretended not to notice as she moved about, dismissing Lucia and straightening pillows and bedcovers. Emma was no fool; she could handle him.

"And while you were at it, you thought you would pull my hotel from under me—take care of things for me, I 'magine you'd put it." Emma sat up against the pillows and crossed her arms over her ample chest, evidently enjoying the man's embarrassment.

"Now, Emma, you know me better than that. I'm not worried about that mortgage; I'm more than willing to wait until you're up and about before discussing it. I just thought you might be wanting to get this place off your hands; it's too much for a sick woman to have to handle."

Emma's snort brought a smile to Jennifer's lips, but she tried to maintain her best businesslike demeanor in interrupting the tirade that was sure to follow. "Mr. Clayton, if you must discuss business, it will have to be with me, but since you brought it up—Emma will be happy to take you up on your offer to extend the mortgage." Gleefully, she watched the banker's mouth fall open. Before he could close it again, she continued, "I think an extension of four months with a quarter of the balance due plus interest paid at the end of each month starting with this one should be sufficient to see the hotel through its present crisis. If you would care to discuss the details, I will gladly go over the books with you—downstairs." She emphasized the last word with a stern look at the chagrined banker.

Emma's astonishment was almost as great as the banker's, but she hid it quickly at Jennifer's knowing look, replacing it with a complacent smile as Clayton recovered his composure.

"Emma, does this mean you are authorizing this child to act in your place during your illness instead of a more substantial member of the community?"

"You have someone better in mind? Madam Dolly? Doc Adams? Yourself? That's about all the substantial you're going to get around here unless you're includin' Johnny Yellowfeather, and I'm not so certain that he ain't more substantial than all of you put together." She cackled at her humor, leaving the banker nonplussed.

He gave a weak smile and a slight bow. "I'm not so certain that Yellowfeather wouldn't be the better choice considering your usual clientele, but if you've made your decision, I'll abide by it. The results of it I shall make perfectly clear to Mrs. Armstrong." He nodded in Jennifer's direction and indicated his willingness to leave.

Giving Emma's hand a reassuring squeeze, Jennifer led him out, following him back to the front lobby. With swift efficiency, she presented the banker with books and budgets, explaining her cost cuts and present payroll solutions, upsetting the banker's notions of feminine inadequacy, and leaving him humiliated further at being put in the position of dealing with her. Convinced the work was her husband's, Clayton questioned her closely in an attempt to embarrass her, only succeeding in embarrassing himself more.

Finally, he gave up and agreed to have the papers drawn extending the mortgage on the specified terms. He would derive no satisfaction in closing the hotel: there were no buyers eager and waiting for the white elephant, and the town needed it desperately if it was to grow as promised. And Clayton had enough invested in surrounding real estate to be interested in that growth. So, still convinced her husband had a hand in this, the banker left with the assurance the hotel would go on as before, but he wasn't planning on holding his breath until the first payment was made.

The days were hectic, but the nights that followed were long while Jennifer lay in the large bed, fingers running longingly over her body as her husband's had, waiting impatiently for Friday and Marc's return. Her excitement grew at remembered touches and whispered words; no longer satisfied as she had been with their first encounter, she wanted more, and her mind worked feverishly at excuses to continue their relationship. If there were truly ways of making love without making babies, why could they not continue their lovemaking until he left?

That he would leave, she had no doubt, and that she would stay behind was certain. The prospect dimmed her excitement, but her mind was made up. In San Francisco she would be pressured into the dreary round of social visits of a dutiful wife, there would be no outlet for her creativity or ambition, and in resentment, she would blame Marcus. In turn, her natural high spirits and outspokenness would not only scandalize her husband, but all society, and he would begin curbing the social engagements he promised her. It could never work; they would be at each other's throats within a month, the only time they might get along would be in bed, and that would only last until she became pregnant. Then, satisfied that she was totally

disarmed and defenseless, he would go out and seek a
more genial companion.

Horrified at the picture she painted in her mind, Jennifer drifted into uneasy sleep, dreaming dreams of passionate kisses and caresses abruptly interrupted by terrible
tremors of fear in which she was left alone with the certainty she was about to be attacked, and each night her
enemy came closer. She prayed for Marc's return if only
to put an end to these fantastic fears.

But Charlie's arrival on Friday removed any hope of a
swift end to the nightmares. Wiping her hands on her
apron as she greeted him, Jennifer's smile faded at his
expression.

"No, Charlie, don't tell me he's going to be late again;
I won't believe it. There can't be anything so important it
can't wait for a few days."

There was no merry twinkle to reassure her as Charlie
shook his head. "The potential collapse of an entire mine
can't wait a few *hours*. The only reason I got away was to
get the instruments I need to figure the best way to shore
it up. He's in there now directing temporary measures,
and it will be some few days before we can get permanent
construction set up. I'm sorry, Jenny, another man might
leave it to his foremen to figure out, but not Marcus. It's
not just the mine, but the men's safety that matters, and
he's just crazy enough to worry about it."

Jennifer could hear the admiration in Charlie's voice
and knew he was right. It was only a small operation, and
Marcus could well afford to lose it, but it wasn't an impersonal transaction to him, no more than the hotel was an
impersonal job to her, and she understood.

"He's also just crazy enough to get himself killed trying
to do all the dangerous work. You better get back up there
fast and keep an eye on him, tell him all the horrible things
I'm going to do once I'm a rich widow." Jennifer attempted a smile but it was a failure, and Charlie's worried
frown did nothing to improve her spirits. "Maybe I should
come up and tell him myself?"

Her joke was half-hearted but the engineer ventured a smile. "You do and he's likely to bring the mine down on both of you. Don't worry, he'll be back in a few days, and you can soothe his ruffled temper again. Keep Lucia away from those maniacs for me, will you?"

"Will do, Charlie, although I think it's better phrased the other way around; Lucia can handle herself very well."

"Yeah, so I've noticed," Charlie rubbed one cheek and grinned sheepishly. "She packs quite a wallop for such a bit of a thing."

"Charlie! Shame on you!" Jennifer laughed at his expression and felt her spirits lift. Marcus would be back in a few days and everything would be all right; there was no point in worrying. "Take back a couple of pies and a bottle and pretend you're here tonight," she urged him, and Charlie agreed willingly.

Only after Jennifer was in her lonely bed again that night did the premonition hit her, and her dreams became more horror-filled than before with the imaginings of deadly dangers confronting her husband as well as herself. Her lungs constricted and her breath came with difficulty as the dread of the unknown pressed down around her. It was as if her unconscious were trying to tell her things her mind would not accept, and she slept little that night or the following.

The weekend kept them occupied, but the miners seemed to have caught Jennifer's low spirits, and there was little merrymaking. Lucia assumed the depression was due to Marc's absence and thought nothing of it, only Jennifer knew the dread that filled her sleep, spilling over into every waking hour.

With the miners' departure, even the haven of work deserted her, and Jennifer wandered idly through the days waiting for the sound of a trotting horse that would indicate Marc's arrival. By mid-week, she gave up any pretense of interest in ledgers or menus, and leaving Lucia in charge of Stuart and Emma, she took a walk up the flower-studded mountain. It was the first time in weeks she had been outside the hotel. Perhaps the August sun would bake her nonsense, and the brilliantly colored fields relieve her heart.

It was a romantic thought, not destined to be. Before she even reached the meadow, a familiar figure dashed down the path, chestnut hair disheveled with heat and wind as he raced to meet her.

"Jennifer! I'd given up on you. Come, we must hurry, you're almost too late!"

He grabbed her by the arm and turned her around, facing town again. Jennifer tugged herself free and firmly held her ground. This was a public roadway; he dared not attack her here.

"Cameron! What are you doing? I thought I told you Marcus was after you? Have you lost your mind?"

Emerald eyes drew together in a frantic frown, and he kept glancing over his shoulder as if fearful of being followed. "We need not worry about Marcus anymore, but if we don't get out of here quickly, you'll be in danger, too. Has he kept you tied up in that damned hotel? I've been waiting for some sign of you for weeks. It's almost too late," he repeated feverishly. "Will you hurry?"

He urged her on, taking her arm again and steering her down the path as if a league of devils were on his tail. Their shoes bit small puffs of dust in the path. His fingers bit painfully into her arm, forcing her on.

"What are you talking about? What danger am I in? Where is Marcus?" Jennifer's words came hurriedly, before some nameless fear could steal her voice and choke her throat. She could feel it creeping up on her now, that suffocating dread she had come to know too well. "Where is Marcus?" she cried again, hysteria building at the sight of the wildness in his eyes.

"Halfway under the mountain by now, I should think." At Jennifer's cry of terror, Cameron halted, and gazed at her with some sympathy. "It's a hell of a way to learn you're a widow, but I've got to get you out of here. I didn't mean for things to happen this way, but it's too late to stop it now. My only hope is to save you."

She stared at him in disbelief, the suffocating blackness encroaching on all her senses until she shoved it back with an hysterical scream. "You lie! I know you lie! Get away from me, Cameron."

Jennifer jerked free a second time, but this time she ran, her skirts pulled up above her ankles and her feet pounding against the rocky path in a frantic rhythm, running as fast as she could go in the direction opposite from which he wished her to go—toward the mines.

"Jennifer—don't!" Cameron cried out behind her, but her feet never slowed. Marcus was somewhere up on that mountain, and this time she would find him, tell him of Cameron's lies and threats. She would keep nothing from him. Marcus would protect her. Everything would be all right, she knew it would.

Cameron caught up with her and yanked her to a halt. "Look, I didn't mean for this to happen, but the man is demented, I couldn't stop him. He wanted revenge and now he's got it. There's still time to save ourselves. I've got horses. We can ride out of here to safety, take the babe with us if you wish. He'll not know we're gone."

Jennifer stared long and hard into the clarity of emerald eyes. They were almost on a level with her own, and there was no amusement in them any longer. There were lines in his handsome face, and a cruelty she had not seen before around his mouth. Yet there was genuine sympathy there, too, and she suddenly knew he spoke the truth, for once in his life.

The sun-filled August day went black and the world whirled in slow-motion. Cameron was calling to her, but she could no longer see him. She could only see Marc's stern, bronzed visage, the eyes now laughing and blue, suddenly clouding and gray. They spoke to her and she heard with her heart.

"Go to hell, Cameron!" She jerked herself back to reality with a screech.

And then in a startling burst of speed, Jennifer fled up the well-broken path, clouds of dust flying into the air as her shoes trod the clods of dirt beneath her feet. Her breath came in ragged gasps as she reached the top of the hill and searched the trail beyond, her heart pounding frantically. She had no idea how far the mines might be, but if there had been some disaster, surely there would be messengers approaching.

Spying the dark movement of horses farther up the road, her feet took wing once more, the pounding, gasping motion preventing all further thought, blacking out the horrifying fears that would fill the void if she stopped. She had to keep going, to reach him, to be with him. Alone, she was helpless, but once she was with him, everything would be all right. It had to be. Together, they were invincible.

Startled at this unexpected apparition, the horses whinnied and sidestepped edgily, but their riders kept a tight rein, steadying the strange conveyance behind them.

Charlie halted his mount at the sight of the dust-covered, breathless figure running to meet them. Dismounting, his hand steadied the wide-eyed, panicky woman in the road. Almond eyes flew from the confirming sorrow in his face, over his shoulder to the travois behind the horses. He grabbed her just as she started to run to inspect the strangely still form on the stretcher.

"Don't, Jennifer. What are you doing up here? Who told you?" Charlie could feel the tremors shaking the slender frame he held, and his gaze traveled involuntarily to the hill beyond. Was that a man's silhouette he had seen there? If so, it was gone now, and his attention returned to Jennifer's frantic struggles.

"It's Marcus, isn't it? What happened? Let me see him, Charlie!"

"You can't do him any good here. We've got to get him back to town. You can ride with me." He held her by the shoulders, preventing her from going near the still form.

Charlie's practical words returned a brief moment's sanity, and Jennifer fixed her gaze on him. "Is he alive?"

"About as alive as a man can be after being buried under a ton of rock." The lines of the engineer's dark face were grim.

Jennifer swayed in his grasp, trying to come to terms with the fact that the towering, broad-shouldered man she called husband was the same as that powerless figure on the stretcher. With a determined nod of her head, she steadied herself, and shook free of Charlie's hold.

"I'll walk." And without another word, she took her place at Marc's side, waiting patiently for Charlie to remount and set the procession in movement again.

Marcus had been strapped in, allowing no movement as the travois slid along behind the horses; there was no way she could hold his hand. But it was obvious he wouldn't have known it if she had. A makeshift bandage had been wrapped about his head, and the handsome face below was whiter than the wrappings. Eyes closed, face blood-streaked and dirty, he showed no sign of life, though Jennifer watched intently for one flicker of a lash, a shallow breath, willing him to respond in some way so she could know he still lived. A dark cloud hid the sun, and there was not so much as a shiver to indicate the presence of life.

At the hotel, Lucia tried to pull her away, but Jennifer shook her off unseeingly, following the stretcher up the stairs as the doctor stood by and directed its placement. The covers of the big bed had been turned down, and Marc's body was gently placed in its center, without regard to dirt and boots. Jennifer made no comment, but the doctor cursed and ordered the boots removed, dunking a sponge in sudsy water by his side as he did so. Jennifer took the sponge from his hands and began the task of cleaning Marc's face, still unaware whether he breathed or not.

The doctor gave her an odd look, then proceeded to unwrap the bandages, ordering everyone else from the room and directing Jennifer to remove her husband's clothing. Obediently, she peeled back the spongy material that lay tattered across his chest, gritting her teeth as it revealed the crushed pulp that had once been smooth, tanned skin. The doctor watched her face carefully as the extent of the damage was uncovered, but she worked stoically, taking his instructions without comment. Satisfied she would be no better off elsewhere, he allowed her to stay on, and they worked side by side into the darkening night.

Gas lamps lit the room with shadows when they finished. With head and chest neatly bandaged and encased in white, arm set and splinted, Marcus still showed no sign of consciousness. Jennifer uttered no more words than her silent husband, and the doctor sent her from the room to wash, shaking his head gloomily when she turned her back. He wouldn't give the man the proverbial snowball's chance in hell of surviving, but if there were any way he could be saved, that girl would do it or die trying. At the moment, he was sincerely concerned with the latter.

Once she had washed and restored some semblance of sanity, the doctor tried to persuade her from the room, but Jennifer adamantly refused to leave her husband's side. In the end, the doctor gave in, collecting the others into the room to explain what was to be done.

Jennifer heard the words: Severe concussion . . . possible internal injuries . . . fractured ribs . . . lacerations . . . compound fractures of the left ulna . . . but they were meaningless to her. Would he live? Those were the only words she lived and breathed for, the only ones that held any meaning. And she sat silently, gripping the arms of the chair, waiting for the words that didn't come. When the doctor stopped speaking, she looked up, startled. He couldn't be finished yet; he hadn't said anything.

She searched the solemn faces before her: they were nodding understandingly, crying, tear-streaked, sympathetic, but not one raised the most important question of all—would he live? Jennifer want to shriek it out and make herself heard, but the words caught and clung in her throat. Tongue gagging at speech, her eyes begged for them to hear her, to voice her question, answer it, explain, but they looked at her with sympathy and tried to lead her away. Jennifer gripped the chair arms tighter.

Marcus had always been there before to rescue her from these panic-stricken fears. He would yell and curse, laugh and torment, lock her up, hold her, anything to drive away the evil fears binding her mind. Now he was helpless, and she must help herself, *must,* his life depended on it, and with a tremendous effort, she burst the bonds that held her tongue, letting the fears fly out by voicing the terror uppermost in her mind.

"Doctor . . ." Hysteria shattering the silence, she commanded their attention.

Brow drawn together in a concerned frown, the doctor turned to face his silent partner. She had been completely calm and unemotional up until now. Was her reserve about to crack?

"Will he live?" The words sounded gruff and defiant in her ears, but they were out, and she breathed again. She could do it, and no one could stop her. She could stand up on her own.

The doctor shook his head. "I don't know; there's no way of telling with these head injuries. He might could survive the others if he ain't bleeding inside or don't develop gangrene, but that blow on the head could have done most anything. If he don't wake up in the next few days, he might just pine away for lack of food and drink. I've seen that happen. We'll just have to wait and see."

"Thank you, Doctor.' Her calm returned. There was hope. If she could just bring him around, make him know she was there, waiting for him . . . Surely, surely, he would want to live. That's all it would take, she knew that was all it would take. And she took another deep breath. "Henry, find me a mattress and put it in here on the floor. Lucia, bring Stuart in here, I will look after him. You and Henry will have to take turns with Emma. Charlie, I need you to telegraph San Francisco and his family."

"Perhaps you should ask *Señor* Stephen to come?" Lucia asked tentatively.

Jennifer understood. "If it will make you feel better, please. If the hotel is going to stay open, we'll need all the hands we can get."

"You're going to keep the hotel going?" Astounded, Charlie couldn't hold his silence.

"Yes, and you're going to keep the mines going. Can you do that?" That would be Marc's first concern when he came to, his mines and his blasted miners. She wouldn't let him down, and she waited impatiently for Charlie's shocked reply.

He gulped and stuttered, then finally agreed. "Yes, I guess. The others are still operating, and I can put men to clearing the collapsed one . . ."

A sudden thought struck her, and Jennifer interrupted his ramblings. "Was Marcus the only one injured?"

The room fell silent, and she guessed the others had already heard the story. She waited for someone to repeat it for her benefit.

"Everyone escaped, thanks to Marcus." Charlie halted, hoping that would be explanation enough, but she waited expectantly, demanding the whole story. He shrugged, and continued, "There were only a few men down there when the explosion brought down the timbers in the center. It was kind of a chain reaction, I guess, as each section went down, it weakened the next. If they'd been in the back, there would have been no saving them. As it was, Marcus held up the last supporting timber before it gave way, long enough for his men to escape. When he let go, there was only time for him to throw himself under the ledge at the entrance. I'm sorry, Jenny, there was no way I could make him leave that mine until everyone was out."

Charlie's black eyes darkened as Lucia fell against his shoulder, weeping, and he held her carefully, all the time keeping his gaze on Jennifer. Her pale face, framed by disheveled auburn curls, remained calm, only the depths of her eyes reflected the flood of emotions released by his words.

"Of course not, Charlie." Jennifer heard the hero-worship in his words, felt the glow of admiration in her heart, but there were other words left unsaid, words that only she and Charlie knew. It was time she faced up to the truth. If she had told Marcus that first time, he might not be lying here now. Whatever it cost her personally, she would see it done now.

Jennifer's eyes met Charlie's. "What caused the explosion?"

It was almost as if he breathed a sigh of relief as he answered. "The beams had just been shored up. There was no one mining that shaft. There could be no natural cause that I know."

He hadn't said it, but it was there. The explosion was set deliberately. All eyes fixed on Jennifer as she paled. The doctor moved as if to grab her, but she caught her breath and came to life again.

"Charlie, you remember the man at the train station?" No one else knew what she was talking about and they looked bewildered, but Charlie nodded, waiting for her to continue. "His name is Cameron O'Hara. He was here again today. His father's name is Michael; they live in San Francisco. Give his description to the sheriff. I'm certain he didn't do it. He hates Marcus, but I don't think he has what it takes to kill. I think he knows who did it, though. Find him, Charlie."

There was strength in her command, but it took every ounce she possessed to make it. She sank weakly to the chair offered and clung to it.

Charlie squeezed her hand, the light returning to his eyes as he gazed upon her. "We'll find him."

Jennifer nodded and closed her eyes, waiting for the others to leave so she might be alone with Marcus and her thoughts.

Only the doctor tarried. "Let me give you something to make you sleep. There is nothing you can do now . . ."

Jennifer shook her head. "I don't want to be drugged when he wakes. I'll sleep."

When he wakes. She was so certain of it . . . The doctor looked at her sadly, squeezed her hand, and left her alone.

Chapter Twenty-Three

The next few days became jumbled memories of confusing interludes: the doctor's visits and the changing of bandages, the tense moments listening to discouraging clucks as he examined the wounds, the tears and prayers after he left, interspersed with the routine functions of day-to-day living. Jennifer refused to leave the room, eating all her meals by her husband's side, watching for some sign of consciousness, bathing his silent form lovingly while talking as if he could hear, conducting entire conversations out loud with Stuart as she tended him, convincing anyone entering that she was on the brink of madness. But there was no madness in Jennifer's mind now. Only complete sanity could pull him through, and she would be as calm and assured as humanly possible if it meant returning her husband to life. She owed him too much to let him die now; she had never even let him know how much she loved him. Perhaps it would make no difference, but at least he should know. And she whispered it in his ear as she stroked his bandaged head, praying that the words would somehow reach him, salty tears falling like rain upon his unresponsive face.

Stephen arrived, entering the room alone and closing the door. Jennifer flew into his arms and burst into tears on his chest, allowing his familiar closeness to comfort her. This was not the man she needed, but he was a friend, and one she relied on, and she needed all the help she could get. Stephen held her until the sobs subsided, then pushed her away so he could see her face.

His rough knuckle wiped away a stray tear coursing down her cheek. "Jenny . . ." He waited until she recovered enough to meet his eyes, but what he saw there stripped away any comforting words he might utter. There was pain and anguish so deep and so complete that no amount of speech could ever encompass it. Only the love that glowed behind it offered any hope, and it was to that he appealed. "Jenny, you cannot kill yourself with grief. There is too much else for you to live for."

"There is no one dying here, Stephen," she answered quietly.

"Then you must act like it, Jenny. Go in the other room and get some sleep, eat a full meal, take a walk. Lucia says you're killing yourself attempting to run this hotel and keep Marc alive at the same time. You have no need to do either; there are others more qualified."

"Lucia is overworried. I am fine." Besides, if she should ever walk out of this room with the memory of Marc's deathlike countenance on her mind, she would keep on walking until she walked over the nearest, most convenient cliff. But she couldn't tell Stephen that. "I get plenty of sleep right here, and I eat what is necessary. Everyone else is running the hotel. I only tell them what to do. It is not a difficult job."

Unbelieving, Stephen searched her face, but she seemed totally calm and controlled now. "All right, Jenny, I will take your word for it now, but this can't go on indefinitely. Tell me how I can help."

"You can help just by being here. You give me strength."

She moved out from under his hands, grasping one and squeezing it before returning to the bedside.

Stephen watched the fine boned hand stroking the still brow upon the pillow and tears sprang to his eyes. Despite their differences, Marcus had always been Stephen's childhood hero, the man he looked up to and admired most after his own father died. To see this man of action, his laughing countenance and brawny frame brought to this lifeless state was like ripping a part of his heart from him. What must it mean to the young wife who loved him in ways no man could understand? Stephen jammed his hands into his pockets and stared out the window until he recovered his composure.

"Jenny, you must tell me what I can do. I would gladly stand beside you and hold your hand if I thought that would help, but I can see that it wouldn't. Let me do something useful."

Jennifer looked up at his stricken face and felt her heart constrict. She would have to realize that others loved Marcus, too, and they needed help as much as she, but it was difficult to think of anything else but the still form beside her.

"You must look after Stuart and Lucia; Henry will be relieved to shed some of the responsibility. If Charlie has any questions about the mine, you could help him. My experience is limited to hotels, and I dare not venture into the mining business. If you truly wish to lend a hand, ask Henry and Harry what needs doing downstairs, and you will soon find yourself tending tables." Jennifer managed a small grin at his crestfallen expression.

"I would have more experience tending bars than tables. From what I've seen, Lucia does an excellent job of not only tending tables, but looking after herself. It is not much to keep a man active."

"Maybe tending bars isn't such a bad idea. We lose a lot of business to the tavern down the street, maybe you could look into that. Unless you have some other suggestion?"

His face brightened with some of its familiar mischief.

"I noticed you have a magnificent bar down there, and it seems a shame a man can't drown his sorrows decently around here. I'll see what I can do." The light fled as quickly as it appeared, and he approached the bed, taking Jennifer's hand once more. "Jenny, I wish there was something I could say, or do . . ."

She shook her head and looked away, then struck by a sudden thought, turned back to him. "Do you think you could wire your mother's doctor and ask his advice? I trust him; he's one of the most sensible men I've ever talked to. Maybe there is something . . ." Her gesture stressed the futility of her hopes, but she couldn't give up any chance.

Stephen nodded. "I will go do it now. If nothing else, perhaps he could recommend another doctor in the area."

He departed, leaving Jennifer alone in the deepening gloom.

Jennifer lay on her mattress on the floor, listening to her son's restless tossing as the sun rose, throwing its golden hues across the room. It was the morning of the fourth day if she was still able to judge time, and Marcus still had shown no sign of life; his muscular body lay slowly wasting away, all color waning to a ghostly pallor, and for the first time the possibility of his death was staring her in the face. Without food, there was no means of maintaining life, no matter how expertly she tended his wounds. There had to be some way of bringing him nourishment. As she struggled desperately with the problem, she became aware of the strange sensation of being watched, and to the sound of Stuart's restlessness came an added noise.

Eyes flying open and immediately finding the bed, her heart leapt at the sight of cloudy gray eyes staring back at her. In an instant, she was at his side, kneeling beside the bed and covering his unbandaged hand with kisses, tears flowing freely down her cheeks as he attempted to stroke her cheek with his finger.

"Oh, God, Marcus, you're alive . . . I knew you could do it." And she buried her sobs in the down-filled pillows at his head, feeling his hand on her hair, the hoarse, whispered "Jenny" that had woke her being repeated again and again.

It took time to recover her composure, but the knowledge of his needs strengthened her resolve, and she dried the tears and took his hand again. There was pain in his eyes, and his face was drawn and pale beneath the bandages, but the answering pressure of his fingers communicated life and hope and her spirits soared. It was like being given a reprieve from a sentence of execution, and she did not know where to begin to express what she felt.

The worry uppermost in her mind took precedence. "You have had nothing to eat in days, Marcus. Could you drink a little broth if I get Henry to prop you up?"

A faint grin flickered across his lips, but nodding his head, an expression of pain took its place. He closed his eyes, and Jennifer caught her breath, but he opened them after the spasm passed, and she breathed easier. There was little that could be done for the pain but drug him, and he needed nourishment more than drugs. She kissed him lightly, pulled on her robe, and crossed to the bedroom door.

To her surprise, she found Henry outside and waiting.

"Henry! What are you doing here at this hour?"

"Heard voices, ma'am. Thought maybe you'd be needin' me." Old eyes searched her face finding the light they sought, and his face broke into a toothy grin. "Reckon the Cap'n might be wantin' a bite to eat?"

"Some broth, please, Henry. I told Harry to make some up the other day." Her excitement could barely be contained, and she struggled to keep from hugging the sympathetic servant. Such a move would probably throw him into a state of shock, and she needed him with all his wits about him, but she couldn't resist taking his hand and adding, "He's going to be all right, Henry, I know he is."

" 'Course he is. Take more than a heap of rocks to bring the Cap'n down. I'll go fetch the soup." Grinning widely, the old man scurried down the hall.

Drops of sweat broke out on Marc's forehead while they struggled to prop him against the pillows, but they soon had him in a comfortable position, and he offered a weak smile when Jennifer sat down beside him, a bowl of broth in hand.

"Tables turned, huh?" Throat dry and cracked from disuse, he spoke with difficulty, but the wry twist of his lips made his point.

Jennifer grinned impudently. "Right. And if you don't start eating, I'll force it down you, and none too gently," she mocked his words and tone with impish perfection.

"Brat," he muttered, attempting to take spoon in hand, but the sudden spasm of pain at the movement caused him to drop the handle. Jennifer took things into her own hands, feeding him a small amount at a time.

"Don't be calling me names. You're the fool who had to play hero and almost get himself killed in the process. Just as soon as you're well enough, I'll give you the tongue lashing you deserve."

He stopped her hand, eyes growing cloudy while his thoughts rearranged themselves in more orderly patterns. "The men?"

Jennifer returned the spoon to his lips. "Everyone is fine but you, thanks to your foolhardy bravery. There's been one or more of them camping downstairs night and day, waiting to see if you're going to make it. I imagine Henry's just sent them off with joyous tidings, and the place is likely to be crawling with worshippers by nightfall." Her sarcasm hid worried concern, and her hand trembled as he took the empty spoon away and studied her struggling features. Tears were too close to the brim to be hidden, and she bit her lips as she returned his stare.

Marcus guessed how much it cost to hold back the tears.

The little girl who never cried had apparently been crying now for . . . days, hadn't she said? And he ventured to guess all the other tears he had heard her shed before were for him, also. And she thought she owed *him*. The pain reflected in his eyes was not entirely physical.

"Jenny, love . . ."

But she had seen the anguish written in his face and set aside the empty bowl, standing up and removing the extra pillows from behind his head.

"Do not talk, Marcus. You must rest until that butcher gets here to examine your bandages. If you sleep, you won't notice the pain." She smoothed the sheets, whispering to herself, "Just don't leave me again."

As if to echo her thoughts, he caught her hand and whispered, "Don't go."

She curled up in the chair beside him, still clenching his warm fingers, smiling bravely. "I won't."

Satisfied, he closed his eyes and slipped into a natural sleep.

The news of Marc's recovery spread rapidly through the hotel, and Jennifer barely managed to get dressed between calls at the sickroom door. Lucia's silent, tear-filled hug and Henry's glowing excitement improved her spirits, and she accepted Stephen's quick kiss on the cheek in the manner in which it was given.

Stuart crawled about the bedroom floor while the doctor expressed his surprise at his patient's remarkable return to his senses. Jennifer scooped the infant up and watched carefully as the doctor unwound discolored bandages, causing Marcus to stir feverishly. The wounds seemed to be festering, pus oozing in ugly yellow streaks, and the skin around them was warm to the touch. Horrified at this deterioration and her husband's anguished groans, Jennifer hastily retreated to the hallway, calling quietly for Lucia.

Surrendering the infant to the maid, she gave further instructions before letting herself back into the bedroom.

The doctor looked up in surprise as she closed the door, but his surprise doubled at her words.

"Doctor, I've received some advice from Marc's physician in St. Louis, and I would like to see it followed. I believe I can carry it out myself if you object, but I would rather work with you if you will allow it." She held out the detailed telegram Stephen had received in reply to his urgent inquiry.

The doctor read the paper carefully, shaking his head in dismay or disagreement Jennifer couldn't ascertain and her heart sank. The use of antiseptics and sterilized bandaging was considered an idiosyncrasy and a nuisance by most physicians, but Jennifer was determined to do anything that would save Marc's life and cleanliness couldn't hurt. The dirt under the doctor's fingernails told her what school of thought he followed, but she had hoped for his cooperation. Without it, her lack of skill or expertise could kill him.

The paper was laid carefully on the bedside table, and the doctor looked at her from under thunderous brows, but the desperate determination in her uplifted chin and the plea in her eyes cooled his wrath. With muttered oaths, he rose and retreated to the wash room, scrubbing his hands with a dedication seldom experienced.

Relieved, Jennifer called Lucia, and they began setting out the prepared materials.

Application of the antiseptic brought Marc back to consciousness with mighty curses, but Jennifer's soothing words calmed him, and though still feverish, he sipped more broth after the doctor left. But the brief interlude of consciousness slipped into fevered sleep, and Jennifer watched mournfully as he tossed and turned, his incoherent cries tearing at her heart.

The next days found him the same, his moments of rationality few and far between while the infection tore at his weakened body. Jennifer managed to pour as much liquid as possible into him, but the fever seemed to worsen, and terror came back to haunt her. It was not fair to see him through one crisis to have him taken by another, and she cursed bitterly at her ignorance, wishing she wasn't so helpless.

Applying cool compresses to Marc's brow, she was interrupted by a hasty knock at the door and Stephen's surreptitious entrance. Looking up, she saw him quietly closing the door, and a puzzled frown crossed her face at his expression.

"What is it, Stephen? You look as if you've seen a ghost."

"I'm not sure what I've seen, but she's asking for you." He came up and laid a cold hand against the fevered brow on the bed. "God, he's baking. That alcoholic excuse for a butcher ought to be hung for this. Here, let me do it a while; I think you better go downstairs and find out what's happening." He took the compress from Jennifer's hand and wrung it in the basin of cold water.

"What's happening? Stephen, what are you talking about? I'm not going down there without some reason."

"There's a wild woman down there claiming to be a friend of yours and saying you offered her a job. No offense, Jenny, but I think she's looking for Madam Dolly's down the street. She don't look like your kind of lady."

"Bess!" Jennifer jumped up, ecstatic, and Stephen gave her an odd look.

"That's what she said her name was, all right."

His expression didn't change and Jennifer hesitated. Stephen didn't know about Delaney, and therefore didn't know Bess saved her life. How could she ever explain Bess's appearance here? For all that mattered, Marcus did know, and she wasn't too sure she could explain to him. She shrugged and smiled back to ease Stephen's mind.

"Don't worry, Stephen. Bess may be a bit eccentric, but she has the proverbial heart of gold. You may just have gained a bar maid." With an elusive grin, Jennifer ran out the door.

Downstairs, the garish red hair and apopletic purple satin gown confirmed Jennifer's guess, and she ran to this majestic spectacle with open arms. The woman hesitated, aware of the suspicious looks she had already drawn, then swept Jennifer into a warm embrace, glaring over her shoulder at anyone daring to express disapproval. Jennifer took no notice of this exchange, but stepped back, clasping the woman's arms so she couldn't escape as she surveyed her costume.

"Bess! I can't believe you came, and you haven't changed a bit! Are you here to stay? Was the trip awful?" Questions poured excitedly from Jennifer's lips as she hooked her arm into Bess's and gestured to Henry to grab the woman's bags.

"Honey, you'll have to slow down a tad bit, I can't keep up with you. You're lookin' mighty peaked; ain't life out here been treatin' you well?" Her magnificent brows drew together in a dark frown as she took in Jennifer's pale face.

Jennifer's smile flickered, and she turned away from that penetrating gaze, only to catch Henry's shrewd look as he gathered up the bags and started down the hall. "No, Henry, take them upstairs. There's a room next to Lucia's that should do. We're not so crowded yet that we can't find rooms for friends." This time she was aware of the raised eyebrows around the lobby, and she spoke defiantly, glaring at Henry's unspoken objections.

"Come on, Bess, let's get you upstairs and settled first, then I'll introduce you around."

The toweringly impressive figure in purple sailed past amazed spectators, still arm in arm with the slight figure in palest green, creating a fascinating spectacle as they glided up the carpeted staircase.

Upstairs, Henry dropped the bags with ill-concealed disapproval in the room indicated and didn't respond to Jennifer's placating smile as he departed. When the door closed behind him, Jennifer turned to find the frown back on her friend's face.

"If I'm going to be causing you trouble by being here, I'll get out. I've got other places to go, you know." Her handsome features wore an air of concern as they took in Jennifer's pinched look.

"No, you don't and no, you won't. Sit down, make yourself comfortable, we've got a lot of catching up to do. How did you get away from Delaney?" Jennifer settled herself into a comfortable chair and waited, leaving the other woman no choice but to sit down and give in.

"Easily. The old crock's been cracking up ever since your man shut down the Magnolia House. I knew the rot was affecting his brain when, instead of leaving, he hung around trying to get you back into the fold again. When he found out you escaped, he went on a month long binge. I wonder how long a binge I'll rate when he finds out I'm gone?" Bess threw off her gloves and hat and stretched out on the bed. "What does your man think of this invitation you've given me? I mean, he's a swell gentleman and all, but he can't hardly appreciate your associating with the likes of me."

Jennifer's face clouded, but not for the reasons Bess suspected. What Marcus thought about the new arrival was not the question. The question was whether he would ever know of it. Jennifer's fingers dug into her palms, and she sent up a silent prayer to once again hear Marc's mighty roars at what she had done now. Aware of her friend's curious look, Jennifer returned to the conversation.

"I'm sorry, Bess, I'm a bit distracted. You've come at an ideal time for me, I need you badly. Marcus has been . . . ill, lately, and I cannot leave him for long. It will mean you'll be pretty much on your own for a while, if you don't mind, that is."

Bess sat bolt upright. "My Lord! Of course, I don't mind. I been on my own all my life, and it ain't going to stop me none now. You just tell me what you want done, and I'll do it. I'm just so grateful to have somewhere to come to get away from that bilge rat, I can put up with anything."

"I told you we couldn't pay much, Bess, not yet, anyway, and we'll probably never match what you made with . . ."

"Honey, I took everything I could off that man before I skedaddled. He owed me for the best years of my life.

Money, I've got plenty of. I'm getting too old for that kind of life now and I want some respectability. If you can get me that, you won't owe me any wages."

Jennifer grinned. "My husband considers my respectability highly questionable, and his opinion will diminish considerably if he should ever learn you're here, but in the eyes of everyone else, I am a paragon of virtue. We will repair your reputation immediately if that is your desire."

"There! You can smile then. Is your husband really such a rat? God, he looked like an angel of a man to me," Bess said almost wistfully, and immediately regretted her words when Jennifer's face fell. "I'm sorry, honey, I didn't mean to upset you. What did I say wrong?"

"You said nothing, Bess. I am simply worried about him. The others will explain soon enough, but I've got to be getting back to him."

"Big man like that can't be so awful sick, can he? What's the matter with him?"

"He's . . . hurt." Jennifer found it too difficult to talk about and avoided the subject. "Don't worry, you have a job in any case, and I'll see what I can do about your 'wages.' You might start by looking through those trunks for a quieter outfit; respectability has its price." Jennifer attempted to distract Bess from the turn the conversation had taken and succeeded. The woman looked down at her glorious gown with dismay.

"Quieter! Why, honey, this is my best, most respectable traveling outfit. Right out of those fashion books from Paris. I thought I looked downright matronly." Dubiously, she fingered the decolletage that revealed the full, rounded curves of her most magnificent assets. "Well, maybe it is just a trifle . . ."

"Revealing. Just a trifle. The men will love it, the bar will be packed every night, and you will soon have enough followers to start a house of your own. Madam Dolly's girls offer no competition. Is that what you want?" Jennifer spoke bluntly. Bess had been the soul of sweetness during her confinement, but there was no doubting her chosen profession. If she wished to continue it here, the hotel would have to be out of bounds for her.

Bess looked dismayed. "My heavens, no. I came out here because you offered me a respectable job and a place to stay. I like the men and all, but I've had enough of that kind of life. I want to be courted and looked up to, just like any lady."

Her childish air of hurt touched Jennifer, and she replied more gently, "Then that is what you shall be. Pin some pretty lace around your neckline, and I'll introduce you to my friends and later we'll order up some more businesslike clothes. Your job will be anything but glamorous, so you'll need more serviceable things, anyway."

Before Jennifer left the room, she stopped at the door and looked over her shoulder at the busily unpacking woman. "Bess . . . ?"

Bess looked up expectantly.

"Did Marcus ever . . . go back to Delaney's after I left?" She hesitated over the framing of the question, not certain what feelings prompted her to ask it.

"Why, honey, didn't he tell you?" The confused look on Jennifer's face answered her question, and Bess made up her mind there was no point hiding anything. "He came back right after you got married. I heard all about your wedding from Delaney, he was *wild!*" Sidetracked by this pleasant memory, she smiled reminiscently, but at Jennifer's expression she hastened to return to her story. "Anyway, your man came back when Delaney wasn't there, and I gave him your trunks and things. He was real sweet, wanted to know if I got in any trouble and if he could help out and all and when I assured him everything was just fine, he thanked me just as nice as ever. You got yourself a real gentleman there; he must love you something awful to do what he did for you."

Jennifer looked startled, but Bess took no notice. "I was so mad at Delaney for what he done to an innocent like you, practically kidnapping you and all, and threatening to sell your baby like you was just another one of his whores, and then when I saw how much that gorgeous man thought of you, I knew I had to do something to make up for the way you were treated. So I gave him all the information he asked for and then some. Delaney was positively *livid* when those articles started coming out in the paper, but he never suspected a dummy like me." Bess waxed nostalgic in her gloating, unable to see its effects on Jennifer.

Murmuring a few appropriate remarks, Jennifer fled back to the sickroom and Stephen's impatient nursing. Marcus was tossing restlessly and complaining, and Stephen was more than happy to give up the task of tending to him.

"How do you put up with the bastard? Pardon the expression, but he doesn't lie still for a minute. He's tried to get out of bed half a dozen times, and I've had to hold him down. I don't know where you get the strength to do it. Even in that condition he's got the strength of an ox. Why don't I hire a nurse to come up here and look after him? You can't be expected to keep this up."

Jennifer took the cold cloth and applied it to a fevered brow, murmuring a few soft words as she caressed Marc's bearded jaw. The restless tossing immediately lessened, and he seemed to slip into a deeper sleep. Stephen stared in amazement.

"He's no problem, Stephen, and I will have no stranger in here who little cares whether he lives or dies. If I am here, I can see that he's being treated properly and with the best care possible. Doc Adams means well, but he thinks I am just a little crazy and would return to his irresponsible practices as soon as I turned my back. Thank you for your offer, but let me do this my way."

"You are more than just a little crazy, but if that's what it takes to pull the fiend through, I can only wish we were all so blessed. Only, don't sacrifice your health for his, we cannot afford to lose you both."

Jennifer gave him a fleeting smile. "I am doing nothing he has not done for me. Now go be polite to Bess; she saved my life once, and I owe her a new one. She wishes to become a respectable working woman and is willing to do all the dirty jobs you've turned your nose up at. Tell Harry he has his dishwasher, Lucia she has her first under maid, and you have your waitress when things get busy. But you must make everyone treat her with the same respect they give me and Lucia or I'll wreak vengeance on them." Her mockery held an undertone of warning.

"Are you sure you know what you're doing, Jenny?" he asked doubtfully.

"Someday, when you grow up, maybe I'll tell you all about it. But for now, take my word and do it."

Jennifer had not listened to Marcus give commands for nothing and Stephen grinned at the familiarity of the tone.

"Aye, aye, Captain," he murmured softly as the auburn head turned back to the still form on the bed.

Chapter Twenty-Four

Another fever-filled week passed and the strain took its toll. Jennifer had to fight back tears each time fevered delirium claimed Marcus after infrequent intervals of lucidity, and the uncertainty only increased the strain. She watched for some sign the infection diminished, but only the certainty that it did not spread gave any hope.

She slipped into a frail shadow of herself, the others watching closely for any sign of weakening, determined to force her from the room for her own good. Jennifer fought against this occurrence with all her resources. To be separated from Marcus now would be disastrous to both of them, she knew it instinctively, and with the wiliness of an animal, she hid the attacks of illness that racked her body daily, leaving her weak and helpless, holding back the fits of tears that struck her at any time, day or night, in fear someone might hear.

At the end of August, the dry, hot weather broke. Rain clouds rolled in from the sea, breaking against the mountaintops, sending purple cascades down mountainsides, darkening the days with gloom and cooling afternoon breezes. None of this affected Jennifer. Her sunlight came and went with Marc's smile, and she lived for the moments when he woke to recognize her, but they never came often enough.

One particularly gloomy afternoon, Stephen entered the sickroom with little more than a polite knock of warning. Startled, Jennifer followed the direction of his gaze as it first went to Marc's lifeless form, then returned to her. There was no reading his expression as she rose to confront him.

"What's wrong, Stephen?" Jennifer sensed the uncertainty under Stephen's usual insouciance.

Stephen avoided the question. "How is he today?"

"No better than yesterday. The fever still rages. That is not what you came up to ask, is it?"

"No." For a moment, he continued to avoid her gaze, then reluctantly, he turned to face her. "That engineer fellow from the mine was just in. He had some news he thought you ought to have, but he wasn't certain how you would take it. So he told me about it, and like a fool, I've agreed to carry the message."

Jennifer's brow wrinkled in a puzzled frown. This room had been her entire life these last weeks; she could not remember the existence of any problem outside of it that could cause Stephen to look at her like that. And then her memory returned.

"Cameron! You've found Cameron." It was the only possible solution and she waited eagerly for the message. How could she have forgotten the danger that had put them here? Had the sheriff found its source?

Stephen grew even more wary at her expression. "Charlie said Cameron's been up here several times to see you. You once assured me he was no more than friend. That has not changed, has it?"

Doubt crept into Jennifer's expression. What was he trying to say? "He is even less than that now, Stephen. Didn't Charlie tell you why he was looking for him? I have seen Cameron only twice, and the second time was the day of Marc's accident. He knows something, Stephen. I want him found."

Stephen took a deep breath of relief and eased Jennifer into the nearest chair.

"He does not mean anything more to you than that? You promise?"

Jennifer nodded, bewildered. "I want to know the man who wished Marcus dead. I want him behind bars before he can try again. Who is he? Do you know?"

"No, Jenny, I do not. I just wanted to be certain this would be no more of a blow to you than that. They've found Cameron. He's dead, Jenny." Gray eyes continued to search her face as firm fingers gripped her shoulders.

"Dead?" Jennifer took a minute to absorb this. Sophisticated, cynical, insincere Cameron, Darlene's much beloved brother—dead. It seemed strange to think of him dead, but there was no pain at the thought. He had tried to poison her life, though she knew not why. But he held a secret she wished to possess. "How did it happen?" she asked quietly.

Stephen nodded approval of her reaction and released her. "Shot. Twice. In the head. They found his body in a cheap hotel room back in 'Frisco."

The news was brutal, but she did not flinch. Something had gone very wrong in Cameron's life. Marcus had tried to warn her, but she had found it out the hard way. Cameron had neither loved nor truly desired her, she knew that much now. So why had he come back for her?

In what way had he been connected with the man who had blown up the mine? Or could he have possibly done it himself?

"Do they know who did it? Was there no time to question him?"

Stephen shook his head. "He'd been dead several days. His killer is long gone. We'll probably never know. What makes you think Cameron wasn't the one to try to kill Marcus? He had enough reasons, I should think."

"It was the way he talked, as if there were another person behind all his actions," Jennifer mused out loud, searching her memory for the reasons of her certainty that another was responsible. "One time, he said 'the man is demented,' or something to that effect. I don't know, I can't remember, I was so terrified." She sighed. It seemed such a long time ago. Maybe it was Cameron who did it after all. Maybe the explosion wasn't even deliberate. Maybe he was referring to himself. Maybe she just imagined the whole thing. "I was such a fool. I could have made him tell me, if there was anything to tell, but all I could think about was Marcus. Do you think there's still someone out there who wishes to harm Marcus? Will he try again?"

Or was there any reason to try again? Sadly, Jennifer lifted her eyes to the inert figure on the bed. She might be worrying needlessly. The killer might yet see his work done.

Stephen pulled her into his arms and gave her a light kiss on the cheek, providing the comfort of a friend's strength when no words could suffice.

Rain pounded on the glass panes when Jennifer awoke to her son's cries, and she rose from her mattress on the floor to comfort him. The depth of darkness in the room told her it was long before sunrise, and she wondered if it were possible for infants to dream. Having just come from one of her own, she knew the urge to cry, and she took Stuart in her arms, comforting their fears together. When he was quieted, she prepared to return to her make-shift bed, but a call from the bed brought her to Marc's side, and she lit a dim lamp to see his face.

Eyes still fevered and bright, he was conscious, but not delirious. Jennifer sat beside him, holding her cool hand to his hot forehead.

"Jenny, is everything all right?" he whispered hoarsely, his eyes anxious.

"Your son is restless, I was just quieting him." She clung tightly to the large hand that reached for hers, trying to keep her anxiety from him.

"You don't look well, Jenny, have you been ill?"

"Don't tell me how I look, you should see yourself." Jennifer smiled lightly, stroking his month's growth of beard.

"Ummph," his lips twisted into a half-grin that didn't reach his eyes as he acknowledged her jest. "Do you prefer sleeping on the floor?" He nodded toward the pallet she used for a bed.

"As compared to what?" At his sharp look, she relented hastily. "I did not wish to leave you alone, so I asked Henry to bring it in for me. Do you object?"

In the dim light he searched her face. "I do. In the morning, tell Henry to carry it out. If we can share a room, we can share a bed. Get in here, your hands are like ice." Painfully, he inched to the far side of the bed, clearing room for her on his good side.

"Marcus, I don't want to disturb your rest. I may harm you with my tossing about." Alarmed at his painful move-ment, she clutched his hand tighter, not daring to admit how much she longed to fill the inviting space.

"You disturb me more by lingering out there. Now get in, I am in no condition to harm you."

His eyes were burning brighter, whether from fever or something else, Jennifer could not tell, slipping between the sheets and snuggling closer to the heat of his body. She continued to hold his good hand, keeping their arms between them as a cushion to prevent jarring his injured ribs.

He sighed and mumbled something that sounded like, "Now we can both get some rest," before drifting back to sleep.

Content to be back where she belonged, Jennifer lay quietly, waiting for dawn to break and praying this time his recovery would last.

But it wasn't destined to be as easy as that, and with the return of morning came the delirium of his fever. Even Jennifer had difficulty soothing him as he cried out, lashing against the torment of fevered nightmares. As he fought against restraining covers, Jennifer bathed his face and dry, cracked lips, tears running down her cheeks.

As soon as Stephen saw her face, he called for Lucia and between the two of them, they cajoled her into taking a break, leaving Henry to take over the task of holding the patient in place. But they couldn't keep her away. After a quick tour to see the changes Stephen proudly displayed in the bar and stopping to greet a now active Emma, Jennifer insisted on returning to Marcus.

At night, she slipped in beside him, hoping her presence would reassure him enough to let him sleep peacefully, hoping if he woke, he would want to find her there. At times, she could feel him groping for her hand, his hoarse groans forming the sound of her name, and she would slide her fingers into his, and he would relax. But three nights went by without another clear return to lucidity.

On the fourth night, his fever seemed to burn more fiercely than before, and his restless tossing kept her awake, her anguished prayers forming a background to his pained cries. Toward midnight, the cries became louder and more distinct as he called her name over and over again.

Jennifer propped herself on one arm and leaned over him, her hair falling forward and brushing his face as she stroked his sweating brow. "Marcus, I'm here. Please, love, let me help you." Impulsively, she bent and kissed the hot, dry lips calling out so painfully.

A powerful arm caught her by surprise, circling her waist, and she had to steady herself before she crushed his bandaged chest.

"Jenny, don't go. I want you to stay." His words were distinct, but muttered with the hoarse heat of delirium.

"I'm here, Marcus, I'm not going anywhere. I'll not ever leave you." Her own words were no less delirious as she kissed his fevered face, soothing his fears while alarming her own. Her lips brushed against his hair, eyelids, beard, then came back to his mouth, finding them eagerly as he sucked her into his madness and their passion grew.

Gasping, she pulled away and tried to disentangle herself from his entwining arm, but with the strength of madness, he held her close, moaning her name, and her heart cried out in reply. So strong and cold and confident, he had never shown any need of her before, and she was filled with the longing to satisfy his desire. How could she deny him in his distress?

Gently, she moved closer and sought his lips once more. Marcus responded eagerly, his one good hand tracing a path down her side, circling a breast, sliding down the valley of her waist, lingering on the curve of a hip, while his mouth clung ardently to hers. She arched against him, hungering for the touch of love that she had been so long denied, and returning it twofold. She could feel the fever in him, his skin burning to the touch, his fingers like dry torches, but it seemed to have no effect on his desires. Marcus matched her passion with a fire from inside, and his whispered urgency sent her blood racing.

With trepidation, Jennifer allowed herself to be pulled across Marc's hips, fearful she would dislodge his stitches, but understanding his demands. As he had taught her many weeks ago, she kneeled over him, opening herself to his thrust. With a moan of relief, Marcus entered her, his swift upward movement taking Jennifer's breath away. But the motion of his body and the pleasure of her impalement left no room for further thought, and she slid into his rhythm, melting into his heat, his maleness filling her with dizzying pleasure. They rocked together with mad ecstasy, an insane joy in this act of life on the brink of death.

Six weeks' separation reached a rapid climax, and Marc's cries now were those of passion and pleasure. Jennifer smiled, satisfied. This all-powerful man needed her, and she could fulfill his needs. It was a startling discovery. Relaxed and sleepy, she slid gently away to curl up at his side. Knowing he understood nothing but the workings of his fevered imagination, she poured out the words that had remained dammed up inside her so long, the words of love that tied her to him forever, whatever their future might be. And Marcus lay peacefully still, claimed by the fire inside him once more.

Pale and waxen, Jennifer stepped from the wash room and halted, her eyes opening wide with incredulity at the sight greeting her.

Marcus stood shakily in the center of the room, his right arm safely in the sleeve of his dressing gown while he struggled to pull the left over his plaster encased arm. At the sight of Jennifer, he stepped forward with an awkward gait, clasping the rebellious robe to his side.

"Jenny, are you ill? I heard you . . ."

She rushed to his side, helping him with the robe as he leaned on her shoulder. "I am fine, but you won't be if you don't get back in bed."

He ignored her words, looking down into her dark-shadowed eyes instead. "You look terrible, and I'm not getting back into bed. There are some things a man must do for himself."

"We just had this conversation, if you'll remember. You are no picture yourself and you belong in bed. There is no use getting independent at this late date." Anxiously, she scanned his face for signs of fever, but his eyes were warm with concern only, his skin cool to the touch.

"I don't remember that conversation, but there is some memory of last night that tickles at the back of my mind." Inquiringly, he searched her face for confirmation of his elusive memory. "I did not hurt you, did I?"

There was a silent pause while Jennifer wondered how much of last night he remembered, then her face flamed scarlet in the remembrance of her forwardness, and she looked away. "No, you did not harm me; I was worried it might be the other way around."

Rejoicing that the memory was more than a fevered dream, he rubbed her cheek lightly, and she looked up at him again. "Your talents astound me, angel, but they do not harm me."

He stepped aside before she could make a resounding reply to his impudence. Marcus closed the wash room door on her outraged glare, chuckling at the flare of color that rose to her cheeks. There could be nothing seriously wrong while she was still capable of raising a temper.

When he returned to the bedroom again with shaving brush dangling in his damaged hand and razor in the other, he was confronted by his solemn manservant and Jennifer's innocent grin.

"Haul him back, Henry. I'm prepared to holler for assistance if he puts up a fight." Jennifer crossed her arms, her grin growing at her husband's discomfiture.

As Henry disarmed his employer and offered a shoulder to lean on, Marcus asked complainingly, "Since when have you become my wife's man, Henry, and not mine?"

"Since she started makin' more sense than you, Cap'n. I be more than happy to scrape them whiskers." Henry slowly inched the larger man across the floor and back to bed.

Marcus collapsed against the pillows, his face gray with the unaccustomed effort expended. "Somehow, shaving with one hand is more awkward than I anticipated. I would appreciate your assistance, Henry." He glared at Jennifer who had flown to his side to smooth his sheets and test his brow. "But you, you conniving little dictator, I will turn over my knee first chance I get. Now quit grinning and find me some breakfast. I'm a starving man."

Jennifer kissed his cheek and flitted away before he could grab her. "You are more likely to get your breakfast if you send Henry for it. A woman parading through the lobby in her negligee on a Saturday morning cannot be expected to be seen again any time soon."

"Better yet. Then I shall get a respite from these constant aggravations," Marcus answered gruffly, eyeing her askance. Then, when she moved obligingly toward the door with raised brow and impish grin, he added hurriedly, "Go get dressed, you silly twit. Henry, fetch both of us some breakfast, if you would. I can see she's gotten entirely out of hand lately."

Henry left, grinning, reassured that things would soon be back to normal.

Well-fed, shaved—with the exception of a mustache he insisted be left, whether from vanity or a desire to save his nose from Henry's zeal was debatable—and exhausted from the morning's exertions, Marcus soon fell into a deep sleep, giving Jennifer time to repair to the wash room for a quick perusal of her own appearance.

That she had lost weight was evident from the way her well-tailored gown now hung loosely about her, a fact not easily concealed from Marc's observant eyes. Her nearly translucent pallor was emphasized by the dark shadows under her huge eyes, eyes that now seemed to dominate her face. She pinched her cheeks and bit her lips to achieve some color, but was forced to agree with her husband. She looked ghastly. Sweeping thick auburn tresses up into a casual tangle of curls, she hoped Marcus would not find her looks too offensive.

Taking advantage of the silence reigning in the sickroom, Stephen knocked at the door, entering at Jennifer's call.

With a quick glance at the sleeping figure on the bed,

he stepped forward and took Jennifer's hand. "Jenny, you look incredible. I heard Marcus was up and the two of you were already at it, and I expected to find you in tears, but I should have known better."

"That you should. Do you have any idea how many times I've prayed to hear him yelling at me again? It is music to my ears," Jennifer confessed happily.

"The man is a complete ass and doesn't deserve your devotion. Can't he see how lucky he is to have a lovely wife like you?"

"Actually, he thinks I look terrible, and I am inclined to believe him." She laughed at Stephen's irate expression. "Oh, Stephen, can't you see? It doesn't matter what he says or how he says it, I am grateful that he is able to say it at all."

"The fever is completely dissipated then?" He ignored the perversity of her reply, changing the subject to one more objective.

Jennifer sat down beside the bed and held a cool hand to a rugged cheek. "It seems to be, but I am waiting for the doctor's word before I get my hopes up again. Or get them too high, I should say," she amended, knowing they were already soaring.

"I think I'll trust your word before that quack's; you've worked miracles, and I intend to tell that ungrateful wretch so in no uncertain terms." Stephen glared down at his cousin's recumbent figure, his eyes reflecting the affection he did not voice.

"Which wretch? The quack or Marcus? Never mind, it makes no difference. Neither will believe you, and I shall emphatically deny it. Now get out before you wake him. He did not sleep well last night." Jennifer waved her hand to shoo him out, but Stephen caught and held it.

"Jenny . . ." His eyes searched hers questioningly. "Is everything all right now? The reports I've heard make me wonder . . ."

Jennifer held his hand tightly with assurance. "Do not

worry about us, Stephen, we have a lifetime together to make things right."

Stephen swooped her up in sudden exhilaration, kissing her thoroughly before returning her to the floor. "You are a veritable angel, Jennifer Lee. Sooner or later, love always finds a way." And with renewed assurance, he strode from the room.

Jennifer watched with a bemused smile as he marched jauntily down the hallway, then turned back to face the room. To her surprise, Marcus lay awake, his gaze resting on her with an unfathomable expression. Quickly, she crossed to his side to prop pillows behind his back.

"Was that my erstwhile cousin's voice I just heard?" He frowned as he sat up, lines of pain deepening at the movement.

"There is nothing erstwhile about Stephen. He is very much present and quite likely to be very much future, so you better become accustomed to him." Jennifer hovered close, weeks of constant proximity not easily shaken, even with the return of his brusque behavior. He was her prisoner for the next few weeks, anyway, and she intended to make the most of it. They had been at odds with each other ever since they met, and it was time one of them did something about it.

Her breezy confidence produced the opposite effect in Marcus. His look became thunderous. "The hell I will. How long has he been up here?"

Surprised by his ominous tone, Jennifer allowed her temper to reply. "Ever since you damn near got yourself killed, you idiot. What did you expect him to do? Send a note of condolence and a 'wish you were here' card? Did you expect Charlie to run your mine and Henry to wait on you and both of them keep an eye on things around here at the same time?"

"You could have sent Stuart and Lucia home. Charlie and Henry could handle their jobs just fine and no one would bother you."

"Of course not. I'm too horrible to look at," she agreed indignantly.

"Besides that, you have a terrible temper and your language is becoming most unladylike."

They were screaming, but there was no rage in their eyes as they watched each other covertly, and this last exchange forced them to bite back smiles. But before either could make a move to stop the fight, Lucia barged in, black eyes flashing with an anger seldom seen in her good-humored temperament.

"I could hear the two of you all the way down the hall! *Señor* Armstrong, you ought to be ashamed of yourself. You have worried us all sick, but look what you have done to Jennifer." She pointed dramatically to her startled friend who was left wordless at this unexpected tirade. "She has been at your side night and day, waiting on you hand and foot, nursing your son, running this whole place from your room. And you dare to yell at her like that?"

Recovered from the shock, Jennifer caught her rebellious maid's arms and quieted her before she could say more. "Lucia, please. Stop before you embarrass me further . . ."

Marcus chuckled and the two women turned to him with surprise. "Lucia, I thought Jennifer had a temper, but I see young Charles is in for a surprise or two."

Turning serious, Marcus held out his hand to Jennifer, his smile gentle as his gaze took in her altered appearance. Jennifer accepted his hand, returning his smile unhesitatingly, teasingly stroking his new mustache.

"My wife may be an uncommon nuisance and the bane of my existence, but I'm not likely to forget what she's done." His eyes crinkled in the corners as he rubbed the itch Jennifer's teasing had created, his gaze resting fondly on his wife before returning to the ruffled maid. "And she's quite capable of defending herself with no qualms about my present unfortunate condition." His eyes twinkled even brighter at this veiled allusion to last night, his grin leaving Jennifer no doubt about the turn his thoughts had taken, though leaving Lucia confused. "Now why don't you get that poor excuse for a cousin up here while Jenny and I continue our well-adjusted, informative discussion?"

"And let you continue screaming at each other? I think I will get the doctor and have you both locked away." Lucia was confused at the turn things had taken, but it was becoming embarrassingly obvious she had interrupted at a bad time. Giving up on the pair of them, she prepared to beat a hasty retreat, but Jennifer halted her.

"Thank you, Lucia," she said softly. "It's just been such a strain these last few weeks—I needed someone to yell at, and you must admit, he makes a tempting target." A faint grin turned up the corners of her mouth. "I will promise to behave, and if he gets too obstreperous, I shall turn him over to you."

"Now wait one minute," Marcus protested, but his argument was overridden.

Lucia grinned impudently. "Should I send *Señor* Stephen up or has *Señor* Armstrong had enough yelling for one day?" Deliberately ignoring her employer's ire, she consulted Jennifer.

"Send him up with strict orders to leave the room the minute any yelling begins. It is easier to get Stephen's agreement than that obstinate creature's." Jennifer nodded over her shoulder in the direction of her husband, who showed every sign of threatening to remove himself from the bed.

Since it was apparent that he wore no more than a half-donned robe, Lucia completed her interrupted retreat, leaving Jennifer to handle the situation.

"You are not to move from that bed until the doctor says you are able," Jennifer turned and scolded him. Then, without warning, she fell to her knees beside the bed and buried her face in her arms, the tears of joy she had been holding back all day finally surfacing.

Thoroughly shaken by this display, Marcus cupped her chin and lifted her face. If he hadn't known how much right she had to hate him, he would swear it was love he saw reflected there. But there was still Stephen to consider, and the scene that had set off this confrontation to digest. He could see where it would be easy for a young girl to fall for Stephen's winning ways, but he would not give her up without a fight. And his jaw set in its familiar pattern.

Jennifer saw the change and despaired, but his next words were gentle and his eyes remained clear and blue.

"No more tears, little one. You are becoming quite as weepy as those tedious young things I used to encounter in St. Louis. Yell at me, hit me, tickle me if you will, but do not weep over me. Come up here and practice kissing a man with a mustache."

Obediently, Jennifer scrambled up beside him, and it was into this loving scene that Stephen walked.

Taking in Marc's state of undress and the woman nearly perched in his lap, Stephen contemplated withdrawal, but a spirit of mischief prevented it. Coughing loudly, he propped himself against the door frame, waiting for fireworks, setting off the first spark himself.

"Now that you've kissed and made up, do you need me for anything?" His tone was entirely innocent, but his appraising gaze was not. Jennifer's blush tickled him, but his cousin's ominous glare provided fair warning of storms ahead.

"That is exactly what I wish to discuss with you. You're not needed for anything around here, so you may as well go back from whence you came."

"To the bar?" Stephen raised his eyebrows in mock surprise, and Jennifer hid a grin.

"The bar! Is that how you employ your time around here?" Marcus appeared a trifle bewildered at this news, and Jennifer hastened to offer an explanation.

"Instead of his customary employment in front of a bar, I have put him behind it. It seems to be working out quite well."

"You mean he hasn't poisoned anybody yet?" Marcus

took this piece of information well, although he continued to eye his cousin with suspicion.

"Did you think any of your men would notice it if he did?" Jennifer laughed, and Marcus grinned appreciatively, acknowledging the drinking habits of his miners.

"Well, it's quite a carnival routine you two have worked up on me, but unless you have something important to say, I think I'll go back down and keep an eye on that Indian. He's a jimdandy carpenter, but he's got a good eye for whiskey, too." Stephen stood up and prepared to depart.

"Wait a minute, I'm not through with you yet. Jenny, would you excuse us for a minute?" Marcus released her waist and waited for her to remove herself.

"No." She hopped off the bed and planted herself firmly in the chair beside it, arms folded and chin set.

"Go on, Jenny, I can defend myself against a one-armed cripple well enough," Stephen claimed mockingly.

"There is no need for you to defend yourself at all. You came up here at our request, and I presume you have conducted yourself with all due respect, and we couldn't have done without you. You owe him no explanations."

"Jennifer, I swear, as soon as I recover the use of both hands, I intend to turn you over my knee . . ."

"You'll have to get through me first, you bully. Now, if there is something you wish to discuss with me, I have no objections to discussing it in front of Jenny."

"Well, I do. If you intend to let this pint-sized female stand up for you, then I'll take her on first. She's a more worthy opponent, anyway." Marcus was incensed at his inability to control this situation, cursing the weakness that kept him from rising and physically rearranging things the way he wanted them, but admiring his wife's self-control. She seemed to have regained some of the spunk and confidence she had shown on the Mississippi and lost in the debacle of St. Louis and their unfortunate contract. She was a constant surprise to him, and he wondered if he would ever get to know her.

Stephen frowned and contemplated Jennifer's defiant expression. "Well, Jenny? You know as well as I do what this is all about, and I'm getting a little tired of playing this charade. Will you tell him or shall I? I can't see that you'll ever have a better opportunity."

Jennifer looked up at Stephen with surprise, then realized what he was asking her. Gray eyes held hers with concern, asking if she had the nerve to tell her husband what she should have told him long ago. If she told Marcus how much she cared, perhaps he would end this jealous rage keeping the two cousins apart.

"Stephen, if he hasn't got any more sense than that, he doesn't deserve to know. Why don't you ask Henry to bring up some dinner? Maybe a little food will give him the strength to clear the cobwebs from his empty head."

"Damn you, Jennifer . . ." Marcus began to protest, but he wasn't given a chance to finish.

"You may be right at that, Jenny." Stephen gave his cousin a disgusted look and stalked off, leaving Jennifer to face her husband's rage.

She stood and waited for the storm to break. "You were saying?"

Marcus caught the look of sorrow in her eyes, and his anger dissipated. Whatever she was, whatever she did, he owed her too much to make her any unhappier. He had interfered in her life too long; it was time to let her make her own decisions. The pain of this knowledge was greater than any physical pain he might feel.

"Nothing, little one. If there is something you need to tell me, I wish you would not keep it from me."

"I am not keeping anything from you that you should not already know." Her voice was brisk and firm as she plumped the pillows, successfully ending the discussion.

That night, as Jennifer crept into bed beside him, she thought him asleep as he had been off and on all day. His system was still too weak from fever and infection to withstand much activity and the constant stream of visitors throughout the day had proved more than he could handle. Jennifer had finally put an end to the steady traffic, and Marcus had dozed off immediately after supper. Now, as his hand closed about hers, it was apparent he was awake again.

He raised her fingers to his lips and pressed a kiss upon them. "I haven't been as easy a patient as Emma, have I?" he asked softly, keeping his hold on her hand.

"Patience has never been one of your virtues, sir," she replied, turning on her side to face him. "But you are not going to undo weeks of work by jumping out of this bed every time I turn my back on you if I have to tie you to the bedposts."

"Strange, how one's words come back to haunt a person," he drawled, chuckling softly in the darkness. "At least, I never tied you to the bed. You've got to give me credit for that."

"You would have if you'd thought you could get away with it. And I'm here to tell you, I can get away with it."

Marcus wished he had the use of his other hand so he might stroke her thick hair shimmering in the moonlight. It took all his energy just to lift himself from the bed and brush a kiss across her forehead. "The day will never come when I need to be tied to a bed with you in it. I was afraid you would revert to our contract after my foolishness last time I was here."

"I seriously considered it, it would have served you right, but it would have been cutting off my nose to spite my face," Jennifer admitted reluctantly.

"And it's such a pretty nose, too." He rubbed a finger down the feature under discussion. "From what I gather out of Stephen's and Lucia's conversations today, I owe you my life. That more than repays any debt you thought you owed me. What would you like to do with your new freedom?"

Stunned by this new development, unable to comprehend his intentions, Jennifer remained speechless.

"I guess I'm not thinking clearly enough to be diplomatic," Marcus apologized at her hesitancy. "That wasn't the way I wanted to phrase the question. Maybe I should postpone further discussions until I am well again." One arm simply was not sufficient. Awkwardly, he attempted to pull her closer.

"Maybe we should postpone them permanently. We don't seem to be capable of simple, logical discussions. There seems to be some ingredient missing between us that renders us unmixable except in bed."

It was Marc's turn to be silent. The word for that ingredient lay unspoken between them and both were hesitant to use it, each for their own reasons. He had told her once he would never love again, not after Melissa had played on his emotional vulnerability with such skill, but even as he had said it, the words had rung false in his ears. No longer impulsive twenty, it was harder to admit that this mixture of feelings he held for the woman at his side could possibly be such an elusive emotion as love, but if that word would bring her happiness, shouldn't he use it? Not only would that be dishonest, there was still the distinct possibility it wouldn't make her happy. No, the time was not right for emotional play-acting; he would have to rely on her practicality until he was more certain of her feelings, and his own.

"Perhaps you're right, angel, but I am sincerely grateful for that exception; many people may never hope to achieve it. Perhaps, with a little practice, we could add on to that exception a little at a time until that missing ingredient shows up. Are you willing to try?"

Smiling, Jennifer stroked his mustache, kissed him lightly, then curled up beneath his arm, one hand resting on his bandaged chest. "I think you are in no condition to try anything for a while, and the sooner you start resting, the sooner you will be able to start practicing."

The soft chuckle sounded again. "You have a lot to learn about men yet, sweetheart, if you think a broken arm and a few cracked ribs will stifle my desires." He lifted her head on to his shoulder and kissed her more thoroughly than she had allowed him earlier, and soon he was teaching her another secret of the gentle art of lovemaking.

Next day, stripping off the old bandages—under a steady barrage of Marc's explicit epithets—revealed considerable reduction in the infection and visible signs the wounds were healing cleanly. The doctor pronounced him safely on the road to recovery but advised constant bed rest until there was no further danger of internal damage or infection. Painting a black picture of what would happen should his words not be heeded, the doctor managed to disturb every sore spot on the patient's body to remind him of the severity of his injuries. Mine dust and galloping horses were definitely out of bounds. Satisfied his threats would keep Marcus from becoming too much trouble for the next few days, the doctor took his leave, feeling his patient was in better hands than his own.

With this good news, Jennifer's health began to recover, and although Marcus still worried about her lack of appetite in the mornings, she was now sleeping well again. The dark circles left her eyes and color returned to her cheeks. Marcus persuaded her he would not disappear if she left the room upon occasion, and the hotel's occupants welcomed her back with open arms. Even Johnny Yellowfeather, their newly hired carpenter, saluted her return with a solemn tour of the repairs made and the partition built to divide bar from dining room. Jennifer was suitably impressed.

Only Bess remained in the background during these receptions, and Jennifer had to make the time to seek her out, cornering her in the dining room polishing the battered silverware.

"Bess! I never thought you to be the quiet type. Where have you been keeping yourself?" Jennifer pulled up a chair, picking up another cloth and starting on the knives.

"Out of the way mostly. I figured you had enough to worry about without people complaining about having to associate with the likes of me. If your husband reacts to me being around like his cousin does, I better be thinkin' 'bout moving along. It was mighty sweet of you to think of me, honey, but from what I hear, you got more troubles than you can handle already."

"Nonsense. Stephen will come down a peg or two soon enough when I get through with him, but the opportunity just hasn't opened up yet. I will plead guilty to not telling Marcus about you yet, only because he raised such an uproar about Stephen's presence that I haven't dared open my mouth ever since. Marcus does not take well to being an invalid, and I'm afraid even the slightest controversial subject will bring him up out of bed. It takes all my willpower to keep him there as it is."

"An active man like that has only one use for a bed, and from the looks of you lately, you found the right way to keep him there." A knowing grin crossed her face as Jennifer blushed. "You don't need to be embarrassed around *me*. A man like you've got wasn't going to put up with that separate bedroom nonsense; it only amazes me that he waited around this long." She caught Jennifer's look of surprise and exclaimed, "You ninny! Everybody in the place knows you two ain't been sleeping together or much of anything else from the sounds of it. I never thought you to be a fool, but how long did you think you could keep your man that way?"

Jennifer had given up any pretense of cleaning silver while staring at her outspoken friend; now her color rose and she laid aside her cloth. "I hadn't given any thought to keeping him, Bess. You know our story, and you know both of us—how long do you think the innkeeper's ignorant daughter could hold on to the rich gentleman forced to marry against his will?"

"Against his will, my ass, pardon my bluntness. That gentleman never did nothing against his will, and I'd bet my bottom dollar on it. He could have had a battery of lawyers and half the townfolk walking all over police headquarters and Delaney's head within twenty-four hours if he'd wanted to. Saved you and the babe and never had to marry you at all, if that's what he wanted. Maybe his pride and his temper got the best of him, but he wanted you, all right. Men don't act like that otherwise." Bess contemplated Jennifer fondly. She could almost see the thought processes whirl behind innocent brown eyes. It was about time someone enlightened her.

"I . . . I suppose not," Jennifer replied vaguely. Marcus had once said something about not having to go to jail if he didn't want, but she had dismissed it arbitrarily. If what Bess said was true, it was only being forced by Delaney that made him angry, not the marriage itself. But that was too incredible to be true. He had told her he had no wish to be married yet. He had described the kind of wife he intended to find. No, that wasn't right; *she* had described the kind of wife he needed, and he had not disagreed. Or agreed. A whole new door opened in her mind, and she was free, at last.

Leaving behind her startled companion, Jennifer traversed the stairway in record time, breaking in on the room where her husband was ostensibly resting. Instead, he held a delighted Stuart in his lap, teasing him with a stuffed toy and laughing at the stream of bell-like gurgles that served his son for language. Surprised by her sudden entrance, his grin grew to include her, too.

"I think our son is developing a remarkable vocabulary. 'Tis a pity we can't understand a word he says."

It was the babe, of course; he had been determined not to lose this child and sealed the matter by giving it his name. But still . . . it wouldn't hurt to think about it a while longer, indulge in the possibility a while before broaching the matter with him and confirming it one way or another. It was pleasant to think he would have married her willingly, given the chance. And her kiss was warm and tender as she sat beside him.

Marcus would have prolonged the moment, but Jennifer was already reaching for the babe, scolding him facetiously. "Shame on you, teaching your father to talk like that. If you're going to use that kind of language, then you'd better learn to do it right." She hugged the beaming infant and fell back against the pillows.

Placing his arm around her shoulders, Marcus admired the glowing vision that was his wife. For weeks now, he had been watching her create order out of chaos: keeping track of the hotel's income and outgo, satisfying complaining guests, making the countless decisions involved in running a hotel and ordering a staff of untrained amateurs, pacifying Emma's need to be helpful, and al the time keeping this hectic frenzy from the island of peace she had created in this room. She changed his bandages with a gentleness the doctor never attempted, cared for Stuart, ate all her meals up here, and never once allowed the needs of the hotel to intrude upon their time together. And she seemed to thrive on it. He had never seen her so happy; there had been no more tearful episodes since his fever abated. Cheerful and smiling, laughing and joking at all times, and at night, loving him with a passion unmatched in his experience, with a tenderness that told him more than could be conveyed by words. Yet through it all, he sensed a sorrow buried deep inside, a sorrow that seldom ebbed except at moments like this when she became almost child-like in her joy.

"He has a reason for strong language. We are both starving while you idle about below. One of these days I will come down and catch you at whatever you do down there." He spoke affectionately, fingering the curl on her neck and brushing his lips across her forehead.

"Then you will find me flouring cake pans or helping Bess polish the silver and I will decide you are well enough to join in the work." As soon as the words were out of her mouth, she realized what she had said, but it was too late to pull them back now.

"Bess?" Mildly inquiring at this new name, he suspected nothing.

Jennifer raised her eyes heavenward and prayed for guidance.

"Bess. She arrived while you were ill and has been helping out ever since."

Her words told him nothing, but her expression did, and a suspicion began to form. "Arrived? From where, St. Louis?"

"Of course. I wouldn't know where else to reach her."

"Reach her!" This last left him totally flabbergasted and it took a moment to regain his speech. "You mean Bess, St. Louis' finest, is here?"

Jennifer's look of disdain would have etched windows, had any been available. "You will refrain from calling her that out here, won't you? The men give her enough hazing as it is and Stephen has become a real prig about it."

Marcus fell back against the pillows and scanned the ceiling. He had just been admiring her efficiency, but had forgotten her insanity. "Jennifer Lee, you are either the most guileless person I have ever had the misfortune to meet, or you are deliberately trying to drive me mad. Am I to assume that you have casually invited Delaney's mistress and the madam of Magnolia House to come and live at this hotel? And that she is down there now, working side by side with my wife and in full view of two hundred miners?"

"She's just a little flamboyant, is all, and the men love her. She knows how to keep them in place and it relieves Lucia of some rather tedious duties, which relieves Charlie, too." Thoughtfully, she added, "I'm afraid we may be going to lose a maid," and shifted Stuart to a better position.

Marcus rolled his eyes, then let them fall back on his wife who sat so innocently nursing their child. She could not possibly be so naive . . . Oh, yes, she could. And he groaned out loud.

Instantly, she sat up and examined his face, anxiously covering his brow for some sign of fever. Marcus opened his eyes and stared back into the childlike brown ones before him.

"I am not ill, although I am seriously considering it.

When you get done with that little pig there, I want you to go down and send Bess up here, *alone*. Bess and I have a few things to discuss."

She stared at him with open astonishment. "Bess and *you*?"

"Do it," he ordered firmly.

And surprisingly, she did.

Chapter Twenty-Five

Now that contract negotiations were settled and Jennifer permanently ensconced in Marc's bed, the sitting room became a nursery for Stuart, and the remainder of Jennifer's clothes found their way into wardrobes and drawers with her husband's. There were no longer the lonesome moments while one lay quietly in bed listening to the padding of silent feet from the room next door, the lying awake wondering if the other slept, or the muffled sobs that couldn't be answered through closed doors.

Instead, they lay in bed together after their lovemaking, talking late into the night about plans and dreams and subjects they never had time to discuss before, had never dreamed of discussing before. Lying quiescently in each other's arms, peaceful and content from passions spent, the words flowed easily and without rancor. As they became sensitive to each other's needs in bed, they became sensitive to each other's feelings in conversation, and they listened more and argued less.

For the first time since their marriage, Jennifer began

to feel married, and found it had as many assets as liabilities. She enjoyed waking in the morning to find this man sprawled beside her, his leg entwined with hers or his hand still caught in her hair from the night before. On those mornings when he woke first, she enjoyed waking to the feel of his lips on hers, reveling in the warmth and strength of his body. She learned he could be gentle and loving as well as domineering, that his sense of humor gave him the wit to laugh at himself as well as at her, and that he made a wonderful father for their son.

This last fact grew in importance as the days passed into weeks, and her sickness in the morning did not diminish as her health improved. Her last "monthly" had been two weeks before the night Marcus had claimed payment of her debt, and Jennifer wondered if the payment might not be more than either anticipated. In the hectic days of Marc's illness, she had thought nothing of missing her time, but now another month was here and she remembered anxiously her aunt's explanations of the facts of life. Since that first morning of Marc's recovery, she had hidden her illness well, but now she began to calculate how soon she would have to tell him.

The thought weighed on her mind as the days passed, and Marc recovered rapidly. By mid-September, he was declared well enough to take his meals downstairs. He wandered the hotel, poking into the kitchen, examining the newly constructed saloon, even entertaining Emma while Lucia ran errands. He was bored and constantly underfoot, and Jennifer seriously suspected he was watching her. Could he have already guessed her secret? If so, he made no mention of it.

Marcus had his reasons for biding his time, but by the end of September, he could no longer bear the uncertainty of their uncommunicative truce. It was time for some answers.

She lay curled beside him that night, her breasts pressing against his side, and he feared the possibility of her loss, but hope was greater than fear and he chose his words

cautiously. "Jenny, do you still harbor your fear of returning to the city?"

Jennifer's heart lurched at this unexpected topic, and
she wondered what lay behind the question. Carefully, she
edged her way around the answer. "I don't fear returning,
Marcus, if that is what you wish. I believe I can adequately
handle the task of being your hostess."

In the darkness, a small smile appeared as a weight lifted
from his chest. "Then you would return to San Francisco
with me if I asked?"

"Is that what you wish?" Jennifer deflected the question.
She had given it much thought since they first discussed
it, and now there were other questions she would have
answered before jumping in impetuously with her reply.
"What is back there for you? You have said your father's
shipping business holds little interest for you. Do you have
some other business there that calls?"

"The shipping business cannot run itself, as much as
Stephen would like to think so. I have considered selling
it for more manageable investments since I suppose
Stephen will not wish to stay, but that is another subject.
Do you think you could be happy if you left the hotel and
returned there?" he asked pointedly, halting further eva-
sion.

Jennifer had her answer ready: there was no other decision she could make. She had nearly lost him once, and
in so doing, learned she could not live without him. Her
life was irretrievably his. "If returning would make you
happy, and I could keep Stuart to myself without a bevy
of nurses between us, I will be content. Emma can always
hire a new manager to help with this place. Perhaps Bess
could help her until the mortgage is paid and there is
extra money for a salary. Bess has no knowledge of kitchens, but she would be helpful. I am your wife, if you want
me; the hotel is not what matters."

There was his answer. It did not include the words he
wanted to hear, but the meaning was clear; it was up to
him to decide what to do about it. She had found the

home and job for which she had been searching, and now she was offering to sacrifice both for his happiness; what other proof could he ask? Marcus pulled her on top of him and kissed her long and thoroughly, his good arm squeezing her tight against his chest.

"I want you, all right. Who else would have a minx like you?" he whispered huskily into her hair, rolling her over and crushing her beneath his weight, rejoicing as slender arms pulled him into their welcoming embrace. She was his, and he would have it no other way.

Morning came and Marc's eyes narrowed watching his wife creep across the room to slip back into bed, curling close to him for warmth against the morning chill. He could count, too, and it didn't take much figuring to determine the reason for her lingering illness. The only puzzle was why she did not tell him instead of hiding the fact. But the reasons did not matter now. He had been debating this decision for some time and last night had settled it.

Toying with her breasts, gentling her as he would a free-spirited filly, Marcus broke the news. "Jenny, I am going into the city today."

Instantly aroused from drowsy comfort, Jennifer's lashes flew up. "Why?" Tremulously, the word sprang out unbidden.

"There is some business there I must conclude. It will not take long, and I shall be back before tomorrow night." He moved to get up, but was held by the uncertainty in her gaze.

"Did the doctor say you were well enough to travel? That train ride is so rough . . ."

"If you have not noticed, I am recuperating nicely, thanks to my excellent nurse. Now let me up, or I'll miss the first train and that will make me that much later getting back." He kissed her lightly and climbed from the bed, pulling on his dressing robe with the inexpert clumsiness of the one-handed.

Not totally reassured, Jennifer wrapped the sheet about

her and went to his aid. "Are you sure someone should not go with you? What if you are taken ill?"

"I have been traveling on my own most of my life, little one. I will survive." Marcus kissed the top of her head and went off to wash.

Jennifer tried not to worry, but this sudden decision on top of last night's discussion did not bode well. She had meant what she said, but she was not eager to see it carried out. They had so many friends here, and too few in San Francisco that could truly be called friends. Unhappily contemplating a future of elegant entertaining with ambitious business acquaintants, Jennifer spent the morning after Marcus left compensating for his dismal future by preparing decidedly inelegant fried chicken and candied sweet potatoes for her totally unambitious hotel staff of friends.

After dinner, Jennifer returned to the sitting room to persuade Stuart to retire for a nap. Over five months old now, the infant was showing signs of a stubborn determination and an active restlessness to rival his father's, and sleeping now was at the bottom of his list of things to do.

That was how Lucia found her, cradling a sleepy infant and a toy clown while rocking gently in a rocker Henry had brought up some time ago. Jennifer gestured for silence and transferred baby and clown to the cradle, indicating they should retire to the other room.

"Where has *Señor* Armstrong gone?" Lucia asked as soon as the door closed behind them.

"Business in the city, he says. It is too painful to ride a horse up to the mines, so he has to find some other way to occupy his time." Jennifer spoke with unconcern, as if there were not a thousand different worries crowding her mind. Among them was one that haunted her most: if it were only a business trip, why did he not offer to take her with him? But she did not linger long on the reasons.

"Is he ready to go back home then?" Lucia asked with more than a trace of anxiety.

"Permanently?" Jennifer noted the maid's uneasy expression with puzzlement. "I'm afraid so. The vacation is about over," she remarked gloomily, settling herself into an easy chair and pulling her feet up under her.

Lucia's normally cheerful smile fell from her face. "Then I am doomed forever to be an old maid and to never have any *niños* of my own!" she moaned.

Jennifer looked up in astonishment and then with sudden understanding. "Charlie!"

Lucia nodded morosely. No words of explanation were necessary. Lucia could not afford the luxury of giving up her job in hopes of the happy-go-lucky engineer someday recognizing her worth.

Jennifer set her jaw with determination and her mind worked quickly. She could not let Marc's obstinacy bring pain to her closest friend. There must be some way to bring the lovers together before she was forced to follow Marcus to San Francisco. And with a mischievous gleam, she pounced upon the perfect solution. What had worked once could work again, if her virtuous maid could be brought to approve and Charlie maneuvered in the right direction.

In a few brief words, Jennifer explained her idea, and Lucia's eyes grew round with a mixture of anticipation and horror. But Jennifer's serene assurances of Charlie's affection calmed the maid's fears, and her own high spirits returned laughter to her eyes. It was better than to return to San Francisco with no hope at all, and Lucia nodded agreement.

Not until the last meal of the day was served and cleaned up did Jennifer have a chance to search out Stephen. There were few guests in the bar when she entered, but all looked up in surprise at her appearance. Ladies seldom found their way into the dark recesses of the newly constructed saloon; only Bess, upon occasion, provided any feminine enlightenment in this male-dominated corner of the world.

Stephen hastily exited his place behind the bar, and putting his arm around her shoulder, guided Jennifer toward the door. "You may be hotel manager, my dear, but you will have to manage from the other side of this door. What can I do for you this evening?"

"Stephen, did anyone ever tell you, you are rapidly becoming insufferable? I would like to talk to you alone a few minutes, if you can be parted from that abominable bar long enough."

"That does not sound like a communication of love, but I will do my best. Where will I find you when I get someone to take my place?"

"Upstairs, in my sitting room. It's about time for Stuart's nightly temper tantrum, so take your time, but if you forget, Lucia will never forgive you."

"Lucia!" Gray eyes lit with laughter, and he kissed the tip of her nose. "I shall be there in next to no time."

There were whistles and catcalls from the bar at Stephen's demonstrative show of affection, but Jennifer ignored them as she sailed though the lobby, skirts rustling behind her. Stephen winked broadly and grinned at his audience, then proceeded to search for his substitute bartender.

The time for the last train passed with no sign of Marcus, but Jennifer had not expected his return. They had never been together for such long periods of time before, and to be accurate, Marcus had seldom been in one place for so long a time since he first left California. His need to be moving and doing must have reached a peak by now, and Jennifer did not expect his return for a week, no matter what fine words he used. Wanderlust, she could understand, but if she should find he was with some other woman . . . the thought did not bear examination.

Stephen appeared shortly after Stuart gave in and fell asleep, and Jennifer hurried him into the room, leaving the door slightly ajar for propriety's sake. As the story of Lucia and Charlie unfolded in eager explanation, Stephen bent understandingly to her swift explanations.

Meanwhile, Marcus cursed the slowness of the late train, ranting at the breakdowns preventing him from arriving at a decent hour. Jennifer would be in bed and asleep by the time he arrived, and he would have to wait until morning to give her his news. It was a cruel trick for fate to play on him: to have everything move smoothly all day with time to catch the last train just as it left the station, and then not get there on time, after all. Checking his inside pocket to see if the papers were still safe, he smiled with satisfaction. It was done, and the papers could wait until morning. It would be good just to be back in bed with his wife. His chest ached abominably from the unaccustomed activity of the day, and a good night's sleep might aid his presentation. The thought of her reaction to his decision restored his good humor, and he relaxed contentedly, making plans for a bright new future with his independent wife at his side.

Marcus was the only one off at the station, and he crossed to the hotel, the well-lighted lobby throwing welcoming yellow squares of lamplight across the raised sidewalks. Inside, the lobby was deserted, but the noise from the bar gave direction to the location of the crowd.

It was too late to expect Jennifer to be waiting, but Stephen would still be around, and he could use a drink to deaden the throbbing in his side. With that fatal decision, Marcus swung into the barroom.

Settling himself on an empty stool and motioning for a drink, Marcus looked around, surprised to find Stephen absent. His cousin had made a hobby out of this place, selecting the woods and decor to be used as the Indian built the partition, insisting on the all-masculine interior over the objections of the women, and occupying the place of honor nightly as he mixed drinks and bantered with whatever stray guest meandered in. Tonight, the bar was packed, and his cousin was nowhere to be seen.

A stranger brought his drink, and Marcus received only a noncommittal shrug in answer to his question about Stephen's whereabouts. The man on the next stool lay down his drink and chuckled. Obviously well along in his cups, he had the appearance of one of the drummers now finding the town a lucrative source of sales since the advent of the railroad. In reply to Marcus' inquiring glance, the man took another drink before speaking. "If you're asking after that young yellow-haired fellow who works here, he has himself another assignation, if you know what I mean." The drunk winked lewdly.

Marcus leaned away in disgust and emptied his glass. If Stephen found time to amuse himself with one of the town "girls," it was none of his affair. He made no comment, but the salesman took his silence for interest.

"Pretty little redhead, she was. Come in here like she owned the place and her lookin' just as ladylike as you please. That fella skedaddled her right out of here, but I seed the way he kissed her and grinned all over hisself and it wasn't too long after he took off on out of here. I ain't no fool, I can put two and two . . ."

But his ill-mannered companion was gone, and the drummer was left talking to an empty bar stool.

Striding up the staircase, eyes fastened on their bed-room door, Marcus cursed himself long and loud. Senti-mental idiot that he was, what made him think any woman could be faithful? At least, this one had been honest and never declared her love, but *damn*—she sure had made a damned good pretense of it. Was that why she'd hid her morning sickness from him? Was the child even his? And Stuart? He'd been so all-fired confident of her innocence, had she even fooled him there? God Almighty . . .

His hand automatically went to his hip as he stalked down the hall, but he had left his guns behind. The gesture halted him. What if they were still in there together? What would he do? Could he cold-bloodedly kill his cousin and his wife? He rubbed his sweating brow with the back of his hand, unmindful of the throbbing ache in his side. He was in the mood for killing, but the crackle of papers in his jacket pocket reminded him of an earlier mood, and he knew he couldn't do it, not even if he could reach his guns. And black despair engulfed him. It was no time to discover how much you loved a person, not when you were on the brink of losing them.

Marcus couldn't bring himself to open the bedroom door; if he went in there now, he'd have to kill them. Instead, he quietly entered the sitting room-nursery where a dim lamp burned over his son's bed. If he needed any more evidence, there it was: a thin cigar lay crumpled and broken on the saucer of one of two coffee cups. Coffee. God, they were cool! Pulling a flask from his pocket, Marcus took a swig, feeling the whiskey burning fiery paths down his throat and into the roaring furnace consuming his soul.

Well, what did he do now? Go sleep in Stephen's room? Barge in on the loving couple and throw him head first over the balcony? Go back to the bar and his drunken informant? Collapsing on the sofa, he took a few more drinks to keep the fire burning, his glance running over the room where Jennifer had slept, all alone, all those merciless weeks. Slept. His eye fell on the foldable bed and he grinned drunkenly. If she could do it . . .

When Jennifer woke in the morning, it was to a cold, empty bed and an uneasy stomach. Comforting herself with the thought that there was no need for silence, she rushed to the wash room and lost the remains of yesterday's fried chicken and last night's coffee.

Her retching did not wake the sleeper in the next room, but the pounding of the wash room door against the end of his bed did. Groaning and running his hand through an unruly mop of hair, Marcus briefly wondered where he was, the truth suddenly dawning on him as the door once more slammed against the bed. Jennifer was trying to enter the nursery through the connecting door, and all the memories of the night before came crashing back with a dismal clangor. Falling back against the pillows, he closed his eyes against the pain.

Scared and furious, Jennifer retreated to the bedroom to pull on her robe before dashing to the hall. There was only one person capable of pulling that kind of trick on her, but she could not imagine why . . .

By the time she threw open the sitting room door, Marcus had dragged himself from the bed and attempted to straighten the clothing he had worn to bed last night. His jacket and boots were the only things he'd had sense enough to remove, and with aching head and aching heart, he pulled them on. Still working on the last boot when Jennifer entered, he grimaced, making no move to stand up.

"Marcus!" Jennifer stopped, astounded at his appearance. Her gaze flew over his unshaven cheeks, tousled hair, and crumpled suit, the reek of whiskey reaching her nose. If it were only that . . . "Are you well?"

"Not particularly," he grunted, bending over and tugging on the last recalcitrant boot. "But then, you wouldn't be either in my condition. There!" Satisfied the boot was on, he stood, and for a moment, as he looked at her, his eyes glazed with pain. But then remembering himself, he reached into his jacket pocket, producing a large packet of papers. "There, madam, your freedom. All signed, sealed, and delivered. I thought perhaps . . ." he hesitated, overcome by some emotion, continuing more gruffly, "but it doesn't matter, you've made your choice."

He handed her the papers with a burning look that reduced Jennifer to ashes. "The hotel's all yours now, do with it as you will. Emma's happy, you're happy, everybody's happy . . ." and he staggered out, slamming the door behind him.

Stunned, unbelieving, utterly crushed by his behavior, Jennifer crumpled into the nearest chair and stared unseeingly at the papers in her hand. Her own hotel, he'd said. Freedom. What had he meant? Tears dripped from her lashes and coursed down her cheeks, unnoticed. She sat there, dazed, staring at the closed door, unable to comprehend . . . Why? Was this her price, then? Was he leaving her? How could that be?

It was unnatural. He couldn't just walk off like that.

Something was wrong. Dazed, she rose and followed him out the door, but he was long gone. Automatically, she returned to the room they shared, knowing it was empty. Sliding the papers into a dresser drawer, she slowly drew on her clothes, searching for the key that would put her brain into action, solve the problem, figure out what had just happened. But nothing worked. He was gone. Just like that.

Bess called to her as Jennifer drifted down the stairway, but she didn't answer. She heard nothing, saw nothing but the look of pain in Marc's eyes as he handed her those papers. It couldn't be true, it couldn't be happening all over again. Instinctively, her hand covered her stomach as she went out the front door. A train whistled around the bend, its wailing holler echoing off the walls of the canyon, but Jennifer didn't hear.

Bess watched her with curiosity, thinking it odd that Jennifer should wander out so early in the morning. But then, she was sure it was Marcus she had seen earlier, heading for the stables. Maybe he had forgotten something. She continued on down the stairs and into the bar; after last night, it would need a good cleaning.

Last night's receipts were still in the register, and Bess jammed them into the money bag Stephen kept for the purpose, wondering if everybody in the hotel had suddenly gone mad. Stephen always locked the cash before retiring, and Bess had no access to the safe; the money had no business sitting here. She would have to hide it somewhere until Jennifer returned.

Money bag in hand, Bess stepped into the lobby, finding it still deserted though it was past time for the day's activity to begin. She could hear Henry roaring in the kitchen, so someone was up and about, but usually Lucia was down here working by now. Stephen often slept late because of his hours, so she dismissed the idea of taking the bag to him. There was only one other choice, and she turned her feet in the direction of Emma's room.

After explaining the situation to the old lady in an offhand manner calculated not to alarm, Bess started down the stairs again to continue her chores. Before she reached the bottom, the front door opened to the jangling of the overhead bell, and Bess came face to face with the demon she had hoped never to see again.

Delaney's elegance had sadly declined as his alcoholic intake increased; any claim he may have had to a gentlemanly facade had long since degenerated. His sallow coloring was more intense, his eyes were bloodshot and wild, and a week's growth of beard told a story of neglect. As his eyes slowly focused on Bess, his lips parted in a tobacco-stained grin.

"You're going to make it easy for me, you two-timing bitch of a whore." With deliberate nonchalance, he withdrew a gun from his shoulder holster, not the small pistol of before, but a large caliber revolver. The madness in his eyes held Bess transfixed with horror.

She gripped the handrail to steady herself. The man had gone totally mad to come here like this, and her panic-stricken gaze flew around the room in search of escape. Where was everybody this morning?

Chuckling evilly at her panic, Delaney gestured with his gun. "Better show me to your room, Bess, or one of your new friends is likely to get hurt."

One last glance told her there was no hope, and shakily, she led the way back up the stairs.

Shoving her into the room, Delaney followed closely behind, locking the door while keeping his gaze fixed on his target. "You and me are gonna have a long talk, woman, starting with where I can find that other red-headed whore of mine. Thought I'd picked her to take your place, didn't you, Bess?" His laugh was cruel as he shoved her into the nearest chair. "You were right. I had my eye on her a lot longer than you ever realized, almost had her once—she was ripe and ready, all right, but that damned Armstrong had to go and do my job for me. Saved me a lot of trouble until he decided to get righteous about it." Delaney spit a wad of tobacco into the corner. "Damned bastard won't even die like he's supposed to. Can't get near neither of them while they're holed up in this place, but I saw Armstrong in town yesterday, so the time's come."

With a cruel leer, he ripped the linen from the bed. "I aim to collect what's mine and you're going to help me do it, lover. This way is even better. I can watch the bastard sweat before I finish him off for good." Delaney cackled at Bess's bewildered expression. Then he methodically set about obtaining the information he desired.

When he left the hotel some time later, his look was anything but smug, yet his gait was determined as he headed for the livery stable. No matter which way his quarry had gone, she was on foot, and he could find her much faster by horse.

Meanwhile, Jennifer slowly regained her senses while wandering at the edge of the field of flowers she had visited so many long weeks before. The grass was lush now with the recent rains, and the remains of bright red poppy heads bowed down under the heavy moisture. The view was stupendous, opening out over a craggy cliff and looking down onto a rocky valley far below to the roots of the mountain providing the backdrop for all this scenery. Jennifer was only dimly aware of the bright pattern of fall color sweeping down the mountainside. She was more acutely aware of the sharp, gray rocks that lay only a footstep away and an eternity below her.

Backing off from the edge, Jennifer collapsed, shivering, on a pile of rock buried in the long grass, her heart pounding with the scare she had just given herself. Perhaps Marcus had been right that night he found her leaning over the rail above the stormy waters of the Mississippi. Maybe she was suicidal. But that was no soft, familiar bed of water down there, and she had no wish to throw herself into the mountain's sharp embrace. It was time she recovered her senses and put them to use.

It was imperative that she figure out what had happened and why, but she didn't know where to begin. Marcus had been so kind, so loving, and he had seemed so happy when she had agreed to return to the city with him. What had happened? When had he arrived at the hotel? He hadn't been there when she sent Stephen off to find Charlie. She had gone to bed soon after that, but unless the train was late for some reason . . . Where could he have been?

Her mind churned over all the possibilities. He had apparently gone to town specifically to buy the hotel for her. But why? She had told him she would stay with him if he wanted. Was he tired of her already? This morning, he looked as if he hated her. How could that be possible? Could someone change so rapidly overnight or had it all been just a disguise? The more she thought about it, the more confusing it became, and Jennifer buried her face in her hands in despair.

Marcus pounded his fist against the wall of his horse's stall, shaking the timbers and disturbing his already saddled mount. It was no use, he couldn't do it. He couldn't walk out without some word of explanation. There had to be a reason. He was so besotten he couldn't believe the evidence of his own eyes and ears, couldn't believe she would betray him like that; he would have to see it for himself, hear the words from her own lips before he could accept it.

Furious at his own weakness, Marcus stalked through the hotel door, into a scene of growing chaos. Lucia's shrieks pierced the air, echoing downstairs and into the lobby, while Charlie stumbled from an upstairs room, shirtless, still pulling on his belt as he staggered across the balcony in the direction of the shrieks. A baby's wail filled the lapses between screams, and Henry came flying from the dining room, frying pan still in hand as he galloped out and straight into Marcus. Other heads and bodies appeared from various doors and openings and with one thought, they all followed Marcus in a mad stampede to the source of the screams.

Hysterically tugging at the knot binding the handkerchief around Bess's mouth, Lucia clung distractedly to her task even as Charlie arrived to calm her screams and pull her away. Above the cutting material, Bess's cheeks were already purpling with evil bruises, her swollen eyes rolling frantically at the sight of Marcus, and she struggled to be free of the torn sheets binding her to the chair. While Charlie and Stephen removed the distraught Lucia, Marcus cut through the bonds with his knife, one part of his mind totally aware there was no sign of his wife in this melee, the other convinced that Bess had the reason.

Whipping the sheets away from the terrified figure on the chair, he demanded, "Where is she? What happened?"

"Delaney . . . he's gone looking for Jennifer. I don't know where she is, couldn't tell him. But she left the hotel over an hour ago . . ." The words gasped out in ragged breaths, urgently, commanding him to run, find Jennifer before that monster did.

Her terror communicated to the occupants of the room, and they milled about frantically, leaving only Marcus with enough presence of mind to make active decisions.

"Henry, go get the sheriff and as many men as he can round up. Stephen, take whoever you can find and head down the trail. My horse is ready. I'm going up toward the mines, tell the sheriff to follow after me. Charlie, hold down the fort and look after the women."

Marcus was already taking the steps two at a time, shouting his commands over his shoulder as he ran. His mind worked, coldly calculating, but fury and anguish ripped at his soul. It was his fault she was gone, wandering the mountain out of the protection of her friends, and he knew, beyond the shadow of any doubt, where she had gone. Sending Stephen down the trail had only been a precaution; there was nothing to call her down that way. But the combination of flowers and cliffs up above would attract her as surely as if they were the Mississippi itself. And he had driven her to it, again.

Chapter Twenty-Six

Jennifer lifted her head from her hands. The sound of hoofbeats echoed over the canyon, muffling the direction from which they came. It could be one of the miners coming or going, but she had no wish to be seen by anyone. Slipping from her rock chair, she hid in the shadow of the surrounding trees. Anyone passing by would never look twice in her direction.

But this rider did not pass by. He reined in, taking his horse farther into the meadow while he searched the area. Not until he turned his face in her direction and the sun hit it from an angle did Jennifer recognize him. At the same time, he saw her.

Spurring his mount toward the edge of the field, Delaney approached cautiously, while Jennifer slowly backed into the sparse cover of trees. The mountain rose up behind her; there was no escape from this boxed in valley except by the path he had traveled, or over the cliff. She could not hope to outrun his horse on the path, and swerving, she edged slowly toward the terrifying drop at the other side. She had once told him she preferred death to returning to him; there was no reason now to change her mind.

"Well, my little pigeon, you seem to have shed a few pounds since last we met. I guess that fine husband of yours has got you properly broken to the saddle by now, hasn't he?" Lecherous laughter followed his words as his gaze stripped her of clothing. "By God, I bet there's a few tricks I could teach you that you haven't learned yet." He urged his horse closer, gloating at her helplessness.

"Cat got your tongue, huh? I'll make you scream before I'm through, though, and not leave a mark on that beautiful body. Remember what you did to me once? Nearly made a damned eunuch of me. Well, I know worse tricks. Only you didn't know it was me, did you?" Hatred glared from bloodshot eyes, hate and lust.

Jennifer was too terrified to understand anything more than the fact that the man was totally out of his mind. This had to be the madman to whom Cameron had referred. But how and why . . . ? He made no effort to get off his horse or touch her, just sat there, hovering above, rambling on with the babble of an idiot. But there was obviously some purpose driving him on, and Jennifer edged closer to the cliff.

"I saw you slipping up them stairs that night, probably still hot from your lover's bed. Yeah, I knew that damned Armstrong's boat was in town; didn't know then he was the man you had the hots for or I would have tried even harder."

The horse snorted edgily as it drew closer, but the madman ranted on, his eyes fixed hungrily on Jennifer. "Grabbed you from behind, had you right in my hands, and you damned near maimed me for life. I swore then I would have you, one way or another." His eyes gleamed malevolently.

Vaguely, his words began to make sense, and Jennifer stared at him, horrified. This was the man who had tried to rape her at the inn, the one who had driven her into Marc's arms, the one who had instigated this entire chain of events. It was incredible. He had changed her entire life, and now he was going to end it. It was as if he possessed the power of God, or Satan.

Pleased that he had finally raised a reaction from her, Delaney pressed on. "I kept an eye on you after that, watching for a way to get you away from that eagle-eyed witch of a mother. Wasn't easy since I only came through that hellhole every so often, but when I came through and found you'd disappeared, it took some fast talking to find out why. Good thing that bitch of a mother of yours is such a pious old bag. Had her eating out of my hand in no time at all, just had to attend that church of hers, wave a few dollars, and pray like I really meant it. Kind of got a kick out of it. Maybe I missed my calling after all. She sold you to the church, my little pigeon, what do you think of that?"

Jennifer grabbed at the bush behind her, the only thing between herself and the limitless space in the canyon below. If Delaney moved any closer, she would be over the edge with only this bush to cling to . . . She prayed it was a sturdy one.

"Then there was that damned Irishman, tried to cheat me out of you, ruined my chance to grab you after I got Armstrong out of the way . . . Put an end to that turncoat, I did . . ."

Delaney seemed totally oblivious to the precipice at his side as he ranted on, concentrating, instead, on the goal so easily within his grasp.

"I been aching to get a handful of that hair ever since I first laid eyes on you. You and me are gonna get along just fine. My mother had hair like that . . ."

With savage delight, he reached for her, catching a handful of auburn tresses, winding it inexorably in his hand, pulling her steadily closer with the pain . . .

Jennifer screamed in hysterical terror as she was dragged relentlessly from her stronghold, her eyes fixed on the horrifying fate awaiting her, the madman's eyes already stripping her of her fine garments and reducing her to the state of whore once again. Her screams rocked the valley, and increased in pitch at the sight of the terrifying sight just coming into view over Delaney's shoulder.

A reckless horseman pounded around the cliff path's curve, his reins wrapped incredibly about a bandaged arm while the other hand raised deliberately, glinting with something metallic in the early morning light. The racing horse swayed dangerously near the cliff's edge, and Jennifer's hysterical screams leaped to a higher pitch. The pain of Delaney's grasp no longer held her in thrall.

Sensing some new cause for terror, Delaney dropped his grip on Jennifer and reached for his gun, grabbing at the reins of his horse too late as it moved under him. The splintering crash of gunshots broke over their heads, and the horse reared in panic. Unseated, Delaney shrieked in terror, and the horse reared again, flinging his hapless rider over the cliff's edge and into the oblivion beyond, his screams echoing down the valley, decreasing in volume with the increasing distance.

Blessedly, Jennifer didn't hear them. As the horse reared above her, heaving its savage rider overhead, her final hold on the shrub loosed, and swooning with shock and fear, she fainted at the brink of the precipice.

Marcus was at her side before her skirts settled, throwing off the sling that bound his arm, sweeping her into his arms, carrying her from the edge of that fatal cliff.

Jennifer woke to the security of the arms she loved. "Marcus!" she whispered wonderingly, her arms responding to his embrace by encircling his shoulders, clinging to the safety of his presence. But as the clouds of fear dissipated in his strength, memory returned, and crying "Marcus!" once again, she hugged him tighter to prove his reality. "You could have been killed! Are you insane? Are you all right? Let me look at you. You terrified me!" Pushing away, her fingers swept over him, examining all the familiar nooks and crannies she had learned so well these last few weeks.

Half-laughing, half-crying, Marcus pried her fingers loose from his injured arm and pulled her head down to his shoulder again. "My God, Jenny! Save your life and you yell at me. Risk your neck and it is *me* you examine. You are the most perverse little . . ." Brokenly, he berated her, rocking her back and forth in his embrace, his voice racked with anguish of words unsaid.

"Marcus, I'm sorry, whatever I've done, I'll never . . ." breathlessly, Jennifer tried to find all the words at once, the words to express her horror and fear, her gratitude, her bewilderment, her love, but he wouldn't let her continue.

Shaking her fiercely, Marcus demanded silence. "Hush, now you're going to listen to me for a change. In my stupidity and guilt I have given you free rein, but I intend to break you to the traces now. There will be no more escapades like this one, my little filly, because I intend to hobble you until I can teach you to love me as I do you. I thought by . . ." His torrent of angry, frightened words was broken by Jennifer's cry of joy, her arms flying about his neck in ecstasy.

"Your lesson is already learned, master, I have only been waiting for your command to display it," she whispered incoherently, salty tears falling down his bare neck. "If you could only know how long I've waited . . ."

Unbelieving, Marcus held her tighter, the tears on his cheeks blending with those on hers. "I command you, then, Jenny Lee, I wish to hear you say it."

Shyly, she whispered, "I love you," then gaining courage from his ecstatic embrace, she repeated more loudly, "I love you," then flinging her head back, she screamed wildly, "I love you!" until the hills reverberated with joyous echoes.

Laughing, running threads of kisses down her cheeks and throat, Marcus added his cries to hers, pulling her backward into the grass until they lay side by side, face to face, wrapped in their laughter and happiness.

But horror was still too close to hand and laughter calmed to tender touches and searching gazes.

"I thought to see you killed, Marcus. That path is treacherous enough, but with no hands . . ."

"Never, my love. My horse knows that path in the dark. I had to reach you before Delaney. I knew what you would do should he touch you." His arms held her tighter and she shuddered against his chest.

"He was mad, Marcus, insane . . ."

"I know, love," he soothed her, stroking her hair. "I know what it is to be insane. I have been in that state since the first night we met; I only regret that it has taken me this long to recognize it."

Anxiously, she searched his eyes, fingers tracing the hard outline of his cheekbones. "Then why . . . ? I do not understand."

"Neither do I, little one, neither do I," he sighed, situating her more comfortably in his arms. "You have been an obsession with me since that first night. I have not been able to touch another woman but you. That day we married, I knew your feelings about marriage, but when the opportunity was offered, I grabbed it, knowing it was against your wishes, knowing I could have hired lawyers to save you without it. I wanted you and could think of nothing else. But when you so bitterly resented what I had done, I regretted my impetuousness and allowed you to force that foolish contract on me, knowing you were not yet ready to accept me or the responsibility of marriage. Keeping my hands off you was the hardest thing I have ever done, and if I neglected you, that was the reason."

Quietly, Jennifer remembered the lonely months of stormy gray eyes when she battled against his will and her own emotions, wanting what he was prepared to give once she was ready to accept it. "But that was not love you were offering me, you told me so yourself. What changed your mind?"

"Nothing changed my mind, Jenny Lee, I only needed to open it. I did, last night, when I thought I had lost you to Stephen. It would have served me right for denying you the one thing you asked of me; it took the knowledge of your loss to bring me to my senses. You are mine, Jenny, I have no wish to share you." Marcus gathered her in his arms again, the wind ruffling their hair, blowing copper strands against his cheek. "I am a jealous fool,

Jenny, but I must know. What is there between you and Stephen?"

Taking his face between her hands, she saw the wound opening behind his eyes, and she knew this one hurt she had the power to heal, and stated simply, "Lucia."

He stared at her in bewilderment. "Lucia?" Searching her face for an answer, he found it in her serenity and the loving glow that lit her eyes, and his face brightened with the joy of discovery. "Stephen and Lucia?"

Jennifer laughed. "Not quite. Charlie and Lucia, with a little help from Stephen. Charlie was too slow and Lucia impatient. Stephen simply added the impetus with a few words of wisdom."

"That damned renegade!" Marcus growled. "I wondered what he was doing in town this morning, but I had no idea . . ." He shook his head in disbelief, but at her anxious look, he grinned and squeezed her tighter. "I always knew you were a conniving little brat, but I never knew your talents extended to matchmaking. I guess we better convince a preacher to set up his booth here if we're going to stay."

Jennifer's eyes grew round as her hands slid from around his neck. "Are we going to stay?"

His gaze heated at the sight of her oval face staring wistfully up at him. "How about a house, right about here, with a picket fence all around and a climbing rose bush, right over there." He made no attempt to point out the location as slender arms encircled his neck again and he received his ecstatic reply.

The sound of horses coming up the trail separated them. Marcus hastily helped his wife to her feet, aware that their joy was based on a tragedy that had yet to be explained. The dust of a dozen horses filled the valley, and they stood waiting in each other's arms while men and beasts swirled around them.

The sheriff was the first to approach, and after a brief explanation of the episode, he ordered his posse to search the cliff for remains. As the others moved away, the sheriff stayed behind.

"I'm gonna have to ask you some questions, Mr. Armstrong, you know that?" A barrel-chested man of fifty in traditional Western garb, Stetson hat and leather vest included, he looked at Marcus with a glimmer of respect, not just for his name and position, but as a man who had done what he thought right and was not afraid to admit it. A man had been killed, a stranger to the town, but a man nevertheless, and Marcus had not flinched at acknowledging his involvement.

"I realize you have a job to do, Sheriff," Marcus stated calmly, his good arm about his wife's shoulders, "but my wife is extremely upset, as you can understand. Let me take her back to the hotel while you do your work here. You can find me there whenever you're ready."

"Don't think there's any problem with that. We don't want the little lady around when they bring the body up. Best thing to do, I guess." The sheriff spat out of the corner of his mouth, wandering back to the cliff's edge to direct his men.

Looking down at the wilting figure of his wife, Marcus was struck by a new worry, one he had forgotten in the midst of chaos. "Jenny, I'm new at this. Will it be safe for you to ride back?"

She looked up at her astonishing husband, not certain if she was reading more into his words than he meant, but the flicker of a proud grin made her heart skip a beat. "You knew! All these weeks I've been trying to protect you, and you knew! I thought husbands were supposed to be ignorant."

"Ignorant, but not dumb." He did not question her protection; he understood now the desperation of loving with the fear of not being loved in return, and he accepted her silence. Covering her still slender waist with his large hand, he grinned. "A girl this time, with hair like yours?"

Basking in the warmth of his gaze, Jennifer linked her hands behind his neck and agreed, "And Armstrong eyes," she whispered, feeling his arms worshipfully surround her.

Entering the hotel, they were immediately caught up in a flurry of people and questions, Lucia throwing herself, crying, into Jennifer's arms, Henry trotting down the stairs carrying Stuart, followed at a more sedate pace by Bess, whose gaze never left Marcus. Charlie and the remainder of the staff soon joined them, all asking questions at once, but it was Bess's neutral voice that filled a lull in the chatter, her stare unwavering.

"He's dead, isn't he?" she asked.

Gravely, Marcus nodded, and Bess paled, unaware of Emma's sympathetic arm about her. "It's better that way." Agreeing with Marc's unspoken thoughts, she broke her gaze, allowing Emma to lead her away.

Before anyone else could speak, the lobby door crashed open, and Stephen exploded into the room.

"I saw Marc's horse . . ." Spying his cousin's tall figure, crying "Where is she?" He pushed through the crowd before it could part to reveal the object of his search. Ecstatically, he swept Jenny up in his arms and spun her around with a cry of joy. "You're safe!"

Putting a hand on his exuberant cousin's shoulder, Marcus brought the spin to a halt. "She's not likely to be if you keep that up," he commented sardonically, appropriating Jennifer into his protective hold.

Unabashed, Stephen placed hands on hips and defiantly faced Marc's wrath. "After all you've put us through, I think some explanations are due. Who or what is this Delaney fellow, and what has all this to do with Jennifer?" Briefly, his gaze rested kindly on Jennifer, but it hardened as he turned to her husband.

Marcus turned an inquiring look to Jennifer—explanations would be difficult and exceedingly painful for her.

Secure in the knowledge of her husband's love, Jennifer felt capable of withstanding anything, and she met his concerned gaze evenly. "We will have to tell the sheriff, won't we?"

"I'm afraid so, love." His eyes were dark with worry. She had been through so much, to have to bring this up now would be an even greater burden. He little cared what it did to him.

"Then perhaps you better include Stephen and Charlie when you talk to the sheriff; I trust them to take it no further." She had no wish to have her shame revealed to all, but Stephen and Charlie would understand, and she could only hope that the sheriff would remain silent once Marcus was cleared of any wrong-doing.

Marc's eyes swept over the crowd of people surrounding them, coming to rest on Henry's understanding face. Henry and Josephine knew, and they still loved her; even if their indiscretion and Jennifer's later predicament became public, he was confident these people here would all give their love and support. Her instincts were right— this is where they belonged. Lovingly, he returned his gaze to the woman who had made him understand what love was about.

Though no one fully understood what was happening, the tension that had pervaded the room evaporated, and everyone began to recall their duties, gradually clearing the lobby until only Stephen, Charlie, and Marcus were left to greet the sheriff's arrival.

Solemnly, the four men retired to the darkened saloon, and while Stephen poured drinks, Marcus clarified Delaney's relationship to his wife. Grimly, Stephen listened to the sordid tale. At Marc's mention of Cameron's position in Magnolia House, Stephen and Charlie interrupted with the news of his death and an exchange of glances. It was evident Cameron had sought his revenge through Jennifer and brought Delaney here to rid himself of Marcus. The sheriff agreed to look in on the possibility of Delaney being Cameron's killer, but no man present dared express an opinion on Cameron's ultimate intent. Marc's squared jaw made the subject taboo.

When Bess was called in for verification of the details, Stephen's eyebrows drew together in a frown, but when the story drew to its conclusion on the mountain, he belted his whiskey and held out his hand to Marcus.

"Cousin, you may be a fool, but if Jenny can forgive you, so can I. I apologize."

Marcus eyed this offering askance, then solemnly gripped his hand and shook.

Quietly, Jennifer entered the room, and all four men came to their feet in a gesture of respect.

"Sheriff, is my husband free of all charges?" Soft and low, her voice managed to vibrate the still air around them.

"Yes, ma'am, Mrs. Armstrong. Body has no bullet holes in it so far as we could find, it was purely accidental. Soon's we telegraph St. Louis for confirmation on a few facts, everything will be cleared up."

"Thank you, Sheriff," and she went to stand by her husband's side as Lucia entered, blinking in the darkness.

Grinning with the delight of new lovers, Charlie pulled her into the room, encircling her waist with his arm and kissing her forehead before turning to Marcus.

"If the time is propitious, I'd like to request your maid's hand in marriage." His laughing eyes expressed his opinion of this formality, but Lucia's loving gaze made it worth it.

Marcus scowled, lifting one thunderous eyebrow at his wife's squeal of excitement, holding on to her before she could fly off, trying hard to maintain his look of disapproval while she wriggled in his grasp, finally giving way to a grin that brought a blaze of happiness to Lucia's dark eyes.

"Well, I suppose," he finally drawled, "if the only way I can keep you content is to give you my maid, I'll have to give my consent." Immediately smothered in excited kisses, Marcus was only able to exchange pleased glances with his satisfied engineer as the women's cries of excitement drew a crowd and the room filled with chatter.

Recovering his wife-to-be, Charlie asked, "If you two are

planning on staying here, do you think you can have the bridal suite rigged up and ready in a month's time?" He squeezed Lucia's waist expectantly.

Jennifer and Marcus exchanged amused looks, both shouting "Bridal suite!" before breaking into laughter to the bewilderment of all concerned.

"Surely," Jennifer gasped between fits of giggles.

"With a solid oak bar on the door," Marcus agreed, and to the astonishment of all, swept his wife into his arms and carried her off, leaving a wake of laughter trailing behind.

Epilogue

Stuart staggered toward the enormous evergreen filling the hotel lobby, grubby hand reaching out in delight as he spied the flickering candles, his cherubic face lit with a glow of excitement more at his prowess in attaining his goal than the fascination of the Christmas tree. Before his chubby legs could propel him to disaster, his mother swooped down from above, lifting him into the air, spinning him around before he could cry out his protests, depositing him into his father's arms.

Marcus set the infant in the curve of one arm and encircled his wife's thickening waist with the other.

"You will soon be in no condition to repeat that maneuver, madam. When are you going to allow me to hire someone to look after this little thug?" He hugged the crowing infant and looked down affectionately at his wife's increasing figure.

Jennifer turned up a stubborn chin. "Never, sir. Lucia and I can handle him well enough without outside help." Despite the disdainful tone, her eyes shone proudly as she looked up at him, love evident in her upturned lips.

Marcus bit back a smile at her defiant air; he knew too well the truth of her words, though he would be greatly relieved if he could find some way to ease the number of tasks she set herself each day. "Lucia may have her hands full soon enough without adding this demon to her burden. Then what will you do?"

Jennifer's eyes clouded questioningly. "What are you talking about? She told me nothing of this."

Setting the toddler back on the floor while keeping a careful eye on him, Marcus reached into his jacket pocket and pulled out a packet of papers similar to those he had produced once before. "The last time I did this, the result was nearly disastrous. I will attempt to rectify my errors this time. Merry Christmas, my love." Without handing her the package, he put both arms around her and exacted a kiss in payment. Their lips met with past experience, warmly and invitingly, but Jennifer's impatience prevented their lingering.

Pushing against his chest, she tried to grab the papers he kept just out of reach, behind her back. "What enormity are you springing on me this time? Give them to me, Marcus!"

He relented, but only because his son was scooting rapidly across the polished floor in the direction of the tree again. While Marcus tackled the toddler, Jennifer scanned the documents he had placed in her hands.

"What is this, Marcus? I cannot make head nor tail out of all these parties and markers and boundaries. What have you bought this time? Another mine? And what has this to do with Lucia?"

Enticing Stuart with a carved wooden ornament from the tree, Marcus left the infant on the floor and took the papers from his puzzled wife. "It is a deed, my ignorant one. You will no longer have to walk treacherous trails to find your fields of flowers. As soon as I can get the house built, you will be able to walk out your back door and find all the flowers you can possibly want, providing I can convince you to ever stay in the house." He waited for her reaction, holding back his excitement until he was sure of his gift's acceptance.

"A house? And flowers?" Catching the undercurrent of his excitement, she searched his face eagerly. "Where?"

His face broke into a smile as he took her in his arms once more. "Halfway between here and the mine so that we may see each other every night and in between if we choose. I'm going to have the road cleared and widened as soon as the weather permits, and you will be able to ride a carriage down it with safety. Does the idea meet with your approval?"

Her eyes danced with excitement. "Then Lucia can have her job as head housemaid, and we can give her evenings off, and will there be room for her and Charlie to live nearby?"

"Of course. Then instead of cold evenings in a camp hovel poring over excavating plans, we can do it in comfort in front of a fireplace with our wives to wait on us." He squeezed her and smiled teasingly. "And instead of listening to another rousing chorus of 'Sweet Betsy from Pike' on Saturday night, we can go to sleep in peace."

"I am so used to the noise, I don't even notice it. I will never be able to sleep without it, now."

"That's because you're usually down there leading them on, brat. Ever since Stephen brought in that damned piano, the place has become a regular music hall." He spoke lightly, teasing a wisp of a curl on her neck while keeping one eye on his roving son.

"Just because you have no talent for music does not mean you should deny others their pleasure. Stephen provides the only bit of culture this poor town has right now. Even Mr. Clayton, the banker, stops by occasionally to hear him play. Does Stephen know of your plans to build?" Jennifer smoothed the folds of his lapel, still thrilled with this

easy intimacy joining them, unable to take his presence
for granted but needing to touch to prove his reality.

Pleased at how neatly he was handling this, Marcus allowed himself a slight tone of self-importance. "Mr. Clayton, my dear, is not stopping by so much to hear Stephen
play as to talk to him. This branch of the bank is due to
expand, and he wants someone here on a full-time basis
to manage it. I believe Stephen is contemplating his offer
of part ownership, and I know for a fact that he bought
the parcel of land next to ours." His grin widened as Jennifer stared at him with disbelief, surprise, then exhilaration.

"He's staying! Oh, Marcus, you could not have given me
a better gift!" And her nicely rounded belly pressed against
his lean one as she threw her arms around his neck, expressing her pleasure in more potent form.

It was on this scene that the lobby door blew in, a cold
gust of wind preceding the animated arrival of Charlie,
who immediately halted his advance at the sight.

"My lord, don't you two ever give it up? Here you've got
company coming and you're standing there like you just
got married yesterday. I should have sent you two over to
the station, and Lucia and I could be here all cozy and
warm . . ."

"Keeping the brat out of the tree." Setting his wife
down reluctantly, Marcus gestured toward his son's
crablike movement across the floor. "Catch him before
he makes it."

Charlie scooped up the adventurous infant and blew
against his neck, sending Stuart into gales of gurgling
laughter. "Guess I'd better learn how to handle one of
these, the knowledge might come in handy one of these
days." He handed the giggling child to Jennifer, who
scanned his face quickly.

"Is Lucia . . . ?" She stopped, the proud light in Charlie's eyes answering her unspoken question. "Oh, Charlie,
that's wonderful!" Standing on her toes, she kissed his
beaming grin, then scolded him, "And you left her out

there in that cold in her condition. You get yourself back out there and bring her in right now. Isn't the train in yet?"

"It's in. I just came ahead to warn you there will be a couple of extra guests."

Before Charlie could continue with his explanations, Marcus took him by the elbow, leading him back to the door. "The guests will introduce themselves. I'd like to congratulate you on your impending fatherhood, but I think I'll reserve my opinion until I do a little calculating. When did you say the child is due?" He turned and winked at Jennifer over his shoulder.

She stared after him in bewilderment.

Grinning, Charlie replied, "I didn't say," and hurried back out the door before Marcus could pin him down further.

"What was that all about?" Jennifer demanded.

"Well, since they've been married only a little more than two months . . ." White teeth grinned blindingly as he faced her.

"You don't need to explain *that!* I'm probably responsible for that. I mean the guests, who else is coming besides Josephine? Did Clare decide to come? I thought she and Mr. O'Hara were planning a trip to Europe." Jennifer waited impatiently for her exasperating husband to explain, guessing he was behind whatever surprise lay at the train station.

"They're probably in jolly old Ireland right now. What do you mean, you're responsible? Unless there's some new development in modern science, I fail to see how you can be responsible for Lucia's condition." Marc continued to grin, stalling for time until the new arrivals could check out bags and baggage and be appropriately introduced to their welcoming committee.

"Marcus, I swear, if you live to see this child born, it won't be because you haven't asked to be murdered." Jennifer stamped her foot and swept toward the door intending to find out for herself.

"The only thing being murdered here is the English language and get yourself back from that door before you catch cold."

His warning was unnecessary as the door flew open again, this time with a flurry of snowflakes and a cherry-cheeked Lucia in the forefront, leading a crowd of heavily bundled newcomers.

Cries of "Merry Christmas!" flew through the air as everyone crowded into the well-lit lobby, damp woolens steaming in the warm air. Jennifer was caught up in an ecstatic hug from Josephine, who threw her arms first around Jennifer, then Marcus, approaching a startled Stuart before turning to allow Jennifer first sight of their remaining guests.

Standing awkwardly silent behind the other exuberant guests were two lone figures, their traveling clothes stained and weary and no match for the stylish Josephine. Stephen and Lucia hurried them forward, and Josephine stood proudly aside, waiting for Jennifer's reaction to her traveling companions.

A familiar smile from a broad figure and the shy dip of a hat from the taller one was all Jennifer needed to propel herself into waiting arms.

"Aunt Trudy! Uncle John! I don't believe it!" Tears fell as she tried to hug both welcome figures at once, succeeding only in bringing tears to the eyes of everyone watching except those of her stalwart husband, who supervised the scene with a pleased expression.

"Jenny, hadn't you ought to be introducin' us to your husband? If it wasn't for him, we wouldn't be here a'tall." Trudy extricated herself from her niece's ecstatic hugs, her gaze quickly finding and assessing the imposing dark-haired man waiting in the background, his handsome eyes never leaving the joyful figure of his wife. Trudy had been in awe of Josephine when they first met in St. Louis, but this man immediately commanded her respect.

Introductions exchanged, Trudy stood before her niece's silent husband, her mind running over phrases rehearsed these last few days. Now that she was facing the gentleman, it was difficult to set her tongue around the words.

"Mr. Armstrong, I want to thank you for what you've done for Jennifer. She's the closest thing I got to a child of my own, and I didn't sleep nights for worryin' about her. Miz Duquesne here told us what your letters didn't say . . ." She hesitated, trying to find the phrases she had formed earlier and not succeeding. "And I know you didn't have to wed her like you did, most men wouldn't have . . ."

Seeing Marc's growing embarrassment, Jennifer stepped into the gap. "And most men wouldn't buy their tiresome wives a hotel to keep them happy, either, but Marcus isn't most men."

"I didn't buy it to keep you happy. I expect a good return on my investment," Marcus said gruffly.

Charlie laughed, staring pointedly at Jennifer's rounded belly. "And it appears you're getting it, the first dividend to be paid in roughly four months, wouldn't you say?"

Jennifer blushed and Lucia hollered, "Charlie!" at her impertinent husband, but Marcus grinned, staring back at his outspoken engineer from under upraised brows.

"Speaking of dividends, I hadn't realized your investment was made in time to be receiving any returns yet," he replied maliciously.

"I was just following precedent by putting the bridal suite to its proper use at an improper time; you should be the last of people to object to that."

Lucia's outraged gasp brought Josephine's sense of propriety into play.

"You two are worse than a couple of roosters crowing; if you can't behave decently, the least you can do is speak with a little respect. This is Christmas; pretend you're Christians."

Jennifer had pulled her aunt and uncle from the midst of the fray so that they might speak privately, but now her quiet words fell into the sudden ashamed silence following Jo's admonitions.

"What do my parents know of . . ." Aware of the sudden silence, Jennifer stopped and looked up to find her husband's gaze on her.

Trudy, too, had turned to Marcus, a questioning expression in her eyes, and he responded by crossing the room to his wife's side and nodding to Trudy.

Her aunt sighed and turned to answer Jennifer's uncompleted question. "I have told your parents of your marriage. I didn't think I could keep such information from them."

Jennifer bit her lip. They knew, but they had not written. They still disapproved of her. It was a bitter blow, but not entirely unexpected.

"Your husband offered to bring them out here with us so they might see for themselves that you were all right and doing well . . ." Trudy hesitated at Marc's frown, but Jennifer's anxious eyes begged for information, and she continued. "But your mother felt it was better this way. She is relieved to be able to talk of her daughter's marriage, but she has no wish to be reminded of it. Mildred has had a hard life, you must try to understand, my dear . . ."

Jennifer nodded slowly. "She is frightened of too many things, I think. But my father, surely, he has some message for me?"

Marcus stood aside as the older woman took her niece into her arms and hugged her. "He loves you as much as ever, Jenny, but he loves your mother more. It has always been that way, and I suppose it is as it should be. Now that you are married, you must have some idea of what it means to forsake all else for the one you love."

Jennifer's brilliant smile reached to the depths of her eyes as she looked to her handsome husband and reached for his hand.

The look in their eyes as their hands clasped answered Trudy's question without words.